OPERATION WANDERING SOUL

ALSO BY RICHARD POWERS

OPERATION WANDERING SOUL

A NOVEL

RICHARD POWERS

𝑤𝑚
WILLIAM MORROW
An Imprint of HarperCollins*Publishers*

P.S.™ is a trademark of HarperCollins Publishers.

OPERATION WANDERING SOUL. Copyright © 1993 by Richard Powers. Excerpt from THREE FARMERS ON THEIR WAY TO A DANCE © 1985 by Richard Powers. All rights reserved. Printed in the United States of America. No part of this book may be used or reproduced in any manner whatsoever without written permission except in the case of brief quotations embodied in critical articles and reviews. For information, address HarperCollins Publishers, 195 Broadway, New York, NY 10007.

HarperCollins books may be purchased for educational, business, or sales promotional use. For information, please email the Special Markets Department at SPsales@harpercollins.com.

First William Morrow hardcover published 1993.
First HarperPerennial edition published 1994.
Reissued in Perennial 2002.
First William Morrow paperback reissue published 2021.

Designed by Diahann Sturge

The Library of Congress has catalogued a previous edition as follows:

Powers, Richard.
    Operation wandering soul: a novel / Richard Powers.—1st HarperPerennial ed.
        p. cm.
    ISBN 0-06-097611-X
    1. Critically ill children–California–Los Angeles–Fiction. 2. Physician and patient–California–Los Angeles–Fiction. 3. Pediatricians–California–Los Angeles–Fiction. 4. Los Angeles (Calif.)–Fiction. I. Title.
[PS3566.092064 1993b]
813'.54–dc20   93–49506

ISBN 978-0-06-314032-5 (pbk.)

21 22 23 24 25 LSC 10 9 8 7 6 5 4 3 2 1

OPERATION WANDERING SOUL

Kraft cruises down the Golden State: would it were so. "Cruise" is a generous figure of speech at best, label from another time and biome still imbued with quaint, midcentury vigor, the incurably sanguine suggestion of motion more forward than lateral. "Cruise" is for the *Autobahn,* the Jet Stream, Club Med. What's the real word, local parlance? Shoosh. Shunt. Slalom.

Freeways, like rivers, age and meander. Lane lines, at this hour, are just a manufacturer's suggested retail, more of an honor system than anything worth bothering with. Relics, mementos, the tourist scratches on the pavement marking the sites of annihilated Spanish missions.

Up ahead, the Blue Angels run interference for an Esther Williams aqua ballet. A lazy, Quaalude cross-drift of traffic skims across Kraft's viewing screen, flow and counterflow canceling out in diffraction pattern to form a standing wave. Several hoods in front of him, sleek little fuel-injected Alpha particle manned by sandalwood-haired guy hugging cellular phone swaps places with convertible Stuttgart-apparatus piloted by blond bombshell lip-syncing to the same song Kraft himself has tuned in on the radio. Eight seconds later, for no reason in creation, the two swap back. The exchange is duplicated all across the event horizon, a synchronized, pointless, mass red shift.

Fortunately, most everyone is a diploma holder here. Driver's Ed: the backbone of the high school certificate. One might emerge from the system unable to add, predicate, or point to Canada on a map, but thanks to rigorous requirements would still be able to

Aim High in Steering, Leave Oneself an Out, Second-guess the Other Guy.

Casting his vision into the advance shoals, getting what his Driver's Ed teacher almost two decades ago affectionately if firmly referred to as The Big Picture, Kraft catches the total, pointillist effect: cars flaking off each other in the steady current, making a shimmering moiré, like sheer curtains swaying in front of a screen. He takes his hands from the steering wheel, passes his extended fingers in front of one another in unconscious imitation. Time (in this country of ever-expanding unusable free time) for an experiment: infinitesimal easing up on the throttle produces a gap between his grille and the nether parts of the Marquis in front of him. The instant this following distance exceeds a car length, the two vehicles on either side both try to slither in.

Proof. This shot-blast stream of continuous lane change is not prompted by anything so naïve as the belief that the other queue is actually moving faster. The open spot simply must be filled on moral grounds. A question of commonweal. Switching into a slower-moving lane gives you something to do while tooling (*tooling;* that's the ticket) along at substandard speed through the work crews surfacing the next supplementary sixteen-lane expansion. Fills the otherwise-idle nanosecond. A way to absorb extraneous frontier spirit.

Kraft tacks west with the cattle trail. He read somewhere, a year ago, while still in the honeymoon, guidebook phase, that a mile of freeway eats up forty acres of land, give or take the mule. The whole idea came from the Nazis. Shoulders, median, dual carriageway, transition-free exit and entry ramps: the total driving environment. How many thousand acres thrashed in Angelinoland alone? Lord, I'm five hundred continuous north-south miles without a traffic light away from home. Throw in the east-wests, the redundant routes, the clover-leafs, the switchbacks and tributaries, and pretty soon you're talking real real estate.

And how many million tons of that double-bulge guardrail, spinning out its hypnotic thread cross-country, shadowing him however the chicanes slip 'n' slide? For a truly nauseating insight, Kraft considers the number of human lives devoted to manufacturing this hardware alone. Somewhere forges run full time just keeping up with the replacement pieces, the smashups, the decay of normal wear and tear. *So what do you do for a living?* Kraft's own answer, the chief career of daytime soaps and evening dramedies, patricidal America's most prestigious gig, half plumber, half God, is embarrassing enough to have to admit to seatmates on planes. But could have been worse. A wrong turn coming up through public school and he'd be answering: I manufacture those guard bumpers for the freeway. No—just the right-hand, convex ones. Although we *are* planning to diversify into mileage poles and overhead signs, the Japanese permitting.

Radio does its thing, successfully distracting him from sustained thought. Tune of the minute transmutes into a synthetically evil, crystal-meth-induced slam metal number about how the sheepman and the cattleman should be friends. Kraft considers pressing the auto-seek and floating to the next station up the dial, but he hasn't the will to discover what's lurking there in the high, truly antinomian frequencies.

He's under the impression, and would like to go empirical on this, that the city's top-polling radio tune at any given minute has a marked influence on traffic's turbulence. Audio Santa Anas, chill melodies blowing in from the vents under the dash along with the AC, raising the collective arm hair in every one of these climatrolled driving cubicles, making everybody just itch to, well, Aim High in Steering. Off somebody. Been happening a lot again, lately: a Man, a Plan, some ammo, blammo—Panama! Somebody's got to scrape together a grant to graph freeway shooting frequencies versus the *Billboard* Top Ten.

The occasional public service breaks on behalf of the president's current call to arms serve only to obscure the narcotic of choice in its many trappings currently being vended by the sponsors' interludes. Sure enough, by the time the next three-minute rhythm gets into full, band-box swing, the flow of control down the pike in front of Kraft settles into the unmistakable ripple effect of gapers' block.

Something has happened. Simple, unmitigated Event, the palpable Here and Now, or as close as we get to it these days—the view through the dash. As one, people slow for a look: not to pin blame on skid or stupidity. Not to check out the parts failure or the make of the shotgun. They want to get a *glimpse,* to see the caller up close for once, bag his ID, collect his ephemeral calling card, gawk at the forgotten familiar, take down the number on his hideous, out-of-town plates.

Kraft has no need. Any survivors of this crash—or the one on the next freeway over—will show up at Carver General almost as soon as he does. He'll hear all about them in living color over breakfast from the Emergency Room boys. The particular inferno he now creeps past might even include a pede case for him to call his own. It's become all but traditional. Family outing to the museum or mall, laid out all over the median strip instead. If not this particular flaming wreck, the one just around the bumpered bend.

He merges right, having long ago noticed that nine of ten pileups originate in the outside lanes. Across the divider, oncoming traffic starts to bottle up too. The drivers smell something burning. Both directions max out to full carrying potential, a premature peak-volume hour. All hours are rush, here and throughout the network. Everybody on earth and his poor relations are desperate to relocate. Kraft can hardly wait until the Chinese can claim what so proudly we already hail: a national front-seat capacity fitting every citizen on the books with seats to spare. The curve of mobility will sidle up ever more intimately to asymptote until that moment at decade's, century's, and millennium's end when the last living road-certified creature not yet on rolling stock will creep out onto the ramp in whatever vehicle it can muster, and poof: perpetual gridlock.

He has lived through evacuations, but never one on this scale. The fabled civil-defense drill gone real, all the more panic-stricken in that everybody in this one acts piecemeal, deep in the dream of free agency. Given the apotheosis of private transport all around him, Kraft finds it hard to credit the shrill fact beloved of the guidebooks, that Angel City once possessed the most extensive urban transit system in the country. The tales of spanking red turn-of-the-century electric carriages smack now of Hans Christian Andersen. Nothing in human ingenuity's arsenal could have staved off this freeway. It is the peak of private enterprise, as inevitable and consummate as death.

"Artery" cuts a figure through his frontal lobes. Southbound artery. Feeder artery. Bypass artery. Exactly the sort of tough, rubbery, spreading net he's transfused into here, tracking the inside lane, the tunica intima. Yet it's impossible to ascertain, in a city as sclerotic as this, which are the arteries and which the veins. Do oxygenated heme groups transport the needed fix out to the Valley, while spent thrombocytes wash the reduced waste back to the Civic Center for reconditioning? Or does the cycle run the other way around? Even the Thomas Brothers aren't saying. Inbound? Out? Yer not from around these parts, are ya, stranger? We're kind of on open circulation here. Arthropod style. This blood doesn't flow. It shooshes. Slaloms.

He merges into the connecting shunt, seamlessly slipping onto the same road by another name. As on any given night, no matter which direction he courses, the congested red platelets pulse off in front of him, the poor venous outflow of spent white-blue plasma returning on his left to fill the spaces he's abandoned. Increasingly these days, he feels the need, deep in his limbic knot, to revert to that cure-all of his surgeon forebears: *Open the vein.* Primitive debridement. Let the infested fluid drain. Bleed this body, too long under pressure. Cut a counterflow, run a detour down that privileged, gerrymandered isthmus straight into the marina. Trust to the Golden State rule: cars will head toward any empty space. And for a few days at least, superfluous pus would spurt superlatively into the bay.

Reactionary, perhaps. But he's not the only one out on the

arboring taboo desires. A hand-lettered sign attached to the hospital exit has for some days fluttered in the semitropical breeze. Slowing dangerously for the third day running, Kraft at last makes out the text. GET OUT OF YOUR CARS.

Sure. Why not? Billboards are scriptural, hereabouts. Billboards for multihundred-dollar tennies, for CDs fiscal and audio, for song collections of searing social protest, for attitudinal adjustments, for advertising firms, for out-of-work actresses, for billboards. Why not a billboard proclaiming a commuters' general strike? Some self-sponsoring eco-terrorist has evidently shimmied up the stainless steel under cover of night, swung out onto the overhang, and, suspended over half a dozen lanes of traffic (flowing, in these parts, even in dead darkness), masking-taped this manifesto in a prominent spot where it is nevertheless entirely illegible to all but the most incurably print-curious.

Kraft holds up instantly irate traffic just long enough to make out a smaller, scribbled footnote that has sprung up the night before. Some second death-defying maniac has taken up the gauntlet, shimmied the pole, and in midair, appended below GET OUT OF YOUR CARS the codicil, AND FIGHT LIKE A MAN. Exercising the old First Amendment rights, which will of course be suppressed tomorrow by municipal hook and ladder at taxpayer expense, in the name of public safety.

He squeezes out of the file, ramping down to surface roads. With deceleration and return to stoplights comes the acrid-sweet, sickly seductive scent of mildewing vinyl. The aroma has gone tainted since he started working this district, as if petrochemicals rotted like living things. Maroon-brown patinas of condensing air each seal an invisible vintage. The noxious residue, the breakdown skeins of hydrocarbon linkages as long as his nasal hairs fall beneath focal notice now. He smells it only on those days when the bouquet is a little fruiter than usual. Even the radio stations have long ago given up warning the aged or cardiac impaired to stay indoors.

He skirts that neighborhood set to the torch one week a quarter century ago. The car insinuates itself down these streets the way Scando-wegian types are advised to walk them, when suicide simply can't be avoided: hands out of the pockets, eyes straight ahead. Keep to a reasonable but not aggressive clip. Act like you know where you're going.

He does, in the short term, anyway: six-month stint at the Knife and Gun Club. Three weeks into the rotation, his unwisely Caucasoid viscera have already resigned themselves to winding up on the wrong side of the retractors, any stoplight now.

Pediatric service at the public No-Pay? Well you might ask. Luck of the draw, his adviser insisted. Already been all over the rest of town, swapped about like a utility infielder whose teams are too numerous to fit on the back of the bubblegum card. Rotation comes with the turf: Onco up in the Hills. Thoracic on the edge of LaLa Land, repairing the Cars of the Stars. Plastics at Trauma-by-the-Sea. The program demands that everybody do some public service, and Kraft's stint happens to be Pediatrics. Thank your deity of choice too. Could have been dealt the ER service out this way. That would have been, well, call it murder.

Bad enough having to listen to Emergency's own Dr. Tommy Plummer go on about it over Sunrise Sandwiches and chocolate-smeared bagels at the Carver cantina. "See, Kraft, it's like this. Distribution of wealth gets iniquitous enough . . ."

" 'Inequitable,' perhaps, Thomas?"

"Whatever. I'm liberal. Point is, wank the bills around long enough, pretty soon every day's a jolly holiday. Guy comes in last night. Big intercostal hack crescenting clear through his pect major. Stick misses the subclavian by about a centimeter. 'My girlfriend, she cut me.' I don't know what these people use for steak knives, but this looked like a number seven recurve. Nice downward slash. I'm sponging the guy off while they're sleeping him, and I come across this big keloid scar just a shade to the side of the fresh entry. Sure enough, it's on his chart. He was in last year. Gotta ask him if it's the same girlfriend."

The usual pecking-order preening: We do the sweat shop stuff while you sissy-mollies lollygag around in Kiddieland. Medima-chismo. What other hobby can you have, when work consists of getting bloodied to a pulp around the clock, than cultivating mas-ochistic one-upmanship? Plummer can afford to wax radiant in relating call night's worst waking nightmares. He too only temps here in no-man's-land. Were this his permanent abode, the man would be begging his own girlfriend to slash and burn him by now. And mind to clip the subclavian this time, woman.

But Plummer's poly-sci cliché: make it an inequity of futures, failed wish distribution, disparity in circumstance so great that it kills all ability to grant even the premise of hope, and Dr. Tommy might be on to something. The breach between dream and deliv-ery has long since gone beyond fault line. Sinkholes in the whole mythology of progress gape open up and down the street, suck down entire retail strips at a shot. Complete *casa* communities vis-ibly disintegrate, crumble into the coreolis of debt and rage each day Kraft makes the commute. The national trope, the Route 66 wayfarer's picaresque, here looks out over the vertical cliffs marking its premature dead drop. The steepest reliefs of belief are shocked into submission when laid against these wilder contours, the chasms between come-ons and their public reality.

He reaches the hospital block, his epitome of failed plot. Been here before, he has, but can't quite place the original. Streets a shambles of hubcap-liquor-weapons shops, nap hotels, beauty par-lors offering quantity discounts, sheet metal wholesalers, blasted transaction booths, purveyors of fine, illegal pomades. The scent of decay emanates from under the sidewalks, behind the baleen shop grates, in the sotto voce wail of that eternal air raid siren, the permanently borrowed porta-blaster boom-box bilingually broad-casting, "Hey, man! Over your shoulder. Behind you, sucker. You look, you dead. Keep the feet to the beat. Cut you. Cut your ass."

Above all this spreading, single-story, dry-rot adobe block party, his tower rises. It shines in imminence, from armed en-trance up to crenellated keep. State-bailed donjon of correctives and cures, unreachable from this side of the counterscarp.

Fix the body, send it back out? Why bother? You must *hear* it. The threat, the hiss wrapping the corpse of neighborhood. The abject rejection of *maybe someday* that animates the warp's woofers and tweeters down here at street level.

He noses his car up to the sealed glacis, fishes through the Rolodex of plastic card-keys his wallet has become of late: one to make phone calls, one to cajole the pump, one to snag money out of the wall, one to consolidate his card-accrued loans, and here—one to lift the parking lot block and slip in. He inserts his magnetic travelogue strip into the slot, and sesame. The world as solvable logic puzzle still operates as designed, one more day, despite the lifeboats all around sliding off the dock, continuously magnum-christened, Crystal Night style.

He skulks up the back stairwell, nursing a fantasy of hot analgesic shower, water pounding away his torsal tie-up like so many barefoot French *fillettes* squeezing out the grape harvest. That's the most elaborate scenario his bilious libido can organize, given the call schedule Carver has had him on. The ubiquitous They spot him before he can even reach his locker and begin at once to black-and-bruise him. Bloody pulp. Professional job, execution style.

Richard, is there something the matter with your beeper? Emily Post for "You turned the sucker off, you bastard, didn't you?" And right here in the gangway they start shoveling him a shitload of new admissions. Seems there's this incredible backlog of seething humanity, and they're going to have to service-station eight mewling and puking little babes in a row just to get the work out, no matter if they have to kill half of the cases in the process.

So it continues both day and night. Some old song he half summons up. Kraft's too fatigued to remember, to name the tune, let alone locate the descant. He gets his shower, about fourteen hours later. But by then his shoulders have been hammered so brittle that he can do nothing by way of encouraging the little French girls except to smile feebly at them and mumble, *Quel est le prix du repas?*

He checks his watch, and then the light from a window, to determine whether that's A.M. or P.M. He crawls on all fours back to his call room where he rummages about for some reading material, some pictorial literature to numb him to sleep. But big-time humor: Plummer and the ER boys have raided all the call room's *Penthouses* and replaced them with *Rifle & Handgun Illustrateds*.

Well, deal with it; he's in no shape for fictively intimate biographies anyway. And he's had enough anatomy, God knows, to last his body a lifetime. So he settles into the May *R & H*, getting no further than the inside cover. A four-color ad: "Take the Law into Your Own Hands." Play on words, see. "The Law" is the name of this little semiautomatic honey. Portentous as the come-on is vis-à-vis cultural decomposition, the spread does yank onto center stage of Kraft's consciousness the question that's been banging about the greenrooms of his cerebellum over the last few weeks. Shouldn't he perhaps get hold of a small arm too, by way of acknowledging the law of averages?

His lone survival trick to date has been to maintain a subterranean profile, to duck under the immediate median. He's got nothing of retail value stashed at his apartment. His moody ten-speed. Last epoch's TV, not even VCR-ready. *Record player,* if you can believe. Two original oils of the Abyss that he couldn't give away. No self-respecting filcher of any nationality is going to bother riffling the dust. Should some enterprising addict crowbar into the place by accident, transposing numbers in the address CB'ed him from Thrashers' Central Dispatch, he'd run from Kraft's postholocaust decor as from a pestilence house. A pistol at the apartment would be as superfluous as any other major appliance.

Fact is, he does not actually go back to his place these days except to pay the utils. He's never spent much time there, and that's tended toward nil ever since he became resident Resident here at Hole of Calcutta Public.

But away from home, here at Carver, reality's numbers are worse than he ever suspected, even in his gloomiest extrapolation. He sees the daily tabulations snaking in human conga lines longer than the most competent admitting nurse can hope to tag and transfer. They amble at him in those cloth shoe-wraps, merging into a multilane free-for-all as amorphously adrift as any expressway. Pimply adolescent gang partisans, assaulters, assaultees, half the underage world winds up in his pediatrics ward. Conscripts of collapsing infrastructure, their gear of choice: Kalashnikov, AK-47, Uzi, even M-16, a tool whose recent sales surge attests to Bob Hope's TV ads about buying homegrown and minding the balance of trade. "You better believe it makes a difference."

And Carver gets only those wounds that are potentially closeable. Kraft's eyes have opened some, living out here in the cash-and-carry neighborhoods, the ones that have been literally fueling the economic transformation miracle, the ones that pick up the tab for the whole ethos of buy now, pay elsewhere.

Why should he sit still and wait for the inevitable? Mornings, this nascent desire to buy a gun seems a silly flare-up, a surrender to his country's prize paranoia. The return of collectively repressed foreign-policy fantasies, writ small. But nights, nights like this one, flipping through the ER boys' practical jokebook while the steady sirens of Incoming wail away like a chorus of Aidas in the tomb, arming oneself seems a case of simple arithmetic. Do the long division: kill ratio into population density. He's not going to last the twenty weeks. He'll be popped walking down to the parking lot, or plugged lazily from the left-hand freeway lane.

The prospect of five more months at this place upends whatever residual progressive sympathies of his survived the Scuttle-and-Run decade. He doesn't need the law in his hands. But a little something in the glove compartment by way of rebuttal? Until such a day as the law stops eating its own?

He slinks off into REM-free sleep, passing through the stages of non-ness without a spike. At four A.M., they break into his room and begin to pound him awake. Six-year-old kid whose gut he sewed up two days ago tore it open tonight on a recap nightmare. Some save-the-world decides that the repair has to be enacted immediately. And Kraft's on call. Go willingly, or be dragged kicking and screaming into that good nightmare? Fifteen minutes after coming more or less conscious, he's sewing. A little peritonitis cocktail greets him, so it's just as well they're back in. As he snips and whisks, the OR radio all the while pipes a little background tune, "Get It Right the First Time."

Afterward, there's no point in even trying to salvage the idea of sleep. Grand Rounds in a couple hours, after the day's opener, the Morbidity and Mortality conference. He can at least attempt to doze through M and M, that weekly proverbial chocolatey mess. But what to do now, now, now? Keep the pace—matter in motion. He'll go wake Plummer from the dead and demand his magazines back.

But Dr. Thomas is up and long since in the trenches. The ER looks like the war zone it is. A chaos of attendings—Milstein, Garber, even Flores—a couple anesthesiologists, scrub nurses running in and out, and Kraft's man himself standing frighteningly composed with his hands horribly enlarged on the TV monitors, poking about in somebody's lumbar, bouncing around flecks of metal confetti like slap shots at the puck in that little boys' table hockey. Kraft rescrubs and checks out the scene.

Plummer greets him, grinning, Cheshire. Always the last anatomical bit to disappear. "See those cops up in the observation gallery? They're waiting to charge this guy with the sexual battery of a woman. I'd like to be charged with the sexual battery of a woman. How 'bout yourself, Dr. Krafty? Say, uh, as long as you're scrubbed and not doing anything to justify your existence . . ."

Kraft stands dumbly, makes him spell it out. "Would you mind bailing for a bit, buddy? Here; just hold this thread. It'll only take a minute."

LESS THAN A month of seniority at this outfit, and he's already garnered a reputation. Not just *a* reputation, which might have been damage-controllable. Kraft's saddled with several. Interesting how a person's public persona varies so insanely from service to service. Whole behavioral morphologies erupt from first impressions and a gentle audience nudge. He finds it too tough to disabuse people of their pet projections. Infinitely flexible, Kraft is. That is, cowardly by another name. Comes from having grown up all over the globe. No matter; for half a year, he can sustain any personality anyone might type him with.

Something about him must emanate this Mr. Potato Head plasticity. Chief of Surgery Burgess, dying a slow, half-century death in this city where reading span is sorely stretched by the instructions on microwave popcorn, instantly imagines that in Kraft he has found a kindred literate spirit, a simile son. Dr. Purgative, as Plummer rechristens him, keeps farming out these convoluted, epistemological novels by Kraft's obscure, young contemporaries. Plow through and report on, over sherry this afternoon, a postmodernist mystery thicker than the *Index Medicus* where the butler kills the author and kidnaps the narration. Damn thing includes its own explanatory *Cliffs Notes* halfway through, although the gloss is even more opaque than the story. What the hell; it's a break from booking for the next wave of board exams.

At the same time, Dr. Milstein, pediatric attending, has been led by Kraft's enthusiastic head-bobs to believe that the new floater resident is a great sailing buff. The man running-bowlines Kraft outside the cafeteria, presses him for a date when they can head out to the islands on Milstein's thirty-seven-footer. Kraft falls back on the ingenious perfect put-off: "I've got call all week." That gives him time to get out to the nearest Books-'n'-Stuff to secure a how-to manual. Between Purgative and the Millstone, it's quite the contretemps keeping Madeira straight from port straight from starboard.

Of the remaining permanent staff, Drs. Kean and Brache— Father Kino and Miss Peach—seem to want him for a whipping boy, a willful child in need of restraint. When we were residents, they used to stick us with hatpins until we suppurated. Loved every minute of it. Made us the exemplary physicians you see before you. Spare the rod and spoil the ortho. Well, no, we don't really *need* you to do seventy-two continuous hours of call. Oh, so you can't do three T-and-A's, a small bowel, an appendix, and a gallbladder in one day? Of course, if you *want* to go into family practice, we can always write some nice letters of rec for you. With these folks, Kraft grins a lot and asks for second helpings of everything they dish out.

And the pede nurses: the sweet cheats somehow conclude, based perhaps on Kraft's baby-face, beardless, brown-eyed prettiness, that he is totally depraved. Whatever the objective truth in that, he cannot match their own aptitude on this score. He skirts past their station on rounds; one of them says into the phone, "Wait a minute. He's just passing. I'll put him on." She hands him the receiver and hello, hello? It takes a minute to realize that they've connected him to Dial-a-beat-off, and there's this growling feminine monstrosity on the other end beseeching him with weird invocations to zipper her skin. Another ward nurse locks him in the supply closet with her, makes him watch as she downs massive doses of cold medicine, then demands to be wrapped in seventy-five yards of surgical gauze. "Come on. Like I've been dead a hundred thousand years and you just happened across me in some pyramid?"

To Tommy Plummer, whom Kraft worked with at Kaiser across town, he is a conspiratorial, blasé fellow-sufferer. *Your* patient, Doctor. Survival requires, as they gather for Morbidity and Mortality, that the knot of his fellow residents, all fast approaching Jesus Christ's age at crucifixion and still in school, hover together by the coffee machine (vicious substance; inotropic agent and elevator of them gastric juices), compare massacre stories and crack bad-taste jokes about the jelly bismarks offered up for public sacrifice. Ritual fortification for the coming ordeal, when they must one by one stand up in front of the assembled surgery staff and announce: forty-two admissions, thirty-three discharges, five complications, one serious. One fatality. And say why they lost that case.

Kraft takes the spotlight, begins the lowdown on a chart that, by the slimmest of roulette-spun grace, stayed on this side of the pale, kept him from having to announce a fatality for his service this week. No blame to itemize; an instructive combination of anomalies, really. Nobody could have anticipated, before opening the kid, that we'd find . . .

Father Kino, the meeting's weekly host, cuts him off. "What ever made you think you could do elective surgery on a child with a potassium level that low?"

Well, how low is low? Isn't that context dependent? I mean, are there guidelines at this hospital for suitable . . . ?

"No one cuts unless K-level is normal. That's N-O-R—"

Yes, but I wouldn't have thought . . .

"You didn't *think*. That's the problem. Consequently, you very nearly killed this boy. As it is, do you know what you've condemned him to for the next sixty years?"

The monotone recital of probable complications drowns out the slighted protestant in Kraft, the voice in the wilderness screaming, *You slimy self-righteous son of a bitch.* April 23. Robinson, fifty-one-year-old black male. Guy comes in with *kidney stones* and goes out on a platter. *Your* patient, Dr. Kean. Kraft ejects the internal heckler in him at the first impulse to shout. Letting himself feel anything, least of all legitimate rage, is self-destructively futile. They have all the emotions countered, covered. Say so little as *I made a judgment call,* and you're wiped all over the canvas.

Kean really gets into the whole TV-doctor shindig, baiting him, waiting for him to utter the first whimper of self-defense. When Kraft refuses to give in to anything but the bare minimum Hippocratic contrition, Father Kino issues a mock absolution that falls flat over the entire room: "Go and sin no more."

Plummer corners him afterward. "Nice show, Dr. Kraft. What *ever* possessed you . . . ?" The rib incorporates a complex mix of sympathy and further abuse. What ever, indeed. Why put up with this horseshit harassment? Five years of eighty-hour weeks at half the salary of a bank loan officer, an aggravated sense of galloping inadequacy and a running ulcer, annihilated private life, dosed out on the varieties of punitive torture, all for the privilege of being publicly humiliated. Where did it take hold, that public-service conviction, the sense that he personally had to hold back the tide of human slaughter? Where did it come from, the terrified certainty that he'd end up squalid and starving to death in the gutter unless he amassed the thickest bullet-proof moral bankroll known to man?

He tries to breach the subject with Burgess, by way of evading the latest, unfinished assignment for the week's literary chat. "Moses complex?" Burgess suggests, all but stroking his goatee. The Chief clearly missed his calling. What's a talking-cure guy doing wielding the big knife?

It earns Kraft hard currency with the boss to lay out the effects of an adolescence in transit on his adult sense of security. He says how continuous military-brat mobilization had him hit all the globe's hot spots by puberty. He spins out the case study of how, by ten, he'd left friends behind on each of four major landmasses. Even with Burgess as lay analyst, Kraft has to lie a little, invent an incriminated mechanism. Make up some plausible cathartic insight into his getting mixed up in a calling for which he never displayed the least vocation, a life of self-denial he could happily have sidestepped, a messianic stopgap that early experience should have told him was ludicrously irrelevant.

Did he never, Burgess probes, dream of a career more adventuresome, more expansive? Well, yes. For years, little Kraft carried with him, three and a half times around the globe, despite the vicissitudes of local politics, his transposing horn. Somewhere deep in the AP archives, a grainy black-and-white glossy shows a scared foreign-service band, evacuated from Lahore at the start of the '65 war to the region's rock-solid American bastion, Teheran. In the poignant foreground, Ricky Kraft, doing his brave little John-John Jr. salute, clutches a French horn case as if it contained the tune the sick world was dying by inches to hear.

The following year, in British Guiana, as it overhauled itself into Guyana, Ricky made his first child's assault on Mozart. By Djakarta, overblowing had taken him into the high registers. As late as his two 2-year stints in what passed for accredited high schools, the terms "valve," "tubing," and "bore" still possessed not the slightest of health-professional overtones.

Simplicity came apart in a single night. That arctic year, back stateside, when it became clear that the energy crisis was not a temporary embargo. The year the president invoked one oxymoron, "the moral equivalent of war," against another oxymoron, "contemporary behavior." The year his father engineered his last international mission.

Bitterly frigid, a February beyond speaking. Four in the afternoon and already pitch black. A twenty-year-old stood on Huntington Ave outside the conservatory, waiting for the Arborway back to his chill flat in Jamaica Plain. His hand froze through his glove to the metal case handle, his breath vapor iced to the hairs of his upper lip, solidifying on contact with air. At that instant, he heard something—cracking mortar between the stones of the building he leaned against, the tensing of the rail at the approach of the trolley, the sounds of an old man being attacked with a baseball bat off toward Roxbury. With that noise—the sound of absolute zero—he would never be able to get warm again in this country.

At his apartment, the power had been out for hours and the pipes had burst. Geysers of water stood in midair, spectral faucet turbulences, ossified, Midased in place. Lying under every blanket he owned, their weave as slack as a stroke victim's mouth, the crystal interstices in his window glass thrown wide open to the outdoors' single-minded cold, Kraft remembered his way to a decision.

The age of music was over. He could play no longer. His horn uncoiled to its unmanageable seven feet. By semester's end, he cashed in his worthless education and headed home to his father, who had chosen North Dakota, the coldest, bleakest, emptiest state in the Union, to be a widower in. There, he slept for six months, shivering out the coma. Waking, Kraft began applying at once to pre-med programs.

Start again, from scratch. Better a few years late than eternally unprepared. University fell, then med school—four years in a pressurized bathyscaphe. Every test was a dry run for the Final Exam, whose hour no man could know but was coming eternally closer, its sole question already cribbed in that one afternoon's sickening presentiment. Assisting at his first coronary bypass, helping to clamp off and excise the saphenous vein from the meat-thick thigh and substitute it for the fouled canal-locks around the heart, Kraft felt only the placid terror of arrival. Not safe, not even here. But the operating theater was as central a station as any in which to wait for that obscure appointment laid out for him.

Even in residency at the most southerly hospital he could break into, the French horn accompanies him, superfluous baggage he's sworn off of but can't deep-six. It sits in its case, arm's length from his unfrequented bed, awaiting that postponed jam session of itinerant orchestra, midnight's clandestine musicians riffing into cleanly earned, twelve-bar sweat over sweet surreptitious saints marching *someplace* in.

And that's why he's a surgeon, Dr. Burgess. What does he win? Reasons, he would tell the Chief, explain nothing. Peculiarly American, this doctoring up of motive after the fact. The M.D. gives him something to fall back on; why not leave it at that?

Only overwork mitigates the sense of rendezvous, perpetually about to be missed. And this job's busier than any in the accepted register. He gives none of this away during Burgess's sherry-and-lit sessions. One does not tell the head of surgery that the career is just a holding pattern. Still, the Chief's got a spot of it too. Cold consolation of supercompetence: earn a breathing space, prolong more lives than one terminates, bilge a patch of the spreading hematoma, nick the parabola, buy a minute, which must be sixty seconds more than nothing.

THE HALLWAYS SWARM with interns today. Each one grins at him from behind a patient work-up, inquiring politely after his potassium level. Kraft, after weeks of running this rat maze and still capable of getting lost in it, follows the colored-floor-stripe Baedeker, the No-Pay's heritage trail, deep into pathology's sanctum sanctorum.

In these halls the human calculus is ceaselessly differentiated with all the rote, overlearned ease of a child doing her lower times tables. Too many bodies even to be blasé over. An n-space, imploded theater-in-the-round. Charity cases line the passages, capitalism's crash-test dummies and quantity grist. They drift, tubed down, stranded, pharmaceutically beached, cobbled up in assorted VA-surplus rolling furniture, talking to themselves, beyond all help but the perfunctory patch job. Emergency gone quotidian. In residents' parlance, SHPOS. Subhuman pieces of shit.

Kraft makes rounds. The first pubescent post-op on the list isn't in his room. Probably off in the can getting high. Perhaps he should join the boy. But today's narcotics of choice are way out of his parlance. Two other must-sees from the same room are perched precariously on the windowsill, where they busily force flaming stuffed animals out through the barred windows to certain death six stories below.

The view from that window reveals an all-points, single-story hacienda sprawl as intricate and comprehensive as mold overwhelming a slice of damp bread. Kraft spots, in the switchback of streets that curl like machine parings, other hospitals, his previous rotations in the Byzantine farming-out that landed him here. The journeyman system has its pedagogic advantages. It lets him sample a mix of varying protocols and staffs. Each neighborhood (a euphemism in this unincorporable metastasis of urban planning) has its exemplary disasters of the flesh. Each round is tailored to its geographical destiny: coronary with the haves; pede with the have-nots. Would that the have-nots had had a few fewer.

Every mini-mall, each net of streets beats its own unique socioeconomic pathologic path. For acquiring a rounded, hands-on account of general surgery, there's no substitute for touring the trenches. Short services are his entrée into semi-autonomous re-

gions just one burb over, those closed camps he could never have
hoped to visit otherwise and survive. Join the army, see the world.
Old idea of the study abroad, the foreign exchange program, the
school field trip. Only this time, the museum is real.

Carver General—Angel City Charity—shows him things that
remain obscene rumor everywhere else. Obsolete, vanquished,
nineteenth-century ailments. Consumption. Botulism. Infections that the texts consign to nostalgia. Paint poisonings. Bizarre, abdomen-filling parasites. He has cured a boy of deafness
by surgically removing a raw chick-pea jammed up his ear. Six
months of public work put him in touch with disruptions of body
and spirit not even hinted at in the random distribution he has left
on the city map outside this window.

If it yielded no other therapeutic insights, the rotation system
would still have provided him with this indispensable view from
above, a key to the patterns of disease traveling through the city,
the wake it traces through the addresses it devastates. Each new
hospital adds to his hands-on conviction: something is afoot just
off the freeway. Something undreamed of by the stay-at-homes.

But these private educational benefits are not the real reason
he is here. Pedagogical payoff is ultimately the cover for an elaborate cost-sharing scheme. Conscript labor is the only sustainable way to staff a freebie hospital on this scale, an institution
otherwise manned exclusively by alcoholics, incompetents, and
saints. Comes down to power broking, horse trading. Folks up
in the Hills will send their boys down only if they can secure in
exchange two pros from Hollywood Pres plus a minor-league
internal leech to be named later.

The knots of this kickback scam are mere ripples in a network of mutual blackmail that dwarfs even the city itself. The
convoluted auction of goods and services depends on a trillion
simultaneous back-scratches all coming off at once. Angel's pal-
aces have been built largely on free riders, illegal taps into Central
Power, unmet overdrafts, slumlording, vapor profits, safety paper
documents erased with dollops of acid, and timely bankruptcies

declared on imaginary underwritings. But for now, and for the next few moments, the whole poker-deck superstructure stands successfully shackled together on gum, safety pins, and signed agreements.

Kraft rustles up the children he must examine, hook by crook. Rounds squared away, it behooves him now only to complete clinic without passing into unconsciousness or its many equivalents. The best way to further this end is to avoid peeking at the afternoon OR schedule until too late for either hysterics or hypotheticals. Clinic is a three-hour, walk-through *Decameron* carved up into fifteen-minute segments during which he must play talk-show host to the afflicted, humoring illness's endless invention.

An aggressively built Latin woman hauls in her seven-year-old girl by both fists. She insists that Kraft excise the child's kidneys right there in the office. He flips rapidly through a pocket bilingual translating dictionary that he keeps by him at all times, as indispensable a tool these days as the stethoscope, although he suspects it of frequently capricious translations. A few confused imperfect verbs later, it becomes clear that the kid is a front: the real problem is a softball-sized lump—the big, sixteen-inch, kapok variety—in the *mother's* pelvic region. Kraft hooks her up with the proper department and, over her departing protests, buzzes in the next guest.

Who is, today, a return from two weeks ago—Turkish kid to whose parents Kraft failed to make clear (no dictionary) that the dressing had to be cleaned. Fourteen days of festering fuses the gauze into a scab-plastered mess more serious than the tumor the cut corrected. Kraft rasps at the leaking, Technicolor wound, picking at the putrid bits while trying to leave flesh, a fresco restorer unable to cut the grime without sponging off half the disintegrating plaster.

Throughout, he exchanges varying flavors of Englishes with the family—verbal bourse signals both opaque and disastrous. Clinic consists of Kraft's finding fifteen-minute ingenious synonym lists for "Excuse me?" Even when language is no barrier, the visitors often have a hard time explaining just what they've gotten themselves into. Exactly why did you leave a rubber band tightly constricted around your little toe for three weeks? Just how did this burned kitchen match come to lodge itself so deeply up your nasal passage?

For grotesqueries, Kraft may be perpetually one-upped by Plummer, with his *Tales from the Emergency Zone*. There simply is no matching live rats in plastic bags inserted up rectums, or even the relatively more mainstream erotic strangulations that get out of hand. Thomas tells with great relish accounts such as that of the woman who was shipped in covered with blood, her throat transversely knifed open. Starting big-bore IVs to stabilize her, they cut her clothes off to discover male genitalia, which doubtless explained the knife wound. No, there is no topping ER for sheer dramatic thrust.

Still, on two scores, Kiddie Karpentry exerts theatrical superiority. First, it is fabulously small, a technological feat of miniaturization. Simply straightening out the gross anatomy of a two-foot-long infant almost requires loupes. And second, Pediatrics—the next generation, wave of the future, America's hope for, etc.—provides the quintessential, unexpurgated view of just where Western Civ's whole project is really headed in its third thousand years.

By clinic's third hour, the traffic of juvenile misery drifting through his office begins to mirror the freeway's aimless lane change. It's as if Kraft's still on his commute here, a ball of fluid sucked along by capillaries' secret adhesions. Clinical existence carries no forward motion at all, only small perturbations, place-swaps, disturbances out on the edge of the crumbling empire. He lives in an afternoon when the old meliorist fantasy gives way to bare maintenance, if that. By clinic's end, Kraft has entered a long, intercalary dark age that lasts until he finds himself swabbing both arms with brown, lathery disinfectant in preparation for surgery.

The factory load is light today, the team relaxed. Somebody's hooked up the optics monitor to receive cable, and everybody stands around watching an infomagazine about how certain notorious primetime bouffant bitches are really lovely, caring people who like to lend their megafame at low rates to assist the Third World. The current duffer intern—perfect man to send out to fetch the figurative falafel—switches between this and a big-budget docudrama about the colossal fireball death of America's space voyagers. Nothing is real until it's been fictionalized.

Opening a three-year-old's chest puts a damper on the party. Something Geppetto-like to manipulating this puppet—paste, papier-mâché, hanging strapped by its face to the anesthesia mask like a fish on a barb. Its purple-coral organelles pump in unconscious coordination, racing all together now for some impossible finish line they can never reach, as if the whole, heaving mechanism needs to get someplace particular by daylight.

Poking inside the cavity, Kraft's fingers move about the place with pride of ownership: All my beautiful anatomical overlays—who *dared* fuck this perfection up? Even when he recalls that he did not design these inextricable meshes, Kraft's hands go on insisting that only those who have looked on the internal works, who patiently isolate the pulsing parts, who even go so far as to reroute or replace them, only this select club of God's on-site warranty service can begin to see through the cast of fantasy figures inhabiting the upper reaches of human consciousness where everyone else lives out his life.

It's all true, what the general public dares not suspect: no one can live with full anatomical knowledge. The heat and pressure of apocalyptic repair jobs transacted in wholesale volume every day of existence inevitably autoclave the heart. After a few hours of call, he does begin to see these needy, shivering bodies strapped to the monitors as so many deli cuts. These days, the freeze sets in as early as the instant he arrives in the theater.

The act of cutting never closes. It lingers on afterward, at the movies, alone over a burger. He replays the tapes of the last session, even in the thick of the next. He sees scars everywhere—perfect physiques betrayed by tiny lateral fissures. Shame-braceleted wrists, throats inscribed with suture-pearl necklaces. In bed some weeks before with an auburn beauty manifold enough to have become The One, he placed his petting hand on what had been soft breast once but now harbored implant. His finger felt the welt of the well-closed insertion slit, and he went instantly as impotent as the best lyric poets. No explanations possible; all he could do was ask her to take her perfect silhouette hence.

Three-year-old ribs retract in front of him, supple and suggestive in their cartilage, the cleavages of subcutaneous wrapping revealing, like tea leaves, the fact that the surgeon must eventually grow inured, restore the veil, return in time to those pretenses that allow casual engagement, human exchange. Every attending, however seasoned and congealed, struggles to forget what was thrust on him during the shock of internship: pus is the spirit's maiden name. Mucus, before anything.

It shocked Kraft, half a dozen years ago, during his first foray into an operating room on the conscious side of the knife, to discover how prosaic cutting's accoutrements were. You mean we just open them up, right here, in the billowing air? A scalpel was the same thing he kept in his kitchen rack, no value added. The cauterizer, just a soldering iron with no purpose except, well, to burn flesh. The wisps of smoke that the searing stick gives off smell—what *else* could they smell like?—like a wonderful steak on the backyard grill of a summer's night. That first time, he had actually salivated before making the induction.

He cycles through his selection of instruments, calling for them by gauges of thickness and weight and curvature, the choice of each a mix of skilled estimate and judgment call. The same basic tools employed since the Babylonians, when the punishment for malpractice was to remove the surgeon's hands. The devices available to Kraft on the sampler tray have gone unchanged for a hundred years: knives, scissors, needles, thread, forceps, retractors, the all-important hemostat. Nor has their use, despite the explosion of tech, graduated beyond the original Vedic paradox: inducing an injury to address an injury. And managing the damage of the injury induced.

What *has* changed, and changed only recently, is the scalpel's leverage. Incursion is nothing now; they invade and stamp about the forbidden grounds, almost at will. The only limits hemming the surgeon in are that abiding trio: shock, self-infection, pain. And of these three, the greatest is pain.

The profession's dream—free manipulation of the interior— was blocked until recently by the need to convince the body that inflicted destruction is better than the alternative. General anesthesia marked hope's first great breakthrough. More. Kraft would promote the discovery to Cornerstone of that imagined city civilization has been building from the start. The ability to baffle life's built-in jettison mechanism divides all history into Before and After: the era of all-annihilating agony and the age of deliverance by constitutional coup. On his best days, Kraft even gets a little glimpse of tenable existence off in the distance.

To crack the cap of negating pain, to rip a hacksaw downward through an expanse of flesh, to mash bone and burrow into marrow without tripping off a single shutdown signal—the chance dismantles the world and resurrects it, redecorates its interior. Life has sat imprisoned by the guard dogs posted to watch the house. Hard to overestimate just how much this advance rewrites the whole human shooting match, reassembles it elsewhere. Philosophy's frilly solfeggios now have half a fighting shot at dictating the terms of a new truce. Agony need no longer always have the last word. One might do more than abide.

Kraft tries to imagine this procedure, the one underneath his hands, coming off without anesthesia. Something pupates inside this baby. They must smash their way in, violating the miniature traceries of rib cage. A few feeble attempts to explain things to the infant, a pint of whiskey forced through a funnel to deaden the surface tingling. Then the blade, so sharp that even gristle melts at its wedge. Two adults to pin the flailing creature to the table, and a prayer that the child passes out relatively quickly. A shrieking worse than any that ever wafted over the death camps, because it screams, *You were my protectors; I trusted you.* Square off the incision and fold back the flaps. Take a fine-toothed jeweler's rasp to the sternum, pull the whole structure carefully apart like a Cornish game hen. By now, the infant brain so floods with torture's telegraph that it begins convulsing. He has read the stats: without dope, seven times out of ten, shock collapses the organism and pulls life in around it.

Then there is the time-honored alternative. Spread the pain out over a couple years, leaving disease free to multiply through the child where it frequently peaks in equally unbearable anguish, this time for weeks. Kill the kid quickly on the outside chance, or condemn it to certain, creeping death, coaching it through on promises of a future, pain-stripped place. There the prospect has stood, since nerve came conscious, until yesterday. That humankind, living through that scene even once, has carried on planning and projecting is almost as much a miracle as the discovery of the chemicals that might make the whole self-deluded, transparent, paper-hat tea party endurable.

Just beyond the folds of his left ear the Millstone, Kraft's attending, breathes epically, like wind sculpting a canyon. The steady oscillation calls Kraft back to the living infant on the table underneath them. Adenoidal in the best of times, the Millstone truly starts to snore when the going gets tiny. Yet better that than Father Kino and his Short Man's Syndrome. ("A short man, perhaps," Plummer frequently jokes. "But at day's end the fellow casts a semilong shadow.")

Together, the team extracts the mass they were after, clamps it off, and hacks it out at its insidious roots. In admiring tones as the gourd is lifted out and laid in a waiting pan, the Millstone marvels, "Hang *that* up on the top of your Christmas tree."

Kraft briefly considers trying to get someone to close for him, but elects against putting his limited seniority to the test. After all, as his mother used to tell him when he went fishing with a low trump, one must never send a boy to do a man's job. He's carried the ball this far. Might as well finish, although it must be obvious to everyone on the team that he's about to go narcoleptic.

He sews like the zigzag accessory on a Singer. His sheep

shanks run as erratically as a tricky halfback, say Sayers or Sweetness. This girl will grow up with Wellington's Victory stenciled across her belly—a thin red line dominating her front. However sultry and beautiful, however high her features, there will be this mark, and her every lover to a boy-man will wonder: *What happened to you?*

Some minutes pass, maybe even half an hour, before he realizes they are done. Quick, now: what day is it? What *month*, for that matter? He knows only that the time has not yet come when he is working for himself.

Outside in the parking lot, it is sunset or sunrise. Low light, in any case. Kino's favorite—day's end. The hour of Short Men the world over.

Could go home a while, but what's the point? At this hour, the freeway's still an open sewer. It will stay a running sore from now until the moment when the red trains are returned of necessity from their mothball bower.

Besides, he'd just have to swing around and come back in another few hours. Here, the meals are already made. A motel room at the Knife and Gun, already reserved in Kraft's name. And when was the last time he could do anything else but slink back to the ward and try to become a better hacker than he has been today, one for whom technique, intuition, and hands-on knowledge might, in some sustainable future, begin to grow almost equal to the body gone wrong, the infinite, anonymous petitions laid at his door?

A girl too small for her twelve years, still pitching from months on the sheet of corrugated tin that took her six hundred miles across the South China Sea, stands in front of history class in the eastern ravages of Angel City and guesses where the lost Roanoke colony has disappeared to. A year and a half of English administered by evangelical Philippines relief camp aides and a battery of weeks stateside qualifies her for the Oral Report, that time-honored ritual of passage. She chooses, for some reason, American history.

She tries to say just what that single word, carved into the bark of a tree, might reveal about the lost Virginian band's destination. She pronounces the word aloud, cuts it into the blackboard with a stump of chalk that disintegrates into pastel sand in her fingers: CROATOAN. She spells the fragment left on a second trunk: CRO. This word, the lone sign of hasty evacuation remaining to greet the colony's governor on his return from a supply run to the mother country, holds for her no impenetrable mystery. It is as English, as Lao, as Lao-Tai, as Thai, as Tagalog, as Latin Spanish as any of the trading currencies drifting through the temporary settlements where she has put up for the night. To every relocation camp its own transitory lingua franca, built up by the accidents of mass migration. And all the mysterious messages ever penned into silent bark come to the same thing: We're off, then. Don't wait up.

Why else would a person resort to words? Words, she has learned in all manner of reeducation programs along her route, have no origin and no end. They are themselves the touring urgency they try to describe. *Barrio,* where she now lives, comes from Spanish, from Arabic, from the idea of the idea of open country. No word could be more English now, more *American,* although all the open country here has been closed for lifetimes. That's okay, because *barrio* is now as plowed under, as built up as that lost open land. It means something else, in the run of time. It means those Arabs creeping northward into Spain like fluid in a barometer. It means the Spanish, unable to stop the Moor advance except by swallowing their science and math and militant restlessness. It means the English maritime offspring, unwisely jumping their own island for something larger, in turn unable to contain the children of New Spain except by eating them whole—their food, their music, their *words.*

This is the outline she was born knowing—how words are the scratch marks of intersecting trails. She still holds in her head a complex map of river linguistics: sound geographies, isoglossaries of all the valley people her own once did business with. Moors and conquistadores and Carolina pilgrims, picked up quickly at the latest trading station, she simply superimposes on the list. She imitates the local playground cries, swapping in the Spanish chants as effortlessly as the English. The two are the same, the nearest of cousins, given the family she comes from. She shares herself between them, speaking an exploratory patois eclectic enough to baffle all listeners equally.

Arriving at this school, abandoned on the principal's doorstep, she wanted only to please—a small enough price for guaranteed safety. Pleasing seemed to involve solving the riddles laid before her. In numbers and planes and problem solving, she tested years beyond her peers, beyond many of the certified teachers. But she could not paraphrase "Make hay while the sun shines," nor complete the analogy "Shoe is to sock as overcoat is to . . ." More indicting, she said absolutely nothing unless forced, and then acquitted herself with the barest minimum of whispered, eerie syllables.

Ceramic, tiny, terrified, she moved about on legs as pencil-tentative as a tawny mouse deer. All four of her limbs would have fit comfortably inside a third-grade lunch box. Her every gesture seemed calculated to evade the incursions of those bigger than she. The school nurse refused to believe the age the little one gave, and there was of course no birth certificate. A problem with number translation? No; the girl marked out her years in sticks on a sheet, silently polite, as if adults required infinite patience. Simple fib? But what on earth could she gain by pretending to be older than she was?

No matter. She *looked* eight, ocean cruise survivor or otherwise. True, she spoke (when she spoke) impressively for a recent acquirer, but no more precociously than other transpacific Asian eight-year-olds played the violin. However well she knew the Roman alphabet by sight, she could barely force her fist to push it into print. Easy cursive, flash card grace, dodge ball without shame were all out of the question. Enlightened pedagogy demanded that she start three grades beneath her age. And obediently, there she began.

Six weeks of field test routs pedagogy. The third-grade teacher allots her a desk, takes an hour to explain the subjects, gives her maps, a math notebook, a compass, and a protractor, and assigns a pristine text from the previous, humiliated decade called *Our Emerging World,* saying, "We'll be working in this." Code, the girl quickly intuits, for "As soon as I teach your fifty other materially arrested classmates how to fake reading."

Misunderstanding, or perhaps just desperate, Joy has the books finished by week's end. Incredulous teacher rejects the evidence. She tests the girl on end chapters, middle chapters, mixing the order, as if the new child were one of those square-root-solving horses from variety TV. Unstumpable if no less diminutive, Joy earns instant promotion to grade four. There, her new teacher discovers that the girl can indeed speak full, correct, even beautiful sentences, only her predicates are always lost to the background radiation of manic classroom.

By term's end, she is kicked upward again. She is made to visit the school counselor, to receive psychological patch-up for what the botched, bounce-around job must certainly be doing to her. Counselor asks her probing but shrewdly disguised questions, such as, Would you rather be a seal in a big seal colony basking on the shore or an eagle soaring all alone high above the cliffs? Seal, without hesitation. Oh? Why? Eagles eat rats and seals eat fish and she has eaten both and greatly prefers fish.

Joy takes pity on this man, helps him get to the point without more embarrassment. "Fifth grade is much better than third or fourth," she volunteers. Yes, yes; how? "In fifth grade, you get to face the street and you can watch people walking by all day long." I see. And what else? "The desks move?" she asks, hoping against hope that this is the right answer.

Do you have any special worries that you'd like to tell me about? Things from the bottom of your secret storage, stories from *before?* Her eyes spark a moment, break for *barrio,* for open country, a place where the smells and sounds that reared her are left a little tropical acreage, where not everyone she loves has necessarily been flayed alive. Before she can control them, her hands fly up like a surprised monkey army breaking for rain forest safety. "Some of my friends here can't pronounce my last name."

The counselor files his report. This girl can be bounced from now until the last institutional foul-up of recorded time and not realize that utter flux is in any way unusual. And yet, the counselor scribbles everywhere on the form except in the blank space reserved for the OCR reader, there are lands around the world where permanent residence, for this child, would be far worse than her list of temporary visas.

In the fifth grade, the bulk of the way back to where she should have been all along, Joy extends her squatter's rights in the New World. She dutifully holds her end of the jump rope, twirling it as she once wound wooden bobbins, in this life singing:

I spy! (Who do you spy?)
Little girl. (What color eye?)
Green eye. Yellow hair.
(What's her name?) Mary Jane.
(Tell the truth.) Baby Ruth.
(TELL THE TRUTH . . . !)

Her chant is a perfect mime except for phonemes slightly pitched, inflected to pentatonic. In the cafeteria, she inquires politely into which foods are acceptable to fling across the room and which are not.

Her academic progress is even more rapid. She has assignments done even before they are given. Some of the subjects she has seen already, at her last roofless holding camp on Luzon. Math and science are just common sense, written in symbols no harder or more arbitrary than the various alien alphabets. She falls in love with map reading: every location, a cross hair on the universal grid. What they call social studies is the easiest of all. She rapidly gleans the generating pattern of history. This country—no country at all and all countries rolled into one—is, like its language, the police blotter of invasions both inflicted and suffered, flash points involving all races of the world, violent scale-tips, constant oversteerings, veerings away from the world's deciding moment.

Her Brief and True Report of the New Found Land quietly maintains that CROATOAN was probably the misspelled name of a nearby Indian clan. No trace of a massacre; no remains. The colonists simply wandered off into the interior, not to escape this foreign force, Joy claims, but to join it. She has found a book in the school library (a lost colonial outpost of progress all its own) that tells how other Europeans, a century later, came across remote Indians with oddly colored hair and speech that bore the inexplicable ghosts of white words, the reverse of those etymological spirits still living in the settlers' canoes, hickories, pecans, squashes, raccoons, corn.

She exceeds her assigned ten minutes, gesturing with her

hands, softly overloaded with discovery, repeating the recurrent theme of this continent. She recites in pitched, open vowels the logs of westward expansion, tales of white Indians in Kentucky, of European languages greeting the very first foreigners to track the upper Missouri. She urges her schoolmates, waving them on in a way she hopes is friendly and encouraging, speculating about the great-great-grandchildren of Madog, a man whose band of Welshmen sailed off the face of the map in 1170 and could have arrived no place but here. This she explicates without the least conception of Wales, or 1170, or Europe, or the Missouri.

And yet, the advantage of the late starter reveals to her what the established are too privileged to see. There are no natives here. Even the resident ambers and ochers descended from lost tribes, crossed over on some destroyed land bridge, destined to be recovered from the four corners of the earth where they had wandered. She tells how a shipwreck survivor named Christbearer Colonizer washed up on the rocks of the Famous Navigators' School with a head full of scripture and childhood fantasies. And she shows how these elaborate plans for regaining the metropolis of God on Earth led step by devastating step to their own Angel *barrio*.

Everything she relates she has already lived through: how that first crew survives on promises of revelation. How the Christbearer mistakes Cuba for Japan. How he makes his men swear that they are on the tip of Kublai Khan's empire. How, in the mouth of the Orinoco, he tastes the fourth river of Paradise flowing from the top of the tear-shaped globe. How he sets the earth on permanent displacement.

Her American history is a travelogue of mass migration's ten anxious ages: the world's disinherited, out wandering in search of colonies, falling across this convenient and violently arising land mass that overnight doubles the size of the known world. They slip into the mainland on riverboat and Conestoga, sow apple trees from burlap sacks, lay rail, blast through rock, decimate forests with the assistance of a giant blue ox. They survive on hints of the Seven Cities, the City on the Hill, the New Jerusalem, scale architectural models of urban renewal, migration's end. At each hesitant and course-corrected step, they leave behind hurriedly scrawled notes: *Am joining up with new outfit, just past the next meridian.*

She would leap across the continental divide, from CROATOAN to the Queen of the Angels Mission for recovering lost souls, go on to describe how this city she has landed in is itself founded by forty-four illiterate, migratory, mixed redskins and blacks, who stumbled by chance upon the rat-scabbed valley they imagined would deliver them. She would woo her classmates, win friends, by telling how the city they now share has within one lifetime served as Little Tokyo, Little Weimar, Little Oaxaca, Little Ho Chi Minh City. Not to mention Hollywood.

But her teacher cuts her off, amazed. Where did you learn all this? "In books," she guiltily admits. "I'm sorry I went overtime."

The teacher—her third in a little under a year—doesn't respond. Doesn't even hear. The adult is wondering how this *bonsai*-framed, walking Red Cross ad in the secondhand Hang Ten tee, whose intact arrival already constitutes a skeletal miracle, who for months (as teachers' lounge rumor recounts) lived on desiccated squid, who has since slept ten abreast on sheets silvery with parasites and counted it paradise to have a sheet at all, who survived by learning to override her throat's retch reflex, whose head had twice to be shaved on return to civilization, how this bit of nubby raw silk, recovered from a forsaken test zone the teacher cannot even begin to imagine let alone presume to teach, could summon up enough linguistic resolve to report on colonial governors and covered wagons and Columbus. How in hell's name could this heartbreak Joy accommodate, let alone decode, the incomprehensible slickie shirts, Slurpees, Nerf balls, Slime as a registered trademark, robots that metamorphose into intergalactic defense depots—all the commodities of exchange with which her every instant on this shore assaults her?

These occult childhood currencies buy and sell the others' oral reports. Andy Johnson gives the fast-breaking private-bio spy's eye profile of this week's slam-dunk, slap-action, singer/actor idol of billions. Pathetic Kelly Frank reports on an afternoon series based loosely on a video game about Armageddon and whimpers witlessly when the teacher informs him that cartoons de facto fail to qualify as nonfiction. The impact of Joy's emergency dispatches upon her classmates is nil at best. Even the sharpest among them sits dazed, too mentally gelded to absorb the first curve of the motions she maps out. If the class stayed amazingly sedate and violence-free throughout her talk, it is the stunned silence of islanders unable even to *see* the first arrival of masts on their horizon.

Bewilderment is always bilateral. The girl's assimilation mounts a makeshift platform rig no wider than the air soles of her jogging shoes. Behind her flawless homework assignments and singsong pronunciation, beneath her mastery of subtle dress codes and cocky akimbo stances, she still floats on the current. She has lived in an open boat since day raids first flushed her from her valley. Evidence slips through the hairline cracks in that celadon-glaze face. The truth is obvious, in the way she hurries over the syllables *joe-nee ap-al-seet* like water over stones in an embarrassed brook. In the way she casts a look out over her audience, a look so afraid of giving offense that all it can do is cower between the muscle twitches of appeasement. She has no choice but to obey the creed of all immigrants: stay quiet, learn all you can, and keep to the middle of the room.

What can the teacher do but give the child an A, tell her the report was excellent, bump her—baffling her further—up to her rightful grade? Promotion solves nothing. They cannot help her here, can alleviate none of that afflicted breathing. The girl is bound fast in the metal burr rasps of jeans, swaddled by clothes that turn her every playground hour into live burial. Her rage for instant adult competence betrays itself. Barbed and intractable, waiting at the bus stop every morning is the scent of saffron, the flake of gold leaf still in her fingers. The temple bells, the lost pitched vendor calls sound, with each additional day-lifetime she serves out in this school-cum-mall, increasingly like a croatoan-note pulling her on toward the next promissory coordinate, deep in the still-unfounded, untouched continent.

There *is* a temple in this city. A classical Sukhothai pavilion stands a dozen blocks from the apartment they have put her in. A *chedi,* squeezed between a video rental palace and WE BUY/SELL/ TRADE ANYTHING. These stepped gables edged in finial flames would once have seemed as foreign to her as the peek-a-boutiques of Melrose are to the Iowa conventioneer. The styles are of another country, a hundred kilometers from her valley, as distant and unreachable as the epic's monkey kingdom. But here, the temple is her one touchstone in a landscape as arbitrary as the language she must use to make her way through it.

Nothing can be assumed here. Total strangers greet you like a long-lost relative, fuss over you, buy you sailor suits, then disappear forever without trace. The price marked on a thing is exactly what you have to pay for it. People leave gaps between them in line, then get furious when you fill them. The water coming out of the wall is drinkable, but ponds and streams will kill you. The dead are not burned, but buried in spacious, decorated plots, while the living set up house on a square meter of sidewalk. Guns are legal but imported parrots are not.

She is saved only by seeing how no one else belongs here either. They catch her eye in the supermarket and look away, confessing. She reads with delight how only Mexico City contains more Mexicans than Angel. She spends Saturdays in the exotic street markets, where a dozen governments in exile make their unofficial homes. Something rustles her ear before she can make out the neighborhood contour: a whisper of how this entire community, even the vested interests, is provisional.

All the property is owned by transpacific gnomes. All the sports heroes hail from the Caribbean. The counter help at the Mr. Icee know no more English than "superfudgebuster." The after-school black-and-white cable classics, their credits packed with foreign drifters' unpronounceable names, always reach the same conclusion: pass yourself off as a local, whatever your origin. The displaced life leads to any ending you like.

Not that she can yet frame the tale in so many borrowed words. Her confusion is primordial. The city she has been set down in is riddled through with time holes, portals opening onto preserved bits of every world that ever saw light. They take her to them on school field trips and church-sponsored socials. That prehistoric, sabertoothed tar pit downtown; the Spanish colonial missions; those Hollywood wax museums; the Wild West storefronts; the sprawling Arab bazaars; the town-sized, live-in, glass terraria arcades enclosing futuristic retail worlds; that magic castle from a medieval past that she would not know from the original thing. These are her reals, her eternally present givens.

She makes nothing of it beyond raw specifics: how to get to school. The inscrutable uses of a library card. The ways of indigestible dried potatoes and bleached sponge bread. A playground where she watches gigglers dig through sand to the center of the earth and come out in China, where people walk on their hands.

The block where she lives, the fourth most dangerous in the city, is for her a garden of almost guilty safety. She sleeps through sirens these days. Even those after-midnight altercations, smashings and bludgeonings in the building foyer outside her room, no longer fully wake her.

The search to avoid attention extends to her choice of three-ring binders, book covers, barrettes, and jumpers. What she cannot afford she constructs facsimiles of—substitute cloth voodoo, clay expiatory figures. She forsakes popularity, a place in the opaque pecking order she cannot even appraise. Joy apes the Angelino offspring only to safeguard her residency permit, that fluke stay of extradition, almost certainly a mistake that will any moment be detected and rescinded.

The tapeworm knowledges she wolfs down only leave her more emaciated. Her virtuoso fiascoes of oral-report earnestness give the game away. Concealed, they fluoresce under pressure.

She covers for a parent back at the rented room, a father who repeats, nightly, in sheer terror, the immigrant litany, *succeed, adapt,
evade.* The girl's show of cheer is so transparent that when she finally appears one day at recess in front of the teacher's desk saying,
"I hurt," teacher herself bursts into tears. Oh God, child, I know;
it kills just to look at you.

But Joy, as always, is something more literal. She points to
a spot above her right ankle. Did you twist it? The girl shakes
her head gravely. She is sent to the nurse, takes a spot in a line
of metal chairs behind the usual strep throats and malingerers.
Nurse detects evident swelling. A little discoloration, maybe. In
her notes, nurse accuses the child, for obscure cross-cultural reasons, of trying to cover up a team-sport injury. As has become
customary, she also misspells the child's last name.

When the sprain fails to heal over the following week, nurse
grows furious. She grills the perverse patient: What aren't you
telling me? She palpates the reticent swelling again, brusquely
but by no means roughly. During this routine handling, Joy slips
unconscious from accumulated torment. Passes out in preference
to crying.

The sense of emergency begins to settle in. Nurse finds no
phone number in the girl's file where her parents might be reached.
A father exists, apparently, but where in the hellish human miasma
he might be found is anyone's guess. A runner sent to the girl's
reported address finds the building uninhabited, uninhabitable,
judging from the husk. The girl is "medically indigent," as the
catch phrase has it. Another underage Medi/cal gal.

The public institutions transfer her from one to the other, bucket
brigade style. At the charity hospital, a roughriding ER paramedic
applies the stopgap, probing just enough to cover his own ass before routing the girl to the pediatric attending, who is, as always,
tied up. One of the service's surgical residents performs the biopsy.
Sinking the shaft, he can see nothing beyond the abnormalities
of his own uncensored imagination—a Rorschach of tissue turning gradually into soft sandwich spread powdered with Parmesan.

The path report comes back stamped "Insufficient Tissue Sample." Don't be stingy, dahlinks. Give us enough to play with, sufficient decent slides to make the necessary stains.

During this whole time, the child's father has yet to turn up. Although voiced only a notch above inaudible, the girl clearly has enough verbal ingenuity to answer the complete history and physical. But when the work-up doubles back on the identity of parent or legal guardian, the girl only shrugs. She is protecting him, by express prior command. The admissions people have seen this before. Dad's another illegal, or maybe a legitimate resident so bewildered by Immigration's cross-interrogating triplicate that he goes fugitive, without the first notion of his legal standing and too frightened to find out on the fly.

But the hospital can do nothing without mature consent. The impasse is resolved only after the pediatric nurse on night duty literally stumbles over the man. Two A.M., and she has gone into the ward to refresh in relative leisure a baby-drip neglected earlier this harried evening. On her way past Joy's bed, she trips headlong over an adult sleeping on an improvised pallet by the cot's baseboard.

The man is wearing a cheap cotton short-sleeve and black pants so loose he has tied them up in front like a sarong. He scrambles awake. A flushed animal, he wavers, torn between surrendering and abandoning his daughter in escape. The moment's hesitation gives the nurse time to summon a massive night-shift orderly who missed his calling as a strip club bouncer. They corner the man, who seems unable to understand their attempts at calming patter.

Soon, the entire ward wakes. Kid Circus spontaneously erupts. Doped, in traction, terminally ill, the imps remain capable of thrilling to a fracas. Sick juveniles aid and abet, to the best of their vitiated abilities, the breakdown of law and order. Staff must resort to riot suppression, the kiddie water cannons.

Questions commence with the return to normal. How did father and daughter find one another with no messages passed between them? They didn't: the only possible answer. How could a full-grown man slip past the whole medical establishment, unobserved? He couldn't, obviously. Yet there is his makeshift pallet, right by her bedside.

Joy, terrified, serves as interpreter for her even more frightened father. The admin nurse in charge says, "Tell him to calm down. We're not the police. No one will hear anything about him. We just need his cooperation, nothing more." She considers adding: *Tell him you might die unless he gives us his signature.*

Negotiations are awkward and drawn out. The man proclaims his innocence. He several times launches into the story of his escape from home, carefully illustrating the persecutions that macerated his family. He lays out their mine-strewn path to the sea. He recites a complex, speculative narrative about what happened to various of his fellow sailors once the craft touched land, their fates, grander or more hideous, enfranchising his.

The hospital objects at every turn: We don't care. We don't need to know. We just want to save your daughter. Both sides have trouble hearing the demure, soft-voiced, simultaneous translator losing strength between them.

Slowly the required papers get hashed through. A staffer reads the legalese and prepares a delicate paraphrase for the twelve-year-old. She in turn constructs a valley dialect version for her father: You agree not to ask them for lots of money if they should make a mistake and something bad happen to me. The old man then launches into an account about a man on the boat who wasn't even a political refugee being given to a rich family up north where all he has to do is skim their pool every morning and douse it with chemicals twice a week. The girl must then translate this story to the objecting staff, silently succumbing to a shame more private and roseate than any bone disease.

The whole transaction is bathed in the surreal sepia of two in the morning. When the signing at last takes place, even that must be mediated. The man inscribes his name in the specified place, but in a Devanagari-derived script that does no one any good whatsoever. The night shift has no idea if the signature is sufficient. They know only that they need *something* from the fugitive before he bolts and vanishes again.

They ask him for a Roman transliteration. Joy must again supply it, reading, sounding, thinking, converting, moistening the ballpoint pensively on her tongue, writing in her bulging, balloon, block printing (she has not yet mastered cursive) WISAT STEPANEEVONG MAWKHAN. Emergency words that will remain behind, carved in this bark, when all this room's transients have moved on, traceless, into the interior.

By what would have been elevenses in another life, the evacuation had run mad. Children thickened alleys into lanes, lanes into streets, streets into high circuses. Evacuee bands swerved across the city, schooling like shoals over lost galleons' hulks. Squadrons swarmed the roundabouts, mobbed junctions, and lined the embankments, throttling thoroughfares in cinematic crocodile lines, past all authorities' ability to administer.

The city was now an orderly anarchy, urgently well mannered, tamed by emergency. *Theatre,* Chriswick had thought, stumbling out to take his part in the overcast September light. The gross, otherworldly theatre of history's gymkhana.

It was as if some world mother had climbed into the lantern of St. Paul's and blown an enormous whistle three times—the signal for home before dark. Only, the motion triggered in delinquent children wasn't homewards now, but out, flung wide, scattering all school-agers onto the sleepy hinterland.

Nothing in the city's two written millennia could match this. The occasional plague, even great fires seemed slack in comparison. Chriswick and his band of assignees, paralyzed on the school steps, watched the tide of London under-twelvers recede before their eyes. Chriswick could not even manage a head count of his own. All Southwark would be emptied by nightfall.

Fifteen years in planning, and the ARP scheme's Friday-morning live run had already pitched the nation into the chaos it meant to prevent. Air Raid Preparedness: within hours, it seemed a cruel joke. Who prepared them for the preparations? No sirens or screaming. No final showdown alarms aside from the gauntlet of Southwark mums sobbing along the escape routes. All the advance warning they had received was headmaster calling assembly and announcing, "Get a move on, lads. You girls too. We're off, then. Do Prince Edward's proud." A picnic on the parade ground of apocalypse.

Chriswick's form sent up a great cheer at headmaster's announcement. Another lark, like the three rehearsal shams they'd had at the end of summer. Anything to escape lessons. The poor wretches hadn't a clue in creation to what lay in wait for them. Not to say that the masters had any more notion; Chriswick himself, in The Palmer's just a dozen months before, had drained an ale at the news of that spineless wonder waving his little scrap of paper around out on the tarmac. The whole local had sent up a pitiful, liquid huzzah of deliverance from evil.

This morning, deliverance disappeared as quickly as the state ration of Cadbury's. Somehow, the typists had managed to produce a label for each child. More miraculously, staff succeeded in getting the right labels pinned to more or less the right human parcels. Then the haversacks, the carrier bags, the personal bundles, and of course the cardboard boxes promising protection against mass chemical death. Chriswick and the other escorting officers donned their humiliating white armbands and away they went, behind a bedsheet banner as if to the bloody Baden-Powell family reunion.

They struck off, although Chriswick hadn't any more idea where they were headed than those idiots on the ARP subcommittee. It had taken the combined intellects of the War Office, Ministry of Health, CID, and—added in a moment of patronizing weakness—the chief inspector of schools to toss off the plan for evacuating four million tinies from the nation's principal cities in seventy-two hours. Unfortunately, no one in the chain of command had thought to inform Prince Edward's, Chriswick's battalion, just how they were to join ranks with that four million.

Chriswick marshalled his contingent on the south playing fields, awaiting word. None coming, he skirted back out among the departing groups and cornered a colleague. "Hunter, where exactly are we headed?"

The swine only shrugged and replied in his best George Sanders, "Why, into the valley of Death, old man."

Returning to his group, Chriswick surprised a dozen boys in the act of putting on their masks, making explosions, and dying noisily. The masks were silly nuisances. How any child could stand the rubbery taste was beyond Chriswick. He'd heard that some up-and-comer at the Air Ministry had put into production bright blue-and-red masks with big Mickey ears—respirators for the two-to-fives in the final struggle against the international fascist subversion of world order.

Chriswick had not asked for this. Teaching had once promised reasonable working hours and a brilliant summer vacation for life. But Chriswick had barely commenced caning his first class for butchering their recitations when the government called him up for the Territorial. And on the very day that he went in to serve notice, school sprung this on him: first shepherd several dozen of London's destitute to imaginary safe havens in green fields far away.

He collected his young and fell in behind the moving masses. The children crocodiled, two by two, as if born to the formation. But despite their exemplary Sunday School marching, his group made no headway through the swells of schoolchild files. Another white armband motioned Chriswick toward a red double-decker at kerbside. He fed the children into the bus, recoiling from the conductor's "You've got their fares, duck?" before placing it as a joke.

In rapid consultation, he and the driver settled on London Bridge Station. The ten-minute ride took three times that. The station was so overrun by evacuees that the bus could get no closer than several blocks away. Chriswick had the presence of mind to leave the children on board and run in himself, to determine the extent of the station's insanity. He milled about in the mob for minutes before locating the makeshift routing table. A foreheadless gentleman skimmed his lists, clicking his dental plate. "That'll be Waterloo for you, sir."

No use even groaning. The whole country had been cut adrift on improvisation. It could have been worse, in any case. Could have been Victoria or ever-weeping Paddington. When he got back to the bus, half the tinned bully beef and potted pears had been downed, and several boys had been sick all over the tartan seats. The furious driver refused to take them any further than back to the school. "Can't be messing about with you all day, guv. I've got a city to save." Good old London Transport; failed to recognize the city even when it heaved all over its upholstery.

Back at Prince Edward's, Chriswick's company rejoined a dozen other rerouted groups trying to get their bearings. To make it difficult for the enemy to hit them from the air, the movements of the evacuation were being kept top secret, even from the organizers. London had become a gargantuan thimblerig, a living shell game. The logistics of shuttling each battalion to its safe destination degenerated into a nightmare Königsberg bridge problem, a problem Chriswick devoutly hoped the RAF would shortly simplify.

The children were growing restive and the morning had not yet reached its worst. No more public transportation seemed forthcoming, so there was nothing for it but to walk. A good hike would at least take something out of the more rambunctious ones. Chriswick opted for Union Street and the Cut. But the way was a disaster. Crossing Blackfriars alone required minor divine intervention.

After an hour on foot, many of the children prayed for a direct hit to put them out of their misery. Almost to the station, they ran across Jansen's group. The sports master was turning the whole incident into a paramilitary exercise. He had his band calling out in drill time, "Are we disenchanted? Not our Prince Edward's! Are we dispirited? Never Prince Edward's School!" On the shout of one, the whole file made a right face. On two, the block-long, two-deep ranks dashed across the street. On three, a left turn restored them to columns. The old tune was right: Britons never never never shall be slaves.

Chriswick had been a fool for thinking things would never come to this. The Bank of England, the BBC—they'd run off to the countryside months back. The other week, he'd heard that the National Gallery was scouting about Wales for idle mine shafts in which to stash *The Fighting Téméraire*. Chriswick's letter box alone should have been sufficient to convince anyone. Wednesday last he'd received a pamphlet with the racy title *Masking Your Windows*. And here they were, his own form, scrambling to evade the fate that until that morning had seemed confined to fairylands like China and Spain. A quarter of visible England took to the streets and turned evidence that we happy few would never outlive this day, nor come safe home.

At Waterloo, ten thousand children seethed about in the waiting chambers and spilled onto the platforms. Mad shouting, panicked tears, bowel and urinary crises laced the main hall. Children were everywhere, laden with prized possessions. They carried school-stenciled portable potties, engaged in last-ditch knucklebones or marbles, and worked out spot wartime exchange rates between *Blue* and *Green Fairy Books*. Chriswick watched as two little girls, no more than six, went about hand-in-hand with chilling composure asking anyone who would listen for help locating the foundlings' group from Samaritan House.

His charges, barely civilised on the best of days, began making elaborate barrow-dances. It seemed best to get them to the trains and let the War Office come try to dislodge them if they were in the wrong place. Ask questions later: the great lesson of historically awakened adulthood needed only this epochal evacuation to at last become self-evident.

The way to the platforms was a study in crowd madness. Another foreheadless fellow with clipboard snagged his group before they could board. "Bit tardy, aren't we? You were supposed to be here hours ago."

"Yes, well, the town's not quite itself today."

"Listen, you. I'm responsible for seeing fifteen thousand children onto thirty trains, each with twenty carriages unloading at over a hundred villages. Don't come snivelling to me."

"Oh, shove off."

"Right. Just so long's we understand one another. You'll be on Platform Twelve, Carriage F." One supposed this exchange would be remembered fondly years from now, a nation pulling together in dark times.

Passing through the throng to change platforms, Chriswick heard an announcement over the Tannoy. All men with strange accents asking for directions were to be beaten senseless. A notice board on Platform Twelve verified that the waiting train was theirs. But neither platform nor notice disclosed anything about destination.

The sight of a virgin car fresh for despoiling should have revived his group's flagging spirit of adventure. But the children suddenly began to cry. It finally dawned on them that the clothes redeemed from the pawnshop, the ruinous knickerbocker glory of the night before, were certain indications of the end.

The train pulled out. In every third garden abutting the line, people were sinking corrugated-steel air raid shelters. Chriswick made a half-hearted effort to patrol the carriage. In front, the girls shouted endless choruses of "Ten Green Bottles" at the top of their working-class lungs. In back, the lads took turns peeing out the windows and squealing, "Watch out! You'll get your willie cut off!" He did not bother reprimanding.

Clearing the city must have lasted several lifetimes for the children, even for those who had never been on a train in their lives. Outside Dartford, an evacuation volunteer finally came through with instructions. "You'll be getting off at Canterbury."

"Good God, man. You're joking."

"That's what it says here."

"Canterbury's another *city*. And it's halfway to Berlin. They'll all be incinerated before . . ."

"Hush, sir. *Pas devant les enfants.*"

It was all too ludicrous. Evacuating children to Canterbury was like, well, carrying coals to Newcastle. The place would be torched for the cultural value alone. It could only be some embittered, Trinity double first's idea of ironic retribution for his clerk's job at the ARP: send a band from Southwark to the holy martyr's shrine.

The children were spent by the time they reached their destination. But the hard part had not yet begun. Canterbury Station was decked out in banners, but any welcoming committee had long since gone home. Chriswick huddled the little ones outside the station. The afternoon began to turn crisp. A terse billeting officer arrived, with forehead this time, but without chin. "We were told you'd be in at one."

"Yes, well, we weren't."

"Evidently." They packed the children on buses and brought them to the market square outside the cathedral gate. There, patriotically obligated villagers gathered round, sizing the wares, every so often issuing a sceptical "I'll take that one," or "Have you got two girls around eleven? We want a pair."

People came looking for cheap labor, replacements for dead offspring, a government subsidy. The Shirley Temple look-alikes went first, to the local child molesters. Some brothers and sisters refused to be split up; other sibs were dispersed to opposite sides of town without so much as a swap of address. The billeting officer made hurried notes of who had whom, but Chriswick knew the scribbling was worse than worthless. These children would never be found again.

Today's trip had already dispersed them past recall, even before the town had turned out to bid for them as for so many second-string elevens. And the solid Canterbury middle class, clucking at Hemming's head lice and the fungus behind Davis's ears: by tonight, these redoubtable folk would learn words long since banished from England's green and pleasant land.

In a modest few hours, an entire nation had abandoned itself to a scavenger hunt with consequences at least equal to those of the world war's latest test match. Was the country counting on being home for Christmas again this time? These children, doled out so freely in the butter market, would grow up away, in the homes of strangers. A whole generation scattered at random, scientifically indifferent, city to country, south to north, Catholic billeted on C of E, Formby fans descending on the lords of the manor, the desperately poor laid out on the thick linen of the privileged. The island had conducted an irreversible sociological experiment at a clap, almost without thought.

By tea, all the potential providers had disappeared, leaving Chriswick and the billeting officer with the South Bank's least marketable. One of the Shillingford twins was wailing that nobody wanted them, while the other shouted excitedly how that meant they got to go back home. The rest of the rejected sat about fiddling with gas mask boxes, all in.

"All right then," the officer declared. "We'll just place the rest of these door to door." This they did, as if delivering milk. They paced the circuit of city walls, knocking on houses with known spare rooms. When the residents resisted, the officer bullied them. The Shillingford girls were split up, one going to a black-and-blue woman whose husband roared from a hidden back room, the other to a widower who had his paws up the girl's knickers before the door closed. The billeting officer mumbled something about correcting the situation tomorrow. Levy went to a mother of five who first ran an interrogating hand through the boy's hair, feeling for horns.

At length, they chiseled the group down to a grim cadre of remainders. The billeting officer sneaked a look at his watch. "Would you excuse me a moment? The wife's expecting me for dinner. I'll be back directly."

And Chriswick was left in the dark, in a strange city, alone with half a dozen dirty, cold, starving, fatigued, senseless children not his own. He ducked into a stall and bought them chips with salt and vinegar, out of his own pocket.

Down the lane, an ancient parish church held out the possibility of a place to sit. At the door, a tiny fist restrained Chriswick by the trouser turnup. "Sir, what sort of church is it?"

"What? Oh, for God's sake, Evans. Don't be an idiot. It's just to rest a minute."

Evans kept from breaking down only by viciously inscissoring his lip. "Really, sir. I can't go in if it's a . . . you know."

"It's a *Saxon* church, boy."

"Oh. Very well then."

The children collapsed in the pews, two or three finding the strength to genuflect. Chriswick busied himself with the tourist plaque—yet another Oldest Parish Church in England—to keep from ulcerating with murderous intent at the billeting officer, headmaster, the ARP board, and Hitler. A sudden, pure-pitched resonance rang out through the church, and Chriswick spun about in surprise.

In silence, while his back was turned, the chancel had filled with choristers. Boys, no older than his own vitiated group, stood decked in white surplices over crimson cassocks. They must have hid in some vestry and filed in while Chriswick wasn't looking. They now formed two reverent banks facing each other in the stalls, and, with no adult to be seen, they launched into a late evensong.

Chriswick rushed to the pews to discipline his group, sit them up straight, or drag them out of the church while he still could. But such was unnecessary. First, there wasn't a soul in the place for his Clink deportees to disturb. Further, Chriswick's children, amazed at a handful of boys their own age conducting an unassisted musical service, sat rapt on their benches, entranced by the sound.

The versicle line fell to a boy who couldn't have been more than fourteen. He sang the plainsong in head tones of a purity that would disappear with the arrival of adult conscience. While the last, long note of his chant still hung about in the vault, its answer arrived in a rush of chorus, slipping off into conductus, flowering full with Renaissance polyphony.

Chriswick knew something about church music, had even partaken once, when younger. But he was unable to place this setting. The moment he thought Dunstable, the piece slid off a further century and a half, to Tallis or Byrd. After another measure, it sounded like one of those imperial, last-century anachronisms, returning to ancient and better days while the world around this island went down in flames.

It started out Latin, but it soon became very Anglican. The text turned into a dog's breakfast—bits and pieces from the Book of Common Prayer. It had been too long to be sure, but Chriswick seemed to make out familiar lines, like forgotten but still familiar faces from old school photographs. Give peace in our time, O Lord. (You'd think they might have suppressed that bit of questionable taste this evening.) Defend us from all perils and dangers of this night. All that are in danger, necessity, and tribulation. All that travel by land or by water. All sick persons, and young children. All prisoners and captives. The fatherless children, and widows. Keep us from the craft and subtilty of the devil and man.

Doubly odd: the setting did not correspond to any service Chriswick had ever heard. No speech—no invocations or readings or prayers. Only this pure singing, from voices of shockingly high calibre. How could a small parish barn, however historic, put together such a choir? Child voices, usually selected for sight-singing ability to perform two hundred settings a year while the trebly tint lasted, seemed here to have been chosen for nothing short of transcendent throats. Every lad in the dozen possessed uncanny musical maturity; they'd been singing for twenty minutes, a cappella, without straying from pitch.

The singing—at the end of evacuation, after hours in flight from the penultimate urban raid, deciding lifetimes by lot—was too much for Chriswick. Those pitches of absolute tone stripped of vibrato cut into his muscle like angel scalpels. A religion that worshipped always like this would have counted Chriswick still among the believers. Freely expanding parts—shared out among twelve boys, the lower voices pitched up into the innocence of airy rapture—interrogated the scar where his abdomen had been.

Assertion and response sounded fifths so clean it made no difference whether the purity was put on or not. This one thing alone of his race might be worth saving from the coming bombs. These soaring, high, head voices said what it was to be alive, to be anything at all. To be displaced, begging temporary address, a choirboy in this alien, bass body, under attack from on high. To be a child from the East End, father a sot, mother numbed by tons of others' washing, a boy duped by a good matric into going on and becoming a teacher, winding up by perverse twist of fate back in the Clink, now subaltern to a war that will send all England to final sleep. To be a functionary, assigned the pointless task of stripping children from their one anaemic chance at temporary home, children by adoption and grace just now discovering too late that all they ever wanted to do while alive on this earth was to sing out blamelessly, however laughably, *Make us an acceptable people in thy sight.*

Alarmed by silence, Chriswick looked up to find the choristers filing toward the vestry. He called out, "Hallo. You boys." The choir turned in unison, as if noticing for the first time that the nave was inhabited. Chriswick's speaking in church wiped away some cobweb restraint from the boys. At the common signal, choirboys and frayed evacuees met in the transept crossing, converged on each other, touching, talking rapidly, collapsing back to their proper ages.

Chriswick found himself unable to take the few steps to where the children gathered. He sat in the pew and gazed on this meeting between mutually uncomprehending races. The choirboys paid court to Chriswick's two youngest girls, giving them chocolate that appeared by magic from cassock pockets. He overheard one of his toughs compliment a singer. "You don't 'alf sound like a host of bleedin' serabim."

Each group sniffed the other, excitedly. The spent children had found a second wind. The day, the evensong had so drained

Chriswick that he could barely open his mouth. From the back of the nave, he called out to the youth who had sung solo, "Are you boys at the cathedral school?"

The boy jerked. "What cathedral?"

Chriswick's surprise was even greater. The boy was American. Imperceptible when singing, the speech was unmistakable. Something in the boy's reticence suggested secret transatlantic alliances, affairs of state ahead of their time.

"Where is your conductor? Are you rehearsing for something?"

"We're touring," the boy replied, in churchly whisper. The Southwark children, awed by his accent, crowded around. The Yank began spinning them a fantastic travelogue, an adventure Chriswick could not make out from the narthex. The chanter handed over for examination a metal pendant hanging on the end of a chain. Some High Church bauble, an excellent Norman copy it seemed from Chriswick's distance. A trumpet-toting angel, but with an astonishing, disfigured face. The street urchins fingered it in hushed admiration.

A fatigue suddenly swept over Chriswick, a heaviness past describing. Sleep penetrated into the rote core that had kept him moving for the past twelve hours. He felt as if St. Martin's were filling with a gas that made him want to curl up and fall blessedly, permanently unconscious. He pinched his jowls with his nails and shook himself. With effort, he stood and left by the west portal, needing air.

He stood in the churchyard, wanting a cigarette badly and a pint even worse. It was pitch dark; English evensong was over. Where was the billeting officer? Where would they sleep this night? Perhaps it would be best to bring the remainder back to London on a night train. They had spoiled enough lives already, condemning those children to the whims of strangers. He did not believe for a minute that any spot on this entire island would be safe from the coming nightmare.

The pilgrims' town was settled in for its night of sacrifice. All across the country tonight, in towns sheltered and forgotten, in

Somerset and Devon and Dorset, in minuscule specks in East
Anglia named Diss and Watton and Scole, in unpronounceable
Welsh stone settlements, on the coastal ports, in Seaford and Hast-
ings and Skegness, steeped in the Midlands, streaming over farms
off the moors and dales and downs, ranging out to Lands End,
Penzance, the project was coming home. Schoolchildren fleeing Manchester, Birmingham, Liverpool, Leeds, Sheffield, and
London scattered like factory workers at history's closing whistle.
From the southeast, over the coast, Chriswick could hear a low,
mechanical hum, still far away but rushing toward the cliffs with
each tick of earth's politics: the blanketing engines, the flotillas of
their common, aerial destruction.

He turned back into the church to gather the remaining children and find at least temporary shelter for them. But the building
was empty, as bare as the old woman's cupboard. Chriswick, in
a daze, checked the niches and sacristy. There were no chapels
where a group that size could hide. He was tired, tired past telling. He could not even remember, from any past so distant as an
hour ago, how many he had come inside with. No one could have
left by the west porch without his knowing. And yet, choir and
makeshift congregation—both gone.

After the doomed city, the impassable Southwark streets, escape's debacle, the chaos of Waterloo, the market humiliation, the
door-to-door desperate soliciting, the last sung service of innocence, the children had shaken loose of the real. The young had
abandoned him to whatever fairy survival adults might still believe
in at so late an hour.

Questions for Further Study

What is the historical background behind these events?

Who is "that spineless wonder waving his little scrap of paper around out on the tarmac"?

What is the source of the allusion "into the valley of Death"? How does this irony contribute to the description of the evacuation?

Where, do you imagine, do the children disappear to at the story's end?

Define: elevenses, matric, Cadbury's, Norman, Saxon, Baden-Powell.

The nationwide evacuation of children described here really happened. Research this strange event and speculate on the impact it made on the life of a nation.

Interview a contemporary who has had to live through a similar experience. Gather his or her life history, and tell it.

They beat him within an inch of his life. While it's too much to say that he loves every minute of it, Kraft does come back for more. Takes a licking and keeps on ticking. Where'd that come from? Takes a beating, comes back bleating. Takes a mauling, keeps on crawling.

And not just on account of the student loans, which he could pay off easily from behind a desk at some university health center, pushing antacids and peddling the bland diet sheet to overwrought undergrads. Something inside him must prefer this, the assembly line of cases spilling out of packed cutting rooms, this dance marathon of service, sacrifice, and salvation. Op 'til you drop. Only intolerable fatigue keeps at bay the worse punishment awaiting him in slack hours. Whenever he's dealt more than three free hours in a row, he winds up on the phone, long distance to lost friends, philosophizing, predicting things, asking acquaintances spooky and proscribed questions.

Idle too long, he dallies with the idea of social reinstatement. A little free time, and he begins to believe he might be able to settle in somewhere. Memories of the place still lodge like lost baggage in the base of his brain. Sky-blue, home free, nights of lazy music while elaborate shaggy dog jokes drift in and out of attention. The kegger tap, the stoked fire, voices in the kitchen exchanging book and movie titles like spent mistresses. Close shoulder-brushes with strangers and intimates. Men to postmortem the latest big-league box scores and international fuck-ups. Women for declaring long unspoken love, just for the hell of it. Two consecutive days off fill him with yearning for the whole forsaken orchestral palette of human contact. Maybe a mortgage, for once, instead of the perpetual twelve-month lease.

When the free hours grow too expansive, he takes Schwartz, the Board cram book, up to the hospital roof. This aerial view, distance perfecting the taillight-as-platelet metaphor, never ceases to calm him with scale. Sheer surface area, baroque Brussels-lace intricacy of civilization's switchboard interconnects, insists that he need never worry about leaving anything undone. It's all being checked off the To Do list somewhere, looked after deep inside this city circuitry. Somebody's taking care of it in a remote strip mall, office complex, or underground research facility out on the periphery. Or if not here, then within another city matrix elsewhere in the megapole, along the freeway, further down the continuous data stream.

During heavy call assaults, his beeper ponging every few seconds, the phone machine LCD stacking up a Sisyphean queue of unpluggable leaks, Kraft tends to stray into the contempt bred of familiarity. (And what could be more familiar than pawing minors' privates from the inside, hands not just on their dollhouse genitals but *underneath* them?) The temptation during unstructured R & R is even more dangerous. Sentimentality sets in, fueled by nostalgia of the worst kind. Nostalgia for events that haven't happened yet.

On the roof, along various rays streaking off from Carver's ground zero, Kraft picks out his recent ports of call: Hollywood Pres, Hills Brothers General, St. Tomography's. The so-called skyline of this city is so low—all the potentially tall buildings demurring at sissy altitudes, each lisping, *After you; No, after you,* what, with all this free land and the Big Quake ratcheting up to unleash any century's end now—that the place names on his résumé spread around him as clearly as the castles on a cartoon postcard of the Rhine.

He can take them in at a glance, opaque oxides and noxides permitting. Photochemical smog, tucked in lovingly by heat inversions, welcomed Cabrillo himself, three centuries before the first car. Ozone in the wrong place, that's all. What we need's a multibillion-dollar bailout, a five-mile-radius undershot water-wheel to hoist the O, back up where it belongs.

Before drifting too deep into the red zone of human empathy, Kraft indulges in an exercise of extended focus. He calls to mind how, in each of these hospitals across the city where he has served time, and in all the numberless institutions where he has not yet set foot—hospitals and research foundations and university labs all the way up the coast from Baja to Livermore and on into the wilds of BC, shooting out across the Aleutians into central Asia, down through the polyglot Indonesian archipelagoes, into the Indian subcontinent, reversing Alexander back to Our Sea and up into Europe, over the Atlantic to North America again, through the government-injected foundation mazes of the East Coast, propagating à la kudzu gulfward, stampeding the Dakotas like an all-terrain, all-weather, year-round ragweed—in all these facilities, one single human woman metabolizes. A strain of her culture inhabits major health institutions all over the planet. This lady, a world and wider, is named Henrietta Lacks, but goes by her pseudonym, Helen Lane.

She's even better known by her nickname, HeLa, that oncological favorite cell strain of researchers the world over. The abbreviation is some cultured microbiologist's idea of literary allusion. Hela, Norse goddess of the dead. This HeLa is the goddess of a spectral eternal life, metempsychosis of the petri dish. Since they scraped her tumored cervix four decades ago, hearty Henrietta lives on in hospices and wayhouses everywhere, even in the bowels of Carver's own Knife and Gun. She splits, respires, ingests, and transforms nutrients—cancerous but immortal. Helen's cells dream the dream of one world, patient in the dense foliage, waiting their cue to rise like rapturous doves.

She is the modern world's oversoul; Kraft will go so far. Her spread is a bitmap index for these million points of hospital light running over the earth's every wrinkle, trying to assemble themselves, spell out some vast declarative that would be visible from

outer space—maybe Schiller's "Ode," an arrow delineating a
continent-sized landing strip, the unit axioms of human geometry, or just another galactic backwater neon come-on insisting
WE DO IT ALL FOR YOU.

Up here, seated dangerously on the unrailed ledge—not even
a handhold should a gust of wind break his tentative balance—
Kraft hears Helen's breathing on the semiarid air. She will make
her run soon, become not only the oldest living human, but the
planet's largest. Her cells, spreading through all longitudes, begin
to reconnect, to learn how to talk to one another again. He sees,
all the way down the Golden State, the local metabolite lines already laying themselves down.

The convertibles are out tonight, sea turtles massing on that one
lunar interval to hit the beaches for an orgy of egg burying. A
desert caravan of them, tops down, flog the blocks below, creeping
randomly, probing, one rider per machine, each with a radio set to
10, tuned to the identical station. They comprise so many stereo
simulcasts that, even from all these stories up, Kraft hears the disembodied messages take to the air and aggregate into a leviathan
Announcer. He leans out over the ledge, daringly far out, tempting
a shift in his center of gravity to change his life for good. Bubbling
up from the cars comes this night's incarnation of the reassuring,
ubiquitous heartland accent, giggling shrilly that there are only ten
shopping years left until the Blowout Clearance.

The aerial overview affords him a glimpse into the neighborhood's after-hours transactions. In the middle of the next block, a
quartet of heavies improvises a counterless concession stand. Spontaneously, the line begins to form, snaking in a direction covertly
understood by all takers. And it's not just members of select under-
classes who join in this evening's bake sale. Practitioners of all the
proverbial races, colors, and creeds, the complete spectra of socioeconomic plumage drop by. Each participant knows the nature of
the real estate. They've come to buy, finding their product without the benefit of megabuck broadcast ads or four-color magazine
spreads. After a bit, Kraft begins to make out the formations in

play—the deep safeties, the cornerbacks prowling out in the flats for the first sign of those who don't belong. A sharp two-pitch trill and the whole carny operation instantly shuts down tight.

And Dopplering gruesomely, audible long before seen, a pack of wailing ambulances homes in from the worst of directions. The sirens shriek through these streets like kids furiously racing to kick the can while trying to yell ole-ole-all-come-in-free-o. With this flank attack, the roof too outlives its expediency for Kraft. Its promise of protection turns out to be as anachronistic as massive ramparts, post-saltpeter. He can go no place, no commute long enough, no hideout where they cannot beep him or obliquely conjure his assistance, his call night or no.

What in disintegrating creation do they expect of him? When will it be enough? Never, comes the siren's singsong answer, the little disco ditty of this minute's shattering accident. There will forever be as many demands on his technique as there are ways of children going wrong, ending up in this halfway hospice of disaster.

THE WAYS ARE many—more than he can keep apart. On Grand Rounds, he maintains the current catalog only by metonymic shorthand. He visits the Rib Metastasis, the Crushed Kidney, the Mitral Valve, the Saturday Night Special. Everyone is pathetically trusting, shouting excitedly at his bedside arrivals, calling his name out confidentially, intimately—*Doc Kraft*—as if urging on a stickball teammate. Pitifully friendly, fast to transfer, ready to love him more than they love their own fathers. Unfair comparison: half of them don't know who their fathers are.

The Fiddler Crab knows. Fiddler's dad decided that the prescription that Mom brought home from the freebie clinic to treat Fiddler's cinder-infected hand was gibberish. The boy's mitt decided otherwise. Now the Crab is back, claw immense and gangrenous, stinking so badly that Kraft can barely get close enough to schedule him for immediate draining.

He cannot linger, but must keep rolling down the roster. Next up, he checks the chart on the No-Face, a prepube whose misfortune it is to have been born with nothing from the bottom of the eye sockets down to the anterior palate. The plastics team has been working him for years, and after half a dozen reconstructions (although "re-" is an overstatement in the No-Face's case) the boy is no longer completely a monster. He still resembles an Etch-A-Sketch something fierce, but he can at least go out in public. Kraft has asked to be allowed to look in on the next buildup. As dues payment, he is given what remains of the pre-op. He visits the kid on the eve of the procedure. The No-Face is fearless, cheerful, but still cowering behind the veteran campaigner's blasé affect.

Leaving the boy's bed, Kraft is replaced, changing-of-the-colors style, by the pediatric psychiatrist from the rehabilitation team. The No-Face breaks into what will one day, after another half-dozen operations, begin to resemble a huge grin. "Dr. Kraft," he calls out, grotesquely polite, the accents of an overrehearsed child star skipping over the years cheated from him, "I'd like you to meet my friend Linda."

Kraft turns to go through the amenities and stalls at his first glance at the woman. Her face is imperative with memory. Her look is full of reminders, pieces of string tied around his finger that long ago rotted off. Brown dominates her register, with jet hair and black eyes that spring continuous surprise from wells of unlikeliness. Her build is assertive enough to make her hospital sack coat look like a poolside party dress. Hands sufficiently pudgy to keep them from preciousness, and calves to kill for.

Linda attacks the No-Face with tickles, laughing aggressively. "And this is *my* old buddy, Chuck."

Chuck, through screams of pleasure, calls out to Dr. Kraft to intervene, stop this madwoman. But Kraft just stands there, helpless with sudden propriety. And probably Chuck doesn't really want any help here. The boy is so completely in love with his physical therapist that Kraft's only option is to get in line behind him and take a number. Linda, oblivious, stops tickling long enough to wonder out loud to herself, "There certainly are a lot of amazing creatures on God's earth."

" 'Creature' is the right word for it," Chuck laughs, pulling a grimace that exaggerates the plastic mounts lying beneath his grafted skin.

Linda drops her whole beautiful, lip-round mouth in mock shock. "Why, I oughta . . ." And she sets to tickling him again. Like sharks smelling a feeding frenzy, the other children in the room pile over to join the altercation. "Yo!" she shouts. "Hold it, gang. Things are getting out of hand here. Okay, all of you: 'I will not assault health professionals.' One thousand million times."

This elicits great squeals of pleasure—the most fun any of them have had all week. For some, the most fun they've had since their mothers set themselves on fire while freebasing. They set to work on the assignment at once. Like the immigrants to this continent that they are, they attack the problem via division of labor. They'll do their punishment in huge, vertical, mass-produced columns, one word each. I I I I. Will will will will. Not not not not. The kid who gets "assault" breaks it into "a salt," and the kid who gets "professionals" isn't even in the ballpark.

"C'mon," Linda says, pulling Kraft by his health professional's sleeve. "Let's beat it while we can." The woman is ample, ample in ways that Kraft hasn't even thought possible in years.

Half from memory of rosters, half from sneaking a peak at her tag, he tries, "Estefan?"

She brays. "Close. Espera. And assimilate that *s* a little bit, huh? My mama's from Dairyland, U.S.A." She clips down the hall, already on her way to the next child on her list. "*Mestiza,* I just met a pretty *mestiza*. . . ."

"Oh Jesus," Kraft mutters, catching the cadence at last, if only a little. "I thought that word went out with the prewar genetics texts."

"Well, we're kind of an army surplus outfit, here. In case you haven't noticed."

"Richard Kraft," he says, sticking out a paw that she is now too far down the corridor to grab.

"Oh, I know all about who you are. Now you're going to ask me out to lunch?"

"Is that the book on me?"

"Yeah," shouts a prematurely gawky kid just slipping past the two of them. "That the book on you." Linda collars the child and tells him when he must show up at her office, downstairs.

"Now. You were saying?" She looks back at Kraft, her chin too curved to jut, her eyes wild with that gorgeous surprise.

"I was just about to confirm the ugliest rumors about me."

"Right. Tomorrow at noon. The cafeteria, where you always meet Nurse Spiegel."

Oh, *that* Nurse Spiegel. Well, yeah. Small world, just friends, etc. But Ms. Espera doesn't wait for any clever protests. She simply states, "I'll warn you in advance, I've got proven soul-saving tendencies."

"Messianic *and* mixed blood?" he tries feebly. "Sounds dangerous." But she is gone, ducking into the next doorway. In a minute, the room issues shouts of more free-for-all scrimmage.

Despite the public poop on him, Kraft has, to his mind, been involved in only three relationships that reached life-threatening proportions. One long followed by two shorts, the Morse letter *D,* if it means anything. It occurs to him, a fact dredged up from adolescent ham radio days, that a long and two shorts followed by another, terminal long would be an *X.* As in X marks the spot. As in just sign on the line marked X. Cross hair. Algebraic variable of choice. Universal placeholder.

Walking away, he cannot suppress a stupid lilt. He passes the nurses' station, where it seems somebody's had her ears to the listening post. Whatever the source of the info, Nurse Spiegel is wringing the phone like a chicken neck and saying into the receiver, "No, Dr. Kraft can't be reached right now. He's in Skulk Mode. Can I take a message?"

He looks up Linda and she *is* there, in his pocket two-way translation dictionary: wait, waiting, patience, composure, delay. In a holding pattern, like the rest of sentient hope.

But he doesn't need to wait long to see her again, to learn why she agreed, his rep rap notwithstanding, to meet him for lunch. The answer comes swiftly, and it's merciless in its disappointment. The woman wants to talk *cases*. She brings her list to lunch, although she clearly doesn't need to refer to it. She knows all these kids, and not just by complaint. Names, dates, the whole curriculum vitae on each one of them, all lodged up in that voluptuous raven's head.

Her mother may have been a cheese squeezer, but daughter Linda definitely hails from somewhere far south of white man's sovereignty. She is a great and constant toucher, handling everything. She fingers the catsup bottle, feels the weave of his tie. "Can you help me at all with Suzi Banks?" she asks, clamping him familiarly by the upper arm. "The girl hasn't spoken a word since you fitted the bag." She dunks her chips liberally in salsa, downs them, brushing crumbs from his sleeve and smirking guiltily at her own healthy appetite. "And Chuck. God. Too brave, the boy. He doesn't have the first idea about what he'll be looking at once childhood is over." She taps the back of Kraft's hand in worried appeal.

"And oh." She grabs his shoulder without a trace of self-consciousness. Propriety wouldn't occur to her. Her nature lies completely beyond more median practices in these parts. She is clearly, constitutionally incapable of worrying about who she is or how she might be taken. She *knows* these things, the way her fingers already know the cut of his clavicle.

He grabs her back in return, on the opposing side. Pinches her a little on what he hopes is a radiating line. "Yes? Oh? What is it now?"

"And oh," she repeats, smiling too strongly to be mistaken for coy, "I need to ask one of you how radical you expect Davie Diaz's spinal thing to be."

That "one of you" gives away his role for her here. "Spinal thing?" he asks, dripping with dryness. What he really wants to say is *Davie?* What's with this first-name basis, Espera? Davie? Kraft would be lucky to place the boy by sight. "You've looked at the chart, haven't you?"

"Of course I've looked at the chart. But you guys are so cagey on paper. Never put down anything they might hold you to. I want to hear the real story, out loud." She footsies with him under the table, her toes on his arches. Her face pleads with him playfully, goofily. And his urge to get up and leave evaporates.

So he's expected to do the consultant physician thing, nothing more. The irony of the situation is not to be missed: across the table from him hovers a face promising all the loveliness of final escape, sensuous lips savoring the salsa, seducing him to deliver. But all she wants delivered is more shop talk. She is the living apotheosis of the paging device. Messianic tendencies indeed. Even sex, the last refuge of free men, is turned to a mere marketing campaign, corrupted by altruism.

But the woman (and here's the frightening bit) is even sexier for all her sainthood. Kraft watches her talk—conjugating with her hands, her flashing pseudo-senorita eyes, her three and a half octaves of voice arpeggiating amazingly from bari Bacall to trebly Billie Burke. And he thinks: Here, perhaps, is a woman even worth playing social worker with. They might make up their own rules as they go along. He twice tries to steer the topic away from child rescue and retrieval toward a bit of rehabilitory salve between consenting adults. For the moment, she will not bite, which is the hell of it, given the woman's dentition. She sticks to business, displaying an impressive knowledge of anatomy, if some of the desired nomenclature is missing. Ah, but he could teach her the technical terms.

Well then, let him see how she looks when self-righteous, blazing, her principles affronted. A bit of Mexican spitfire shouting how you doctor bastards are all the same: you all think treatment ends with sterile bandages. "Linder," he scolds her. A too-affectionate name derangement for the first half an hour. But she smiles at the liberty, a glorious, asymmetrical, arousing flare forming in her brow ridges. "Linder, all this holistic medicine stuff. It's all a tad too type A for me."

"You—! Not to be believed. *I'm* type A? You little boys arrange it so that you can stay up all night—"

"*Night?* Singular?"

"Go ahead. Prove my point, why don't you? Stay up all week, then, with a dozen spinning plates up in the air at once. Big tray full of shiny, sharp tools at your beck and call. You make this colossal mess and then leave us to clean it up over the next several years. Talk about MI candidates. You're so wound up from constant jolts of fourth-and-inches stuff that you probably can't even hold up your end of a decent dinner conversation."

"Try me."

"Only if I get to pay."

"See? Type A. I knew it. Crying shame too."

"Come on. Consider it a little payola. You let the drug company pimps take you out to floor shows and things, don't you?"

"I have never let a drug company pimp take me to a floor show in my life."

"No? But you accept the little bribes? The pens and key chains . . ."

"Nope. Nada."

"The note pads with prescription logos up top?"

"Uh, well . . ."

"Well, okay then. This comes to the same thing. I take you to dinner. You do little favors for me."

"I would love to do little favors for you." He finally manages to slip in something of the old cadence.

A glaze spreads across her face, impish: "Yeah? Really?" Coquette, perhaps, but bathed in unmistakable pleasure. Surprise? Impossible. Looking the way she does? How could she have come this far, with those shoulders, that rib taper, these cheekbones, and not know what she does to half the men in every room she enters, and a handful of the women too?

"Yeah," he says. He'll let her pay for dinner. They'll alternate every other lunch. She can pick up the theater and symphony tabs, and he'll square the Maui vacations. The mortgage they'll do proportionately by incomes. They can split the cost of the double funeral down the middle.

They both behave themselves admirably, right up until she must go keep her afternoon appointments. She amuses him with stories about having to prove her citizenship the last time she did a day trip over the border. "They started asking me all these questions I haven't thought about since sixth grade. I panicked and confused Francis Scott Key with Julia Ward Howe. Finally got in by naming three of the U.S. Olympic hockey starters."

"Oh, hockey is it? So you go for the rough stuff, do you?"

"I'm sorry. I can't help myself. When I see those enormous guys body-check one another into the boards . . . Mmn!"

"Do psychological bruises count?"

"Afraid not. They've got to be real, flesh and blood owies." When he suggests that they watch some surgical study videos together, she slaps his upper arm. "I may be perverse, but I'm not sick."

Exactly: whole, hearty, vigorous. Which is why she shines out in this place, a minister of health touring a plague house. She agrees to a movie date. But it has to be a commercial release somewhere, about teenagers bopping forward to the future, or loved ones coming back as ghosts.

"By the way," she adds as wistful caveat. "You may want to keep in mind, I do happen to be ten years younger than you."

"Which one of us are you warning?"

THEY MEET OUT at one of those hundred-and-forty-four-screens-under-one-roof places. The requisite separate cars, of course: it's a Pacific Rim first date, and they want to do things right.

Kraft loads his beeper for the evening with the weakest batteries money can buy. He picks Espera out from across the packed lobby, like there's a moving flood spot glued on her. They're both a bit buzzed. Linda buys enough Milk Duds to keep the Vienna Choir Boys dosed until all their voices change.

When they seat themselves, she launches into what for her passes as the most self-evident coming attractions topic in the world. "Davie Diaz is in extraordinary pain. I know you said that a certain amount was inevitable for the first couple weeks, but I don't even know where to start with him. The Wilson girl, on the other hand: you seamed her up so beautifully that she barely even needs me."

She speaks quickly, as if needing to squeeze more syllables out of her finite column of air than pneumatics allows. "What's your take on Joy?"

"I'm in favor of it."

"You juvenile. Are you sure you're a decade older than me? Twelve-year-old Asian female, presenting with severe incursive . . ." Her words are like Care's ushers, roving up and down the aisles, swinging their flashlights. "Joy, with the impossibly long last name. Cambodian or something."

"Pali," he murmurs. A memory from across immense distances sounds out the edges of his mouth. But the look is too foreshortened to be made out here in the darkened hall. "I mean, the name is Pali. Joy Stepaneevong."

She looks at him as if he has just revealed himself to be the Gretzky of grief interdiction. "You *are* a doctor, aren't you? Oh, Kraft. What in God's creation are we going to do with her?"

"I've not actually met her, tell you the truth. I've looked over the . . ."

"*Cojones!* You're slicing into a little girl's foot on Friday, and you haven't been down to see her?"

The trip to Maui is off. The double funeral too reverts to separate tabs. Exuberance dies on the vine, replaced by a hard little spoor case of disappointment. "I suspect I'll get around to it," he enunciates.

"Sorry. That was out of line." She clams up, curls, braces herself for the worst. Her flip side is instant, and the withdrawal has something brutal and expectant to it. She tosses a raven's lock with one hurt hand. Faster even than their first flirtation, the whole promising lanyard unravels. Her chest heaves discreetly, tender lip trying not to quiver, to be found out.

"No," he rushes out. "My fault. It's that time of the surgical cycle." He gets her to snicker, despite herself. Oh, Linder; do I need you already, a perfect stranger? "It's just that . . ."

Say it, then. It's just that, if you knew all their names, if you staked your heart on the prognoses of even those most likely to survive, you'd keel over with the bends, die of decompression sickness inside a week. What can she possibly know of the technique, of the essential, deadening distance from accident that one must preserve? Her kind of care would kill the death-defying skill instantly, if ever once admitted out loud.

"Linda. Maybe it's indicated by all the studies, but I just can't do the hand-holding thing."

At these, his words, a second change smooths her surface. As drastically as she dropped into vulnerability, she is back. She cups her all-protecting hand, crooks her pointer at him. "Com'ere, little man. Let's see." His cardiac muscle bangs up against the chassis like an adolescent's. She takes his hand, stretches out each of his fingers in turn. She folds his palm into hers for the first time, holds it as if embracing the prodigal son. "I'd say you do all right." The house lights dim on cue and the feature begins.

During the film, she is wonderful. She organically annihilates the armrest between them. At certain key points in the plot, she nudges him and scribbles circled numbers down on a note pad produced from her purse. Afterward, she extemporizes at length the thoughts that each number stands for. Number one is that according to her, people don't really talk like that. Number two is that they should have had the Russian and the American switch briefcases by accident. Number three is she wants to know how high the feature's leading love interest ranks on his personal lust-o-meter.

"Know what?" she asks, vamping for him. "If you stay on this side of the lobby, they don't recheck your ticket." She casts him a challenging nostril flare, suggesting they partake of a hundred and forty-four films for the price of one. Well, what the hell. He missed this kind of thing the first time around. So they take to screen hopping, rolling from one anthology of images to the next in best tragical-comical-historical-pastoral style, giggling at all these eternal middles of stories, each one ludicrously stripped of any sense of beginning or end.

They watch, in converging splices: the story of a woman who gets gang-raped in a bar, a reexamination of Chicago mobsters and one of quiet Nazis living in Cleveland, a stock market scandal torn from yesterday's headlines, the real-life events of a horribly disfigured kid, a heady biopic of the discoverers of DNA, one of an early film mogul, of an early automobile antimogul, the pioneer astronauts or folks very much like them, Billy the Kid or a pack of teens very much like him, teens triumphing in historic sporting-event re-creations, teens inadvertently starting the Third World War, aliens inadvertently starting the Third World War, and adults advertently starting the Third World War. Every one a virtual fact, actually dramatized. Based on a true story.

Stories like you read about, and all included in the price of entry. They do the Scheherazade thing all over again, only this time it's not just the beautiful child-bride who's gonna lose her head if the spell of narrative slips. Should the film break or the power brown out with the last unpaid bill for fossil fuel, should the projection booths simultaneously proclaim themselves autonomous republics acting in the name of fundamentalist revenge squads everywhere, should the two of them be caught and sent home on movie probation, the death sentence will at once fall not just on this one double-dutch evening but on the whole heterogeneous experiment in migratory, free-market, fiction-consuming, two-car-date democracy. This multimovie complex will take its place along-side ziggurats, galleons, the colonial pith helmet—all the museum bric-a-brac emblems of lost eras in the world's blind expansion.

Linda laughs, drags him by the arm into another show-stall. At the peak of her giddiness, he feels out her mouth with his.

She stops laughing long enough to kiss him back. The sneaked interval reveals just how many years there are, in fact, between them. It synopsizes the drama of two health professionals who have only just met, out on a mobile Saturday night, testing the myth-edge of accessible, Valley happiness. Yet he cannot help but wonder, despite lips whose novel turns compel his full attention, despite the plot complications hinted at in the feel of her hips, despite her hand wandering across his back, tracing out a story thread that could lead anywhere at all—he cannot help but ask himself how, exactly how things are going to end this time.

GOTTA GO SHOPPING, he announces. Sort of thing a body needs to resort to every now and again.

"Shopping?" Plummer echoes incredulously. "As in *food* shopping, you mean? You realize, don't you, that grocery stores have become the exclusive last resorts of hopeless reactionaries and the desperately poor?" Common knowledge, man. Who in this self-respecting world eats at home anymore?

They sit in the Sauna, a gritty cross between locker room and on-call lounge, so baptized because of the uninsulated heat pipes that hang out of the ceiling, peeling the wallpaper and misting the furnishings with a light coat of mildew. Ordinarily, well-offs like Kraft and Plummer would have to pay big bucks to do this kind of slumming. But here in the charity rotation, it's just one of life's simple fringe bennies and franking privileges. Add to this the rooms Plummer has christened the Squash Courts and the Jacuzzi—obscure maintenance function facilities now employed by residents in competitive rituals of moral toughening—and one has a complete home away from home.

Plummer, hands down the toughest among them, has food stores in this neck of the world's woods pegged. The places are hopeless archaisms. Ordinarily, Kraft has no trouble avoiding them. But when, the thousand and one movies having all ended happily, he asked the lovely Linda for a repeat engagement, he could come up with no restaurant suggestion that she found both edible and politically correct. "Why don't you cook something for us, Ricky? That'd be different."

Different indeed. He hasn't brought a foodstuff under his roof for months, aside from the odd soda cracker packet and single-dose PCB tub of marmalade pocketed from Carver's subsidized eatery. And yet, the prospect of rolling around in the deeper spots of his shag with a woman of mixed ancestry who is still in her early twenties is enough to make him want to suffer the whole avuncular hunter-gatherer charade, and like it.

"You going alone?" Plummer resorts to muted, deputy-sheriff intonation. "Good God, buddy. Be careful out there."

Kraft, to keep from having to give the forced grin, asks what his blademate is doing for sustenance this evening.

"Is that an invitation?"

Absolutely not. Read my lips, as the commander in chief likes to say, in an era when actions no longer speak louder than even the softest subvocalizings.

"Well," Plummer wheedles, "I've kinda had my eye on that cast-off of yours. You know. That Nurse Spiegel? What we used to call sloppy seconds when we was kids?" The uses of loneliness rear their ugly hydra heads. Is Kraft himself the last person on this coast who didn't realize he and Nurse S were an item? "I figure she's had enough time to get over you, but not enough to resist the temptation of a sudden and insensate rebound relationship. Maybe ask her out to this little candlelight place on Far Point Pier . . ."

Far Point was wiped out by storms last spring.

"Was it? I never heard. I've been busy. Well then, that Dish-pansation place on Ventura?"

Torched by the cattle-rights activists.

"Holy jump-up-and-sit-down. What the hell's happening to this place? Drugs, Mr. Rico. Tell me: just how responsive might everybody's favorite RN be to the Tastee-Freez phenomenon?"

The grocery store, when Kraft at last faces it, is its usual, fluorescent humiliation. Food Warehouse, that stately rollerdrome, smacks of historical emblem. It seems the penultimate whistle stop on the Big Parade from pickle barrel general store to palatial Hot-to-Go emporium. Standing in embarrassment in the produce department as they weigh his goods, Kraft fights the urge to shout, "That's okay, I trust you." At the meat counter, he sees this woman in dark glasses who he thinks may have been the oldest daughter in an ancient family sitcom, a formative, masturbatory fantasy of his. She warns him off with a "One word and I'll radio the SWAT team" look.

Half the food packages bear, on their printed labels, black, fake "Actual Price" numbers, inked out by the same press run in red, the universal color code for Discount. The afterthought text reads: "Your Price: Only . . ." How stupid do they think we are? Or rather, how stupid are we obliged to be? Kraft forgets to weigh his bulk lentils, and the cashier makes a tremendous pedagogical show of sending the sack back with a runner, personally apologizing to the line behind him for the man's hopelessness.

Only when he gets the ingredients home do things really start to get fun. It's been years since he's cooked anything except with the cauterizer, but this seems child's play. Why haven't I cooked more often? I mean, they tell you all the necessary ingredients right up front. Then they step you through exactly what you need to do to put it together. Just like assembling that old one-to-whatever scale model of the *Graf Spee* with Dad.

He thinks: If I can remove and reattach a living, three-inch kidney, I can certainly shuffle a nine-inch dead soufflé. Christ; anybody can cook. All the essential vitamins and iron, plus the perfect seduction thrown in for grins.

She buzzes. Kraft casts a last panicked look around the efficiency. He's had the foresight to stick everything in the utility closet, and the place is looking sharp. Standing tall. But Ms. Espera is not even halfway through the door before her face makes this incredulous O, like she's just witnessed a murder. "You *live* here?"

Why? What's wrong with it?

"Oh, nothing; I'm . . . just a little surprised, that's all. Say. How much are they paying you, anyway? Do you have a lot of debts from med school or something?"

Not the first impression of choice. But he still has his culinary trump card with which to win this woman's undying affection or six months' worth of lust, whichever lasts longer. The soufflé comes out looking like the Thing from Three Mile Island. He can't understand it. He goes through a Morbidity and Mortality session with her, talks out the recipe, insists that he did exactly what they said to do. Linda explains to him the difference between beat and fold, a semantic differential he had attributed to the pursuit of rhetorical variety.

"But it's delicious," she objects. "Hasn't affected the taste at all." And she laughs with her mouth full, blockading the bits of exploding food with a gesture hazardously endearing. She insists on washing the dishes right after they finish, before the microorganisms can claim their eminent domain. And she invokes all the magic little rituals the female will make of the slightest procedure.

"Now," she says, drying her hands gingerly on his lone dish towel, "are we going to do some aerobics for a little bit, or what?"

The assorted alarms pounding through him flush a rush of neurochemical pheasants into the air from out of their cover in the undergrowth. "I believe we are."

She nips variously at his face. They lower each other slowly to their knees, hands blindly reaching out at violent angles for support. Then they are sitting sweetly in one another's laps, gently necking, mouths in each other's mouths.

This has no precedent for him. Adrift, cut loose, a little more blessedly free, at the mercy of the equatorial currents. They begin to explore in earnest, hungry but shy, like pre-meds set loose with *Gray's*. What is her waist's wave, the taste of her undulating armpits? How does the scoop of her scapula surprise, the taper of her calf turn imperceptibly into ankle? He all of a sudden knows nothing of anatomy but the gross outline, the generic stamp. Form is uniquely overhauled again in her particulars.

She is so alien, so deliciously not him. That's it, that's why his body craves her foreignness. His appetite for sexual pleasure kicks in, follows its intimate program to rediscover—again and again—the heft of this new *instance*. Vintages, mint conditions, proof bouquets. Her parts are as unique as core samples of fading sunlight. They loosen another notch, from sitting to slouching, ever nearer the carpet. There seems to be always one more buckle to her. Her hand, lighter, longer, lets its tensors clamp against him in a way he has never before mechanically known. She curls girlishly atop him on the floor, and through her body's otherly weight, he recovers his own.

Flavors, he decides. Life at any time of year always comes down to flavors and focal distances, magnifications, the concentration of waves into visible, scalding frequencies. The textures of the silky cotton he strips away from her are infinite. The smells extruded from her body's many passages form a complete concordance. What will her next anomalous patch of skin be like? The wayfarer's question, the only one worth wondering about, extends indefinitely.

She begins nosing him all over, eyes closed, head tilted intoxicatedly forward. Sniffing him like a truffle hound. Her eyes bat, her succulent lashes lap his neck. Her hand grips his trachea; thoughts of Plummer's ER tales of eroto-strangulation flash through Kraft's soaked medulla. What might he and she try out upon one another? How easily might dress-ups, all manner of exotic clothing, get out of hand. There is nothing they might not discover in themselves. She brings her mouth up to his ear. What taboo words? Could be anything, and in imagining the forbiddens she is about to try out, he fills almost to the point of spilling all over her.

"Do you like me?" she whispers, wrenching violently on him in the dark. She holds his head in some decimal fraction of a nelson. In another minute, she will rug-burn his scalp. "Do you?" Answer me. Is it the extension of Linda into stranger spaces, or some cruel multiple, a sinister substitute teacher, her identical twin?

"Do I like you?" Stupid parroting.

"That's right." She tongues the question as through a police bullhorn. A growl issues from underneath her sternum while she pins his face in a three-point takedown. Yes or no. Let's hear it.

How can he begin to say? The shot seems to dolly slowly above this postprandial wrestling match until he stares down on the whole teeming planet from on high. Her question becomes the one thing anyone asks anywhere at this minute, in all time zones. It interrogates every home, hacienda, hut, *Haus,* health spa, and hovel in the world's directory, and a fair chunk of the underground addresses. Superpower summits sashay around the issue. Corporate heads put it to pitiful proxy votes. Silver anniversary vets lip the litany over hurled crock potsherds. Internationally acclaimed actresses, the fluffy chenille of mass wet dreams, plead it with unseen audiences in darkened halls. Nurse Spiegel petitions Plummer with an unguarded glance as he makes his bluff pass at her back at Carver. Even Plummer's pass is a crude paraphrase. Terrified children of the ward, half hardened criminals from birth, demand something in writing from parents who never show. Rebuffed, they seek it from surrogate candy-stripers just now tucking them in for the night.

And this woman under his hands asks *him,* outright, in so many words. She threatens, as if his answer will tip some electoral balance. A yes might persuade a fraction of forsaken global plebiscite that paths besides abdication are still available to them this evening. She wants to hear that they are booked for the comprehensive journey, if only in steerage. Does Eligible Bachelor Number One, in efficiency number 1275, in this honeycomb of tasteless prestressed concrete on the sovereign, sunnyside corner of Mission and Delivery drives, D-5 on page 77 of the fabulous cartographic compendium of this entertainment capital of the world's largest self-undermining semifree-trade zone, on the cutting, jagged edge of all that is left of what liberal democracy must yet become in this emblematic, exemplary, guiding high beam of a high-ground nation, all but amok now that it has outlived its onetime prime motive and moral force, its colonizing adage,

> Use it up
> Wear it out
> Make it do
> Or do without,

does he, this lone fifth-year surgical resident (having exiled himself to his field only on the belief that cutting and pasting was the one profession that might keep him from backsliding into the existential aloneness his horn in F no longer protected him from), does he *like* this undulating orchid that he has plucked and pinned corsage-style to his designer gold shirt for the nonce, for the old beloved one-night time being? Do you recognize? Know me? See me? Approve?

He cannot answer her and escape with his life. Cannot say that it chills him already when she smiles, when she turns her head in a certain arc, when she kisses him like a deranged adolescent, when she laughs like an arrested preteen at the self-same movie kisses, when she attacks professional problems with the earnestness of one who still believes in healing's ability to at least break even. He dares not say how she promises to salve his inevitable next bloodying, to brush away like cobwebs the scrub-suited gang of thugs that wait for him, trimming their nails nonchalantly with number seven recurve blades at the end of the alley. Just to look at the promise in her features chills his gut as solid as the old tennis ball dunked in liquid nitrogen.

He looks up at her from the floor where she holds him pinned. So clean, naïve, those fantastic arching eyebrows, her expanse of cheek built up from subcutaneous muscled fats as flexible and unassigned as empty last-century maps of the poles. She is one of the lights, the breeze-borne weightless people capable of taking pleasure directly from the air. He at last manages to get out: "I love your face."

She tenses, her fists clenching against compromised parts of his body that she could do genuine damage to if forced. "My face? What's the matter with my face?"

The theater-hopping, roller-skate-voiced kid from the first date vanishes. All trace of that supercompetent child-rehabilitator steeped in her rounds, the pro he first asked out, is gone. A piccolo trill of authentic fear struts front and center in her voice, above the hundred-piece marching band. *Nothing the matter,* he wants to say. I *love* your face. There is something in it I can't quite place.

But he can say nothing out loud. She twists her neck nervously around, like an icy Hitchcock blonde looking about for the blunt instrument. Only, her hair is coal-blue, her skin tinted iodine for purposes of international intrigue. Then she pounces, using on him the same trick she used to seduce the boy with a crater where his nose should have been. She begins tickling him, the same frontal attack of hands that will forever make her the No-Face's first and only love.

Kraft, like the boy Chuck, is wildly, sickeningly ticklish. He buckles, tries to throw her off, but she uses some kind of Eastern center-of-balance thing to keep him under. He is twice as big as her, and in the throes of torture. The woman knows exactly what she is after. He screams for mercy, but she just skritches him on the floating rib, his truly sensitive spot, grinning, "Go ahead. Yell your baby-brown eyes out. Who's going to answer? Screams from a single man's apartment, in this neighborhood? Not even the police'd be stupid enough to mess with that."

She levers down his wrist with her knee, grazes his flank with long strands of hair until he starts to hyperventilate. Slowly, agonizingly, she voices over, "I don't know why I'm letting myself get involved here. I hate doctors. I swore to myself to make it a rule never . . . You're all deranged. You're probably a real sicko, aren't you?"

Her face to his exposed nipple, just dribbling little spurts of air across his horrendously sensitized flesh. She has him flailing, laughing in agony, his eyes like Zeeland after the dikes were bombed. "Oh, you poor sick little baby. You little crippled baby child. Does it hurt? Come on. Give in. Occupational rehab. You need it bad. Trust me. I can help you."

The quick flurry of feints and ambushes slowly flutters home to the prime roost. Her infant flank attacks gradually mature, mutate into effleurage, tapotement. *Yes, here,* her fingers say. We know. Act it out. Do your worst. No one can hurt anyone else. A little physical therapy is all. Just what the psychiatrist ordered.

You must believe, first, in the leaping cure. In this more than anything, even though the children's ward is its living denial.

Espera believed already while still a schooler, long before experience dulled the bloom of rehabilitation theory. Two years into her first job at a place where gleaming machine panaceas are less than laughable fictions, her faith in the method is accredited. The treatment of choice here consists of a little light exercise and a few read-alouds. Pragmatics allows no other therapy. All she can do is rally the routed field trip by returning it to memory's locales, the place it might even now call home.

She cannot hope for state-of-the-art here at this public spa, given the art of the heavily indebted State. Procedures that clinics just over the freeway consider barest livable minimum are denied her. Funds for physical medicine—vague promissory notes dangled in front of her team from quarter to fiscal quarter—fail to meet even need. In place of Hubbard tanks, they get hot showers. Their muscle-zapping machines look and sound like bug lights. Even her exercycles and wobbly massage tables were picked up on the cheap from a supplier indicted in an elaborate scam involving large-scale plundering of Salvation Army drop boxes.

Lacking the requisite physiatric high tech, she must resort to restorative tricks. Each of her jerry-built cures is tailored as far as possible to the specific destruction set before her. In this, the indigence of her clients actually assists. Where the cash transaction is the exception, ordinary accounting is, if not waived, sufficiently relaxed to permit experiment.

Carver is one of those places used to launch careers or generate articles that land real, paying jobs. She does her flood control under ranking Pediatrics administrators, M.D.'s who see no children anymore, not even their own. Linda alone of them would put down permanently in health's Hooverville. In her heart, she already exercises her option to buy. More counselor than physician, she masters the tissue repair and recoordination, the schedules of heat and exercise behind all makeshift disaster relief. But these she supplements with pure play, coaxing out recovery on tempts and teases. She sails through this shoestring outfit conducting sing-alongs, assigning mock punishments, doling out treasures, improvising her own recuperative scripts. Open stage—every night, amateur night.

How many ways can a child go wrong? Leave aside the chromosomal, skeletal, and congenital disorders. Forget the untreatables, the ones even she could never repair. Count only those acute enough to force institutional treatment. Forget the nightmares of the preemie nurses, the inexplicable arrests, the sudden circulatory collapses late on winter nights. Pinpoint the preadolescent, her specialty, if she is allowed the luxury of having such a thing.

Begin with the classic infectious checklist—the potentially fatal poxes that her college texts elitely insisted were eradicated in industrialized countries. Add in the respiratory infections, the bouquet of asthmas, cystic fibrosis, miliary TB. Endo, myo, pericarditis. All known blood disorders, book length in themselves. Lymphoblastic leukemia, that spring lodger come to spread its putrefying possessions into each limb of the playhouse tree. GI failures, renal annihilation, precocious or arrested endocrine systems, convulsive disorders. Palsy and a legion of other lesions and tumors, meningitis, diabetes—a list of lethal birthday party invitees that would cripple the coolest clinician to think twice about.

Espera has studied enough Latin nomenclature to tear the short-answer soul out of any semester's final exam. Daily practice leaves her in sufficient command of *Stedman's* to return surgeon-speak in spades. And yet she swears still by an artesian aqua vitae free of all pharmaceutical sediment. She has watched the watery

placebo work with her own eyes, even in the death dormers of
this sick building. She has softened the root tumor—that secret
thing all childhood illnesses share in common, whatever their
differential diagnoses—with leaping treatment. Has seen hope
open like any iris to the light.

Figure in the assaults by things that as yet have no medical
name. No matter; every injury is of a piece. The precise etiology
of reality's strike is almost irrelevant. All impairment flows from a
shared subterranean source. Her pedes are broken by a first disease
long before they are hit by the particular trauma that dispatches
the ambulance. Malnutrition, psychodisorientation, pellagras,
anemias, dementias, the regional varieties of abuse distinctive to
city hospitals: all leave traces, a common pallor that shellacs her
every child's skin.

That culprit, the *Ur*-wrong, underwrites even accident, the
leading destroyer of under-eighteens. It lies beneath the hungry
ingestions of household poisons, the handgun mistakes, the training wheels spinning their mangled aluminum sidewalls in the air
after a hit-and-run. Even burns are at best secondary: she's read
the study showing that half of all arsonists are children looking
for love.

Among her floor and outpatients this week, she has Chuck,
the child born without a face; Jorge and Roberto, twin preteen
overdosers; the girl Joy, darkness creeping up her ankle; the brutally ectomized Davie Diaz and Suzi Banks; a new boy, Nicolino,
wasting away freakishly; Ben, the double amputee. She has only
a single treatment to bring them all back. And she *will* return
them, as far as they are willing to run. She can do nothing for the
parts irreparably lost. But she has something to leave in the dark
reaches, the space in each one where the earliest, inviolable fable
of self still stands intact, ready to respond to a little food, workout,
heat, and play. She can plant a start in that place waiting to be
proven wrong, a plot that will still heal at the first touch of fresh,
outrageously naïve narrative.

She possessed the germ well before the six years she spent up north, studying by the bay. It was built into her posture already as an undergrad, that era of cotton and arm down when she lived in a state of permanent expectation engineered by temperate breezes. Her personal knowledge turned heads from across the medical quad. It lent her a come-on, broad-based cheerleader appeal without any of the attendant, affected sorority girl contempt. She knew, just by living, how to thrive in the health profession, without once having to book for a single hourly in the subject. She was born knowing it, the single greatest advance in contemporary medicine, the one that at last set organized care on its unfolding path: the discovery that healing only begins with treating the wound.

This was the breakthrough forced on an industrialized world by the arrival on the doorstep of a permanent surplus of maimed child veterans who, for the first time, survived their treatments in numbers beyond ignoring. She gleaned it by second nature, even while her professors mouthed the formula from their operating theaters. The kindergartner who shoots screamingly awake from an anesthetic dream to find a huge, paste-oozing, suture-stubbled, crimson gashwork down the length of her abdomen tends to resort to her original conviction, buried under ancient keloid scar tissue: I knew it. You tried to *kill* me. You cut into me with *knives*. Fail the patient here, fail to talk that scream into remission, and all the mediating incisions, however beneficial, will remain forever open, pussing subcutaneously until final discharge, the hour of the child's second street death.

How best, then, to reassemble what the king's combined cavalry and foot labored over impotently, powerless to transact? (She wonders, mouth twisted in healthy skepticism as she reads that rhyme out loud, what, pray tell, *horses* were supposed to contribute to restoration.) If musculature alone were at stake—relearning how to swing a bat or kick a sprocket—a few simple professional references would address everyone. Even the subtle ruddering of a pencil—that immensely complex navigation across empty expanses of paper—can be brought back from nowhere, relearned in committee.

Warmth, water, a little oscillating current, passive tensor-flexion aid, and a sprinkling of weights can work wonders. As much as you can, as steadily as you can. You learned it all from scratch once; you can repeat the process, from crawl on up, with whatever parts fortune has left you. That much is simple routine. Rigorous, brutal, overwhelming at times, but straightforward. A little technical know-how, some trivial persistence, and that would be the extent of the job description.

Still-forming bodies can heal, sometimes faster than she can prompt them with suggestion. Baby bones refute excision. Unripe brains reshape to compensate for lost capacity, almost as if youth still remembered the starfish and lizard trick of regenerating lost parts. Near-full functionality returns almost as quickly as it was struck down. Espera's infallible algorithms even return words to the mute. She has taught pseudolaryngeal speech to a roomful of croakers barely out of tadpole stage. Suck in a gulp of air, swallow it like food. Belch it up from your esophagus, shape it with gullet and nose and tongue to produce real *names.* Ready now: in unison. She's had them singing, industriously belching out "Up a Lazy River." And she would have yanked them kicking and buzzing through "Flight of the Bumblebee" had they not used up their available esophageal supply on gales of laughter.

Walking, swinging, singing, eating, bending, grasping, blinking, breathing, peeing, flipping, sitting, seeing, shouting—all the procedures of earliest urgency can be taken out for a reconstructive spin. They can be approximated by brute, repetitive, accumulating rote no different than the afternoon hours upstairs with a music stand, wood-shedding on *the clarinet, the clarinet, goes doodle-doodle-doodle-doodle-det.* But her job is to carry off that old joke: to get them playing the instrument again, even when they'd never played before.

There is a catch. All destructions dip layers deep. Knives sever through much more than muscle, than mere mechanics. Every child who shuffles up her office ramp is a shattered hierarchy.

Whole systems have been shaken loose, one from the other. The skeleton may move impeccably after a year or three. The circulation routes generously reopen, but the larger links are lost. The simplest gesture, the pressure of an overhand curl contracting the hand into a wave goodbye, no longer means what it used to. Will becomes detached, as cleanly as retinas in a playground brawl.

The leaning, eager hesitance of ducking through a jump rope only begins in the feet. The legs are just the first fuse. Once quadriceps do their buckle and flex, a spark must spread outward, catch fire. The real rope skip is desire. Motive must magellan its way across the cerebral map until the whole quorum organism grows ready to hurl itself through the rotating whips. Try to teach *timing,* the delicate diplomacies of depth perception and projection. Instruct in wish, give daily classes in confidence retrieval. Try to instill want, the belief that shooting through the twirling ropes has some primal significance. Convince them that the brandished, braided lasso cycloiding its playground arcs, wobbling like the precessing equator above a navigator's head, is not glass infested, will not slice like the collector's scythe. Ah! To teach *that,* one needs an advanced degree.

What's more, the skipping per se is trivial. The tribal jingles that go with it are the tricky part.

Who are these children that the surgeons palm off on her to recondition? Here, in the sunny Southern Caliphate, they make up a smorgasbord of least-favored nations. There's not a single schoolbook innocent among them. She's had little girls who needed propping up in bed, glaze-eyed and indifferent to everything but broadcast. She has treated the spreading allergies of the underclass, those puffed black bruises that can be only one thing. She converses with furious patterers who growl in hyped-up rhythmic pidgins she cannot understand.

Her clients belie every story she would read to them: wasted torsos inscribed by gang insignia. Scurvied spines that slump appalled by their first balanced dinner. Ten-year-olds who food-process their eyes with homemade weapons. Who put their faces through the windshields of cars they were stealing. Who, by junior high, replay in miniature their parents' lifetime criminal loops—expulsion, record, parole, repeat offense. Who spit into drinking glasses and clean their teeth with salted index fingers or the corners of scummy undershirts.

Yet she knows them all by name and history, almost before making their manila acquaintance. She can recognize each half-*compatriota* from her own sixth-grade studio photographer's composite photo of a suburban school grotesque in its Wisconsin, fairy tale privilege. The might-have-been lives not yet extinguished in their faces seem to her the bewildered remakes of safeguarded Julie Axelrods and John Lartzes, prophase faces frozen for little Linda Espera at the age when she last saw them. She knows: every one of these visaless deportees would kill for the chance to regress to afternoons of benevolent chutes and ladders if they could.

The disease, the accident that brings them to her is just the tip of a spiked pithing stick lifetimes longer than the few years these victims have been given. She has brought children back from the point of despair, returned them to whole except for a refusal to urinate, or an uncontrollable need to pee around the clock. Or eat until unconscious, or starve into airy nothingness. Or scream at certain colors and pitches, or buckle over from imaginary pains. Or refuse to talk, or lose all ability to stop. She has seen a child pinch off his finger in a folding bed rather than let himself be discharged back home.

What medicine can she possibly slip them, during the few weeks when the state will pick up the tab? She needs the psychic analog of antimalarial paste from thirteen buttercups. Brown sugar and beets for whooping cough. Bandages of spider webs, cobwebs, puffballs, for binding up wounds. Powwows for burns and bleeding. Nothing less than immigrant folk remedies will help. Leaping cures for those abandoned to a newfound land.

A single checklist informs her every therapy. If their legs jitter, she takes them jogging. Longer and longer circuits, through the wards, up and down the emergency stairwells, around the parking lot, in neighborhood runs swelling incrementally until they are off, no turning back, gone. If their voices catch or slur, then it's amateur forensics, debating gowns scissored from surgical scrubs, the stage curtain stenciled with the hospital logo. A season of speech, and they begin throwing off the podium yoke, exiting into the imaginary wings in search of more *in situ* material. If they still scream in their sleep over torched apartment blocks, then she assigns them to a design team busy drawing up an entire utopian city from the fireplugs up. Those who have fallen out of perfect pitch she recruits to carol the geriatrics, and if their "First Noel" comes out more sinuous mariachi or reedy street Arabic than Eurodiatonic, then it's that much more medicinal for the chorus.

Reading out loud helps as much as anything. Hardly among her official requirements; not included in what they ever-so-modestly pay her for. It's strictly volunteer, candy-striper activity at best. But nothing can touch it for building collateral trust. When the parents go home (yes, she repeatedly tells the slumming doctors, even welfare mothers notice when one of their dozen is missing), after her own official rounds are over, Linda sneaks back into the sick bay, setting off shouted requests. Box scores, pop lyrics, soap opera synopses, fanzines, miscellanies, believe-it-or-nots, books of video game clues: they demand any printed word whatsoever from the outside world.

The reading therapy is as much for her as for them. It restores her to prepragmatics, when she still believed she might somehow make a living out of the communal pleasure of words. At eighteen, the mystery unfolding around her like a convoluted orchid, the erotics of social prosody suggested for a semester that English lit might be a legitimate, maybe even a responsible major. In those days the fate of the West at its pivotal, wavering moment seemed to depend on what the word "still" meant in the line "Thou still unravished bride of quietness." She hears it again now, out loud—

poetry, antique verse so strange and illegally alien in this place that it holds even hardened and dying children spellbound for the scope of a few stanzas.

Read-alouds, the oldest recorded remedy, older than the earliest folk salves: these are her only way to trick her patients into downing, in concentrated oral doses, the whole regimen of blessed, bourgeois, fictive closure they have missed. Tales are the only available inoculations against the life they keep vomiting up for want of antigens. She reads them things she herself would have grimaced at at eight, knowing that without at least a taste of that outrageous fable of return in their deficiency-distended stomachs, they will never survive their own recovery. Children already lost to inherited addictions sit in a rapt half-circle, listening to their moonlighting occupational therapist reading from a book she has found in the ward library, a volume rescued from God knows what improbable secondhand shop of anomalous trinkets fetching absurd designer prices for hysterical campiness—tea trays emblazoned with saluting fifties hostesses or wall lamps made from the front ends of fatuous Chevy sedans. She plows through the spine, ticking off, one by one, the tales from that anthology, *A Country a Day for a Year.*

Tonight's story is from the distant North. How is it—the primary mystery for students of children's literature—that in all eras, the richest hints of hidden destination derive from the North? The differential is wider than the gap between brocade and flax. She has her private answer: the South insists on the child as embryonic adult, while the North has always known that the adult is just a displaced child. Is it freezing climate that crystallizes imagination, or is there some Southern Andersen or Grimm that her anthology has not yet discovered? She reads to them tonight about an innkeeper's wife on the North Sea, who dreams of unspendable treasure to be found outside the bourse of the big city. There, at the bourse, a broker laughs at her gullibility. "Why, I myself have dreamed of a fortune under the bed in an inn on the North Sea." The woman rushes home, tears up her floorboards, and finds her kingdom. This is the key to narrative therapy, the cure of interlocking dreams.

That surgeon she has foolishly flirted with comes into the ward on autopilot, stands and examines her. She feels herself a girl in this moment, reading. The anachronistic tableau fades as he watches, a freak five-point snowflake melting in the hand. She keeps her cadence up for half a story before he withdraws, thinking himself unseen. Outside the hospital window, even in the failing light, every listening child can see it is still East Angel City, a neighborhood a year or two away from setting itself on fire, exploding again under the pressure of daily unanswered need, routinely violated due process, random strip-search and seizure. They need only shift their eyes to see a skyline rushing to void all the clauses of the social contract it has but acquiesced to until now. Each thing she reads them tells in code how they are rudderless, at the mercy of their own unchecked unfolding, racing to event's end.

Story Hour is strictly giveaway. Tax wars in a country that considers public payment to be an infringement on private liberty guarantee that all costs remain hidden, shunted off on revolving credit until the unpayable lump sum comes due. Linda never got around to economics in school. Perhaps that's why she, almost alone, sees that society's every advance up to this minute has been paid for by liquidating principal, mortgaging the unborn. It takes no special macroeconomic smarts to see where the curves of expenditure and cost will intersect. She reads them another tale, one where life exists entirely off wishes and interest.

Where necessity goes unpaid, she must donate her time, extending physical medicine until she becomes half teacher, half trainer, half director, half coach, half psychologist. When she reads out loud to too many, too long into the night, when the story safeguarding her listeners against actual awfulness is too Northern and icy in its enchantments, when the sense of its foretold ending grows too immediate and real, she begins to draw up, by story's end, a report card for the entire delinquent human project, a teacherly evaluation of this global little handgun victim, curled up invalid in front of her for the evening:

MATH AND SCIENCE: A. Student possesses enormous aptitude. Advancing rapidly on all fronts now . . .

LANGUAGE ARTS: B–. Although gifted here, student remains undisciplined. Lapses into fits of inarticulateness when excited. Penmanship a joke.

SOCIAL STUDIES: C. Disappointing. Despite every opportunity of late, fails to rise above provincialism. Shows little sensitivity to foreign affairs . . .

ECONOMICS: C–. Extremely uneven. Impressive progress in some areas, at the expense of others. Has not yet figured out the basic principles . . .

CIVICS AND POLY SCI: D. Don't even ask. Pleads no contest on final exams.

MUSIC AND ART: B +. Student constantly surprises. Varied and restless. Creativity really coming to the fore. A big overhaul may lie in wait.

HISTORY: Incomplete.

HEALTH AND PERSONAL HYGIENE: F. Five million children dead each year of *diarrhea,* for God's sake.

With such mixed grades, can the creature ever dream of graduating? Could any tutoring, any therapy at all work at this hour? *Radical surgery,* her new perhaps-beau might whisper to her. No program short of total slash-and-burn has any chance in hell of helping.

Fortunately, she's never been one to worry about the odds. One reaches an age when being realistic just isn't practical anymore. The work she does all life long may save no one. Even for the limb-clipped, organ-stripped preschooler with the IV walker, she may do nothing but cake-makeup a scar that the crippled child will never walk away from whole. She may at best only delay the night of full payment, the helpless screaming fit of fear laid down in personality's pede ward, in the so-called formative years. But whatever she gives them will be more than they arrived with.

And if she shares her professional conviction—say with this new man, at thirty-three already too worn down by fact ever to follow her, this jaded practitioner of a career she should know better than to mix with, a man who clearly prefers that she not learn the first thing about him—if she shows him the clinical trials for this secret healing charm, would he get it? Might she make even her new surgeon see that to *pretend,* to live as if life might yet lead all the way to unexpected deliverance, is the best way to keep from dying in midfable? Could she get him to sit in with her circle of stricken, listening children and take part in the promise of fiction, the *pleasure,* our one moral obligation?

He is no older, no more decimated than the worst of her children. And she has only this, this cobbled, worn ministration, to show any of those stubborn enough to remember how they have been dropped down in the middle of a plot that is only waiting for them to follow the lead. You are going somewhere. *You are going somewhere.* Sound it out, exercise the phonetics, the rhyme, the muscular spasm, the shape of the storied curve—beginning, development, complication, end. It is the point of being, the thing bones were built for, broken by, the land all leaps aim at, the link, the hovering conclusion, her whole-body therapy, the reading cure. A tale at night. A country a day for a year.

(Night 57, Japan.)

This is how the world begins. At first, the All was no more than a blurry egg, full of seeds and shaken together. After a time beyond telling, the heavier parts began to sink down and the lighter floated upon them, forming the plain of high heaven. On this plain, three gods were born of no one, lived out an eternity, and then vanished back into nothing.

How you gonna be born of no one? Everybody got . . .

Shh. Come on. It's a makeup; that's how it opens. Next there came about, on their own, a few pairs of gods who lived in the drifting middle of nowhere. The youngest couple among them were called Izanami and Izanagi, or She-the-Inviter and He-the-Inviter. She and He were ordered by their elders to collect a solid world from out of the shapeless, muddy waters that flowed beneath the high plain of heaven. They stood on the bridge of the sky and dipped a jeweled spear into the sandy broth below them, stirring it slowly. They pulled their spear out of the waters. A drop of brine sticking to the shaft fell off to form Onogoro, the first island.

She-the-Inviter and He-the-Inviter climbed down onto the island and began exploring it. They circled slowly around one another at the pillar at the center of the solid world. Slowly, they discovered each other, and learned that they wanted one another.

Uh-oh. They in trouble now. When my daddy found my big brother and me . . .

No, sweetheart; it wasn't like that. Remember, these two gods had no parents. Slowly, by experiment and chance, She-the-

Inviter and He-the-Inviter learned how to make a baby. But their first child was born with something wrong with it. Because She did not yet know the rules of courtship she accidentally broke them. So the first infant who laid eyes on the world was born deformed.

Heh. Like me, you mean?

Yes, Chuck, my man. A little like you. She and He named their boy Hiruko, the Leech Child. They didn't know what they were supposed to do with him, so they built him a boat of reeds and set the boy adrift on the open sea. So you see, the very first child *ever* was abandoned. As soon as the Leech Child drifted out of sight, his parents began making other babies, more deities to cover every walk of creation.

Among their new children were the eight main islands of the world. She-the-Inviter was burned to death while giving birth to her last child, Fire. Gods spilled out of her dying body. Other gods arose from the tears of her husband's eyes. In a rage, He-the-Inviter swung his great blade and cut off the head of Fire, his son. From out of the bleeding neck of Fire there sprang Thunder, with several more gods.

The soul of She-the-Inviter went down into Yomi, the land of darkness, where He-the-Inviter madly followed. He wanted to find her and bring her back to life. But his wife had already eaten food cooked in the land of darkness, so she could not come back. The dead She warned her husband not to look upon her. But he disobeyed her command. He looked at her face, and saw something horrible. His wife was rotting. Maggots covered her. Shh! Yes, like the ones in old garbage. He-the-Inviter ran back up into the world in terror. She was hurt and angry, and She sent a pack of Furies to chase after her husband.

When He reached the surface once again, He sealed up the entrance to the land of darkness with an enormous rock. His wife became furious. She threatened to kill a thousand of their children every day that He kept her trapped. But He just sneered at her. He said that He would father fifteen hundred new children for every thousand that She killed. She and He knew they had come to an end.

To purify himself, He bathed in the waters. As He washed, more gods sprang from him. From the water sprinkling from his left eye was born the Sun, and from his right the Moon. Out of his nose there came Susanoo, the God of the Wind and Storm.

His nose? Gross. But what about the boy in the boat? The Leech?

It doesn't say. He must have floated for a long, long time. Reeds can be very watertight in these stories. But the ocean can be pretty big too. The Leech Child probably drifted in the current for years, farther and farther away, into places where land was completely unheard of.

Maybe the boat was held together by little metal clasps. That's it; I once read something like this. He pulled one of these metal strands loose and fashioned a bit of tinsel from it, which he dangled in the water just to amuse himself, because it looked pretty. And that's how, by accident, he learned that fish will bite at a hook. And he figured out that by eating fish, he could live pretty much as long as he needed.

Yeah? Well, all right. It's possible. Read us another one.

(Night 139, central Italy. Twin infant sons of a vestal virgin and the God of War are sentenced by the king to be drowned in the Tiber. Miraculously, the cask they are put in floats. They are found and suckled by a wolf more loving than human parents. The foundlings grow up to invent the West.)

Go on. We want more.

(Night 21, the Near East. Another terrified tyrant orders all the male offspring of a certain tribe to be drowned to death. The mother makes a little reed ark for the boy, and lays him in the rushes on the riverbank. The tyrant's daughter finds the infant, and hires the boy's own mother to nurse him. The boy grows up to bring God's law to . . .)

Why drowning? Why water all the time? Why little boats?

Yes, that's odd, isn't it? Happens all over the place. Look at this:

Night 308, the Mississippi. Night 145, Norway. Night 98, Kashmir. Night 114, Zimbabwe.

(Across the planet, attempted drownings, tiny bound bodies thrown deliberately back into the sea. All through the time line, vanishing into the current, carried along by the undertow. Every other story in any anthology—children sealed up, locked in casks, keelhauled, strapped on rafts, sucked down by the departing tide. A few miraculously saved, for future purposes.)

And some mom and dad always want to kill them.

Yes, true! Notice how the stories always blame some evil step-something, or foster fathers, or kings? Guilty conscience, I'll bet you anything. These cats have something to hide, I'm here to tell you. If they're not putting the kids out to drown in chests, then they're leaving them on church steps or by a roadside out of town. Or here, look: dropped off deep in the woods, bricked up into cornerstones, rolled over on in the parents' shared bed . . .

(. . . swaddled too tightly, delivered with a club to the skull or butterfly slit in the trachea, wrung with a bit of old cloth, or, for maximum efficiency–Night 3, Greece—eaten.)

Awesome. Any that stuff really happen?

(Night Before Last, Pacific Islands: two thirds of offspring. West Africa: any twins. Sarawak: boys strung up from trees. China: daughters given instant turnaround chance to return as sons. Germany, Italy, France: 1.8 "live birth" males to one female. SE England: "Three drowned in pond, two in well, five buried, two suffocated by pillow, two left in ditch, one thrown on dung heap, one slammed against bedpost, two twisted necks . . ." Chicago; Houston; Portland, OR: discreet suburban fatalities, malign neglect, everyday police roundups dribbling out of radio speakers in the dark, on all-night talk stations turned down low, between choruses of that old folk tune, *I am no stranger to your town.*)

Why?

(Tales 101 and 343: postpartum birth control. *Done because we are too many.* Tales 45, 83, 162: quick cures for deprivation, ille-

gitimacy, incest. That historical run in the 200s: merciful assists
of nature, stifling the half-lunged, leaving the acephalic to starve.
All but the hardiest arctic infants turned onto open pack ice. Mass
infanticide—the simple extension of the battering and abuse cases
right here in this listening ring. Folder 219: "She wouldn't love
me, the little four-year-old slut. So I burned her feet with a cigarette." One step further, now. A last-ditch, or oven, or well, or
pillowcase effort to extirpate the thing that will always remain
a heartbeat outside control. Children are evil creatures. A devil
lives in them. You can recognize changelings by the way they cry.
A child needs both bread and blows. We must terrify them into
being good. It was going to outlive me, so I killed it.

(These night-sirened final roundups are just the latest parental
attempts to ward off prophecy. To kill the still-bewildered child
in themselves that their own parents failed to finish off. The word
goes out from the Imperial Capital, or is initiated by some two-
bit, provincial governor: damage-control the old order. Issue the
slaughter papers, mandate the stopgap massacre, book boxcar passage free of charge for every imminent threat to the status quo.
Invested power faces no greater danger than these revolutionaries
incarnate—every breathing body under voting age.)

I don't know, sweetheart. I wish I did.

Come on. Read. Keep reading. Give us one of those really wild ones.

(Night 12, Palestine. Herod's storm troopers, fathers from this
part of the empire, conduct their house-to-house sweep in the
dark. Students of political terror, they know that the random
knock on the door works best at two A.M. These hatchetmen
blindly follow orders, not much motivated by national security.
Theirs is a saturation search-and-destroy. To get at the one potentially destabilizing element, the incumbent commander in chief
is willing to expend all innocent hostage bystanders. The troops,
agents of the State, work in willed ignorance, butchering in the
dark—trapping toddlers in back alleys, encircling a knot on the
plaza, mopping up pockets of resistance in the poultry market,

methodically dispatching children as in some dream of urban renewal.

(Grotesque tableau, but the troops are now too deep into the tale to withdraw. Crack phalanxes rip open the province's newly toilet-trained. Erotic charge ripples once more through the professional soldier class at holding prepubescent flesh on the unsheathed sword.

(How is it that the account seems so familiar, as vivid as recent newspaper coverage or some further dead reckoning slated soon to be remembered forever? June student genocides, shooting up always on the other side of the world like so many lab strains of miracle rice, are here, by November, spread outside, flowering underneath the pediatric wing window.

(The redemptive germ kernel—how one fugitive family slips out the back steps, how one infant escapes the bloodbath to found the new order, the slaughtered little ones promoted to eternal blessedness—the end of this late-night read-aloud is decided by the time it arrives. The road to the future is paved with fourteen-inch corpses. That is their magic, incantatory function. All the teen poverty brides, the single mothers escaping another screaming mouth, the cunning merchants unwilling to invest in daughters: all serve as mere manipulated ignorant pawns of delivering prophecy. However they are killed this time around, the infant pilgrims form the race's blood sacrifice, progress's solid rocket fuel.

(What hope, when story outstrips the outside horrors her read-alouds are supposed to ward off? Raw nightmare will rule the ward tonight. Every splatter of Herod's maces into these sapling chests provokes its imitative blow here among the eager listeners. A group of four gladiators, incensed, hack wildly at each other's surgical dressings.)

Kwishhh. Whack. You a dead pers. Yeah! No, sorry, don't. One more, one more. We'll quit, we promise.

It's late. Come on, kids; bed. You'll get me in trouble.

No! Another. Okay, if you don't want to read no more, just at least tell us what happens to that boy. The deformed dude, in the boat.

Well, I'm not sure. What do you think? He . . . just drifts. His boat holds water, he fishes, alone on the surface of an endless mirror. He slips along on the ocean current. Every so often, although time doesn't mean anything to him, because nothing changes, he sees another boat far off on the horizon. But he never signals or calls out; he just stares, not really knowing what it is. At night he falls asleep and dreams of a whole universe full of intelligent creatures, just like him, only . . .

. . . on land?

In hospitals?

All over the world?

Exactly. You guys are brilliant. But because he has never met any other creature . . .

. . . except fish . . .

. . . except fish . . .

. . . and octopuses . . .

Octopi, you igno-twerp.

Because he has never met any other humans, he doesn't even realize he's alone. He doesn't know the names of the oceans, and he cuts right through the boundaries of territorial waters. It's just liquid to him—deep or shallow, cold or warm.

Does he pick up more children along the way?

Well, sure. Why not? But not right at first. At first, when he draws close enough to solid land to figure out what it is, it scares the daylights out of him. The Hard Places, he calls the islands. He sees right away how incredibly dangerous they are. You can't sail on them; a boat would get completely stuck, or else it would be torn apart as soon as it touched. How you possibly gonna fish in such places? The hook would just lie there on the Hard Stuff, worthless.

He keeps to the wider currents. His eyes, over a long, long time, grow so strong from staring down into deep water searching for fish that he can see shoals even when they are a mile below pitch-blackness. You see, he has nothing else to look at except cloud and wave and the occasional piece of giant kelp. Years go by without even a mast. Slowly, he trains his eyes, learns how to see over the curve of the earth.

Get outta my life.

No, really. And his hearing sharpens too. There are no distractions in his whole world. So even the tiniest sound is worth concentrating on. He gets so that he can track the songs that whales sing to one another. He concentrates until he can hear even the pingings of corals. He can hear noises coming from all over the place. And one day, after several ages, he hears, from a thousand leagues off, and then he sees, long before it becomes visible over the horizon, a very weird thing.

Carrier fleet?

Jet skis?

Jet skis? For crying out softly. You people are hopeless, you know that? Absolutely lost.

A message in a bottle?

Now there we go. Only, not just one little message in one measly bottle. He paddles his reed boat closer, his eyes squinting to focus. He notices the water change temperature, color. These clear-gray flecks accumulate, growing denser until they form a solid swarm bobbing on the sea around him. He picks one up. He has no idea what in the world it is, but he thinks that if he knew what bottles were, this would probably be one. He tries to count all the bottles he can see, using the system he invented for sizing up schools of fish. He loses count at a thousand million glass bottles, each bobbing upright, congregating into the still spot at the center of the swirling ocean.

He's in the Sargasso Sea!

Now how did you know that?

I saw it on a map.

It's okay, sweetheart. I was just asking. Anyway, that's where he is. A sea inside the sea: the drainage point for the entire watery pinwheel. They all collect here, bottles from every port of call in this half of the hemisphere; messages launched from West Africa and Spain, the Canaries, Azores, Madeiras, Iceland, the mouth of the Senegal; notes from Paramaribo, Port of Spain, San Juan; letters pitched without hope from the Keys and the Carolinas, dropped in secret into bays by Baltimore, Brooklyn, and Boston, or lofted off the sides of ocean liners . . .

   . . . *crippled subs* . . .

   . . . *downed private planes* . . .

Each of a billion flasks has been swept up through the loop for a few cycles. Some have been circling for decades. Some spell out emergencies that have been over for centuries, and others come from as late as that morning. Centripetal force sucks them all into the Sargasso center. All this glass—smoky, green, gray, turquoise, sky-blue, magically transparent—just floats motionless. It's an elephants' graveyard of SOSs.

He opens one up and looks at the slip of paper inside. Of course, he doesn't know how to read, and he sure wouldn't know any of these foreign languages. But he's got a lot of time. Slowly, he teaches himself.

Impossible.

Who you calling impossible? I tell you, he's got a *lot* of time. He works on the first message until the words come out, "Tulip smiling wobbly Friday evaporation." He thinks, *Nope; that can't be it,* and he starts again. He keeps working until the message reads, "Come help me." He tries a second bottle, and this one says, "Come feed me." Bleeding on Barbados. Grounded in Greenland.

Each scroll of paper carries its own miniature map. X marks the spot. He figures it out: the globe is packed full of other creatures, exactly like him, only in trouble. Through these notes, he learns about human society. And he sees that he is nothing more than this one lone figure in a tiny, open boat, looking out over this expanse of bottles spreading across the sea. More requests than even a god could read in a lifetime.

He thinks that maybe the best thing to do would be to sink

the whole herd of help messages. One by one, fill them up with water, unread. Send them to safety on the ocean bed, where they can wait until the day when they might be answered. But there are too many, even for that.

He decides to follow one of the maps. His eyes and ears, grown superpowerful on emptiness, point the way. He matches up the languages he has learned to read with the distant, background chirpings he always assumed came from some kind of land bird. The map and the sounds and the sight of land beyond the horizon take the Leech up close to a continent where something big is coming down. He picks it out of the air, this feeling of awful expectation such as he has felt nowhere else along the whole continuous ocean coast.

The Leech pulls up a safe distance from shore, trying to figure out what huge, silent shake-up is under way. Every petty principality in this patchwork landmass, every inhabitant from emperor to crook seems to be running around, trying to beat the clock. The people of the continent themselves haven't figured out what's up. Something's unfolding, although so slowly that it is still lost in myth.

Everywhere on the continent, children are chucking these bottles into rivers, where they wash down to the sea. The Leech can hear it all from his anchorage offshore. He can hear the noises banging around villages and cities. He hears people counting down the days, waiting for something that seems to get nearer with each delay. He sees the signs and wonders springing up like weeds. He watches packs of outlaws, soldiers, scholars, and peasants cut swaths in all directions.

Everybody is terrified of waking to the news they hope for most. Castle walls sprout all over. From the scorched western plains all the way up to the frozen fjords, dancing manias break out. In some provinces, everyone under twelve gets caught up, dancing for weeks until dropping. From off the coast, it's obvious: the entire continent is scared, something fierce. Inflation, unemployment, the Plague. Things are so bad that entire countries take to outra-

geous remedies. Boys become bishops. Whole towns are entrusted
to their youngest residents.

On the extreme corner point of this continent, the Leech
makes out another abused, deformed child who has built a lookout tower from which he can stare out across the sea, looking for
a way to escape.

Henry the Navigator?

Now how in the world did you know that? Somebody's actually been paying attention in school. By staring for weeks at a time
from the top of his tower in—where was it, again?

Portugal.

Right. By staring from his tower in Portugal, the Navigator
has trained himself to see beyond the curve of the earth. He is
convinced of reports of a River of Eden somewhere just beyond
the next landfall. He is trying to see just past world's end, around
the next cape, where the coast turns.

But that morning, in midsurvey, the Navigator gets a shock: an
island off the coast, one he hasn't noticed until now. On second
look, he sees it's no island, but an open boat. And there's a kid
in it, dark, shrunken, deformed. In another minute, he and the
ancient boy make eye contact. The boat child stands up, and the
Navigator gets a second shock: it's the face of an old friend of his,
from school days. The Navigator has known the face for so long
that he can't place it.

The Leech seems to recognize too. He breaks into a big grin
and begins to wave, great scoops that begin down by his knee
and end up cupping air over his shoulder: *Come on! What's keeping you?* It's all the proof the Navigator needs. The boy is clearly
from the East—hair, skin, eyes, everything—although the Navigator has never seen an Oriental except in imagination. If the
Easterner has come over sea, then the Navigator has guessed
right about his route. He lets out a whoop, audible all the way to
Lisbon. He waves wildly back to the Leech Child: *Hold on; we'll
be right there.*

It's the signal to break out. The children of Europe at last have a surefire escape. They can leave home. They start to pile into boats, whole families, whole countries of them. . . .

But that's not, that's not how . . .

(Night 366, Angel City.)

Oh God. Joy. I'm so sorry. I wasn't thinking. I completely forgot. Oh, child, forgive me. It's only a story.

He has a theory about the pathological popularity of hospital shows—the butt of resident humor and abused needle of a nation that pretends to have no professional relations with death. Those continuous discharges of polyphonic drama and alarm, where gangs of surgical staff career through hallways shoving cadaver-sized rolling tea caddies full of code blues (or whatever entertainment calls them these days) owe their lurid clamp on imagination's binding sites to the emotional methadone maintenance they offer the home audience.

Kraft has this image of nuclear families everywhere, camped out in the den, lapping at disaster's nipple, squeezing it dry of the recommended daily nutrients. The pans and dissolves of affliction's visual clichés have become as foggily familiar as high mass once was from the back of the choir-screened nave. Small wonder. Every schoolgirl knows exactly how the Incomprehensible goes. She has seen it on her hand-held color LCD set, dramortized, chanted over the commercial airwaves with the ease and frequency of jungle gym jingles.

Lots of messages batch out over the public band at the same time here. First among them, Kraft wearily concludes, sitting in the decidedly unphotogenic call room, still replaying his latest real-life docu-dramas on mental video, is that total apocalypse differs from the usual domestic shouting matches and traffic collisions only in decibels. Shows also suggest that no disaster is so real that it can't be reduced to ritual emergency.

Serialization tames in exactly the way that table manners obscure the ugly reality of eating. Inevitably, around about minute

49, the runaways come back, the Hitler dads break down in tears, number one junkie son kicks the habit (shaking like blazes for a whole forty-five seconds), and the little girl in pigtails crawls out of her iron lung to do the verse about how wishing makes it so. The upshot is that *your* plotless, personal frame tale will reach its significance, its rare closure, in the run of time.

Reality—he might tell the scriptwriters for a small lifetime consultant's fee—is infinitely quieter. Nobody yells. Cases come in like sacks of mattress money reluctantly signed over to a bank teller. The showdown stays imperceptibly prosaic, deathly silent, as the cliché goes. Breath persists perversely in the barely living lumps, wood-grain isobars under the nicks of a beaten-up bar table.

Even down here in the bowels of the building, the emergency entrance, the residents' little sovereign state of siege, all the rushing around is done so mutely, so close to normal speed, that it's easy to miss. Accident's selected recipients, holding their eyeballs, still grasping their blackened, necrotic thumbs by the severed tendons, shuffle in quietly. The paramedics, the police escorts are quiet. Teen gang kingpins, their faces carved up, have already had their say.

If a spouse or next of kin accompanying a victim does, under the otherworldly pressure, begin to jackknife off the high dive of despair, they stay well south of sotto voce or they too are quietly escorted to another part of the medicinal forest for a sedative all their own. Large gelatinous pulp may extrude from an open skull, but the room remains demure, methodical. The leading players issue nothing more than a diplomat's "No comment." Never any word about the here and now, let alone about what happens next.

With a minute's dead time in the middle of wider emergency, Kraft flips through memory's dial. He amuses himself by running casual Monte Carlo simulations on his own prime-time roulette. He does this concurrently with committing to memory the newest complications from out of the *NEJM,* and dictating into a matchbox-sized microrecorder a rambling, unpostable letter: "Dear American Savings, Thank you so much for yet another of your thoughtful monthly statements. Perhaps none of you realizes the value of these regular reassurances. . . ."

Multitasking holds him occupied all of ten minutes. He begins browsing the latest off-the-rack genre remix from the staff library: *The One-Minute Messiah, or How to Survive the Next Sixty Seconds*. He holds the paperback with his left hand, while with his right he doodles aimlessly, scribbling Chinese calligraphy that he imagines reads, "Serve the People" and "Fight Self."

He retreats to his makeshift office, and the desk he has been avoiding. Tommy Plummer ambushes him there, pasting up a newsprint, ransom-note quote for Kraft's benefit:

The young child which lieth in the cradle is both wayward and full of affections; and though his body be but small, yet he hath a great heart, and is altogether inclined to evil. . . . If this sparkle be suffered to increase, it will rage over and burn down the whole house.

This is in reference to the third prepuber pyro that Pediatrics has had to reupholster this month. "Those seventeenth-century docs knew their stuff," Thomas tells him. "Only way to save the structure is to torch it preemptively, with the tyke asleep upstairs. Where did modern medicine go wrong? Huh, champ?"

Kraft can't really call Plummer a friend, but of all the surgical starters, the man offers the best prospects of human diversion. Even the torture of companionship beats the alternative today. He must prep to go drag-line fishing in the ankle of that twelve-year-old Asian refugee princess, and the prospect has completely shot his usual aesthetic distance.

Thomas tags along behind him on the way to the OR. He seems to have nothing better to do than play this episode's side-kick.

"Truly shitty job," says Kraft, up to his elbows in disinfectant.

"No, little Richie. That's the small bowel resection, later this afternoon. This one's slimy."

"Shitty." Kraft ignores him "Pitiful. First you flush the family out of their village. Then you take the village off the map and put them in a camp. Then you overrun the *camp*."

"What's this 'you'? I was busy that year, I'm pretty sure."

"Lead them to believe that an open boat . . . Sure, a boat, with this little puking *kid,* across half the Pacific . . . Toss her around assorted holding pens. Relocate her *here,* of all the godforsaken, fast-food-franchised, tar-paper-and-antennaed—"

"Doesn't she have to get raped by Thai fishermen first? Don't they always get raped by . . . ?"

Kraft just stares at him blankly, beyond everything, even disgust. Plummer's shoulders flex an indifferent little *eh.* Perhaps boat people jokes are no longer *au courant* this season. He rifles his repertoire for comic crumbs about South American cattle prods or starving Ethiopians.

Kraft begins enunciating, always a bad sign. "Welcome to the United States." Something in the pitch suggesting that Plummer is the cultural case in point.

"What, what? *We* didn't murder this kid's bone marrow for her. McDonald's didn't fuck up her leg. GM didn't. Okay, Dow Chemical might have had a little hand in the matter. But tell me, champ. What the hell would of happened if the little china doll had stayed in Cambodia—"

"Laos."

"Whatever. If she hadn't gotten out, hadn't escaped, hadn't been allowed over here out of the pure magnanimity of the State Department? You tell me what'd have happened if she'd come down with this creepy leg-nibbling shit in her country? Those jungle cutters would have smeared her leg with a little betel nut and taken the whole thing off at the waist with a machete."

Gravity crumples Kraft by the trapezius. He is several rounds of shock therapy past caring to answer. His insides are arid, desiccated already by ten years of apprenticeship en route to this continuous call. When he does get around to speaking, he talks to some captive audience nowhere to be seen.

"She's the picture of eager docility. Talks in tunes. Lies in bed studying, because she doesn't want to fall behind the class at school. She asks the nursing staff for books on the procedure we'll be using. They say to her, 'Wouldn't you rather have something to color?' She shakes her head, but respectfully, to keep from embarrassing them. She sits up in bed doing algebra, history, answering all the sample questions at the end of every chapter, never peeking, writing the answers into this little spiral notepad. Doesn't even flinch at pain—"

"Tell me about it. I pulverized the girl's foot in ER the night we admitted her. She just looked up and smiled forgiveness all over the damn place."

"And then she goes and loses it completely, decompensates at the first little sputter of the traffic reporters hovering over the Harbor Freeway."

"Is it true that they found her old man cowering under the bed in the middle of the night? Hiding out from Immigration? That they had to use the kid to talk him into authorizing the release? I heard that he signed it 'Murrican.' Only he wrote it in Lousish."

"No." Kraft's eyes trace a migratory route around the operating theater, acquainting himself with the emergency exits. "The word was 'Mawkhan.' Regional dialect. A professional title. It means the man is a physician."

"Oh, right. Absolutely. If that guy's a doc, then I'm a . . ."

"We all know what you are, Thomas. We're just waiting for the State Certification Board to figure it out."

"Come on. No shit? The dude's a doc? What's his field?"

"Certified in cures involving the recall of a person's errant soul." Kraft exhales. *If I remember the term correctly.*

"Holy Om! Get that sumbitch to scrub. We need someone like that down in the ER."

"Speaking of which." Kraft, holding his hands clean, crooks an inviting elbow at the theater where the little girl is already put down, gassed on the table, like the evening spread out against the sky.

But Plummer takes the opportunity to bow out hastily. "The least I can do for you, Kraft old buddy, is to let you go on me owing one."

Kraft puts off his clever comeback until he gets a chance to think one up.

The next thing he knows, he is cutting, following the surveyor's chalk line, mushing the blade too softly into the brown anklet, forgetting everything he's learned about the superiority of slicing over sawing. His eight years of examinations are suddenly as irretrievable as states and capitals or presidents. Of the five-hundred-plus skeletal muscles, he'd be lucky to be able to name ten and visually identify a half dozen. All the sophisticated scientific sheen strips off, leaving just the procedure right now under his hands. Strange pellets, bits of evil living gravel are loose, growing inside this girl. He must locate them the only way possible. He probes around by touch, making out structures both benign and insidious, things that would have been a marbleized blur to him this time two years ago. He loosens the invader trace, chases it with his rubbered fingertips, differentiates it from the pulpy, pink, enveloping striations of the host.

The shock of first gaping into an open life rips into him again. The landscape looks exactly as it must. What else *can* it look like? A streaky piece of marinated porterhouse, only pulsating. Lurching a little to one side every second or so, then falling aside. He works his way down through the dermal layers, pinning them back, edging closer to where he can slit whatever sickening pupa they might find free of its attaching gristle. How is he to describe this *stuff* except through today's state-of-the-art material metaphor? Here's your problem, ma'am. Leak in the fuel line. Bad IC chip. Evil spirits inhabiting the system housing. But breaking the seal may void your warranty.

The body overhaul shop is not a one-man operation by any means. What they intend to pull off this morning is yet another miracle by committee. Surgery is the most unlikely, corporate, bureaucratic cure since the King James translators. An entire relay team passes the baton continuously between the autoclave and the open body. All decisions, however cosmetic, demand referenda. Kraft is just one of a half-dozen functionaries milling about in the room, and far from the most critical player. The position of center forward probably belongs to the lady with her eyes on the monitors and hands on the gas valves.

But the person wielding the working knife at any given moment becomes the guy with the ball. Just as an audience sometimes mistakes the virtuoso in the pretty party clothes for the composer, even the surgical team may conflate the one sticking his pinky up inside a valve with the design engineer.

Today, Kraft is the international cartel's front man, their carrier, the one they send out to slip past the douanes, to violate the border and dart back across with impunity on forged diplomatic papers. He fights against his innate, human ham-handedness the way those Ice Capades chimps struggle to stay up on skates. Whatever dexterity he can assemble depends on a stockpile of technical knowledge baroque in both mass and ornament. The quadratic can be solved by anyone of superior intelligence with the necessary patience and perfect retention, plus a dozen available years to sink into indentured slavery.

Kraft fidgets with a retractor. Here they are, making base camp just above this little girl's foot. They're in the absolute hinterlands, Hibernia, the outermost reaches of life, as far away from the core of the self-administered mystery as circulation permits. And yet, the terrain is already appallingly gorgeous. Sinew rivers cut their canyons down through layers articulate beyond the subtlest medical illustrator's ability to survey. The color, texture, distensibility, tensile strength of the conduits and struts and cables, the delicate interfaces of ligament and capillary connecting inimical tissues, all the middlemen of this fabulous political economy, mirrored in their complexity at every level all the way down the stacked hierarchy into invisible collagens, the excavated living preteen laid bare, lies touchable here, flush against her encasing wall, yielding yet giving away nothing to her correspondents, his groping, invasive tools.

A slit dead on the offending mass, and Kraft might stop further incursion. Hit it spot on and he could give this girl a birthday present of sixty more years' worth of scrapbook particulars. Or make a slight backhand nick, almost identical, another cut straight out of the textbook, only this time the anarchist disease somehow escapes and her foot goes cold.

He's not built for these constant judgment calls, continuously maneuvering in the millimeters between condemner and redeemer. Working his way by touch along the cut, Kraft stumbles up against a tactile hint of that tacit trade secret shared among all surgeons. A few years of this, and he will be lost forever to social contact, to all involvement in personality's twists and turnings. What interest can outcome still have, once he has held outcome's engine up close and arbitrary in his own hands?

Proximity to the bared root runs away with him. *Merck's* countless pathologies expand into an involuntary party game. He cannot shake a stranger's hand without making out tumorous mountain ranges under each mole. The lips of everyone he converses with twitch around the edges with impending Jacksonian seizures. The sound of stomachs ulcerating soars above the noise of this room. And even now, as he glances at the anesthesiologist, he can see the vein walls in her brain toy with the idea of collapse.

Even stretched, the tent of human skin seems insufficient to span the faces of the assembled surgical team or bind together their insides. He can see beneath, to the hideous, fatty slabs just dying to squirt out all over. Beneath the pretty sausage casing, webs of nerve niagara in spraying veils. He has peeked beneath the packaging and become hardened, like a kid disabused of Adventureland by accidentally glimpsing the motor underneath the talking puppet Plasticine.

Kraft knows already how he will end. He will wind up worse than the vegetarian butcher, the agnostic priest, the book-hating professor of literature, the notary forger. His destiny lies several notches lower than the lowest of these. It feels as if there's no derailing, as if he's already halfway there: the hypochondriac doctor. The misanthrope volunteer.

The Evangelist, it occurs to Kraft as he tucks back a reticent bundle of tibialis anterior, did not know his ass from the proverbial pothole. Nothing that the nervous system is capable of believing can withstand a hand shoved deep inside the wound. Only those on the conscious side of the general anesthetic during an operation will ever know the true reading of that parable. Nothing will devastate a man as much as a fist pushed wrist-deep into the open side, all the way up to the hilt. Kraft would jimmy the punch line just a little, to restore it to truth: blessed are those who believe, even though they have seen. And more blessed are those who haven't seen, and are thus still free to believe anything they please.

These thoughts last for about one systolic flip. Then the sound of his team's gossip drives them out. The background broadcast in the room lifts him into a trance of nonthought. He follows procedure in a coma of concentration, like a batter waiting out his pitch. When he reaches the region in upheaval, his clipping turns conservative. He feels himself taking too little tissue. Every tooshallow scrape misses a bit, risks having to reopen a few weeks from now, higher up the limb. Yet his blade goes diffident, almost flirting with anklet indifference.

The trick is to disengage. He must read this beating shank of foal back into pure, anatomical model. The green cloth hide-a-screen built up around the wound works a marvelous trick. But he must do the rest, must imagine, as he plucks out the most obvious infiltrating pellets, that he takes a grappling crane and clears out the Golden State Freeway, dumping every sleek little import into the bay. When the lay of the land makes it increasingly difficult to pluck out the offending logs, he shifts fantasies. He strokes the pink fiber with the flat of a blade, and it feels for all he is worth like satin against the back of a hand.

A bit of brain bails out of the image-forming cerebral cockpit, and he finds himself lying full-length alongside his private physical therapist, her dark cross-border eyes lit up like the point coils of a space heater. Oh, Christ, Linda: give him one more chance, if you are still alive, if you still remember him, if he can survive this procedure. This, the most tenuous fantasy of all: if their rapidly collapsing social order makes it through until his next night off, he might see her again.

The fantasy plays itself out. Linda will ask him desperately how it went, and he'll respond, casually: Joy Stepaneevong? Oh, yeah. The boat girl. Well, we pulled the thing out without having to clip anything that belongs to her. What did I tell you? It always pays not to get too alarmist in these matters. Whole procedure was pretty straightforward, actually. She's spanking; disease-free. We cleaned her completely with a few flicks of the whisk broom.

To win the woman Linda from the awful accident that waits for her like a lover at the next dark street corner, he must file just such an all clear. To keep her from the worst case is his only desire. He would hand her the perfect prognosis, pristine as a rash valentine and twice as reckless. This particular case, above all others, is the one she wants. Yet for his cutting hand, following the standard operational excision, to know the stakes means courting disaster. The case must mean no more to him than any other in the cattle call of lives he has already decided. Should he feel its specific weight, even in theory, he and the girl are both dead.

Autonomous lieutenants propel his fingers, destroying as little of the innocent-bystander tissue as they can possibly get away with. He knows he's pushing it. He can hear his misses register in the Millstone's tortured, adenoidal breathing. The man hovers over his shoulder, displacing whole air masses with each exhalation. Vast frontal systems blow down from the man's Arctic Circle directly into Kraft's inner ear.

Only, wait: it can't be Dr. Milstein whom Kraft is—as the euphemism goes—assisting here. Milstein's down in San Diego for a conference. Kraft's had a minor TIA, or he's suffering some overwork/deprivation combo phenomenon that someone in neurology could probably get a paper out of. Brain volleying up a little spatial-temporal racketball is all. By process of elimination, if it's not the Millstone under the cap and gown wheezing behind Kraft, then it must be Father Kino. "Shorty" Kean. Little Napoleon.

Kraft snaps aware to that fact just as the said attending launches himself into an administrative shit fit. "Cut something. Cut *something*, goddammit. Not there. Why the hell did they ever let you through med school? What did you do, *buy* your way through your internship? What are you afraid of, son?"

What indeed? If Kraft is afraid of anything, it is of exactly what happens next. Dr. Kean starts flailing about in a fog of frustrated authority. "Here. Give me that." And darting out, he grabs Kraft's *hand,* of all the shit for brains maneuvers. Kraft manages to fight him off with a combination of reason, diplomacy, and testy resistance.

Kean will complain to Burgess this afternoon, and the Chief will have Kraft in for a talk tomorrow, ever so delicately reprimanding the insubordination before asking for impressions of the multivolume copy of *The Man Without Qualities* that Burgess lent him last week. What would the profession be without a dose of the obligatory Good Dad, Bad Dad syndrome? Even satanically real medical mills must stick to the script of TV General.

They close the girl, Father Kino still blasting the assburning afterjets. Kraft feels that he has given the girl a reasonable chance while leaving her the better part of her foot. He has not once, throughout the procedure, gone up north to have a look at her face. That'd be the last thing in the world he needs just now. The already unbearably familiar iodine tint of her skin around the wound is disabling enough. All he has seen is the taper of one calf, a shape remaining as distinct across the populations of the globe as faces, build, or hair. But this particular polynomial taper he could trace freehand. He knew it by second nature once, in a previous incarnation, before this profession took up subcutaneous residence in him.

He stitches, punching his needle laterally through the complex ecosystem. He loops up the layered Dagwood sandwich in a way proven to leave behind the least surface scar. As he sews, an overlearned jingle skips trochaically through his head, a singsong rhyme he memorized once while learning the alphabet. Not that anemic, twenty-six-letter, tell-me-what-you-think-of-these. His tune taught an alphabet that flowed forth in more than four dozen symbols, a scatter pattern of phonemes too subtle for nonnatives to hear, let alone grip properly in their glottis. A poem, a song actually, in a language where all poems turn into songs because all words are pitched.

His was not the girl's language, but the next dialect over. He spoke, once, a first cousin to the one Joy's father used to sign away his rights and expectations. Learned it when exactly this girl's age, the age when industrious children of this once-blessed mainland must typically commit their mental resources to acquiring that "We the People" paragraph and a half. The syllable rhythm lies intact in him, but long since irrelevant—a letter of intent forgotten in a strongbox until long after expiration date. Ratty, riddled with holes, fragments of the alphabet chant reassemble themselves. Gratification swells him, collapsing immediately in distress at how many letters are now beyond recovery, with no words to slip into the blank melody slots.

The bits he can recall lie like surf-polished shipwreck, detritus from the semiconscious coast of a place he inhabited once and left while the leaving was good. He hums the chewed residuals of the tune, one that might as well buzz about in his brain, staving off the latest rhythm-arrested, mega-euro-yen-dollar, ten-second singing sales spot for cola–cum–life insurance coverage. He hums: *g* as in chicken. *K* as in egg. The tune takes him through treacherous *ng, bph*—sounds his tongue still recalls but cannot talk the muscles into anymore. *Y* as in mythological giant gate guards. *H* as in owl, who hoos across the borders of all time's alphabets.

JOY COMES TO: much . . . *later,* is the word she has swung loose from. The first thing she asks, when she recondenses out of the anesthetic, is how much time has vanished since she was last awake. The missing hours are more important to her than the missing bit of foot, still swaddled. She does not wonder "How did it go?" or "Will I walk again?" Meekly, she asks a nurse, her voice sounding from miles down a well: "How many days have I been away?" Worried, perhaps, about what trouble she might have made, or where she has been off to during the unaccountable interim.

She gets an answer that does not answer. No matter; she is back now, returned from the place that leaves only a ribbon-scrap in her recollection. Here, on this side, she must again work for a living. The girl's industry returns as the pain suppressant ebbs. Furious with diligence, head bent over the hospital bed-desk, she writes out a thank-you note to her surgeon.

She uses wide, three-lined paper, the two outer lanes solidly marked, the median strip a faint, encouraging dash. Urgent schoolgirl style transforms the letter into one of those commissioned classroom pleas on behalf of some Polish boy who decided to defect despite his returning parents, or for the first-ever panda born in North America. The scope of the project forces her to dare cursive, although she is still several thousand practice ovals and half-Immelmanns shy of mastery.

"Dear Dr. Kraft, thank you for snipping the incursion out of my leg." She copies the word carefully out of the material she has made the woman therapist give her. It's not a long word, shorter even than her last name. To a nonnative speaker, it is no harder a word for the creature hiding inside her than any other. "I am sure you have done a most satisfying job and that the incursion will not come back. All my expectations are for the future and pain is so far low. I am sorry you had to do this but glad that you are my doctor and such a good one." At the bottom, she draws a winged creature, midway between giant gate guard and guardian angel. She folds the thick newsprint in quarters and delivers it suspiciously to a pede nurse, making her swear up and down that she will deliver the note swiftly.

Pain is so far low: the note reaches Kraft interleaved among X-ray envelopes, incisional biopsy reports, the fan-fold printout of the week's new admissions, an unsigned memo requiring all staff to get inoculated against the latest epidemic, and police notification of several recent assaults in the underground parking garage, one of them fatal. He unfolds the newsprint, reads it without comprehension. What are they asking him to do now?

He is still clutching the text when he next comes to, in his call room, that Motel 6 just off of the surgical interstate. He tapes her note to the cinder block wall above the bed, where he can glance at it from time to time from over the edge of the *Rifle & Handgun Illustrated*. I'm sorry you had to do this. I'm sorry you had to do this.

He falls asleep for the specified hundred years. While he is out, the shoots and tendrils of time's parasitic vines overgrow the entire city, clamping in place all vehicles, transports, relays, and faxes, freezing for good all liquid assets and every medium of exchange.

"THE MAIN THING, as I see it, will be keeping her from laterally stressing the . . ."

The lovely Linder throws her hands up in exasperation. "The main thing, as I see it, will be keeping her X rays clear."

She is a touch bristly this morning, and perhaps with good cause. Kraft takes a deep hit of the Condition Six air and tries to settle into another tone. "Look, I've seen you in action. I know you're a pro."

"Thank you." She is as close to acid as her temperament allows. "I'm delighted to hear it."

"And it's not that I'm trying to tell you what to do."

"Just how to do it?"

Okay, okay. Ordinarily, by the tender ground rules they've already established, he'd be the one trying to steer their rationed conversations toward fondue recipes or furniture refinishing or anything at all rather than let this last remaining candidate for his One Good Thing be infected by more medicine. But today, in these few free hours with each other, they flirt with major role reversal. Kraft can't seem to keep from nagging the Stepaneevong post-op. He has brought up the girl's case three times in as many blocks, and the ring of the refrain's bad-conscience rondo is about to put a royal burr up their afternoon's ass.

They are walking—yes, *sic;* as in "on foot"—down Melrose, he in jeans and a clean scrub shirt, she in this marvelous, clingy, soft rose silk shell the likes of which he'd years ago forgotten existed. They indulge in that favorite national pastime, after-shopping. An hour earlier, Linda bought a clock radio and now she is industriously devoting herself to belated comparisons, seeing how well or poorly she did. Kraft simply tags along by her side, desperate not to be left alone for an unstructured hour.

He tries not to hang on her, while using her as moving shield. Only under her wing—half bare, and beautiful as a fashion model's—does he dare witness the final twenty-four hours of this EVERYTHING-MUST-GO clearance close-out. CRAZY CAL SEZ: WE'RE SELLING THE FARM. GET YOURS NOW, BEFORE WE COME TO OUR SENSES. Ten thousand groping, bewildered years of recorded culture go out in a windup FIRE SALE blaze before them. All they can do is walk, basking in the full glow of the apotheosis of retail.

"Let's duck in here," Linda says.

She indicates a tasteful little theme boutique called Cop a Buzz. It gathers together, for purposes of trade, diverse objects with no conceivable use all partaking of the slenderest of common denominators: the ornamental Insect Motif. Big this year. "Can never have too many locusts," Kraft says enthusiastically. Espera knees him gently in the kidney. "Incidentally, did I mention to you that there's a danger of her hyperextending her . . . ?"

"Hey," Linda says, taking him by the shirtslack around his collarless collar, clamping him to her, pulling him down a little, toward her bared teeth. "Whatever happened to that cavalier, jaded, you-mow-'em-we'll-sew-'em hack I've come to know and love?"

"*Love,* you say? Don't get much call for that around here, lady." You still got the sales slip? You must have the wrong shop. Wrong theme. Wrong strip mall."

"Listen, Richard. Joy is an angel—too good a patient, too good a child to be true. She detests the very idea of crutches, and I wouldn't be able to keep her on them even if I wanted to. And why would I want to? What's to protect her from? Nothing she might sprain would be any worse than bedsores. Her outlook is worth a dozen of ours put together. Who's gonna know better than she what the foot can do, and when? If there's any danger with her at all, it's . . ."

"Yes?" he throws out, supercasually. What, *me* stiffening?

"If she has any problem at all, it's with her spirits."

"Spirits? What the hell is that supposed to mean?"

"Easy, fella. I'm on your side, remember?" She refreshes that memory with a finger-brush across his floating rib. "This is one powerful little girl we're talking about. She has sent for her schoolbooks. She sweats at plane geometry for hours at a stretch. When she stops, it's only to start in again on the High Middle Ages. Then she asks *me* to grade her homework."

Kraft stands absentmindedly stroking a Rive Gauche oven mitt with that cockroach look and feel. "So what's the problem?"

"Do *you* remember the difference between Louis the Fat and Charles the Bald?"

"I could probably tell them apart in a police line, if that'd help."

"We'll ignore the clown in the back of the class. Ricky, it's too strange. She smiles politely while I read make-believes to the other kids. Then I ask her what she would like to hear next, and it's *The Wealth of Nations.* She never laughs, never gets excited or spooked or impatient. It's as if she simply has no idea on earth what's happening to her."

Tell her, then, he wants to say. Tell her the chances of their hav-

ing to go back and take more leg. Tell her what drugs or rays will
do to her doll's face, her hair, her schoolgirl exercises in concentration. Tell her the odds against her sticking around long enough
to graduate from junior high. Tell her how quietly it comes on,
no threatening shout, no siren of stylized alarm. How can people
live? How can we live?

"But as long as we're on the subject," Linda segues, sweetly
tentative. She tries, now that he is suddenly volunteering all over
the place, to enlist him, as simple comradely buffer, in cases every
bit as heart-rending as Joy's. Joleene Weeks, who refuses to talk
except by pulling the string and releasing random messages from
her Chatty Cathy doll. Markie C, who likes to plunge silverware
deep into his prosthetic limb in cafeterias, for the sheer pleasure of
the public whiplash. Kraft listens politely, as demure as the little
Laotian girl listening to tonight's fairy tale.

They roll on down Melrose's Babylonian bazaar, these miles of
continuous stalls at a street fair of surpassing strangeness. Shock
troop merchandising here reaches its peak. Science determines de-
finitively how to part a buck from the bottomlessly blasé. Riches
from the Orient, booty from the Crusades, fatiguingly inventive
combinatoric treadmills of commodity-churning high funkiness
are rendered salable by their utter implausibility. The pyramid of
nudge-and-wink, what-the-hell impulse buys at the cash register
aspire to a high weirdness, even a conceptual art of death denial
just now in the run-up to its greatest, most decadent *fin de* yet.
Electric rare-earth jackets. Magnetic monkey's genitalia for the
dash. Farmer's hats reading "Kafka." Digital executive barbells.
Self-help bathroom scales. Programmable mascara. Solar-powered
rain announcers. Clothing bearing every conceivable legible message except "Please stop and talk to me."

Stay sick, Kraft says, almost out loud. Stay in bed. Never get up
and walk. Never go outside again.

Fashion, it strikes him, is even more insidious than the planned
obsolescence people imagine. It involves engineering into each
good or service a time-delayed precipitate of alienating ugliness

so that the desperate purchaser will wake up one day from his incredible bender and say, "What *ever* possessed me?" Then head out with the electronic money transfers to go score a little hair of the dog. Every glass of refreshing, consumable product must be laced with hidden salt water, inflaming the need that it promised to placate. The point of fad is to provide tomorrow's refuse and the day after's marked-up nostalgia. And we will not stop climbing, laboring, assembling, trading, making, marking down, and closing out until there's a credit card form attached to each harnessable dissatisfaction, a coin box inserted between every somatic anguish and its real salve.

Perpetual carnival out here: a Rio of retail. Improbable as it seems, in all these theme boutiques—the flightless-bird shops, the split-crotch panty shops, the 'thirties, 'forties, and 'fifties shops (Kraft sees the day coming when his abysmal young adulthood will be bottled as campy vintage, the collision curves of trend and retro slamming head-on into each other), the information shops, the shops turning Stalinist lapels and hemlines into spangly kitsch, the Day-Glo designer industrial-waste outlets vending pet elements from beyond the actinide series—in all this synthetic needs-mongering, Kraft and Linda stumble upon a bookstore.

"Hey! Look at this. It's just like the scene in that movie." Every movie about the distant, disastrous future ever made. "You know, where they come across the half-sunk Statue of Liberty buried in the sand?" And Jesus, it's been *Earth* underneath there all along.

They go in and browse, evading the public promenade of fears for a moment, hiding out from the end of time. Even this old sanctuary is overrun, already prostrate, everywhere infiltrated by the titles of malevolence: *How to Think and Act like Genghis Khan, Learning to Love Your Dysfunction, How I Went from Fanny Farmer to Firmer Fanny,* and *McMassacre! The Inside Story.* No matter; this is all that is left, all the refuge the two of them will ever be allowed. They are trapped out here on the threshold, the absolute cutting edge of the dream's realization.

Kraft and Linda split at reference, each turning to trace out favorite, obsessive routes through the racks. She starts in travel, proceeds to fiction, and ends up in food. He drifts to music, scans the picture books, then sinks down into biography. Each takes a small treasure through the cash register, showing the other only when outside the shop, embarrassed at the names of their personal reading needs.

"Wait a minute," he says, remembering something a few yards down the sidewalk. "Wait for me right here." Squeezes her shoulders, semaphore pleading. Here; don't move, or we will never find one another again.

He runs back into the shop. She loses sight of him through the glass front as he scrambles about trying to negotiate a category that has become alien to him. He comes out again bearing a wrapped package, which he accidentally tears open in presenting to her. *The Secret Garden. Alice in Wonderland. Oz. Peter Pan.* "Give her these," Kraft coughs neutrally.

"Oh," Linda says, fingering the volumes to keep from looking at him. "Oh. The classics. Do you think . . . ?"

"What? Something easier? Something a little more current?"

"No, no. Only . . . Hold *still* a minute, can't you? Don't be cross. Pull in your lip. I haven't hit you yet." She puts her hand to his neck and smooths him. "I was just going to ask if you thought it might be better if you gave them to her yourself. She thinks you're God, you know."

Kraft makes ready to bolt at the monosyllable. In point of fact, he has bolted already, silently gone, back on call. "You do it for me, will you?" Just this one thing. For my sake. For God's sake. Slip her a children's book, for once, while she's not looking.

Has read them all once, time was, several lives ago. Thumbed his way about in, climbed down through the portable portals, every one an infallible *Blue Guide* to a parallel place, unsuspected, joining the town and just at hand. Maybe's municipalities are always: the illustrated pastel covers deliver this shocking evidence to his cortex's tangled bit-bundle as he handles the books again. Immediate, closer even than the known, so close he must have constantly stumbled over the entryways without seeing. Children are forever falling through, almost by accident. Right *there*. Over the high hedge. A dead drop out the nursery window. Behind the heavy wall hanging. Just inside the next pastel binding.

They were, by all accounts, places much like the place he inhabited, the one you were supposed to play, wait, work, grow up, or lose yourself in. They doubled reasonably for the land at large except with one rule tweaked, one natural law finally understood for all it implied. There, everything would be exactly the same, everything except perhaps that aging would turn out to be a myth, disease vastly overrated, time a steady state, and thoughts real.

Adults, de facto, could neither locate nor recognize the layout. This followed tautologically. Once naturalized and issued a green card, once lured into believing in the possibility of a long stay, once you'd accepted the terms of lease, just the idea of going abroad on speculation became too ruinously expensive. To have an address *here* embargoed trade with dislocation's private provinces. But to a child brought up on customs checks and absentee ballots, to a reduced fare in terminal transit, to a boy raised on tales of a blessed country unreachable except by eternal detours through every makeshift sultanate that ever swabbed the upper decks of the General Assembly, these secret gardens and lost domains, these accounts of wonder- and neverlands were simple extensions, travel brochures from sovereign states just past the next Passport Control.

Hidden valleys were commonplaces to a boy who had been twice around the world before breaking his first bone. (The bone was a clavicle, cracked in a fall from a jackfruit tree that he had scaled in a doomed attempt to spy out the Nicobar Islands from the Indian mainland. He came to consciousness two days later in a field hospital bed, clutching a regiment of his beloved toy Gurkhas.) His parents moved every couple dozen months, whether they needed to or not. They took large leaps in small integer multiples of time. The boy always moved with them, deferring to their wishes as in most incidental matters.

In such a life, the roll of real places was as mysterious as the secret, stowaway locales his books laid out. Until the age of eight, Ricky nursed the impression that his father worked for some multinational oil company. He held on to that orienting fiction long after the evidence failed to add up. For another few years, just before adolescence set in in earnest, he was content to tell people that the man was with the Foreign Service. After that it was Air America, or "I don't know." Then the topic simply stopped coming up.

Whatever the name of his father's true employers, they demanded frequent and radical relocation. Each time that the family struck the set, dismantled the current household, and loaded it into shipping crates, reading excitement came and riffled the boy again, awakened by the standard hopeful anxiety of being left behind in the shuffle. He would find it for good this time—the wayward path, the wandering door that had somehow blended in invisibly with the surrounding grass and stone.

Veteran repacking campaigns left him a quiet child, capable of sitting still for endless, uprooted stretches. If he could live through the tedium of reaching the next stopover, he might recognize the new place on arrival, instantly find his *way,* the way that both imagination and his biannually decimated library swore existed. The next stopover never lay along the usual picnic routes given in the *Michelins.* The year in Seoul and the six months in Buenos Aires were mainstream compared to a few of the more remote refueling overnighters that made the family checklist.

He was an only child, the lone ward in his parents' caretaker government. Little Ricky had already come across, in bed, by flashlight, years ahead of the event, accounts of what would become of the folks: taken by cholera up in the Punjab. Pricked by a hail of cassava-tipped arrows. Swept from ship's deck by unseasonable eagerness on the part of the Pacific south equatorial. They would either return a lifetime later with tales of a strange inheritance or they would not: the books were reticent and divided on this matter.

His parents made up for his isolation by sending him through a slew of international schools. Sometimes private tutors would catch him up to the levels of learning in the local time zone. Schools too various to keep track of arrived new every year or two. These drilled him in all the lessons of peer terror, violent schoolground rivalry, and systematic spiritual search and seizure. Yet the one great payoff of continuous upheaval was that every two years it wiped the slate clean. Thus he acquired all the lessons, with none of the long-term liabilities, of human contact.

In every new temporary home, he was allowed all the books he could amass. But by the end of the stay, at the next inevitable move, the boy had to pare back his library to fit into one packing crate. Toys, of course, accompanied him along the way: when very young, a small, weight-driven walking cow that he let traipse over a cliff in the Andes. When slightly older, a View-Master with a handful of reels that brought the death of Pope John XXIII into vivid 3-D. In some countries the family compound was overrun by house and yard pets: one-eyed dogs, a sadistic gibbon that swooped down to attack from the roof of the servants' quarters, a myna bird that he taught to shout "Burglars!" in three languages.

His own myna mastery of the regional dialect would appear within weeks of arrival. By steeping and imitation, he'd start to jabber with the new round of street vendors in an innocent and indiscriminate mix of Farsi, Korean, Urdu, and bastard lingua franca Carib, jumbling and enjambing words, forgetting where each came from and where in the world each might successfully be used.

Terms appeared of themselves, even in conversation with his parents. (Even as an adult, he sometimes dreamed in words that were lost to conscious recall.) French was frequently helpful, but with so many obvious mother-tongue cognates, it was too trivial to be considered foreign. He could count to a hundred in three different Chineses, could pray without comprehension in Arabic, and could swear sufficiently to get himself hanged from multiple major branches of speech's tree.

Once, they did accidentally stumble upon an entrance to the Alongside. Puberty had not yet hit him in earnest, and so he was still clear enough to recognize at once the most beautiful city he'd ever seen. Geography had been absurdly generous with the setting. The city arose from an arena of hard stone as white as bleached sheets, the perfect material for raising pure linen towers next to a turquoise sea. A naturally protected port made it a prime spot for jumping off from, a base for thirty centuries of enriching trade.

A bracing, crystal climate left the city in year-round early summer. The air contained antidotes for most debilitating infections. Food spilled off trees and animal flanks into markets that sprouted everywhere in a pristine street maze. Ricky could sit for entire afternoons in the piled-up terraces among idle ancients. The men would drag lazily on their water pipes and keep the boy in fizzy drinks and figs so long as he would sit and listen to stories of rocs and roving thief bands and sunken Phoenician ships long overripe for salvage.

Here was a city given enough time and sun and wealth to have come perilously close to transcendence. It was halfway to becoming the thing that all cities are seeded to be. With easy benevolence, it had grown into a gathering place of scattered people. Syllables of Arabic, French, Turkish, English, Italian, and Kurdish bargained with one another through the commercial districts. Life disturbed the silence of crusader churches, milled about the mosaicked mosques, and picked through the Roman ruins lying just across the rim of hills outside of town.

Sitting in the smoking cafés, listening to the reports that the old men gathered exclusively for him—accounts of wandering rocks, intelligent ships that could sniff out ocean currents, wine tuns that seeped full again overnight—the boy realized: this country was the zero milestone from which all migratory sweeps set out. A life posting here would be beyond luxury. He could snorkel forever for sea urchins in the coastal grottoes, surviving on goat cheese and lamb and olives from the azure-dry mountains.

But after only nine months, the boy was yanked away. Ricky's father came home one day and issued the familiar packing orders. "No future in this town for the likes of us. Situation hopeless. We've been moved out." Further business was contraindicated. The home office threw in the towel.

As always, his father's insider prediction turned out to be worse than prophetic. Within weeks, the first trickles of smoke, still invisible to all but trained eyes, began rising from the airport, hovering over the harbor, and seeping through the back streets. In another five years, with the usual outside assistance, Beirut would be torn irreversibly apart. Over the next two decades, the shining white foundation by the sea would be mortared down to a quivering stump.

It had been the one inevitable place, a city that moved steadily for three millennia toward the goal of a livable kingdom here in this life. This capital that had teetered on the edge of final deliverance disintegrated before reaching it. Over the years, the boy watched from a distance as it descended into a spiral of factional violence from which it would never recover. He committed the lesson to long-term memory, and confirmed it repeatedly. Paris, New York, Tokyo—all would fall as quickly and completely, all the blessed islands of the world, sucked down.

His family's evacuation from a still ravishingly beautiful Beirut was banal, expected. Departure arrived as quietly as the standard strange tenant always arrives in Chapter Two. The boy took banishment in stride. By this point in his life, he could be packed to leave anywhere, forever, in a matter of a weekend.

After Beirut, the family floated about the Near East for a handful of stays, short even by his father's standards. They headed temporarily for rock-solid Cyprus. There, under a canvas tent, on a portable television with sound drowned out by a gas-powered generator the size of a small munitions plant, the three of them watched a grainy, unidentifiable machine bump up against an even grainier, more unidentifiable landscape. Through the cloud of soundtrack static, Ricky thought he could make out a man saying, "Uh, Houston?" He heard the urgency of disbelief in that endless pause, a wait pregnant with every incredulous question that technological restlessness would never be able to address. Words full of the stunned, wondering irrelevance of speech: How can one ever announce this? "Eh . . . Tranquillity *Base* . . ."

He thought it a toss-up as to which of those two words was more implausibly surreal. Both were imaginary constructs, pointers to a lost colony off to airless nowhere. One small step, one low-G caper that extended the infinite series and converged on a tranquillity, on an extraterrestrial base that the boy had never once in all his years doubted would be reestablished in his lifetime. His father told him to remember this moment for some future, comprehensive, behind-the-wheel exam. He smiled at the advice. Remember? He had never forgotten. He'd only been waiting for the landing to catch up to him.

Master this. Make a note. This one's important. His school was a hands-on social studies project gathered from the hot spots of the globe. Portable generators in a strikable Cypriot tent; blackboard and chalk propped up against a schoolhouse-sized baobab; a freak-show museum of formaldehyde jars in Sunday markets across Asia; a whole natural history every time he purged sub-Saharan water parasites from his system. Each chance reassignment became curriculum. Formal education was where he could scavenge it throughout his formative years.

And Ricky was an honor student in this erratic school. He rarely needed to look at a problem twice and never stooped to homework. The traditional round robins of algebra and economics, the model electric circuits, and the posters of the stages of alluvial fans were child's play compared to the shifting rainbow coalitions of recess or the occasional mandatory religion classes where he hadn't an Eskimo's chance in hell.

In sports he was too fair ever to rise higher than mediocre. He liked pickup multinational World Cups, but tried to engineer all the matches to end up ties. He learned the tensile strength of the local teak or cedar with near-native fluency, jackfruit disaster notwithstanding. A ball's parabolas could be extrapolated from kapok to rattan. But compete? Why? It didn't *lead* anywhere.

His schoolmates came, like Ricky, from families adrift on the world circuit. Sons and daughters of servicemen, missionaries, field agents for well-intentioned but forsaken UN agencies. For sustained companionship, small schools in insignificant villages were the best. People posted to off-track places tended to stick around longer. Big cities had notoriously high turnovers.

His friends disappeared faster than water down a *wadi*. When they were not being reposted, Ricky's buddies simply died on him. He lost two São Paulo streetballer mates to kidnappers, and his best friend in all Indonesia was found convulsed in bed, clutching a plastic sack of inhalant. Like those unmapped mansions on deserted roads, come across by chance during late-night storms, his friends vanished before he could return in daylight to look for them. Faces of all nations rushed past as furiously as a perverse dodge ball whose torture was never even to graze, never hit him at all.

He rapidly developed what his father called personal capital. Self-reliance: the reputed byword of his national character. He knew nothing about the mythic States. What stunted access he did have to homeland ways only mystified him further. The sight of Mrs. Carmichael or little blond Dennis-san speaking Japanese or Hindi on decrepit black-and-whites with abysmal reception kept him laughing only until he'd learned enough of the local idiom to be baffled by the lines.

To fill all the hours of a day, he drew complex maps or invented games he could play alone. He taught himself to play reed organs and talking drums. There were always gardeners or cooks who now and then had time for him. From these adult friends he learned endlessly useful things like how to treat lemon bark or how to coax a coconut tree into giving up its milk, palm cabbage, and sugar.

But none of these activities filled the expanse of time assigned him. A child abroad, at large in the unlimited confines and corridors that Air America served, he could almost palpate the concealed country he stood flush up against. The land he looked for was the only one large enough to accommodate native speculation. He read about it at night, in the maps and travel accounts of the local children's literature, not yet outgrown.

In the last summer of his childhood, Ricky's mother and father, out of parental obligation, took him to tour his unknown home. They felt that the boy should possess more than just a picture-book, View-Master acquaintance with the Lincoln Memorial and Yosemite. Ricky liked the States, where people were tried only for alleged crimes and no one need ever get out of the car, even to eat. The vaudeville system of weights and measures did give him trouble, however. And surprisingly, despite supermarkets the size of entire autonomous guerrilla regions he had lived in, Ricky's countrymen had not yet discovered anise coffee poured over crushed ice, or the pleasures of dried squid tucked in the back of the cheek all afternoon. Some mornings he would wake up too early, anxiously wondering, until consciousness took him, what had happened to the street vendors' calls.

The visit was of obvious symbolic importance to his parents, and the son tried his best to make it a success. Not long after their Atlantic arrival they attended a national folk festival called Opening Day. His parents took him to his first baseball game, between what his father kept calling "the new New York team" and their bitter rivals from Chicago. They sat in the upper decks next to a Chicago family who, although it was the first day of the season, unrolled a bedsheet that read, WAIT TILL NEXT YEAR. Ricky asked his father to explain the banner but the man only sushed him, embarrassed.

The get-acquainted session with his national sport was a disaster. Ricky listened intently to his father's intricate explanation of such violences as the suicide bunt and the hit-and-run. He shouted out a few well-meaning Spanish encouragements to all the Latin American players. But he wound up, during the tense tenth inning, under the bleachers playing fighting tops with six equally bewildered foreign-exchange students from the Balkans.

Rebuffed but forgiving, the folks took him to Niagara. There, Ricky agreed enthusiastically that the falls were truly impressive in volume, although of course not anywhere near as tall as Angel or Cuquenán. He enjoyed putting on the raincoat to ride the *Maid of the Mist*. The spray and spectacle and liquid statistics were all staggering, but the thing that most entranced Ricky was a scrap of yellowed newsprint pasted on the wall of the gift shop:

MIRACLE AT FALLS
Boy, Age 7, Survives Pitch over Horseshoe

He carefully added the age of the miracle survivor to the age of the clipping. The numbers summed to precisely the figure he expected. A boy his age had fallen over the impossible water cliff in a two-person dinghy. The hundred-sixty-foot dead drop had

been child's play; the consummate, stone-eating churn at the bottom had killed the boy's sister instantly. But Ricky's contemporary, after a three-minute gap lost in molten madness, had bobbed
free, beaten into pulpy unconsciousness, each one of his body's
twigs shattered, but fished out inconceivably alive.

No one except a child could possibly have survived the Horseshoe's pitch. Ricky reread the account, confirming in his mind the
only available explanation of the miracle: those three unaccounted-
for minutes, away. A boy his age, saved by falling not into the
rock-drill undertow but somewhere right alongside it.

He asked to buy the clipping, but it was not for sale. So he
stood in the gift shop, committing the account to memory. His
parents had to come tug at his sleeve, pull him away. He would
not leave without a last look at the landmark chutes, one more for
the road. But even alerted to the spot, he could not see where the
boy had temporarily pushed through.

The family campaigned their way westward like Indian fight-
ers, cutting a path through all the patriotic must-sees. They had
had the Old North, Liberty, Independence Hall. Now it was on
to Gettysburg, and out to the GM assembly lines. At the one-
third point, in one of those C-cities in Ohio, after standing at polite attention through a guided tour of some presidential home, he
talked his mother into taking him to the natural history museum,
where he hoped to find some mummified birds. These had been
a favorite of his ever since Egyptian days, when he had caught the
school bus each morning next to the mouth of a cave network
where teenagers had recently discovered seven hundred thousand
embalmed ibises.

The museum's collection was woefully deficient in the sacred
bird-corpse department. But the Egypt room did house the trans-
fixingly tiny, bound body of a three-thousand-year-old juvenile.
The three of them stood looking at the diminutive god-king, his
father eager to get on with things American, his mother yanking
him this way and that so as not to stand in the way of other fami-

lies who might want a look. Finally, in his summarizing voice, Ricky's father gave a contrite shake of the head at this creature, five hundred years older than Socrates. "Not even a teenager!"

His mother sorrowfully replied, "Isn't that a shame?"

With this exchange, Ricky realized his parents were of no help to him. And in that moment, he became an adult. He was here alone, in the middle of the strange place name stamped on his passport. From all sides, Mayday snatches from lost boys bombarded and bathed him in garbled shortwave. He stared at the hieroglyphs on the inside coffin lid until they seemed to move. The oldest picture book in existence: he should have been able to read it the way he breathed. But he could not make out the first illustrated sentence.

Late in the summer, just before heading back overseas, the family took their now high-mileage rental down a demurely paved two-lane track running through the considerable empty bit between Mount Rushmore and the Grand Canyon. Ricky had greatly appreciated the enormous stone noses, large enough for a man to live in. He asked his parents ingenuously if the nation had any plans to add the current president to the mountain after he died. They laughed evasively.

They steered toward the southwest, following a connect-the-dots of Park Service gazebos laid out for public display. Glass cases the width of the entire desert displayed their attic residue: dinosaur teeth, arrowheads, pony express hand cancellations. Stereopticon slides of the mayor's wife playing at squaw, the redskin papoose slung from her head. The dress the little native girl was found in, made from a flour sack taken in the fatal ambush of settlers' wagons.

Several hundred blank miles from the nearest registered monument, the car began emitting soft, enigmatic chirps. They had driven the vehicle clear across the country and apparently it had had enough sightseeing for this combusting lifetime. Ricky's father nursed them another dozen miles into a station with no

identifying trade sign. Its only marking was one of those movie
marquees where battered black letters lined up like a brigade of
unruly railroad-building coolies:

HAVE YOU HEARD THE ALL-SAVING WORD?

Snacks, Gas, Reading Matter

The ancient proprietor's wife took it on herself to entertain
the boy while the other three adults puzzled over the intractable
antiphonies of the four-stroke engine. The woman claimed to be
one-quarter Indian, and he asked which quarter.

"Last folks to come through here," the woman told him, "had
one curious story to tell. This was late last Thursday night. Young
couple, newlyweds, out on a backroads honeymoon. Now just
you think how astonished they must of been to see a lone girl, no
older than you yourself, hitchhiking down this roadside hundred
miles out in the middle of nowhere. In a beautiful Sunday dress. It
so astonished them, they said, that against their better judgment,
they picked the child up. Plain as a coyote's call, something had
frightened this girl into running. They say she sounded like she
come from far away too." The woman whispered sympathetically
to him; her voice was full of a conspiratorial forgiveness. "Foreign
as you yourself."

The boy did not correct her. Nor did he interrupt the quarter-
Indian woman to say that he already knew the end of the story.
How the girl hitchhiker insisted on getting in the backseat. How
she sat in party dress, answering all questions politely with no
more than a yes or no. How, when the couple turned to let her
out at the requested crossroads, the backseat was empty. How
there was no trace of the girl, nothing to indicate where she had
come from or where she had gone. "Far as anyone could say, she
dropped down on this stretch of road from out the Airy Above.
Went back to it too, I bargain."

Ricky knew better. To his experience, very few girls his age dropped out of the sky, and fewer still turned around and vanished back into it. And when they did, they rarely needed to hitchhike in between. She must have come from somewhere. Everyone did; that was the one core geography agreed upon by every school he'd ever attended. More clearly still, the girl had been headed someplace very specific. Most certain of all, she had found it, arrived while her ride wasn't looking.

The right map, the appropriate triangulation might narrow down the vanishing point the girl was after. Cartography would reveal a surface pitted with sinkholes that drew drifters across this gift plain, lured them in and pulled the covers over. He had seen, from the air above half a dozen continents, how the map might work. The surface of the earth, a continuous, dense, originally igneous curve, was wearing down and building up at different rates. Water, wind, and sun slowly threaded it with veins, favored or despoiled spots with various soils, left behind regional features that shuttled between blessing and curse over the run of time.

Planet-sized convection currents in the mantle churned up the crust and dealt it out again. Some places got granite, others obsidian. Lime laid down. Rock buckled into brittle ridges. The length and twist of a flood basin, a mountain range blocking or bestowing rainfall: these explained the secret, specific horrors of every place he'd ever lived. Weather spilled over the divide. On one side, forests formed; deserts dusted the other. The world surface was pimpled with unequal well-springs of wealth—tiny trees standing for timber, mocha ovals announcing coffee, triangles depicting tin.

Geography was the sole explanation anyone had yet given him for wars, trade, starvation, color, language, custom, mortality rates, the westward gravitation of power, tropical poverty that could not be dislodged. Geography was why that Hausa tribe found his hair so bizarre that they were compelled to stroke it as a good-luck charm. Geography sounded the thunk of darts thrown against the walls of the Singapore Anglo-American Club by civilizedly stewed civil servants upon whom the sun had recently set. The reason for Things as They Are lay quietly in tables of average temperature, salinity, acreage, snow, wind speed, altitude, fertility.

If, under the mesa edges, out here on the dry scrub range, a life had shaken loose, if one young hitchhiking girl had procured an exit visa, beautifully forged, it was to escape the local prejudice, the unfair play of forces flung from the earth's spinning axis. Travel companions he would never meet, friends with road tales far outstripping his streamed from spots all over the wrinkled planet surface like carbonation bubbles sprouting from invisible crevasses on the walls of drinking glasses. Places deep inside these continents must steadily absorb the stream. That was the only explanation how, fanning out from their font at the Nile, flowing atypically north to a delta a world wide, pitching over Niagara in a dinghy, the migrants could disappear back into desert, at night, on a nowhere Dakota road.

"This girl," Ricky asked the part-Indian woman politely, "this hitchhiker. Where did she ask to be dropped off?"

"She never did say. Just like, 'Wherever you're headed is fine with me.' Course, there aren't too many places out this way *to* be dropped. . . ."

"Was she carrying anything? A knapsack, maybe? Books?"

The woman just looked at him strangely, patted him on the head, and went to check on the repair.

On the plane westward over the last stretch of coast, Ricky thanked his parents for the vacation. Yes, he agreed cooperatively, he was an American, as he was sure would become plain as soon as he had the chance to spend some time there. Yes, he hoped he would, someday, for college, perhaps. Where would he most like to settle down? Oh, St. Louis would be fine. Or Portland. Newport News. Sure, Asheville. Abilene. Anywhere. The Airy Above.

He settled in for the flight, a whole day-and-night affair, to a place whose native name was Angel City, the capital of a country called, locally, the Land of the Free. He had brought along a book for the ride. *Where are you?* the hurt voice, the wounded tone of this year's story opened. For whole pages, for the entire lifetime of the book's little boy, it searched down a chronic ache, a place agonizingly near in every way except for the passage there. Kraft looked up from his reading above the dead center of the Pacific, realizing, suddenly, that he had outgrown fiction.

A Sapling Learner's Classic

PETER PAN

By J. M. Barrie

Printing History

First published in 1911 under the title *Peter and Wendy* and in 1921 under the title *Peter Pan and Wendy*. First American edition . . .

ISBN number . . .

Do you know that this book is part of the J. M. Barrie "Peter Pan Bequest"? This means that J. M. Barrie's royalty on this book goes to help the doctors and nurses to cure the children who are lying ill in the Great Ormond Street Hospital for Sick Children in London.

bequest: *noun.* A gift of money or property arranged by a person's last will. Also, the act of making such a gift.

royalty: *noun.* 1. The position of king or queen . . . A member of a royal family. 2. A portion of the money earned by the sale of a book, the licensing of an invention, the performance of . . .

Barrie, Sir James Matthew (May 9, 1860–June 19, 1937). Scottish author of *Peter Pan.* Barrie was one of ten children born to a country weaver. When he was six, an older brother died in a skating accident. The family never recovered from the shock. To Barrie's mother, the dead boy would remain a child who never . . .

Chapter One. Peter Breaks Through

All children, except one, grow up. They soon know that they will grow up, and the way Wendy knew was this. One day . . .

. . . Mrs. Darling put her hand to her heart and cried, "Oh, why can't you remain like this forever!" This was all that passed between them on the subject, but henceforth . . .

henceforth: *adverb.* From this time forward. From now on.

Chapter Three. Come Away, Come Away!

"But where do you live mostly now?"

"With the lost boys."

"Who are they?"

"They are the children who fall out of their perambulators. . . . If they are not claimed in seven days they are sent far away to the Neverland to defray . . ."

perambulate: *verb.* To walk about. . . .

perambulator: *noun.* 1. A baby carriage. 2. A rolling wheel used to measure distances.

per ardua ad astra: *Latin phrase.* Through difficulties, to the stars.

. . . and she was just slightly disappointed when he admitted that he came to the nursery window not to see her but to listen to stories.

"You see, I don't know any stories. None of the lost boys knows any stories."

lost-wax process, lost tribes, Lost Sunday, *Lost Steps, Lost Manuscript, Lost Legions,* **Lost Generation,** *Lost Domain,* **Lost Colony, lost . . .**

Peter the Hermit (?1050–1115). French preacher of the First

Crusade. He fought in the siege of Antioch and rode victoriously into Jerusalem alongside . . .

Peter Pan. The boy who wouldn't grow up, hero of J. M. Barrie's . . .

Peter the Wild Boy (?1716–1785). In 1724, a savage child was found scampering about the trees like a squirrel in the forests near Hamelin, in what is now Germany. The boy was taken to England under the protection of George I, where . . .

CHAPTER FOUR. THE FLIGHT

. . . they drew near the Neverland . . . not perhaps so much owing to the guidance of Peter or Tink as because the island was out looking for them. . . .

Strange to say, they all recognised it at once, and until fear fell upon them they hailed it, not as something long dreamt of and seen at last, but as a familiar friend. . . .

névé, never, never ending, nevermore . . .

never-never: 1. *noun.* The Australian desert outback, especially the Northern Territory. 2. *adjective.* Imaginary or fanciful. A never-never land is a paradise that exists only in the mind. See also: Utopia, Eden, Canaan, Cockaigne, El Dorado, Shangri-La, Arcadia . . . lotus land, wonderland, dreamland, fairyland . . . promised land, kingdom come, millennium.

millennium: *noun.* The thousand-year reign of a triumphant . . .

Millenarianism, a form of eschatology (**eschatology:** *noun.* The study of last things . . .), addresses the purpose and final prospects of the human community. It asks: What will be the final destiny of this world and its inhabitants? Will mankind ever succeed in reaching the earthly paradise that it perpetually approaches and expects? What are the final prospects and purposes of the human estate?

(**estate:** *noun.* 1. A piece of land or property . . .)

In its specifically Christian version, the millenarian formulation takes two forms: pre-and postmillenarianism. In the first, a shattering return of Christ will end history and usher in a last, thousand-year period of transcendent righteousness before . . . In the second, worldwide unification of faith will climax in Christ's return and a final harrowing. . . .

Belief in the imminent completion of the world infused the early Church, and predictions of the fast-approaching end of time erupted repeatedly throughout the Middle Ages. Yet millenarian expectation has increased steadily in modern times, concurrent with the bewildering expansion of human affairs. The settlement of the United States is shot through with millenarian models: the City on the Hill, Manifest Destiny, the Social Gospel movement, "The Battle Hymn of the Republic," Fundamentalism in its many forms, the War to End All Wars, the New Frontier, the Great Society . . .

Colonialism, imperialism, and the various industrial-age crusades to establish a world order typically sport messianic hallmarks. Marx's historical apotheosis of communism, although secular, bore an obvious millenarian cast. Hitler's Thousand-Year Reich was a revival of Joachim of Fiore's medieval apocalyptic vision. The radical political fervor characterizing the present international community—from the Red Guards to the Islamic Revolution—is perhaps best understood not in economic but in eschatological terms. . . .

Throughout history, millenarianism has centered on common themes. First is the belief that we have entered end time, the last days, and that portents visible around us warn that the completion of history is a matter not of lifetimes but of years. Although despair and excitement flourish around the ends of centuries, the date of the end has been variously set at 948, 975, 1033, 1236, 1260, 1284, 1367, 1420, 1588, 1666, 1792 . . .

Formulas deriving the onset of the new age tend to produce dates on the immediate horizon. Millenarian feeling is often accompanied by an upsurge in occultism: belief in reincarnation, purification rituals, visits from otherworldly creatures, out-of-body experiences, alternate dimensions . . .

The most common hallmark of millenarian thought is the conviction that civilization is just now entering its moment of truth, an unprecedented instant of danger and opportunity, of universal calamity and convergence. . . .

Militant expectation flares up in periods of social upheaval. The transforming stress of the nineteenth century produced an extraordinary number of prophetic cults from divergent cultures. The Mahdi of Sudan dealt the British empire several spectacular defeats and established an Islamic millenarian kingdom before being crushed by Kitchener in 1898. Isaiah Shembe, the Zulu messiah, preached the coming of a New Jerusalem exclusively for believing blacks. The Ghost Dance of the Plains Indians awaited the floods and whirlwinds that would level the earth and remove the threat of annihilation. Tens of thousands of American Millerites awaited the Second Coming on the night of October 22, 1844. In Europe, a gathering sense of end time infused the anarchist uprisings, theosophy, salvationism, the . . .

The most devastating millenarian movement of the century was the Taiping Rebellion. A failed Chinese civil service candidate named Hung learned in a vision that he was the younger brother of Jesus Christ. Proclaiming his Heavenly Kingdom of Great Peace, Hung gathered more than a million devoted followers. With this militia of believers, he surged down the Yangtze Valley and captured the city of Nanking. The move precipitated a decade of civil war during which the millenarians nearly toppled the Manchu dynasty and wrested control of China. By conflict's end, half the country was wasted and as many as twenty million lives had been lost: the second bloodiest war in human history, just behind World War II, itself an eschatological Last Battle.

Our own moment of dislocation has produced a wave of imminent expectation, from New Age movements to island cargo cults whose jungle runways and ritual wooden planes guide the Delivering Spirit safely to earth. . . .

The idea of a *progressing* history may itself derive from the hope for a new heaven and earth. Prediction of the end, like historical "progress," is eternal. And yet, millenarian eschatology is not static; rather, it may steadily escalate. Just because expectation has been wrong up until now, the faithful maintain, does not mean it will be wrong forever. . . .

Millenarianism is born in the longing for confederation and the fear of collapse, in the desire to know where the world is going, in the need for closure. We seek consolation of our own otherwise-random histories by linking them to a common destiny. But our end, eschatology insists, lies in the seed of our beginning. Predictions of Parousia frequently feature children as central protagonists. History is a propagating myth of missing innocents, carried by catastrophe to their forgotten bequest. . . .

(**bequest,** checked off in minute, ghostly pencil.)

Surely no plot could be so sadistic as to end, arbitrarily, its sole chance at continuance. The epidemic of child abduction, abuse, and exploitation taking place throughout the world seems to many to be that long-awaited harrowing that presages the return of final innocence. "A holocaust of children," shouts Captain Hook, one of the quintessential millenarian reapers. "There is something grand in the idea!"

Chapter Seventeen. When Wendy Grew Up

. . . as if from the moment she arrived on the mainland she wanted to ask questions . . .

He was a little boy, and she was grown up. . . . Something inside her was crying "Woman, woman, let go of me. . . ."

. . . and thus it will go on, so long as children are gay and innocent and heartless.

heartless: *adj* . . .

A girl is screaming. Through sheets of graphite, conducting air, annihilating paradise darkness, a scream trickles. Something young, as green as freshly cut grass, panic-whispers over night's dead receiver. Sound seeps into the eardrum, too curdling to face, too remote to locate or answer.

Its grace note mimics a playground giggle. But by second syllable it twists, like that beautiful young line drawing, into the hag hiding out inside it. Rattling clamps itself hideously to his building walls. It inches along the brick, reaches and taps at his bedroom window like a man clutching the outside of the rushing room as it speeds through midnight's mountain tunnel. The scream taps at awful intervals as if already dead, a hand automatically nail-scratching the glass, its twitch reflex still beating feebly against the pane to be let in.

Panic, as always, pitches itself up into soprano, a voiceless terror stuck in treble. A reedy panpipe issues from a girl lying in the deserted street, her legs snapped back over her neck, her belly stenciled by a tire tread. Or moans at gunpoint, stifling a shriek that she knows will make her panting assaulter kill her. A girl calls out from under a column of countless cubic feet of water, the words past making out, wild in the upper registers.

Chooses night, naturally, the old narcotic, always eager to assist in these matters. The wail taunts, under cover of darkness: Come try your inalienable rights, your annual increments to the GNP against *me*. Come measure me with your little pencil marks against the kitchen wall. With one hushed high-pitched snag, the weave unthreads. Disaster laps at the corner of his block, and he must shoot up, *now,* not even stop to dress, but run out and avert the unthinkable.

Fear freezes his tensors, holds him prostrate, drugged. Impossible; his least move will wrap the raving around his head. He can only keep deathly still and wait, pinned in terror to the soaked linen. Ghostly gas seeps through the casements—chloroform held to his nostrils on a greasy rag. He is immobilized by what he would see if he ran shouting to the window: pale straw child in burning dress, albino on fire. Naked black baby bleeding from a furrow drawn clean across its face. Asian, dazed, fresh from out of the teleporter, wailing clueless through neighborhood after neighborhood until her feet swell into pulpy spades, her skin unsheating.

A second paralyzing cry follows in the first's wake. This one is softer, a bleat of hunger or numbed grief. A child stands screaming at the end of history's downward, disintegrating spiral. It mewls in petrifying ravishment, *This is not right. Where are . . . ? This is not . . .* An animal, a feral creature, wanders loose in the apartment, bred in a basement under the city's subskin, raised on mold and leaded water, freed for no reason except horror.

The noise wavers between cries of distress and sighs from an acid bath. The one child becomes two, alternating their howls at fading intervals. The two start to stagger their shattering screeches. How many are they? A whole community, calling out from impalement a street or two off.

A scream that spectral—here, spooned into his ear—strips off the rules, shreds them like cheap paint. Safety breaks into pasteboard pieces. Shock chooses its hour, when anyone who might resist is docile with sleep and confusion. A girl at night is beaten senseless in a street where every other plate window bears the crime-stopping palm, that secret Mason's sign of Neighborhood Watch. A girl's screams return his nervous system to randomness, his heart to clammy panic. A shout at this hour . . . a single small girl, this late . . .

Exhausted ambulances fail to appear. Sirens don't even bother going through the motions. East Angel City lies within ear-shot, hustled awake, listening, eyes pressed together, night-lights smothered, firearms at ready on the bed stand. Civilization, the soul's slum clearance project, rolls over and plays dead. Practice suicide.

He tests the air. His nostrils would core-sample the room if he could find it. He has been asleep for an epoch and a half. Just on the verge of falling. Still under. Eternally coming to. To what? He must be on call, Motel Residente. The Millstone and Father Kino, at work, have skipped a crucial step, general anesthetic. The scream issues from the operating theater, which they have some-how miked so that the howls . . .

But it can't be the hospital. The room lacks that chemical aroma of rotting flesh daubed down with Listerine. This must be the house he has just bought with that beautiful . . . No, an-other. A house he never should have left. How long? Where in the world? The shriek pierces him again. It penetrates his drums like poison. He hears, coldly mechanical, a hundred times more lucidly than waking.

An aural virus slips between the crystal interstices of window glass without needing to break in. Laboratory toxin, sprung from its test-tube home, disperses a fatal help-me through his apart-ment air, waiting to sink a million microsyringes into his lungs in the dark. It slinks up, unkillably small and needy. It makes of his brain a downy bed.

It implodes him. Girlish terror injects itself, becomes his. Fear worse than he has ever known, beyond the power of memory to compare. Anthrax fear, frenzied, thrashing but still. His corpse-to-be locks up with dread, except for a heart slamming on a buf-fet of vasodilators. Grotesque scenarios tear through him, teasers before our feature attraction. Millisecond Rorschachs, the deep stuff, the mound burials: the girl's face, eaten away by bamboo rats. Her methodical ravaging by Green Berets. Fat shit-kickers slithering over her with mucused razor blades.

His brain screams, *Save her now.* But the least twitch of his muscles would incinerate him. His spine fuses down its length. Commands to contract refuse to travel to his outer reaches. The constant emergency of his days has been drill for this moment, when he alone must decide all outcome. But now he seizes up against an unknown outside the threshold of control. The scream might be *anything*. Fictions proliferate. He cannot move.

He cannot look. He knows already who it is, come here for help past giving. She has hobbled across town, over the unfordable expressway lanes on foot, one already dead. She hobbles this way to tell him that the nightmare case already races beyond his worst possible expectation. His core self, the real Kraft—the one before all deliberation—kicks in. And at the sound of moaning just outside his door, he lies still in the dark and dissimulates, denying that this is his address. The hit-and-run urge takes hold in him, with everything now on the line. And the rest of his life, spent explaining away . . .

With each second, the charade of stillness gets harder to shake. Every click condemns him further into shaming it through to the end. She will die out there, hanging onto his window. With luck, she will be blown off by daybreak onto someone else's lawn, to decompose before the police can trace her back to him. He snuggles up to final deniability in the snickering blackness.

Something inside him, some uncondensed background radiation, bursts. White light cuts across the phosphors under his lids. He pushes up, shoves for all he is worth against the ice floe lovingly drowning him. And sudden as a saturated circuit breaker, he snaps.

Gravity, switched on, smashes down on his pelvis, doubling him over. He bends erect at the waist, firing perpendicular like a spring-loaded doll. Untongued, an inarticulate blur tries to tear itself from his lips, but his face muscles stonewall it with one last veto. Voice box, throat, gauze-lined mouth refuse to mobilize. He has had, is right now having a stroke, a neural storm. The stuff-arrested word, a shed piece of floating birch bark, pilots its way through, issues out in a *nnnn-yy-aaeoo No.*

His own scream swallows up the girl's, eradicates it, but not before the rasped treble turns to a more domestic alarm, closer to his ear. He is awake, yelling out intervention, calling for emergency procedures, the extraordinary stopgaps he knows by rote. Thoughts come to him one after the next, tin soldiers pouring through the breach in a battered syllogism. My bed: break from it. Feet to floor. My room. My apartment. Door that way, one o'clock, north-northeast. Get to it before it seals shut.

Something reaches out to snag him before he can bolt. A hand, another human being in his bed. "Ricky?"

Arrival comes as suddenly as had violence's burst. The street torture stops the moment that Linda—artlessly naked, here, next to him, his on ephemeral credit—changes her breathing. The screams are no more than slight obstructions in her nasal passage, amplified by his ear up flush to her breath. Terror comes of closeness, the way single cells reveal an Armageddon under the microscope.

"Ricky? What's the matter? What's happened?"

He collapses into her, breaking a harder fall. Nothing. Nothing's happened. Exactly the sort of featureless, unnoticeable night he prayed for in secret as they fell asleep a lifetime earlier.

"It's all right. I'm . . . okay. I just thought . . ." Thought that the girl had come for him, like a little slaughtered bride. "I just remembered something. Really. Go back to sleep."

"Sleep?" she says, incredulous, smiling, scolding. "Ricky, you're shaking."

"True," he concedes. Body-long tremolos, at intervals, replace the now-silenced cry. "Hypothermia?" comes his lame proposal. And yet, partly true; he is freezing, shivering to death in this heat sink of human compromise that he's chosen expressly for its hothouse climate. "If you'd just quit stealing all the covers . . ."

"Covers?" her bewildered syllables race in all directions, furious, afraid of him, like children scattering in front of the blindman in a game of bluff. She holds him to her over his protests. She cradles his head to her bareness in half comfort, half nelson. "You *sure* you're ten years older than I am?" And worse than her most hopeless case.

Dark in her limbs, her skin an inexhaustible chamois perfection, a taut heat treatment everywhere against him: Linda. She has come to keep him from recall. They've sent her at just this critical cusp to release him from his deserts. Grateful for that much, he considers telling her. She, if anyone, could leave the scream explained and housebroken. *Listen.* Your breath sounded to me like the last child left on earth, after all the rest had been taken.

But even should he confide in her, they would be alone. Both of them, unbuffered, clothed only in this *faux*-residential calm, hurtable now in more ways than can be cataloged. He would only freeze her, leave her as chill as he is if he told, if he held her any longer. Already her naked nipples go gooseflesh, pucker like an alum-punished mouth. Or does something else arouse them, something aside from the desert cold? Some desire awakened by his pure fear, the chances of unlimited suffering at this hour when personality is discarded as a worthless blind?

He tests the gooseflesh, puts his tongue to it. He searches across her body for hidden hiding places among her moraines that must have heard *something,* must have registered. And Linda, half blood, flexing like a jaguar, spooked by him now, of all he might do to her, moans. Then more, she calls out in strange languages—yes, *there*—uncaring who hears them through the thin walls. Love abandoned to the cries of adjacent devastation.

THOSE NIGHTS WHEN the need to pass out completely marauds through his so-called consciousness like a clubfoot waltzing on parquet, nights when not even the last blast could wake him, he must still prop himself up at this twenty-four-hour convenience casino, tape his eyes open with pharmaceuticals, and deal out continuous all-or-nothing hands of one-card stud. And on those other nights, the ones that rotation magisterially allots him to go blaspheme himself with sleep, he cannot. It's no less than a form of sublimated impotence (the real thing so far blissfully spared him), imaginary. Yet from out of deepest, ripple-free Stage Four nothingness, advance warnings of alarm and visitation make the thought of even a couple hours of lowered vigilance unthinkable, even obscene.

Fortunately, work supplies a variety of substitutes for narcosis. This morning, they rebuilt Tony the Tuffian's ear. Tony's parents initially tried to deny ever having seen him in their lives when the police dragged him bleeding to them, the half of his head opened up in a street misunderstanding, as pink and wet as an Independence Day picnic melon. Only when the officer swore that the investigation had nothing to do with the folks' own improvised retail operation did the mother start wailing. The woman promptly sponged and bound the boy up with root extract, about as helpful as cornstarch to a contractor.

Couple of absolute tenderfoot cops brought Tony and his severed left outside awning to the ER. "Iced," according to Plummer, "but get this: with the ear *inside* the bag of melting cubes. Thing was total mealworm meat. I wouldn't even have fed the pup to my horned toad."

This was a couple months ago. During the time it took for the side of Tony's head to heal enough for Kraft to consider working it back into shape, the cops, unbeknownst to anyone outside their autonomous little fiefdom, were paying visits to the Tuff, telling him that they had forbidden surgery until Tony told all. They got their names, and Tony got scheduled for his first-stage ear reconstruction, convinced that he had the magnanimity of the American law enforcement system to thank for it.

Going into surgery this morning, the Tuffian expressed some regret that he would lose the instant status that his blunted left stump had earned him with the rest of the kids' ward. He seemed almost thrilled to hear that he would wake from the procedure with another scar, this one across his lower thorax, where Kraft would remove the bit of cartilaginous framework needed to form the new external spoiler. The transplant will hold until Tony loses the hardware again in some prison brawl.

That one is Kraft's only cut-and-paste scheduled today. Work has been his one topical balm against the thing that has steadily coagulated since he went ankle fishing inside the boat girl. And fortunately, the job drones on, long after the sexy procedures are over. The hypercompetitive med schools ought to make it broadband knowledge: the career of professional shamanism these days consists of equal parts corrective injury, scut follow-ups, and brute bookkeeping. Having bloodied up the Clean Room enough for one day, Kraft still has the blessed canonical troika of distractions—logging, filing, and retrieving—to keep him from replaying his latest library of debilitating mental cassettes.

Documentation is everything. Data and protective paperwork. By this point, Kraft has learned not to say so much as "Lookin' good!" to a patient without making a shorthand note of the date, time, and physical circumstances. As a result, he's saddled with a hell of a lot more scrap- than scalpelwork. So much more that even Beirut General must give him a desk to bury in forms.

He sits in his requisitioned cubicle, plucking messages back out of a Dictaphone and pinning the phrases, like formaldehyded lepidoptera, to official reports. He keeps the corridor door open; otherwise, it gets deceptively restful in here. Now and then he comes up for air, to guard his flank by throwing a quick look hallward. Somewhere around the millionth such routine inspection, he just about jumps through his own cranium. A diminutive super-oldster in Dodger cap and baggy cardigan has crept silently into the doorframe and just stands there, staring at him.

The guy has been there a while, by all evidence. One of those balding, skin-flappy, underinflated men you see shuffling around in Griffith Park carrying a paper bag and stick, talking to pitiful cocker spaniels in tongues found only in hidden mountain villages that appear but once a year. The old fart just gazes at him from myopic mine shafts on either side of his hook nose. Kraft, deep in his usual Latinate fog, can't even summon up an officially inquisitive "Yes?"

Before Kraft can determine What Is Wrong with This Picture (This here is Pediatrics, sir. You want Gerontology, Floor Four), Gramps spits out, "What's it to ya, buddy?" and disappears. The midget Walter Brennan pads rheumatically down the corridor, looking for all the world like a gargoyle punching out at quitting time, packing up shop and lumbering stonily down the nearest flying buttress to catch the bus home.

The old geezer's voice shocks even more than his beaked features. The codger-style diction is just about in line with his general level of senescence. But where Kraft had expected a kind of Lionel Barrymore gravel, there's only this disturbingly treble whistle. May in December. Weird, unplaceable, disconcerting. But hey. Like the man asked: What difference does it make to you? Leave it. Not your specialty; not *this* rotation, in any case.

Kraft sits another minute, pursed over the Dictaphone. Checks the doorway again. Has sleep deprivation progressed so far as to deliver visuals? All at once the click of differential diagnosis hits him. He blanches and stands up slowly. Hutchinson-Gilford disease. True progeria. Visible after a year or two of normal infancy. Onset of full-fledged symptoms around six. Sixty years old by the age of ten. Kraft falters over to his bookshelf, flips through the references catatonically, already knowing what he's going to come up with. Only four dozen known occurrences in the entire world literature. Kraft lurches back out into the corridor, but Gramps, one of creation's rarest ancient children, is gone.

A Hutchinson-Gilford, here, at a freebie institution that can barely handle tonsillectomies without sending the kid out on a tray? A hospital where half the senior staffers are alcoholics and half the residents have doctored their transcripts? How on earth can Carver even think about handling such a case? The minute the kid walked in the door, they should have airlifted him straight to Boston. There's something not quite Hippocratic going on here. Either the admitting physician doesn't know what he's looking at—impossible; that pinched nose, the vanished hairline, the jaundiced, ravaged, medieval parchment skin—or the shriveled boy has been sucked up into some medical Barnum's bailiwick.

It doesn't seem conceivable: a child rushing toward advanced old age at this wildly accelerated rate without having attracted the attention of research's power players somewhere along the line. Even the family physician, however blunderingly inept, certainly must have noticed when the kid picked up a decade between six-month checkups. Then Kraft returns to the reality check and remembers where he is. The bulk of this outfit's clientele couldn't pay for a periodic physical, even if they knew what such a thing was. But surely the school nurse, the boy's teachers, the neighborhood social worker . . . ?

Drop it. Lose the whole matter. Run closed-lidded in the other direction singing "The Star-Spangled Banner" while cupping your hands over your ears. This admission obviously has no bearing whatsoever on surgery. As such, it lies outside the only shorthand calculus Kraft has for years been able to afford: *Impact on immediate work load? Need deal with this by self?*

But the wrong, awful rarity of the thing haunts him. A boy a third his age, except twice as old. That uncannily sick face. A great-grandfather's face, superannuated and wasted, yet with half a century still to go before retirement age. A half century it will never make. An extraterrestrial face, para-human, a mask violating the fixed sequence of innocence to experience to decay, mixing up the stages of growth in monster parody. The tragic by-product of a mad invention, a bio-ray, some visionary machine invented to blaze open a transforming shortcut but botched horribly, locked up deep beneath the earth's crust, forgotten by everyone except a few children who, not noticing the CONDEMNED sign rotting over the entrance, wandered down into the shaft while playing and accidentally absorbed the full, cell-accelerating blast.

He tries work again. But no matter how often Kraft rewinds and replays the burst of urgent nonsense on his Dictaphone, he cannot transcribe it. He puts the machine down, exchanges it for the phone, and dials an extension fast becoming as familiar to him as the lab technician's. "Espera, please."

Another shuffle, and a voice like home whispers out of the

receiver, "Squeakheart?" Giggling at his decorum. "Zat you? I thought I told you never to call me at the office."

"Linder, listen." To what? To a transcript of ultimate unlikelihood. To wild suppositions. To the track of a background song going hideously lost. To the blood coursing as audibly as surf through his ears. To the dead silence on his end of the line, the pyre of questions piling up on his police blotter. "I just . . . This kid, this *old* kid . . ." The disease's proper name refuses to come out of the technical tome and unfold itself.

"Ah. You've met Nicolino."

The word convinces him of the utter hopelessness of dealing with this woman. The gap between them—almost a full generation, by the standards of developing nations and the clientele down at OB-GYN—is trivial compared to this. Their incommensurate pasts would be resolvable. Even the unspannable chasm of sex, the two of them dosed with mutually unintelligible hormonal cocktails, would be a little leap. But this, this *equanimity* of hers in the face of the unassimilable makes her another genus. Alien. He can't even begin to talk to her.

He has called to enlist her aid in comprehending this fifty-to-however-many-historical-billions shot strolling around loose, unprotected, Dodger-capped in the corridors just outside his door. But Linda—he might have known that she would already be on a firstname basis with astonishment—makes of this boy an order of magnitude rarer still. Just one. One, out of all the cumulative billions that do not stop today but go on growing toward some terminal forever. He might have known it'd be "Nicolino."

"Linda. Do you have any idea *what this kid is?*"

"Yeah. He's a cheeky little brat. He came in for his first appointment with Physiatry and propositioned me."

Kraft's resentment of this woman vanishes in a flash, replaced by murderous rivalry directed at a preteen, dirty old lecher. "What did he say?"

"He said, 'Va-va-voom.' Or words to that effect. Then something or other about lamenting his vanished youth."

Kraft has to snort, but painfully, a solid, undislodgable mass in his trachea. "What in hell is he doing *here*?"

"Trying to get medical attention, I think. Sor-ry." She suppresses a guilty laugh. "His folks don't want to turn their little boy into a rolling research freak. 'Just fix Nico up and send him home. Our only child!' Soon as I heard that, I thought, aha! So that's why little Nico is spoiled. But know what? It turns out he's *not* an only child. He's got about a half-dozen sisters. They don't count, apparently. Is that some kind of Islamic thing, or something?"

"I wouldn't know."

"Kind of a specialist, are you?"

"Did you tell these people that a little research might help the next kid who decides to go geriatric overnight?"

Linda sighs, exasperated on both sides. "What do you want to do? He is their kid, after all. Oh, Nico himself would love doing the pony show, I'm sure. He'd jump at the chance to sass the country's leading medical investigators. But Mama's the bottom line, wouldn't you say? 'Give me a new generation of mothers, and I will give you a new world.' "

"Run that by me again?"

"Nothing you'd know. It's from a *book*. And not a manual. Don't worry, it won't be on the Boards."

Hang up now, and the tiff will propagate. He can feel it already, building toward chain reaction. He doesn't even feel like intervening, smoothing things over. Even throwing the offense back at her takes too much energy. Sullenness is too obvious, though. Would only give her more occasion to egg him on. He needs to find some neutral, not-too-icy politeness, and get out.

But he can think of nothing more to ask. He doesn't even have to inquire about the reason for the admission. Median age of death: thirteen. Few true cases make it to the adulthood that mocks them. Cardiovascular crack-up, arteriosclerosis, heart disease, vessels pissing out of the parched scalp, systemic deterioration of the organs. The kid's body clock is simply shutting down early, like an office on New Year's Eve, pitching it in after only half a morning's work. Nicolino is dying of a parody of old age. No other name for it, unless, like the newspapers, you go with "natural causes."

Linda is insouciant, oblivious to his tangles. When Kraft doesn't fill the silence, she does. "You any good with Dodger statistics, by the way?"

"You're asking the wrong guy." Wrong in every way. Linda; leave me. Don't waste another day of your twenties on this lost cause. Come back when you've worked your way through the rest of the state, the men who like to do things at night, the ones who'll match your bursts and stoke you up and make you flash on and keep you as alive, as supple as you still are. Come back when you're ready to go stiff, to end things. I won't have moved.

"Oh, sorry. That's right. You led a deprived childhood, didn't you? I forgot. Mowgli, the jungle boy. No Sweetarts, no juice-filled wax vampire fangs. No national pastime. That explains everything."

He feels his muscles initiating the shove-off, biceps starting to reverse-curl the thousand-pound receiver back onto its cradle when he hears her ask, "Sleep any better last night?" Her words shine with confused, hurt highlights, a banished *me-neither* tone—can't you guess? Hearing it, he can no longer help himself. He needs her otherness. He hangs on her every distraction the moment work stops. Addicted already, and following the viscous, familiar path of habituation, he will soon need her even during daylight hours. A fix, a whiff, just to start moving in the mornings.

He loves her absurdly, immaturely. His blood hops up with the high schooler's full panoply of anticipation and dread. He would tell her now, but for Kean working in the next cubicle to his. And yet: he will not say so, even in their next night-long privacy. How else except by silence can he hope to keep her all along his length, always, and when the hour comes, still a permanent stranger?

She does not ask, as her voice hints, *Are you on call tonight?* Instead, her words assume the courage neither of them has. "There's nothing to be afraid of, you know."

But there is. Is everything. All the world must be run from. Little girls stump for miles on severed stems across a wasted city to come ambush him in the dark. Old golden-agers a lifetime beyond his roam the pediatrics ward, dying on him in the prime of childhood. How can he tell her, and not drive her hastening away?

HE KNOWS NO more about progeria than he can afford to learn. And he can afford to learn no more than he needs to string along and pass the next certification. What's it to ya, buddy? Absolutely nothing.

Nobody, it appears, has even a game show's clue about the thing's etiology. Without a shred of supporting evidence, a little one-room school of thought lays suspicion on a hereditary cause. Sure, why not? Throw it on top of the "congenital" heap, the fuck-ups in the master switches twisting the body this way and that like hideously abused Raggedy Anns and Andys. The intermediary gaps between "Ann" and "and," and "and" and "Andy" fill with any number of permutations on battered puppethood: microcephaly (pinheadedness in less polite circles), protrusion of the meninges and neural elements out the rear of the little baby back ribs, the whole salad bar of androgynies and cretinisms, endocrine leaks and overflows, organs on fire or attacking themselves, hips and limbs and skeletal connectors pointed every which way but useful. Or simply missing. Stolen. Never delivered.

Genetic disorder is Kraft's absolute first nightmare category. It is corruption at the source, at the point of manufacture. Obscenity nuzzles up close to molecular innocence, suckling its infantile teat the way flies lap at a running sore. If purpose can be scattered already, even here, then what's the point? The morning's first shadow casts itself over his ward. And worst of all, all these

specific charts—the No-Face, the Nephrosis, the Septal Defect—
they have all been born just hours before the breakthroughs that
might have saved them.

They are, perhaps, the last generation to be struck down before
the arrival of the ultimate gene-weaponry. Cures are coming,
just around the corner, all but here. Fantasy treatments, fictive
fairy diagnostics, complete in-the-womb screenings, packets of
substitute chromosome segments to replace the defective instructions. His successor physicians will have every intervention imaginable, thought-designed curative texts placed into action simply
by specifying the right combination of magic words. Kraft and
the rest of the last graduating class of witch doctors have only
their blundering surgical corrections, bulling about with knives,
helping sometimes but always at crippling expense, buying the
necessary patch job at ruinous rates the day before a massive, half-
price giveaway.

No firm evidence proves that Hutchinson-Gilford is, in
fact, a twist in the master narrative. And yet, lumping it with
congenital disorders beats the pathological alternatives. Bald,
diminutive, withered twelve-year-old kid, his skin yellowed
like ancient newspaper, his whole circulatory system corrod-
ing to worthlessness. We're clearly not dealing with infectious
disease here, not even one of the truly exotic. And if it were a
contagion? Kids passing progeria around, picking up communi-
cative old age as easily as croup. Whole playgrounds turned to
pensioners in a matter of weeks. Lawrence Welk hastily recast to
include Saturday morning cartoons. Now there would be a real
plague, one worthy of Kraft's day and age.

An environmental cause is at least conceivable. Some erratic,
unidentified toxin accumulating in secret tissue. But it has no
geographical outbreaks, no stricken communities like the ones
becoming mundanely familiar even to those, like Kraft, who stu-
diously avoid the nightly scoop operas. Nutrition, perhaps. God
and the social workers only know what specialty dishes they're
feeding youngsters in the town's eastern marches this season. But

if age were ingestible, Southern California—the whole holistic *concept*—would be awash in juvenile octogenarians.

Perhaps cause lies somewhere on the far, sinister end of the spectrum. Chance micro-hit. Physical injury. Damage incurred through the placenta or sustained at birth. Regulatory mechanism wiped out in one systemic shock. A blow to the head, deliberate or—always that ludicrous euphemism—accidental. Accidents do happen, but the stats don't jibe. Ten American children are killed each day by handguns alone. Yet only fifty of these little old men have appeared in the entire historical record. If it is injury, then strange, reticent, internal, even molecular—not one of the more expedient violences of this increasingly adept twilight culture.

Etiology cannot help Kraft, as is so often the case. How this freak, this *Nico* happened to put on six decades in as many years is of less interest than what to do about it. Thank the bureaucrats that be that Kraft doesn't have to deal with the case. How can anyone hope to treat the kid? He's brittle, beaked, dry. Dermis like phyllo. Only, it's *not* old age. No senility, no wasting of the CNS. Half his organs are untouched. The kid's got spring in his legs yet, even if he looks more third-base coach than runner.

Jesus, the kid's a kid. Whatever else it may or may not be, freakish aging is a childhood condition. And there, precisely, is the whole hopeless situation in a handbag. The would-be Department of Pediatrics, Dr. Joseph "It's Under Control" Milstein presiding, is about as mythically monolithic as that twenty-five-language empire on the other side of the globe, at this very minute breaking into a caldron of contentious turfs. Their service is no more than a Jack-and-the-bean-curve, a wide-load Gaussian with Infancy on one end and Adolescence on the other, with a class of cases fat in the mode-peaked middle for which English has no good word.

Pediatrics is not a discipline. It's a default, a catchall. Kraft cannot connect even its two main provinces. The bins themselves are hopelessly coarse: from birth to vertical, and from vertical to near voting age. What, pray tell, is the common denominator between pyelonephritis and Munchausen syndrome by proxy? In one, the kidneys drive the parents crazy; in the other, the parents drive the kidneys insane. The specialty is designed by one of those guys who go into bookstores and order a yard and a half of red hardbacks no taller than eight inches. As Dr. Brache once told him (and irony lies outside the bounds of Miss Peach's rhetorical modes), if you can crack a fourteen-month-old's chest, than you can wean a fourteen-year-old off crack.

The international community, from Kraft's third-hand vantage, is currently engaged in some intensive R & D, smoking up several delicious monster scenarios for the coming collective blowout. Things are definitely on the march. Nightly news lays out its attendant horrors in a series of thought-eradicating, three-minute music videos. Ice caps melt. Fuel reserves push toward asymptote, with nothing anyone can do about it. Debt amasses faster than global capital. IRS computers threaten to trigger the long-teetering global financial shutdown by issuing checks and debits essentially at random. The president's astrologer joins the Secretary of Defense in clicking off the Patmos checklist of critical warning signals. An Angel City, an incredible place to live for Those About to Die, has about a decade and a half's jump on all other up-and-comers.

But Pediatrics supplies Kraft with an alternative wrap-up scenario. The department nurses, whom he tries to avoid for reasons not sufficiently buried in his checkered past, report this tremendous spike in preemies, SIDS cases, placental substance dependence, inherited autoimmune deficiencies—slopes ramping up for an assault on the airy altitudes above the graph-paper tree line. His imagination is entranced by the chance of an annual power skid in the male-to-female ratio, not just statewide, but throughout the euphemistically labeled developed countries. A Pink Shift drifts demographics measurably away from snips and snails, sugar-and-spiceward. An almost imperceptible but steady 0.1 percent reduction in males per live birth per year, when coupled with the recent slight *increase* in male infant mortality rates, and the shift reveals nothing less than the steady girlification of the world, with its inevitable—although belated—precipitous drop in procreation.

Wouldn't that be the ultimate kicker? After all the high-visibility threats, the dire predictions proliferating like food stamps, the concerted forward two-and-a-halfer over the brink of willful critical mass, to wind up perishing slowly from irreversible sex-ratio drift, brought on by some invisible drinking-water effect on gamete motility? Sure, it smacks of wishful thinking on Kraft's part, when faced with the grab bag of aggressively masculine apocalypses, to hope that the species might sink into a more benign disappearance, a surfeit of female.

But until the collective end of choice arrives, or until he finishes this service and graduates to the next one—the VA, a weekend cake promenade in comparison—whichever comes first, he is compelled to make his minor mitigations for those sufferers who share nothing in common except their unripe green. Monsters, freaks of gene or accident or pathology, race up and down these halls in relays, in fifty-yard dashes leading to no medal, no record, nowhere. Files of them, parades of shell-shocked, half-staffed pilgrims. What's it to you?

"OKAY. NOW ROLL over. Move your arm like this."

"God. Lay off. You're killing me."

"Don't be such a baby."

"Stop. Wait. No, really, Linda. I *need* both my arms. It's a professional thing."

"Oh, come on. Why is it that men start shrieking at the least little hint of therapeutic pain?"

"Who you calling a man? Jesus. I think you dislocated it."

"Then it probably needed to be dislocated. It's for your own good. I've never seen anyone with more restricted mobility."

"Yeah? Well that comes from years of conscientious discipline."

"Discipline? You ungulate, you. I ought to teach you the meaning of the word."

"I'm sure you could."

"Do you want me to fix you or not?"

"I ain't broke."

"That's what all the boys who come see me say. Your little mascot these days, Tony the Tuff? Diminutive little machismo thug. He sits in my office whining that it hurts when he grimaces."

" 'Don't grimace?' "

"No. Don't get your ear cut off next time. Now, if you want to talk about real bravery . . ."

"I'm supposed to sing 'Sank heven vor leetel gerlz' now, right? Speaking of which, did you give them to her?"

"Give what to who?"

"Joy. The books."

"Of course I gave them to her. You think maybe I fenced them for their street value?"

"What did she say?"

"When I brought them to her, she just . . . I'm sorry. You know, those eyes. It's like: 'I have to protect *you* from what you don't know about the world.' She thanked me profusely, and begged me to thank you, and looked up to me, deadly serious, and said, 'Do you want to read them out loud to me?' Like that's the only official way of doing these things. Like they were part of some . . ."

"And what did you say?"

"Will you shut up, please, and let me tell this story? I asked her, 'Would you like me to read them to you?' To which she very tentatively suggested, 'I think I would rather look at them carefully during my free time.' "

"Free time? Free time from what?"

"From her self-designated study periods. We have to graduate, didn't you know?"

"Oh God."

"Here. This way. A little radial . . ."

"And did she read them?"

"She took what is for her a leisurely stroll through them, compared to the day and a half she usually takes to polish off the histories and almanacs. Then she tried to return them with the usual politeness. When I told her they were hers, she said she had a few questions. 'Why does that boy, when they wheel him into the garden, say *I shall live forever?* That other boy, the one who never grew up: How is that possible?' Not your typical twelve-year-old concerns."

"Utter failure, in other words."

"Oh, I don't know. Who can say what Joy's imagination is capable of? That she's kept pace with *reality* is astounding."

"Not her. I mean me. Utter failure in selecting titles."

"I wouldn't say that either. Okay, now the planar axis."

"Ouch. Oh Christ. What are you doing to me?"

"I'm not sure. But you love it, don't you? Admit it. Admit it or I'll twist your little wing right off."

"Anything. Anything."

"Undress me."

"What? Here? In the middle of . . . ?"

"Come on, come on. Am I going to have to do this myself?"

"Espera! Oh holy. Shh. Stop. People will hear."

"So what? They'll just think, Hmm. Old Dr. Kraft in there, bashing the bishop."

"Old?"

"Enough to know what he's doing."

"Oops! I'm afraid that's my beeper."

"Look at him grin. I hadn't realized you could make it go off just by wishing."

He does not say good-bye, or set the time and place for finishing what they have started. He does not tell her that far more than the foot is in danger, that getting away with just the calf would be deliverance. His old saving grace: say as little as contractually necessary.

And when he sees the child next, for a set of scans, she welcomes him with a smile that would be shy if it weren't visibly shaken. He thinks: The pain. It's starting. It will wring her until she cries out to be killed.

But it is not the pain. Not yet. Something else drives her brown-petal face ashen. "Dr. Kraft," she tells him excitedly, swallowing the consonants in a ghostly holdover of lost Asian highlights. Ghostly for them both. "I have seen him. He's *here*, right here on my floor. The boy. The boy who never grew up!"

(A softbound text works its way to the top of the To Do stack. Its ocher cover mirrors a map maker's fantasy: the Land of Faith, the Land of Infidels, the Promised Land, all bound by the Unknown Ocean, crossed bravely by two intrepid small craft and a spouting sea monster. An ink noose tightens around the book's title, The World Awakens, Part III. *The loop fills with snorer's zzz's. The spine is split and a sewn signature of pages slips loose.)*

. . . occupational rescue work in a dark time—the stopgaps that a people summon at the moment of collapse—would make a profitable study. The psychology of decline, the realization that progress has reversed and that history is entering upon a long, perhaps terminal decay, must be one of the most revealing of civilization's convictions. But such speculation lies beyond the scope of this endeavor. . . .

. . . a narrow span of nine years in the Europe of the early sixteenth century. Few periods have been more ambivalently explosive than the years 1527 to 1535. The dissemination of printed matter through movable type, rapid expansion of trade, advances in medicine led by Paracelsus's epochal surgical manual, a density of artistic genius such as the world never again produced, and the daily exodus of ships embarking westward on a salubrious footrace of nations were cause for the highest optimism.

Yet the underside of the era's developments more than kept pace. The scale of political intrigue and social dislocation stripped conviction from even the age's most gifted. Signs and portents— the comet of 1531, the Gnostic calculations pointing to the fifteenth centennial of the Savior's death, Columbus's prophetic fulfillment in gathering together the globe's scattered races (a collision from which the world has yet to recover)—become the basis for a more substantive chiliasm. The renewed Turkish incursions, Müntzer's Peasants' Uprising, the endless roles of famine and crop failure, returns of Plague, horrific distribution of wealth, the sundering of the sole institution that had held Europe alive for the thousand years since the collapse of the Western Empire, and Luther's new timetable for the perpetually impending Visit all attest to a climate of frightened expectation.

For one highly cultivated, multinational confederation the size of Western Europe, these years truly were the end of history. Pizarro and his two hundred soldiers sprung their ambush in Cajamarca town square, captured the Incan emperor, and slaughtered his four-thousand-man bodyguard. The Cuzco hegemony fell, and an empire as remarkable as any the world has seen vanished into legend.

From the home ports, a fabulous, golden land seemed to rise up from the sea in the nick of time expressly to solve intractable over-population, inflation, stagnation, unemployment, and restless violence. Yet the overnight infusion of new goods—tobacco, tubers, maize, gold, human lives—only increased the disruption of populations. By 1527, all Europe was crisscrossing the seas in carracks and caravels. Assembling a fleet became a nation's rite of passage, a frenzied, peripatetic hunt for commodities and resources. But by a process that has become historical law, a sudden, often inflationary increase in the material stakes brought about a proportional expansion in the risk of disastrous . . .

(A passage obscured here by vigorous Crayola spirals, scarlet, canary-yellow, Adriatic blue-green.)

. . . had angered Charles with the Cognac maneuverings. The emperor's response was to incite a force of mercenaries under Frundsberg. We are fortunate to possess, almost intact, the diary of Michael Klotz, a Lutheran lance commander in the *condottiere*'s band, a remarkable document providing, like Cellini's on the other side, a firsthand account of the Sack. Klotz writes of the devastation the *Landsknechte* cut on the way through Lombardy, where they merged with the duke of Bourbon's army for a combined drive down the Via Emilia upon the Eternal City.

Privately, Klotz favored the last-minute attempts to patch up a truce between pope and emperor. But the terms offered by Clement and accepted by Charles's agent were too niggling for the twenty thousand German and Spanish troops, stoked by promises of pillage and booty. Klotz could no more sway his own brigade than Frundsberg or Bourbon could restrain the force as a whole. The army now advanced on the capital of Christendom with an independent will.

By April, Rome at last realized that it was the object of the march. On Easter, a crazed recluse ran through the streets, calling on the bastard children of Sodom to repent or be destroyed. Desperate defense preparations commenced, but these came too late. The pope's guard were outnumbered at least five to one. Skillful use of the walls and existing artillery managed to thin the attacking squares. Soon, however, the pope was forced back upon the Castel Sant'Angelo. Cellini tells us how he single-handedly . . .

(Two more pages of florid Crayola, now a jeweled, sunken garden through which float disembodied figurines, boats, fireworks, and several uppercase Hs and Os, alongside a chorus line of amorphous shepherd's crooks.)

The task of safeguarding the endless inventories of artistic splendor in the papal treasuries fell to the younger Antonio da Sangallo. Antonio, nephew of the great Sangallo architect brothers, then headed the building project whose funding schemes—excessive taxations, selling of papal indulgences, and the like—had precipitated the calamitous unraveling of the Western world. . . .

Many of the treasury objects were melted down rather than allowed to fall into the hands of the Northern invaders. Cellini himself (who derided Antonio as a tasteless woodworker) personally destroyed unique masterworks of his own art, as well as works by his greatest contemporaries and predecessors.

But Sangallo had another plan, equally outlandish, one that

meant to preserve the achievements of civilization from the storm. The shape of the secret measures emerges only from gaps in the record. The master builder worked around the clock in the confines of the Vatican, packing sandbags to fill Sixtus's private chapel, hoping to protect the Botticelli, Perugino, and Ghirlandajo frescoes from falling mortar and to absorb the bombardment's shocks to Michelangelo's already world-famous tabernacle to Creation. Antonio worked steadily and without much hope to preserve the triumphs of the imagination from reality's latest onslaught, stacking sand in the full knowledge that this was neither the first, nor the last, nor even the most senseless of politics' annihilating sieges.

Antonio's daring plan was carried out on the night of May 6, as the invaders poured through the breached walls in a turmoil of fog and artillery fire. He assembled, in the now-barricaded papal apartments, as many of the quarter's juvenile homeless as he could find. Street urchins were the ideal cover, the last bodies that a pillaging mercenary would think to shake down. On his own initiative, Sangallo doled out priceless medallions, cameos, portraits, reliquaries, vessels, precious glass, and jewelry to this band of cutthroat children, instructing them to carry the fortunes away and threatening them with God's eternal damnation if they should fail to return so little as a single piece of sacred art after the danger subsided.

And so it came about that a considerable part of the richest collection of artifacts in Europe passed into the impoverished streets inside the torn shirt seams of children, not one of them privileged enough ever to have attended school. . . .

Klotz relates, with fascinated horror, the events of those eight days. His professional soldiers degenerated into a blood-drinking mob, killing at random for sheer pleasure, ransacking churches and libraries and *palazzi,* destroying the university, starting fires with irreplaceable manuscripts, looting anything that looked pawnable, carrying off all movable painted surfaces and destroying much of the immovable out of spite, torturing eminences, parading about in cardinals' vestments, desecrating altars, proclaiming Luther the pope, forcing nuns and young women and girls into the Piazza del Popolo at sword point for a promiscuous carnival of violation.

(The word "promiscuous" clumsily circled by crude exclamation points.)

In one senseless indulgence, marauders entered the orphanage of Santo Spirito Hospital and slaughtered all the helpless who had assumed sanctuary there. The pope was held prisoner in the Castello; law and decency had come to an end. It is little wonder that the Sage of Rotterdam saw in the Sack "not the destruction of a single city, but of the entire world."

Klotz's share of the spoils, if we credit his account, was modest. He spent the first two days attempting to restore decorum. As papal resistance dissolved, he roamed the streets trying to reduce the brutality of his men. He writes at length about rescuing a tiny boy and girl from the hands of a loot-incensed cavalier. The soldier had discovered brooches in the children's possession—an encrusted filigree pin, a Romanesque silver winged grotesque, and a Florentine terra-cotta. Klotz killed the molesting soldier with some evident satisfaction.

There follows a long, sometimes pathetic passage in which Klotz describes taking the children under his private protection during the fierce, waning days of the Sack. His harrowing inner battle between the altruistic impulse to protect these wartime refugees, followed by what seem to have been repeated, ungovernable bouts of baser . . .

(Two pages cleanly excised by razor blade or moral equivalent.)

. . . upon Klotz's return to Germany and his rise through the ranks of the imperial armies. Eight years after the Sack of Rome he was involved in another siege. This time, he was deployed against the Catholic capital's very opposite: the Anabaptist stronghold of Münster, the protestant New Jerusalem.

The Anabaptist movement, a loose uprising of millennial sects, gained momentum in Germany and the Low Countries during the troubled late 1520s and early 1530s. Hans Hut, a bookbinder turned prophet, died mysteriously in an Augsburg prison in 1527, having prophesied Christ's return for the following year. The wandering visionary Melchior Hofmann gathered a wide following, preaching a period of woes that would culminate in revelation in 1533. And in that year, mass expectation of the End began to turn the prosperous Hanse town of Münster into a grotesque parody of the City of God on Earth.

In early February 1534, the merchant Knipperdollinck and the Dutchman Jan Beuckelson (John of Leiden) ran screaming through the city's streets calling on people to repent. They managed to provoke an armed uprising of converted Anabaptists, who took over the town hall. The council, weakened by infighting and filled with Lutherans eager to protect their own freedom of worship, did nothing to oppose the revolt. Assisted by the arrival of his spiritual master, the gaunt, bearded ascetic Jan Matthys of Haarlem, Beuckelson rapidly took over. Armed mobs ejected all misbelievers from the town, appropriating their property and condemning to a February snowstorm a stream of dispossessed, including expectant mothers and infants.

The Dutch proclaimers of the Second Coming were left to establish an absolute theocracy, a divinely inspired island of the Chosen amid history's final deluge. Matthys began implementing the utopian communalism that would for a few months turn the city insane. Private money was abolished, and property was commonly distributed. All books except the Bible were set ablaze on a pyre in the cathedral square. Public execution of dissenting voices took place to the accompaniment of hymns.

To restore order, the bishop of Münster threw up earthworks around the town. But his forces were too weak to lay a fully effective siege. On Easter, Matthys, now absolute dictator of the city, claiming divine assurance of success, rode out with a handful of men to scatter the besieging army. Matthys and his suicidal squad were sliced apart without mercy.

Back inside the walls, the cloak of leadership fell to Beuckelson. Obeying mystic revelations, he implemented a strict rotation of labor and appointed a governing body of twelve elders. He instituted polygamy and compelled all women under a certain age to marry. By year's end, polygamy had devolved into a kind of mandatory, rampant promiscuity. Beuckelson so inflamed his little garrison of two thousand men that they repeatedly withstood the attacks of episcopal forces several times their size.

In September, a goldsmith named Dusentschur stood in the Prinzipalmarkt and announced that God had chosen Beuckelson as king of kings, ruler of all the nations of earth, and Messiah of the Last Days. Such was Beuckelson promptly ordained, to increasing murmurs among the fanfare. Streets, gates, days of the week, even children were all given new names. An ornamental coinage was struck, and Beuckelson surrounded himself with the trappings of an ornate fantasy court. While requisitioning goods from the poor to pay for this splendor, the new king assured them that the day was at hand when stones would be turned to bread and mud into gold. The Third Age was here, when the Children of God would inherit an earth richer than their wildest dreams.

Sympathetic Anabaptist uprisings erupted across the North. At last realizing the scale of events at Münster, the states of the empire joined together in sending money and soldiers to topple Beuckelson's messianic kingdom. By the time Klotz arrived to seal off the blockade in January of 1535, life inside the city had descended into a last, macabre nightmare. Fantastic feats of stagecraft were devised for the starving populace—athletic tournaments, masques, obscene masses performed in the cathedral. Trumpeters went about delivering concerted blasts at all hours, the signal for townsfolk to assemble in the square, under penalty of death, and listen to the king's latest inspirations.

Much of what Klotz describes, however fantastic, is corroborated by sources inside the walls. In May, Beuckelson began resorting to mass executions of his starving, hysterical subjects. Many believers were ready to be transported up to heaven along with him. At first, those who came to their senses were allowed to leave the city, but the imperial forces refused to let them through the siege lines. Klotz describes how these creatures crawled about like animals in the moat between the city walls and the besieging earthworks, grazing on grass, begging to be put to death. These were the lucky ones; subsequent defectors were quartered and nailed up about town.

Klotz's task was to shell the northern ramparts along the Buddenturm with cannonades of leaflets, imploring the citizens of the town to turn on their king and thus avoid a massacre. He reports that by the siege's gruesome end, the desperate garrison had been whittled down to starved children. When the besiegers finally pierced the city and overcame the last, fanatical defense, they had to pick their way through carnage beyond imagining. Stacks of corpses lined the streets, most so mutilated by execution, scavenging, or disease that the aged could not be told from the young.

The surviving Anabaptist leaders, Beuckelson and Knipperdollinck, were singed to death with red-hot irons. Klotz reports that the king made no sound during his torture, nor did he recant. Their bodies were hung in lead cages from the spire of the Lambertikirche.

At precisely this time Michelangelo, old and misanthropic, embittered by history, returned to the Sistine Chapel, now free of Sangallo's sandbagging, to add to his ceiling's Creation a transforming footnote: the horrifying *Last Judgment,* that most pitiless work in Western art. . . .

(Crayola flowers, houses, their chimneys curly with Prussian-blue smoke, some simple words, a girl's stick face, a fighter airplane spewing pudgy, rainbow caterpillars of bullets . . .)

Well, yes: of course. Through the arabesques of innocence's syllogisms, the conclusion grows obvious to him. Her insight shines as brightly as the pool of early reader flashlight under the covers at night. Kraft backtracks through the steps of her logic. And she has it weirdly right. Still adept, Joy infers what he has missed. The codger in the Dodger cap is not a little boy propelled into a sensationally aged body. Exactly the reverse. The new kid on the block is the Laotian myth-equivalent of Methuselah, a spirit older than entire generations who perversely refuses to detach himself from boyhood.

The explanation she comes up with is simpler, closer to the bone. A child shriveling from the husk inward still stays green in the core. She asks the boy's name. Kraft tells her, as if he, like Linda, has known the tag all along. He sees her roll the clinical syllables around on her tongue. She tries the name out loud: "Nicolino." Beyond doubt, one of the lost boys. Fell out of the perambulator in Kensington Gardens. Corroded by time in outward stuff, while remaining essentially untouched. All children, except one, grow up. I've seen him; he's just flown in the window of the ward.

"That book you gave me . . ." He knows what she struggles to protest: every word of it, the literal, documentary truth.

Kraft considers giving her Hutchinson-Gilford disease to add to the pile of homework assignments she keeps by the side of her bed. Progeria's Pan, the ward's most fantastic invalid ever, might outdo all the study texts she has so meticulously assembled. The boy who never grew up: brutal practicality leaves her no fiercer a fairy tale. Joy will need myth much more outrageous—absurdly, magically more—to live through the mystery ahead of her.

 She will need to believe far worse, and wilder. Kraft can't even compose faith's prerequisite list, so deeply has measurement encroached on his own credence. She will need to hope that escalating pain has some surprise, hidden by design until the redeeming twist. She will have to keep believing that the physician she adores is not poisoning her for pleasure with sloe nausea fizzes and chemo chasers. Let her believe. Let her escape the exam constraints this once, buy in, subscribe to any prognostic faith that helps her account for the nursery damned. Believe any transparency at all rather than come to the one unskirtable truth Kraft himself would still deny if he could: that all children will grow up, except this believing one.

 And forty-eight hours suffice to prove that her take on the new boy is in every way superior to Kraft's own. Nicolino is not a child; he is a phenomenon, a hell-raiser of perverse proportions impossible for anyone under retirement age on what Linda still insists on calling God's earth to achieve. He moves in with both overnight bags blazing, and before the week is out, he not only owns the ward, he's backdated the deed. After ten days, he's ruling the rotting, disease-infested roost as if that's the way things have been since time out of mind.

 Joy is right: this is no geriatric boy. He's an incontestable old-timer, hanging on to the sandlot by his gnarled claws. Linda's not the only one to get solicited. The better part—and Kraft has to admire the squib's taste—of the female staff assembles with bewildered frequency at the ward nurses' station comparing incredulities. Did that kid say what I think he said?

 On rounds, Kraft himself hears the precocious lecher come on to Suzi Banks, the Colostomy Girl. Asks to see the lump under her dress. And virtually in the same breath, the mini-mogul hits up on Joleene Weeks, whose response to acute lymphatic havoc has been to drift into a kind of self-induced autism. "You're cute," he tells her. "When did you first do it?"

"Do what?" the girl manages, her first, faltering verbal steps independent of the Chatty Cathy in more than a week.

"Coy one, are we? I like that in a woman. 'Still waters run deep,' and like that."

Still waters? Kraft's pretty sure that catch phrase died out with democracy in America. Where the hell does this kid come from? Kraft tries asking, with a kind of verbal head-pat, in their first conversational exchange. So, uh, you're not from around these parts, are you? Nico snaps at him. "Right down the street. Read the chart, Dr. Killdeer."

Time-scrambled sass, and weirder than it is rude. Who taught this little Spanky to speak? The diction instructor is revealed after a few days when the little old guy produces, from out of nowhere, several gross of comics—a major-league library of them. Complete, contiguous series span the whole illustrated spectrum from classic demigods down to diluted, contemporary, adolescent chelonians. The collection incorporates everything from old *Arthropodmen* and *Vigilante Patrols* to *Tender Traumas, Tales from Beyond Terrors,* strips starring inflatable bubble-figures, *Masterplots Illustrated*s (including four-color, frame formats of *The Ambassadors* and *The Magic Mountain*), the adventures of Amie and pal Jim-jam (at a ridiculously recently integrated Brookvale High), Green Stingers, Dark Cowls, cartoon anthro rats, cats, and wombats—all the perennials, and some titles so obscure they barely lasted through single numbers, not to mention a European department complete with a Gallic imperial pocket of resistance, two Fleming kids constantly getting one another into big-time trouble, and a cowlicked cosmopolitan news reporter somewhere between fifteen and a hundred fifty years old.

Nico unpacks not only this Rabelaisian *bibliothèque,* but also a thick, loosely bound Blue Book of his own devising that accompanies the collection. In it, he has carefully cross-listed, in the block letter capitals of a spastic on a muscle stimulant, every single issue number, its publisher, date, and point of acquisition, a synopsis of the adventure, and, of course, the volume's fair resale price. The pricing scheme has only one foot, size 2½, in the realm of supply and demand. For instance, an old *Cosmic Sentinel* scarce enough to command the bulk of an upper-middle-class ten-year-old's annual allowance even back when Kraft was doing his own international assets trading costs roughly the same as a buck-a-bushel dentist's office throwaway.

His market yardstick has nothing to do with peddlable rarity. It's something altogether different—use value, readability, the catalyzing spark, or some other subjective look under the hood. Whatever his pricing formula, Nicolino imposes mercantile order upon the naïve economic anarchy of the pede department. Every item in his comic inventory is available for open circulation, but only after the book value has been coughed up.

He establishes a cashless barter system. "Gotta watch it or those Fed creeps'll be on our cases." Other kids' comics, from parental care packages once shared out freely, are kicked into the kitty according to a rigorous system of swapped debits and credits. He'll take any currency: broken hand-held LCD games, Mars bars (unwrapped are half value), singing rings—anything with resale potential. Nico introduces new commodity wrinkles from day to day, producing, by spontaneous generation, bulk shipments of cinnamon-soaked toothpicks, iridescent kaleidoscope disks, or silly sand. Rooms of the demoralized listless soon start to hum with the biggest trading racket since Green Stamps.

He is utterly scrupulous; he will not skim or scalp. If a *Fantastic Forces* returns to his pool in roughly initial condition, it will earn back its original price or the equivalent in, say, multi-colored water-pistol pens. Yet he's dead firm on the rates of exchange. He's not going to trade a good *Saviors of the Universe* for anything less than two middle-weight ghost yarns plus a knock-off heartthrobber. In this manner his catalog steadily grows. But somehow, so do the smaller satellite stockpiles of his trading partners. In a form of perpetual motion, the ward's magic cottage industries begin to generate wealth.

But this free-enterprise zone is the least of Nicolino's impacts on the nation of sick children. He forms the inhabitants, both terminal and transient, into voting blocks, loose political parties that he then coerces into running referenda on the kids' choice for chief nurse and head resident. He presents the results, scribbled in pencil on a nubbly-edged sheet of shabby spiral-notebook paper, to the staff. When the mandate fails to produce the demanded changes, the new ward boss—his own constituency more or less ensured—starts talking hunger strike and sets himself up as People's Government in Exile.

He gradually picks up the tempo of the place until it lags just behind his own. He cannot keep still long enough even to do up his laces. He rallies his troops, splits them into rebus-solving R & D teams. He sets them to work prototyping escape vehicles. He enlists them in cracking jigsaws—a 1,496-piece *Garden of Earthly Delights* spread across the top of his bedcovers, for want of enough flat space anywhere else. He teaches them to sing innocuous verses that turn obscene when sung as rounds. He organizes gangway-long grudge matches of Smear the Queer with the Ball. He awards the highest-ranking, most loyal of his cadres with revolving titles, offices, and privileges. He designs gambling ladders, plays out pools on sporting events using tons of colored golf tees as the stakes. He endows taffy pulls, paper airplane competitions (prizes for both outrageous design and distance flight), potato-printing marathons—activities selected exclusively for their ability to leave a trail of carnage in their wake.

He doesn't sleep. Some voice must somehow rag him into trying to thrash time while time is still his to thrash. At ridiculous hours, he appears at the bedsides of all-too-willing friends, whispering "Are you awake?" until they are. Then come the first of the expeditions, slipping invisibly past the adult night watch to whatever destinations they might pick their way into without tripping alarms. They shoot for the roof heliport or raid the inner kitchens as if they were Prester John's lost kingdom or the source of the Nile. There they fall upon whatever loose prizes they can carry off undetected.

In less time than it takes him to age another decade, Nicolino wins over the whole turf. Those who had been most frightened by his beak and baldness become the most devoted. That's the source of his manic power. Convince them there's nothing to be afraid of. That you're just one of the gang. The only place where this one's ever going to be inconspicuous is front and center, in the brightest light. In days, Nico comes into his own, kingpin of these victims, the race of those singled out for damage, barred from public playgrounds.

The boat girl alone treats him with a mixture of suspicion and astonishment. "What's with What's-her-namee-vong?" Nicolino asks Chuck, the No-Face, whose fantastic handicap, despite his angelic good nature, promotes him to Nico's second-in-command and senior partner in crime.

Chuck shrugs. "Think she had to have some stuff taken out of her ankle."

"Not *that* matter, Cluckie. I mean, how come she's got her head up her bunghole and her nose in dictionaries all the time? We're working some *great angles* here. And where the crud is she? Studying."

"Maybe we move around too fast for her. She's still a little wobbly. . . ."

"Wobbly? Hah. Ben here is your basic beach ball. Double amputee, and *he's* in on just about every operation we run."

"I don't know, Nico. Maybe we . . ."

"Maybe we better go have a talk with this chick, that's what. Let's see. Think she'd go for one of these?" He riffles through his stash of illustrated fiction and produces a *Sergeant Shrapnel,* all about hand-to-hand fighting on a Pacific island infested with subterranean networks of enemy burrows crawling with giant bamboo rats. A hesitant pause from Chuck makes Nico throw up his age-wasted arms in exasperation. "Come on! Gimme a flipping bee. This is one of the best 'zines I got."

He pulls out the Blue Book as proof, but Chuck stands firm. "Uh-uh, Nico. I don't think so. She likes to read those . . ."

"I know what she *likes* to read. That's exactly the problem here, isn't it? Wait. I got it. Here's the ticket." He rummages around in the piles of noncomic trading booty, at last locating a plastic bag no bigger than his fist. "Come on, Cluck. Let's go have a word with this femme."

Preliminaries are awkward. Or, rather, there are no preliminaries. Joy watches them approach from the horizontal, frightened and expectant, as if she has long known that this visit was inevitable.

"Here," Nico says, when they reach her bedside. He thrusts the buy-off peace offering into the boat girl's hands. The boss remains unflustered despite the suppressed giggling on all sides. But it does unnerve him a little when this Joy creature refuses to ask what the present is, resorting instead to label reading.

The bag is full of tiny, brown bulbs that shuffle about as if alive. She watches hushed as the lumps of animate popcorn bang randomly with increasing vigor as she takes them into her hand. The label reads:

MEXICAN JUMPING BEANS

Born into the only home they will ever know, gradually expending their finite supply of food, these tiny larvae hurl themselves continuously against the walls of their constricting prisons. . . .

"Immense, huh?" Nico prompts.

"Intense," Chuck is quick to ratify.

But Joy looks up after a moment's incomprehension. "Sad."

"Sad?" Nico fails to keep the note of moral outrage out of his dignified tone.

"Very sad."

Chuck jumps in, the hapless moderator, eager to show the merits of both sides. "Yeah, but, I mean, they can't be unhappy *in there*. Huh? Because they've never seen anything but the inside. They don't even know about, they can't even picture . . ."

"Then why are they trying so hard to get out?" Joy's interruption, awful in its certainty, is soft to the point of disappearing. But she looks forgivingly at Chuck; he, at least, is doing the best he can.

"Holy jump up and sit down. Listen to this, will ya? Get outta my star system. Get outta order. I've never heard such drivel. These things are utterly cool. You got to be completely whacked not to see that. And they're illegal too! Any idea what it takes to slip one of these babies past the Agriculture agents they got posted all up and down the borders?"

"Half the children in this hospital have slipped . . ."

"Wait a minute," Chuck intervenes. "They must be able to get out. If they can't get out, then how do they . . . ?"

"How what, you weed weevil?"

"How does the species, you know . . . ?"

"Procreate?" Joy suggests, at almost speaking volume.

" 'Procreate,' Cluckie? That the word you're looking for?" Nico shoves his buddy, almost spitting with smirk.

The question returns Joy to the magic beans with new intensity. Perhaps there is more to this prison than the identifying label lets on. "Thank you. I'll take care of them," she says, looking into the eyes of the man who never shed boyhood. A nervous treaty, but the one he came to establish.

"Great. You do that. Now tell me one thing. How come you just lie here studying all the time?"

"My leg hurts."

"No, the studying part. I mean, Louise. You're on vacation here."

"We still have to graduate."

"Oh wow. You are spoo-ky. Graduate? Why?" Nico tries to wipe the sweatband of his ball cap without removing it. "Okay, never mind that one. Suppose, just for grins, that I humor you. So what do we have to know for the exam? Go ahead. I'm asking. Graduate me. Learn me something."

She gives him a strange, probing look. Her eyes tell him: You can drop the disguise. No need to pretend with me. I've read your biography. Twice through. And this is where I'm supposed to teach you the end of the story you were eavesdropping on, outside the window, late one interrupted night.

The look, the accusation—I know who you are—rattles him. "Hey, Cluckie. C'mon. Let's blow this peanut stand. We got work to do."

Chuck hesitates a moment, his bandaged face trying to twist into an explanation wide enough to appease everyone. He turns to trot after the boss, when Joy calls them back.

"Wait a minute. 'Lino?" She swallows the first syllables in ignorance or first, awkward attempt at familiarity. The summoned boy returns to bedside, nice and casual like. "I wanted to ask you." She reaches, without letting him from her steady scrutiny, for a thin volume that she has kept at her side since receiving it days back. She fixes on the ancient, taut face, hoping to surprise it into dropping its disguise. "Do you know this story?"

If she flushes out the revealing muscle-flinch she expects, it does not show. Nico takes the hundred and fifty pages, thumbs through it back to front, reads the dedication and the title page. "I'll swap you two superheroes, a sci-fi, and a kissy thing of your choice."

He looks up. His eyes challenge those of this overlathed dowel, this vanishing girl. "And I'll throw in a mint-condition chocolate cream egg. Just because I'm a nice guy."

FOR OBVIOUS REASONS, the premature pensioner becomes Linda's darling. Any kid who not only puts up willingly with her amateur therapy reading but actually ad-libs asides is a patient after her own heart. On her rounds, she quickly learns how to get the maximum rile-up by calling out to him, "How's it hanging, old man?"

He glows under the sobriquet, puts on a palsy act, laces his already disconcerting voice with parody tremolo, and warbles back, "Can't complain. Well, I could complain. In fact . . ." Or: "Hanging? Wait. Lemme check."

Well, she asked for it. This afternoon, Linda finds Nico and a fraction of his gang camped around a TV. "What's up? What's on?" Perfect chance to get them to tell *her* one for a change.

"Stupid so-called show about some cartoon future that the friggin' cat dragged in." Nico's betrayal of the spell that has held half a dozen of his cohorts enthralled causes several wounded faces to jerk in hurt incomprehension. His better self, protesting pitifully from its perch on the traditional right clavicle, causes Nico to repent his rudeness by the time honored method of re-doubling it. "Yeah. You heard me right. Dumbshit program here, gentlemen."

"Nico," Linda growls. Quite the little performance he's mustering for her sake. A shame that kind of strutting is restricted to the young, or the old, or whatever her potty-mouthed courtier actually is.

"Oh. Sorry, ma'am. I mean dumb-fu . . ."

"Cut! That's enough out of you. Somebody fill me in."

But the other kids are too cowed now to give a synopsis, and His Nibs is pulling this royal sulk to punish the woman. So just kick back and watch a while. Linda settles in, tries to catch the drift of this installment's saga. It's set in that obligatory, endless High Chaparral of Space. She can tell it's the outermost Outer, because the guns, bombs, and assorted vehicles of outrageous intricacy are all proton-powered. Wider and wilder skeins, eternally higher levels of energy manipulation: that's, like the immortal hokey-pokey, what it's all about.

On the one hand, they've got the matter transporter—the be-all and end-all of the whole civilized shooting match. On the other hand, galactic destiny still comes down to a slew of hand-to-hand combats with what amount to electrified meter sticks. The story takes place in two different worlds. One world just doesn't cut it with discriminating audiences anymore. Seems on one of these two, there's this combination architect, civil engineer, and voice crying in the wilderness . . .

"Hold it. Who is this guy? I can never understand it when they talk through those echo machines."

Suzi Banks peers up suspiciously, steals a glance at Nicolino and then back at Ms. Espera. "Beezaholi," she murmurs, in a coy, little-girl drawl as impenetrable as the cartoon sound effects.

"Say who? Beet-aholic? Would you mind spelling that?"

A violent shush from Nico cannot quell the ranks' revival. Suddenly, paraphrase flies at Linda from all directions, almost as if recounting gives as much pleasure as watching the wrinkle of event unfold in the first place.

"Beezaholi."

"He's *evil*."

"He's not evil. He's the one's gonna save M-31."

"What's M-31?"

"That's where the Dromedaries live."

"Andromedans, pissbag."

"Oh, them," Linda says. "I remember them. We go way back. What's bugging them this time?"

Childhood's hair-trigger tone detectors threaten to set off a chain reaction of suspicion, jamming all the communicator channels. Linda is rescued by the beautiful Chuck, who says, "They're facing Galactic Heat Death something fierce."

"Sun blowing up on them?"

An exasperated quartet shouts, "No! Dying out slowly." Dummy. Get your stellar thermodynamics straight.

Their spark is going cold, motionless, still. A race against the last ticks of the thermal buzzer before life fades into the freezing vacuum. The fable's appeal is as familiar as the planet-encroaching ice caps visible even from here, in the smogged semitropics of Angel City. Every day, a little trickle of available use escapes irreversibly through the cracks of the system. Cars slow, appliances rust out, neighbors capitulate in a hush. If Linda herself feels it, these kids must be frantic. These, the fresh heat litmuses, the thermostatic coils still factory mint, must long ago have registered the approach of absolute zero and are left to go about astonished that the planet makes no preparation.

Beezaholi chooses this lull to mumble to himself: *"The Cyclogeneron must be assembled on a scale no one has yet imagined. It must span the entire diameter of the star system! Only then will it be capable of accelerating particles to the velocity needed to give us final power over the very laws of . . ."*

"What's a Cyclogeneron?" Linda asks.

More irritation at her unending trouble with the obvious. But facts are as boundless as their unassuageable underpinning. The more they give to her, the more they have.

"It's this humongous metal ring . . ."

"More of a torus, really. A doughnut."

"I'm sure. A galaxy-sized metal doughnut. Give me a break."

"Arm or a leg?"

"And it's lined with these awesome hyperelectric solenoids that accelerate these subatomic . . ."

"And truly brutal cosmic forces come shooting out the other end."

"End? How can a doughnut . . . ?"

"Beezaholi tried to tell the 'Dromedans about it. But that Rathgor, who's got control of the Planetary Radix . . ."

"Not just Rathgor. All the Phagolytics. It's like they simply don't want to . . ."

"The whoozy-whats?"

"Rathgor," Beezaholi says, *"you must listen. If we don't begin at once to redirect the energy we squander on Amorphicoms into the construction of . . ."*

"Did he say 'Amorphicom'?"

"They're like these immense private jets. . . ."

"I thought they could transport themselves."

"The vehicle part is just a fringe bennie. They're really these ultra-cool live-in pods that you connect yourself to for the most intense . . ."

"Give up our Amorphicoms, Beezaholi? You're joking. Why, the mere mention of the idea at the People's Council would . . ."

"Right on, R. No way! The Amorphi is the coolest thing this side of . . ."

"And why should we give them up, you bellowing old fool? Just to humor your delusions?"

"Beezy's right. They need the Cyclogeneron, or it is Heat Death City. The end of M-31 as we know it."

"Our people will never surrender the pleasures they have struggled so hard for centuries to secure. People will kill for the possession of an Amorphi. To bodypilot is the most rewarding experience known to . . ."

"They are wickedly wasteful," Jorge concedes.

"And addictive as sin," adds Roberto, Jorge's twin and some-time needle sharer.

"A massive drain on the Grid."

"The Grid?" Linda whispers.

"It's no use. Even if I managed to win over the whole Planetary Radix, we still wouldn't possess more than a fraction of the energy we need to manufacture the Cyclogeneron. The entire tappable Grid wouldn't provide . . ."

"Could someone tell me why he needs an accelerator the size of a . . . ?"

"Man! You get particles to that speed and collide them: you can Do It All. Make a new star. Create new forces. Name it."

"Only—one hope—left. Must—renew interplanetary contact—with Heliotria."

"I give up."

"Heliotria. The other world."

"That's it! I *knew* it. Bishop Perpetuus. The Touring Monks. The Ikonankh."

"Sure, Mr. Massive Brain Case. I could have told you that a half hour ago."

"Much has changed since Andromeda last made contact with Heliotria. The good Bishop Perpetuus must have died generations ago."

"Will somebody please rescue me?"

"Shh! A long time ago they hyper-tapped this other planet, where these monks went about in robes chanting all the time and the head abbot gave them this jewel thing. . . ."

"More like a little metal statue."

"And so long as they had this figure from the monks on Heliotria, the Andromedans could open up the space-time fabric between the planets. Only that was in the past, and now it's the distant future."

"I must return the Ikonankh to Helio . . ."

"Don't risk it, dude. You'll never get the thing back."

". . . where it will act as a powerful beacon, drawing into our galaxy, across the space threshold, all those with special abilities. The ones the Heliotrions call . . ."

A minor emergency with Suzi Banks's new hardware precludes Linda's witnessing the polychrome passage of the Ikonankh through the opening it tears in space. She returns just in time to exclaim, "Oh, lo-lo-look! See what it's doing! How come the thing is only going after kids?"

"Because"—the shortcut Methuselah at last condescends to address her—"that's the core commercial market for this kind of bullshit. *Real* adults don't waste their lives watching this Gerber drool."

"Well, *you're* still hanging around."

"Dodgers don't start for another two hours," Nico says, with the barest giveaway glint. "Quit. You tickle me, lady, you die a slow death."

"Wait a minute." Linda breaks off the brawl. "I just got it. They're all *ancient* there in M-31, aren't they? They have no . . . ?"

"That's right. Nobody knows how it came about. It's always been that way."

"Oh." The monosyllable comes up out of her throat, a bit of phlegm wrapped around an acid lemon drop that went down the wrong pipe. She will choke on it, on the image of this bewildered Thursday afternoon class, huddled around the fable-fire for whatever feeble electron-beam spark it might still emit, whatever slight stay, its half-hour postponement of heat death. Not one of them knows. Look: look now, what the primitive metal casting does. It stands still while Heliotria's ravenous fads slither past in reflex after-spasms, faster than she can track. It draws toward itself hands still raw from thumb sucking, gathering them up with the crisis touch, catapulting them, adding their increment of ergs to swell the eternally just-insufficient Grid.

The Ikonankh swims in front of her to fill the screen. She watches as the summoning trinket burrows through the tube's phosphor trail and lands in this room. It materializes, pulsing, beating its metal wings, come to recruit a last-ditch rescue for the universe's doomed omnipotents, to enlist these ignorant psychics, robust in their innocence, to put them to work assembling, arresting, assisting in the most desperate invention necessity ever mothered.

MEANWHILE, IN ANOTHER galaxy just around the bend, Kraft is performing sloppy seconds on an emergency repair cobbled together by Plummer on an eleven-year-old male who was riding semifigurative shotgun in a car that a couple club brothers had taken out on community loan. Ably assisted by a cordial that subsequently registered all kinds of exotic blood concentrations, the driver power-skidded the vehicle into the rear end of a tomato-motif, twenty-four-hour pizza delivery van. The kid cohort happened to be picking his teeth with a wooden skewer at the moment of impact.

His cruising buddies would give no name for him aside from "the Rapparition," a title they claimed he'd legally earned in brilliant public battle. The boy was past interrogation, so that was the handle that went down on the ER paperwork. Plummer's initial repair consisted of removing the larger bits of toothpick from their resting place in the boy's soft palate. The Rapparition's first slurred words upon swimming up from under the anesthetic were "The movement lives on; you can't slash it down. You can't even long to make it gone."

The scrape of the sutures makes him wretch, but the Rapparition gets the words out. By the time Kraft inherits the kid
for all the rest of the patchwork, he's become Carver's blessed
peacemaker. When Tony the Tuffian and that Rib Fix from the
Crack Pack go tearing each other's sutures out in a territorial
blood dispute, the Rapparition interposes himself between them,
declaiming,

> This is a plea
> For u-ni-ty
> Between the He and the We
> And the Me and the She.
> We're on a mission
> Here, so don't start dissin'.
> Ya got to listen to the Rapparition:
> Use your God-given powers of analysis!
> We *got* to break through this crip-pl-ing paralysis.

Kraft could not have put the matter more succinctly. Today's
follow-up procedure is aimed at repairing a bit of the damage
Plummer's stopgap palate patch-up has done to the Rapparition's
dactyls. Nothing life shattering. In fact, almost opera buffa fare
compared to much of what society has been shoving under Kraft's
blade as of late. But it is, nevertheless, a long, grueling, painstak-
ing, delicate transaction of considerable consequence to one who
has chosen speech over any of the deadlier assault weapons in
aggression's arsenal. A constructive bit of craftwork, placing it in
the decided minority of piece labor assigned Kraft in this place.
   Still under the influence of the Rapparition's cadence, half
desperate to convince himself of the feasibility of a Lindaesque
lightness in the face of wounds beyond fusing, or maybe just
punchdrunk with overwork, Kraft notices an upbeat, potato-
chip rhythm using his cerebrum as electronic drum pad while he
closes. The pernicious little beat goes: Let's have a jammer (*uh*), I
said let's jam (*rest, rest, rest*) in the slammer. And mixed in there,

like undercoatings of old wallpaper forever unsteamable unless one is willing to gouge out half the drywall along with it, the phrase's Renaissance counterpoint: Lulla lullaby, my sweet little baby. What meanest thou to cry?

He senses something expected of him, a rendezvous all arranged and penned into his agenda by unknown secretary. He feels it, the weight of specific disaster, of predetermined public breakdown settling in for the evening, locating the point of perfect parasitic attachment, homing in with all the inevitability of an earnest grade-school mathematician employing approximate roots to close in on an irrational decimal. Armies of omens assemble themselves, fall into the only formation he affords them these days—the short roster, the cursory catalog standing in for a more comprehensive account of approaching capitulation. Generic alphabets, glossaries of collective pathology you do not want enumerated at greater length.

What is this place? The lightest attention limns it: the evidence is everywhere, widening with the decline of light. Poverty in positive feedback. Cascade of chain-failing banks. Earnings not even enough to cover debt service. Volume discounts rewarding the spree mentality. Illiteracy passed down as the only family heirloom, actually cultivated by every trick in the marketing book, because merchandisers, like politicians, prosper from a maimed electorate. Ten-year-olds who can tell caliber and make of a handgun by sound alone, especially in the dark. Toxins trickling down into the aquifer, from which they can never be filtered. All the while, the index of leading indicators—wealth measured by the ability to wage disaster—doctors itself until its message is bearable, even downright rosy to the ears of the self-proclaimed best-informed people on earth. Of the two alternatives in the ancient grudge match, Thanatos clearly has more future in it.

Pale, cheap, and prosaic, this doomsday laundry list. Kraft feels it grow glib under his suturing fingers. He takes facile pleasure in confirming his worst fears, talking himself up onto the hospital rooftop in his bloodied surgical robes to wait for the arrival of this year's all-obliterating comet. Anemic, stripped even of outrage. The bleakest symptom on his list is less than quotidian. They are easy, breezy, light conversational cocktail gambits sung to the swish of a vein-skewering swizzle stick. Thus all the more horrific. When collapse becomes aperitif, it must be here at last. When the end is announced in silence, in blasé acquiescence, then it must truly *be* the end.

Polyphony pounds through Kraft's head as he shoves the point of the needle in and under, punching repeatedly through the drawn drumskin that lines the soft insides of the Rapparition's mouth. Let's have a jammer—*uh!* In the slammer. Lulla, lu la la, and lo, alas! Behold what slaughter he doth make, shedding the blood of infants all, sweet Savior for thy sake.

He can feel himself running aground on bone shoals that haven't been named, that didn't exist until he blundered against them with his field sewing kit. The voice-leading of his obsessive ditties grows too dense for him to keep the competing lines straight. His repeated, rustling whistles—a dozen notes at a pop, each ritornelloed perhaps a quarter of a thousand times over the course of this operation, alternating fragments forced through the tiny crack decades ago chipped in his central incisor that for some reason he's never had capped—are getting on the nerves of his fellow team members something fierce.

He knows how much these cheerful, trilled flute-de-loops must be driving the whole surgical crew up the blessed institutional walls. But he can't help himself. That's the sound. *Uh.* That's the sound. The sound of his horn, his oldest continuous possession aside from birth certificate, neglected, long unplayable, but still sitting at the bottom of the closet in that apartment standing in for a more permanent abode. The sound of something out of his own fading repertoire, a bit of musical past he impels himself to conjure up from the scrap heap. A tinny, treble, obbligato *rescue me,* pitted against the short list of inevitables. The idiot whistling is some reincarnation of saving playground charm. Or perhaps it just traces a random resonance, a tone-row association triggered by the accidental conjunction of prepuber repairs thrown at him as of late, of lulla, lullaby.

Recapping in miniature the general blackout between Kraft's preteens and his thirties, the operating room vanishes. The set gives way to one of those membership discount stores, his city's most distinguished contribution to world betterment. The place is crawling with self-proclaimed discounts, but only for those who put up enough grubstake to secure the photo club card. The fee is trivial—just high enough to screen out the underclass. The only illegals allowed within spitting circumference of the showrooms are hired under the table to swab the decks perpetually with blisterproof paint.

Closing the Rapparition, changing out of the scrubs, heading down to the subterranean lot, blasting his automotive escape out of Fortress Carver, negotiating the freeway, finding his way to this warehouse, and flashing yet another private badge to win entry: all these steps fade to a blur at best. He has a generic memory of the overall process, the recall of one who has read the crib notes but not the book. He flails at his belt to check for his beeper, but does not feel it there. All the same, he feels queasily certain that he must still be on call.

Memory loss: a thing that virtually every text Kraft has ever been made to memorize would unhesitatingly classify as No Goodish. More alarming, he can't seem to get worked up about his brief disappearance. He's willing to flow with the symptoms, string them along with the hope of staying supple for a potential shot at the broader diagnosis. And yet, how far is he going to get without a complete work-up, beginning with a decent history and physical? He's become exactly the sort of patient he most dreads, the stuff of Plummer's rolling burlesques. Childhood diseases? M-maybe. Any trace of this in your family? You mean, like, mother, father . . . ?

He hasn't a clue in creation why he is here. Here in this store, that is, let alone any wider, more imponderable locale. At this point, he can't even recall why he paid for membership in the first place, except to prove that twenty bucks would still buy him into some anesthetizing club somewhere.

Well, let it be retail then, the sheer, diversionary power of the stuff. And harbor the hope that here amid the available merchandise, one might find the best place to hold vigil against the quiet pogrom already under way. One or another clearance trough in this charnel house of bargains must cradle the ticket item that he'd been after when the lights went out. Track it down, kick its unholy can, freeze the statue maker, bluff the blindman, all-come-in-free-o!

Problem is, the commodity he is after could be anything, anything this heartbreaking, magnificent mess of a country marks down in today's race to clear inventory. Perhaps he's in pressing need of some processor or another—word, data, food, sound, trash, or love. Could be this here artificial-intelligence beer-can Thermos ring. Or this: a mock-membrane-pad simulation of a security alarm system to fasten to his front door, instant advertisement to smart-shopping, card-holding break-and-enterers that his home is in fact prostrate and defenseless. A key chain that comes when you whistle? A tape recorder that starts recording eight seconds before it is turned on? An own-yer-own, home version of some private-reserve cinema classic, say, *Seven Brides for Seven Samurai*?

He figures it can't be this last, as he'd have to buy a player first. He has so far failed to do so, knowing that whatever device he might settle on would be obsoleted (as the English-obsoleting term of the moment has it) ten minutes before he could tweak the thing's pots. Nevertheless, home electronics alone keeps his speculative faculties happily suspended for over an hour. He stands gazing, in fascinated stupor, at a gargantuan image thrown up on a flat-screen, wrap-around, wall-sized, live-in, digital stereo television larger than his apartment, larger, in fact, than his entire bet-hedging, twitch-appeasing leisure existence. The eerie, green-shifted specter waltzing around up there seems weirdly familiar, despite the chromosmear. It moves when he moves, ducks, shadowboxes in perfect synchrony, and hey! Howdy, Dr. Kraft. I'm on TV.

His first thought is: How'd they know I was coming? And how'd they get me on video in the first place? Utter idiocy lasts long enough for Kraft to feel the sensation of dancing to yesterday's ballet, as if *he's* the mario-martinet doing the tag-along, aping his screen alter ego's choreography class. Once he figures out it's live, he almost twists his neck off trying to look directly at himself. Why can't he get his eyes—either this or that pair—around and past the side of his head? The problem's not with any obstruction in his face, any blockage in the old universal joint. It's just that the screen is here and the camera is over there, and that's why, he decides, every picture tells a story. And every story lies at right angles to itself.

He picks up the Handycam, fiddles with it. He points it around the store, at the other cameras, at a nearby mirror, holding the mimic at arm's length and gauging the effects on screen. He points it at the screen itself. Big mistake. He loses another god-knows-how-many minutes of his life, image-mapping the edges of recursion's all-devouring hellmouth.

A bank of demonic monitors runs along the back aisle and out of sight. Several hundred of them superimpose their simultaneous soundtracks into a cacophony that makes Ives sound like monkish homophony. The massed picture screens make up a mammoth grasshopper's compound eye. They trawl at random for a half-dozen picture signals and flaunt these in assembled, inscrutable patterns. One block of picture beam, interrupted by another, resumes as an irregular trapezoid just down the plane. For Kraft, the channels congeal into a single, wide-gauge program whose theme any stringer pediatrician would recognize at once: children adrift, out of doors too late at night, too far from home, migrating, campaigning, colonizing, displaced, dispersed, tortured loose, running for their lives.

He has stumbled onto one of those half-hour slots reserved for dispensing pitched bewilderment. They're doing news again, as they do around the clock these days. Image chorus line. The sight-bite *Zeitgeist*. One signal block has been hijacked by an emergency update on this year's flash point, one that Kraft has until now only dimly registered. He focuses in on the account, amazed at how quickly this one has slipped from precocious to precarious. The language of direct confrontation—the contempt for the public behind all action in the public interest—cranks itself up to a pitch past the usual theatrics. The endless, impotent, international diplomatic game of chicken in Dad's car begins to embrace its casualty rates. Grim foreign secretaries shaking their heads Live at Ten rule out negotiation, basking in an electrified aura of imminence that, because of the network-wide inability of home audiences everywhere to sustain concentration, will once more turn to boredom by the dismembering end.

This evening's particular head-on high noon has been busy escalating, introducing new twists and chicanes while Kraft's been away. All sides accuse the others of disinformation, a spiral of ever more sophisticated muddying of the waters. Claims of historical mandate crash up against new world orders. Preacher beseechers on a competing channel tick off the prophetic countdown to Megiddo Revisited. Nebuchadnezzar is returned to power. Engineers work at constructing life-sized living models of Babylon. TV-steered TOWs stand in for angels of incineration. Infidel legions mass for final face-off against the emissaries of evil expansionism. Does have a familiar ring to it—the old high road to simplification. Details available in this million-selling handbook; order now by calling the toll-free number on your screen.

Where's the Rapparition when we need him? The pint-sized poet could defuse this whole self-powered keg with a few well-placed hypermetrics. You know, a little sync along the lines of:

Some say this madness is the workin' out of scripture,
With Belial and Nemesis taking up the picture;
You tell me the unlivable is better than okay
'Cause we're heading for a showdown like the Good Book say.

Yeah, set the kid up as equal-time evangelist on the alternative station and we might just get enough market share to survive. But Kraft himself has only recently put the boy to bed with a mouth full of bloody fudge ripple.

On another block of sets, glitz-punkers probe the anarcho-disintegrating underside, pretending (like the solitary man trekking across the Gobi followed by a hidden documentary crew of two dozen, or the first-ever flimsy plane touching down on a deserted island, as shot from below by the disembodied camera) that they aren't part of a million-dollar, cake makeup, multiple-take, posturing, slick production number. Another, adjacent slice of the color carousel busily spins out its insistence that the universe can be saved only by constructing a doughnut the size of a galaxy.

An oval nimbus above this row of screens spews out one of those *Unsolved Celebrity Mystery Tonight!* samplers. Today's real reenactment includes the lavish particulars of Eva Braun's unquenchable and probably unrequited crush on Robert Taylor as well as Sukarno's lifelong ambition to sleep with Marilyn Monroe. Both utterly true, the anchors swear, so help me Broadcast.

A movie *verité* police-blotter public service announcement about the recent epidemic of vanishing little ones—two million annually, a full two-thirds of these abductions masterminded by estranged parents—dissolves from a gloss of the Missing Children Act into an advertisement for Home Litigation Workshops. This offer, void where prohibited, is flanked on both sides by banks of full-length shots, each in slightly different tonal registers, of a devastating Brit girl, fourteen at the most, telling her Yank soldier that she isn't going to do it, war or no war, unless they do it standing up, the best contraceptive method available. He leans her gently against the wall and provides her with stirrups by sticking two Coke bottles (empty) in his khaki back pockets while the cameras cozy in for this bit of shared intimacy in the endless, interchangeable, beautifully textured darkness at the edge of time.

This brief cross-sectional spin through the dial's mandala suffices to remind Kraft of what incontestable research continuously discovers and covers back up: the species is clinically psychotic. Pathetic, deranged, intrinsically, irreversibly mercury-poisoned by nature, by birth. And what more could one expect of a cobbled-up bastard platypus, a creature whose spirit is epoxied to its somatic foundation? Mental thalidomide cases, every last mother's son, as far back as accounts take things. On one cadre of tubes, slithery androgynes belt out a hardcore rendition of the station's signature slogan: "We nail your eyes to the screen." Just kitty-corner to these, the minority bank of "educational" monitors takes things back to a past whose name is somehow familiar to Kraft, although the face evades him.

At first he mistakes this signal for more current event. But a minute's wading in this current and the waters open up just upstream of the present. A cavalcade of years from—how long ago? What time is it now? Kraft stands staring in review at events he witnessed once, some of them firsthand, when he was still young enough to weave them into the semblance of sense. The replay unfolds in front of him, hurting afresh, the second bite of remorse.

Watches a river rising, somewhere in the Sunny South. It has swollen before, overflowed even, but never like this. The Flourishing One, survivor of countless previous auguries, the jerkwater money-lenders' town that rose to respark the West, is going under. Florence's shaky alliance with its pulmonary artery has been severed. Nervous black-and-white hand-held cameras make their way down the mud-plundered streets-turned-sewers of what was once the most angelic of angel cities.

Crude floodlights play over the Old Bridge or huddle under a loggia. Here and there, spors of sculpture bob above four meters of water. *Piazza* becomes *lago,* and eight centuries of art's aid and comfort are lost. Distraught *signori* from the National Salvation Board tell how they have given up on the mosaics and frescoes and are concentrating on porting as many priceless paintings and papers as possible out of reach of the rising ooze. All those not busy saving themselves are conscripted: inmates, the army, whole schools . . .

On that sound cue, cut to another, simultaneous mudslide. North now, October of the same year. From the center of history to its exploited edge. Pitiful little Welsh mining town, population too small for formal census. The view of disaster from inside the doomed schoolroom. How they looked out, looked and saw a mountain rise up and roll down its own slurry of slag, settle in and simply annihilate this building like a felt hat left on a chair. Inside, the town's entire next generation, one hundred and sixteen studious would-be graduates, most of them slated for the mines, hard at work doing sums and grammar and history—the Blitz, the famous Evacuation—look up for a minute before they are mass-buried, swallowed in one spasm by the sliding earth. Look up and see a tribe of faces their age, peering in the schoolroom window, coaxing them desperately outside, elsewhere, beyond safety.

Now is already too late. Mudslide slips elementally into sandstorm, a desiccating desert war. Boy soldiers in that same epochal year once more march into the town of God's Foundation, while other boy soldiers flee the sacred city through secular back streets. Everywhere, scripture is fulfilled faster than it can be written. At the same time (now what, Kraft wonders, can that absurd little phrase possibly still mean?) as this holy showdown, student armies face off on three other continents. The call for victory of belief over doubt wipes away with one sweep the last cobweb cling. Half a dozen simultaneous dream liberations are declared by those young enough to have nothing to lose but the childhood already denied them.

A six-year-old black girl fire-hosed from the streets of Birmingham is replaced by a crowd of her contemporaries, singing into the city center. Teen rioters vent their birthright terrors even here, just down the block from Kraft's alma mater. He watches them stand off the State again for a while, until the inevitable body bags decide matters. The newsreels veer to the shadowed half of the ball. There, in mass placard marches, Maoist high school dropouts cow a quarter of the planet. French, Spanish, Chilean,

Indonesian, and Rhodesian school-agers blunder through the revolutionary calendar, staunching their way toward year one. A fly-fanged, glazed-eyed, successionist, baby Ibo exoskeleton flexes its stick-limbs, twists to reach a mother's teat no larger or moister than a shriveled mole.

No possible connective thread explains, let alone excuses, this shock-wave assault of images. The obvious answer—Chronology, Your Early Years in Review—appalls Kraft with its arbitrariness. Okay, so the pics in this sampler of disintegration all took place in the space of—what? A small-spanned handful of months? A shared time frame still reveals nothing by way of explanation, nor says what possessed the show's rambling editor to string these random spots together. Empty syllogism, domainless variables: this *then* this *then* this . . .

His nostrils flare at the remembered stink of a certain institutional-green, paint-plastic coating, a pocked, porous, cinder-block lunar landscape. He feels the impression of it, close up, smashed against his face during some drill—fire, tornado, raid, political collapse. He and a few hundred others, crouched down for hours, giggling and dry-heaving by turns, compacted into the stingy angle between wall and floor. The smell sticks in his throat as if newly coated, memory's phlegm brought up by this cough of cavalcade. If these film bursts share anything at all, it's the thread running through all the other free-associating open channels. The one distributed middle, the only available theme: tender-foot decamping, refugees on the run, issuing from cities set ablaze by those no closer to legal age than they.

Angel Cities: well, he is getting warmer now, much. That must be it, the link he's supposed to recover. But what can this panicked pleasuredom, this theme park of loosely confederated, strip-malled membership stores—self-asphyxiating, self-immolating, drugged, gelded, joyriding, willfully slipping back into the worst of Third World crippling sinkholes—what can his current address possibly have in common with the first one, the city Kraft once spoke to in its native language, before his facility with languages withered away to pocket translating dictionaries?

It comes to him with the force of first discovery. He lived once in another place by the same name, yet spelled in a far more ample alphabet. A city called the City of Angels in a country called the Land of the Free. A people called the Free People, although the outside world knew all three only in clumsy transliterations.

And this picture parade, the infinitely extensible police lineup of intermediary staging grounds for those Crystal Nights all school drills promise: Florence, Aberfan, Madrid, Detroit, Prague, Paris, Hong Kong, Hanoi, Newark, Belfast, Harare, Jerusalem. Each a namesake, yet sharing something steeper, deeper down, beneath names. All are celestial suburbs gone wrong. Single steps, separate arithmetic means between the shining seraph of his own childhood and this place, its follow-up succubus.

His confirmation comes in one quick cut, almost faster than he can frame his guess. There it is, on three dozen diffracting screens at once, each appliance assorting its yoked electron sprays into patterns that whisper of geometries past the axiom, corollaries beyond the freshest new crop of Euclids' ability to prove. He sees her on the screen, *her* beyond all reasonable doubt, running naked through cratered streets, clothes singed off, taking her skin with them.

She runs in blind panic from something dropped out of the sky. She limps, favoring the ankle he himself has only recently excised, a girl unable to outrun the leading edge of her own animal terror, running both from and right into the next descent of aerial rupture. Running dead on, in another minute perhaps dead, into the impartial lens (but a *man* behind it, some picture scavenger, standing there filming). She runs into a world-famous image, one arrested forever a dozen years before his little girl is even born.

And she's not alone. The whole canon of ward cases accompanies her, in shot after shot. The No-Face fills the screen, his features miraculously whole for a moment before they are smashed in again by a Chicago policeman's cudgel. Then the Rapparition, laying down a Frelimo battle celebration in Bantu-Portuguese. Joleene Weeks holding what at first seems to be her Chatty Cathy doll but horribly isn't, mother and child both panting, breathing through their ribs in—well, could be anywhere. Remember these places, does he? The day's Biafra, the day's Dhaka?

Even if he has blunted the exact coordinates for a couple of sedated decades, he cannot fail to recognize the next face, as fresh in his mind as if he'd seen it for the first time just days ago. It's the newcomer, the old kid, a year or two further along, yet a half-century younger. Still bald, or rather, shaved. Led out of the subterranean prison where he'd been buried alive. Turned about for the camera like a vertical rack of lamb, his body molded all over with blue flash burns, a Roquefort grown in caves on copper wire skewers.

And this one does not come from out of the bowels of some provisional capital a day's forced march from the Chaco. This one's from closer to home. As close to home as can be, as flush, as smack up against it as video and imagination permit.

WITH INTERLUDE AGAIN fuzzy to the point of nonexistent, Kraft is back at his flat. The freeway bit is totally missing. He has negotiated those masses of lanes with no recall, even from what he hopes is only a moment later.

But he knows he's home, because the lady across the way—used to call them neighbors back before the West Was Won—female, mid-fifties, non-racially distinct, slightly dyspneic, partial to ceramic goods with ironically upbeat printed messages on them, a radical mastectomy within the last year—is standing in his doorway asking him to sniff her chicken fillets. She is the first human he can recall seeing aboveground and outside an industrio-retail complex in he can't remember how long.

"I just bought this from the Food Parade not two hours ago, and it smells rotten to me. Does it smell rotten to you? Tell me honestly, because I don't want to bring it back and have them tell me I'm crazy."

Kraft takes a whiff. He smells nothing, neither micro nor macro, animal, vegetable, mineral, nor any of commerce's more recent hybrids. He can't even smell the chicken *an sich*. "Yes," he says, surprised at how clinically he carries it off. "You may be right."

"Are you sure?" Sung to the tune of the old NBC triad. The living color peacock preens in front of him.

Then, he's still standing at the same door, but opening it for a second buzz, time lapse style. It's the woman, Linda, arms full of packages, volumes, damp and aromatic paper sacks. When he fails to make way for her, she slips past him with a playful nudge of the shoulders. "Hi, baby. I came straight from the hospital."

"Hosp—? Are you all right?"

Her eyebrows curl over her eye ridge, two caterpillars racing to reconnoiter the bridge of her nose. Her neck stem straightens in residual reflex. Half a beat, then she giggles. "Oh, I get it. Hospital, sick. Funny stuff, there. I stopped on the way and got some grub. I was seized by caprice to eat Chinese."

"Eat Chinese?"

"For God's sake, sit down. Open your mouth and close your eyes, and you will get . . ."

After dinner, she jumps up and says, "Stay put. I'll do the dishes."

"All right." He's in no position to move anyway.

"That was a joke, dope." She crumples the eternal plastic plates and multiple sacks, makes of them a single wad that she sinks with a twenty-footer into the trash. He is still sitting motionless, staring at the spot the meal had occupied. She smuggles around behind him, kisses the crown of his head.

His spine convulses, half of the famous galvanized frog's legs. "What?"

"What, 'what'? Relax. Assault waves are over for the day."

He jerks his face around to look at hers. Assault? How much does she know?

"Tough one for you today? They do you with the rubber hoses again?" Her fingers go deep, directly into his shoulders. It's good, relief beyond description, revealing what he hadn't known had been festering in that knot of confused tissue. At the same time, the pain is excruciating, worse than the one it exorcises. Retaliatory surgical strike he has no choice but to submit to. And she hasn't even slit him yet. Just the prep, the antiseptic scrub.

The rubdown expands, deeper and wider, radiating outward from his sternocleidomastoids like dioxins through the food chain. She must feel him succumb, because her cadence starts to do the *Ben-Hur*-galley-master-with-the-timpani thing. "Bare your privates, huh?" she coos in his ear. "Make them available for female consumption."

These words don't seem to issue from the Linda he knows. But maybe it's the answer all the same. Now that push comes down to shove, his hormones flush from his system with cruise technology: accurate and massive, even from a great distance.

But release is no relief. Worse, that state of blurred conviction returns to him, locking up his receptor sites. Some attempt to attract his macerated attention hovers around his apartment's seams. That tribe, that band of eyes outside the school window, waving madly, hurry, come away. The massed, perhaps coordinated movements of minor militias, an agenda afoot already, stretching forever through time and space. A single overarching pattern doubles back repeatedly on two names, words that camp out in the deflated oxygen tent that once fed the language center of his brain. The first, a place name, already ascertained. The place of his own childhood mobilization, the same name as the place where he now euphemistically lives.

The second is not a where, but a what. It is the tag of that first strategic maneuver—emblem, metonym, the name people revive every time history rounds up its usual innocents. He can retrieve nothing of the original—not its century, nor locale, nor public motive. Somewhere there must be an account he can turn to, to recover the contour of an event he is not even sure ever actually happened.

He rakes his rooms, mine-sweeps the shelves where the general encyclopedia should be. Nothing but a wasteland of medical texts, back issues of *Morbidity and Mortality,* offprints on new tech-niques, Board review workbooks, in-service exam crams.

"What you looking for, sweetface?" Linda asks, scenting con-cern.

He does not stop to answer, but goes on searching. Who can he phone? There must be an 800 number, elected state rep, one of those public service outfits that deal with radon, gas smells, dead squirrels in the walls. He will take anything, any account what-soever, even the docudrama version, the reenactment, the Based on a True Event.

Desperate, not even knowing what he is after anymore, he turns to the loose material the woman has dragged in with her. Her overnight bag. Has it come to that? Are the two of them an item, shacking up? Is this—good God—this near-girl, a little lolly-popper not more than two years out of her teens, spending whole nights, sleeping here? He'll get busted, booked, institution-alized, sentenced to a life of continuous, punitive tonsillectomies.

At odds' ends, he roots through her pile of print. The hot new issue of her own trade journal, *Practical Physiatrics Review.* Who names these things? A beach party bit of light reading, *Postopera-tive Flexion Restoration.* Next, a ridiculous grab-bag of field tools for the over-dedicated. Picture book, *A Country a Night for a Year,* which he whips through in a frenzy, but without success. One of those magic water-release books, half brushed in by a wildly inac-curate saturation painter, perhaps forced to hold brush in mouth. A pack of stiff-cardboard-bound comics.

"Oh, I traded Nico for those. You'll never believe what that kid asked for them."

All at once, there it is, lying bare in front of him. In the middle of the pack of illustrated funny magazines is the glaring ringer, one of those Treasure Chest Illustrated History Classics, the *You Take Part* series. He might have known that transported tribe would sooner or later throw the thing in his way.

"I had to swap him two pieces of . . ."

But Linda stops at the sight of what has come over him. His

hand is stroking the glossy cartoon cover, an elaborate medieval crusader column, puerile, weaponless, stretching unbroken to an infinite horizon. In a voice not even a close impersonation of his own, addressing not her but fleeting figures just outside his window, some boy inside him asks, "Who *are* these . . . ?"

His tongue tags along after the word it can't catch up with, the one that skids away just in front of the snare set for it. These kids. These children.

A picture book narrator, perched in the sky, looks down from miles on high onto a map where ink-etched ocean boldly wraps blocks of continent in currents of purest palette. Successive frames gradually pull the eye in tighter, until gross features firm. Steel-gray ice caps, bleakly gorgeous, rim the borders. Coasts cut seaward under a swirl of cloud. Waters stretch away until they arrive beyond the bounds of knowledge, spotted here and there with details for the scrupulous squinter—occasional sea monsters, the puckered face of the blowing wind, the blanketing expanse of a midsea mass that might be anything but to the practiced audience outside this paper portal, pressing faces to the square-paned windows that ladder across these pages, becomes a flotilla of bottles so closely packed that they form a single decanted help message, readable only from ten thousand feet above.

But this forsaken armada of bottled petitions is only a fanciful flicker, a curl of the illustrator's nib, a slight tint-change in the hazel carpet spread over the surface of doom's deep. Castles perch on cliffs, visible before they should be at this magnification. Monasteries pock-mark the shore, devout in tenuousness. Walled ports, minuscule but intricate with masonry, their plowed fields and fiefs heaped up like carpet remnants around a throne, are as yet exceptions, small halts in continuous wood and wildness.

The storytelling eye hangs suspended in midair a little longer, a surveyor's speculation wider than these fortified hills allow. Then, renouncing its bird's-eye, it nestles down like a silversmithed, dove ciborium lowering itself to the surface of the sin-steeped world. The panels take on earth's tangent, a pilgrim's view. Focus falls to the roads below, ways swarming with travelers, one for every conceivable reason in religion's calendar.

Here, at ground level, belief marches through the year in brief. Each discrete frame is a new saint's day, another motive for mass migration. Across a quilt of color-strewn squares, searchers shake down Santiago de Compostela, assault Amritsar, Lumbini, or Ayodhya. They venture off to venerate Saint Peter's bones in Rome. They scale Mount Abu, wend to Canterbury. They figure the four sacred mountains, the five thrones, the seven sacred rivers. They close in on Buddh Gaya, Lourdes, Assisi, Sarnath, Turin, Goa, Tours, Nankana, Guadalupe, Kusinagara, Fátima, Marburg, the hills of Parasnath and Girnar. The world pictured is a surging hajj, one that every believer must make at least once, if only by proxy.

Contritional, reverential, purgational, memorial, devotional, salvational: the motives for moving sweep an arc as wide as the swing of these walkers' staves. Cartoon figures, burgundy and forest-green, journey to the source of all grace, the spring of all politics, the birthplace of history. The tour is slow but urgent, desperate enough to have demanded this illustrated guide in the first place. It is as if, the drawings insist, only a thousand miles on foot will ever set things right again.

The paneled page tags alongside this parade to those expanses that are a little more sacred, a little *closer,* if only because they mark the resting place of some grotesque bloodletting. Ink and watercolor snake into lines of supplicants ready to sacrifice all purchase on earth to reach their holy sites. And there, at page bottom, farther than they can hope to see, the luster of goal: a temple, crypt, battle site, the empire's earliest universities, wandering schools where they might matriculate.

Tinted print starts to hover just above the frames. Just the spidery shape of the letters speaks of a moving desire, an impulse bedded down below the soul's water table. "Pilgrimage," the captions begin, "is the path of a single life made visible, replayed in the space of a few days." Beneath these words, a band of travelers passes close by a familiar, inviting house en route to the far land-scape. The very next picture is the window casement itself, drawn from the inside, the sight of the receding band insisting that the stay-at-home eye chase it down, join it. *Go* somewhere. What does it matter if you're not back for dinner? The suffering and cold, molestation, looting along the way are mere softened pen-strokes dipped in crimson and gold. The story stakes you only this one round trip, this one staged set of oases leading ever higher up into the mountains, this one chance to recap the embryo's first adventure overseas.

"A single hope, if never more than secret, stabs at the heart of everything that is awake." Flowery voice-over for a child's trea-sure chest album, but the accompanying astonishments of artwork vindicate the text. Who reads these preliminary bits anyway? The proof is all visual. Wait, walk long enough, and you will arrive. The hinted-at place is just around the next hillside. It will appear in your lifetime, in another half page or two.

Fresco-inspired friezes, severe yet sensuous, tell of the need to replay the whole itinerary in miniature. Swelling rectangles add up to a radiant, full-page display, the fabulous rivals: Mecca itself, and, *en face* across the stapled spread, Jerusalem, the Holy Sepulcher. Each story panel moves the seeker closer to that ulti-mate end, the scale model City of God on Earth. From a great distance, it appears only as a gathering, anxious crosshatch on the horizon. Still miles away over the plain, the towers become vis-ible, then the walls. Then, at long last, the mammoth gate appears and opens, sparkling with celebratory stone revelation, ancient promises—detailed and intricate—carved everywhere into its cy-clopean surface.

The dress becomes clear now, the style, time, and place. It is that interregnum of great faith, when most of the world knows this habitation to be almost spent. The globe is degraded; it cor-rodes only to be restored soon to its old original. Its oversoul migrates through a slow loop, one that narrows its noose to ar-rive at final things. Crisis cultures, cargo cults, nativistic movements, messianics: everyone on this road-strewn surface survives the present by naming it a station, an inscrutable detour on the way to the next age, the next image, the next frame.

The passes to the shrines of the blessed martyrs, the languishing trade routes are charged now with danger and salvation. An emerald mix of fear and need lights the spired horizons. Pen and color do not dare guess yet at topography's terminus, the shape of the hastening finish, except to fan the palmer's hope that arrival must surely be near, the end of the day of wandering in sight.

The Tour Guide—the Anointed, the Mahdi or Twelfth Imam, the Mahayana redeemer, the Nanabush—is shown preparing his many returns. In every town that the processions pass, the old order is smelted off. The *novum* is set to make its break. Strange, reified contours, miraculous and unexpected, get ready to rise up out of the earth's destruction. "Come the Fourth Kingdom . . ." the supertitles predict. "Come the Third Age . . ." Come the revolution, the return, the liberation, the overthrow, the transforming renewal . . . The mass pilgrimage rolls across these ocher hills, stopping for alms at all the pox spots of civilization. Suddenly, the stills reveal all: this disguised, private campaign, this jihad by another name, draws toward the emblem of all foretold spots, the city at the end of the world.

Illuminated saga retraces the eye's first excursion. To scan these lavish psalter sheets is almost to see through the panels from the other side, to surprise the reading youth under the sheets at night again. Arrows leading from square to square mark a flagstone picture path down which the strip's original owner raced by flashlight to reach story's end. The way is a seven-hundred-year shortcut back to an ancient destiny.

Back to boyhood, back to that moment when the medieval West sits inside a defensive moat rapidly filling up with rubble. The Christian world has restively expected its impending end for twelve hundred years. It waits at this very moment, more certain of *now* than ever. God's tune rushes to cadence.

"True," a series of recapitulating panels concedes, "prior clock-watchers have been wrong." Many expect the old heaven and earth to burn away just as the Anointed, Antichrist Sylvester II, pronounces midnight mass on December 31, 999. Comets blazed brilliantly in advance. At the sound of transubstantiation's bell, people across the continent drop to the ground, expectant. In reprieve's let-down, hurried calculations produce another thirty years of grace. And when that extension also expires, seers settle on a new due date.

Numbers prove pliable. Sooner discard the calendar than the drift toward cartoon apocalypse it was built to predict. "Not the *year* 1000!" a Gnostic calculator proclaims in his cold stone cell, the astonished correction coming out his mouth in a speech bubble as old as Romanesque ecclesiastical comics. "The thousand-year reign of majesty here on earth!" Then two frames, scalloped to show they come from his monk's mind's eye: crypts opening, the martyrs resurrected to serve as kings in the new world's political machine, perfected at last.

Broadly announced now, bruited about all lands in caption and image: the Last Emperor, the ultimate successor of the Frankish kings, will soon assemble a host and make the long passage across the Middle Sea to recover by force the earthly sign of heavenly metropolis. There men will prepare the way for the Second Coming. Pilgrims return molested from the Holy Land, cries of protest filling the air above their heads. When a bubble-call for help comes from Pope Urban II, standing on a balcony in the South of France and beseeching a crowd to turn its random havoc into a single, sanctified, militant pilgrimage, his *"Deus volt"* is magnified a millionfold. All ranks and social stations catch fire. Europe launches itself into the new age it has long been predicting.

But the fall of the Holy City fails to bring on the last battle. Muslim and Jew are duly slaughtered to make way for Jerusalem's new inhabitants. Sovereign states are drawn up on the Levant map, diamonds designating the cities the pilgrim generals dole out among themselves: Antioch to one, Tripoli shores to another, Acre and Beirut to a third. No sooner is the new world order established than Zangi, Nureddin, and Saladin mount holy encircling maneuvers of their own.

The West, flexing itself in foreign contact, launches another wave of its eschatologically charged faithful into the World's Debate. France and Germany, the princes of Bohemia, Swabia, Poland, and Byzantium join forces under the cross. Armies of incompatible nationals pour into the Near East. But rival millennial expectations among allies prove fatal. The Second Crusade ends with a senseless attack on Damascus, executed in a disastrous fade to indigo and black.

The City of Heaven on Earth, ruled for a while by a thirteen-year-old leper, teeters on the brink, shattered by sectarian bickering. The crusader armies mass yet again for Armageddon, and are once more destroyed. Jerusalem falls again and is lost before God has a chance to install His transcelestial bureaucracy. The end of history is postponed for another few pages.

A third call for a God-willed showdown sounds across a catholic confederation too sophisticated now to hear it the way it first did, a century before. England's Lion-Heart signs on, along with Sicily, Flanders, and the Danes. They grab Cyprus as jumping-off point. Frederick Barbarossa, a furious seventy, leads the Germans cross-continent to a brilliant victory, only to drown—in intricately inked irony—crossing a stream.

Spiritual fervor degrades into a cynical race for fiefs. Holy war gives way to political shrewdness, the deftly drawn fourth campaign. The international hammerblow aimed at recovering Jerusalem, deflected by backroom Venetian power broking, ends not in sieges of infidel strongholds but in a brutal sack of Christian Constantinople. The soldiers of the cross succeed in tearing the two churches apart forever. They shatter and slice up Byzantium—beautifully penned in strategic and tactical views—the jewel that for so long formed the first line of defense against encroaching East, dealing it a wound from which it never recovers.

All this unfurls in four and a quarter pages, a dozen hand-colored rectangles per side. Then focus narrows another notch.

The centuries-meandering road cants into a valley where the story's boy hides this time. (Watching these accounts of upheaval pour in, the flashlight reader marvels at how it is always *them,* the brigade of the displaced, each time out with the same names, the same age, the same slim chance of ever arriving by candlelight, let alone getting back again.)

"In the spring of the year 1212," a text box authoritatively interrupts, "a young boy no older than you tends sheep in a pasture near the tiny town of Cloyes-sur-le-Loir in central France." Two hundred years from now a little girl saint will lead an army through this hamlet on its mission of salvation. "A boy on the threshold of his teens, Stephen, who has never needed a last name until now. Soon the world will know him as Stephen of Cloyes." His flock is agitated and expectant, despite the sweet weather.

He lives in fabulous times, although he cannot know it. Deployments are everywhere in the air. Just outside his cleanly inked borders, towns busily receive city charters, universities spring up, cities band into trade leagues. A fever of new building spreads like flowering weeds across the champaign. The last westwork of Our Lady of Paris and the first stones of Rheims are laid in place even as Stephen keeps the two-year-old ewe with the weak left fore from sliding down a pebbled pitch.

He cannot write or read, has never even needed to sign anything. Simple arithmetic, certainly: lambs, ewes, rams, weight gains and losses, hours spent grazing. His grasp on medicine, meteorology, even natural history has all the finesse of a field practitioner. He can recognize 113 varieties of plants, diagnose fifteen different illnesses, and predict the weather for the next four hours. He once visited Vendôme, and last St. Mark's Day he attended a Litana Major in Chartres, a chance service that will charge the conscience of the race. He takes the flock out after sunrise, ranging them from field to field until hail or darkness forces them in. He converses with his animals, calling each by name.

For a frame, he prays, singing psalms to himself. But now that the flock is safe, the dog content, the weather solid, the spring too sweet to admit danger, he sleeps on the sly, fifteen minutes this afternoon, his attention unneeded. The dog wakes him from his secret nap, barking in confusion at a dark figure climbing their remote rise up the path toward them.

The figure is not his father, nor any acquaintance carrying alarm from the village. Stephen can think of no reason short of catastrophe why anyone would hike all the way out to these fields. Thieves would wait for dusk; others are bound to their labor.

As the apparition approaches, Stephen makes out a pilgrim's cloak and cap. The man must have strayed miles from the cathedral route. And alone! Stephen calls out to the wanderer, thinking to set him straight. But the man preempts him, cuts off his speech bubble with another, and greets the startled shepherd boy *by name*.

"Who are you?" Stephen asks as the man draws closer. "I don't think I know you."

"Don't you?" the stranger smiles. A shiver runs up the boy's spine. "I woke you?"

Stephen manages a terrified, close-up shake of the head. The Pilgrim scolds him gravely with a look. "I would like you to deliver a letter."

"I can't read," Stephen blurts.

"A messenger shouldn't know how. But I will tell you what this note says. 'I have seen the Lord's City, arrayed as for her bridegroom. Why fail her now when the feast is so close?' "

Stephen taps his staff against the dog's flank, to keep her from snarling. "It's in code?" The traveler grubs about in his sack. He withdraws a moldy crust, which he shares with the boy. The man's poverty boosts Stephen's confidence. Thanking the man for the food, he asks, "Where should I deliver the letter?" He adds hopefully, "The village is just that way."

The Pilgrim places a parchment, heavy under its seal, in the child's hands. "You will bring this to the king of France."

At the touch of the man's hand, Stephen falls to his knees and begins crying. Sucking air, he manages to gasp, "Why me?"

The Pilgrim, already halfway down the rise, calls out the answer that Stephen most dreads. "I choose one who follows my profession." The innocent sheep kneel as one beast across the field, praying for absolution.

At night, after bringing his flock in, as his family gathers noisily around its late meal, Stephen announces into his soup, "I must go to the city."

His father bats him across the head with an elbow, automatic, businesslike. The younger ones snicker, and receive similar treatment.

Comic interlude turns into clamor when Stephen clarifies. He doesn't mean Vendôme or even Orléans, an already-impossible fifty miles away. "I must go to Paris." Father looks wearily at mother to discipline the outrage. She brains the boy and washes his mouth out with scalding lard. Dinner breaks up early.

He could tell them of the message and the man who set it in his hands. One word, and his family would fall at his feet and beg forgiveness. Instead, for reasons left undrawn, he chooses to slip out early, before daybreak, stealing the best pair of trekking shoes and some stale rinds destined for the feed bin. He ties the letter firmly to his forearm. He runs from the farm in the dark, choosing a random direction, running anywhere, so long as it is away and unseen.

When it grows light, Stephen stumbles upon a village and orients himself. He points himself northeast and keeps walking. It will take weeks to reach the goal he's been given. He wanders alone at a time when the average adult traveler would not last an afternoon against human ingenuity. "The Pilgrim would not have sent me off without providing for my safety." He puts up for the night in a hayrick, his belly nagging like a scythe wound.

An angel wakes him at daylight. Graphic match: a beautiful girl, perhaps a year younger than he, shakes his shoulder, calling, "Wake up! What do you think you're doing here?"

He begs some milk and a bit of bread, which his angel supplies with scorn. Then he tells her, whispering, that the Savior has sent him to the king of France, bearing a message about the end of the world. She hisses at him until he pulls up his sleeve and shows her the letter fastened there. She touches him gingerly on the muscle, and a delicious pain shoots through him, a change he can't understand. She studies him, amazed, and begs to be allowed to come along.

"Go on, then. Collect provisions, as much as you can carry. Then meet me down by the stile." She returns with a sister, also inflamed by the cause, carrying food, clothing, even a blanket. By midmorning, they are five, having met and bragged of the goal to two of the girls' village friends along the road. They sleep in an open field, together, happy as they have never been, singing religious tunes until they pass unconscious.

They travel in greater safety now, occasionally stealing an egg or two for the Lord's breakfast. To the rare adult who stops and challenges the little band upon the route, the girl lies sweetly, "We are cleaning the weeds off roadside crosses." Stephen cannot help noticing: her face grows beautiful, flushes rose with excitement when she invents the truth. They are joined by a boy named Luc, richer than all of them combined, and another named Henri, who has a dog that knows the useful trick of digging up carrots. They share all things among them, as needed. At night, they trade off standing watch.

Before the week is out, they number twenty. Stephen finds it steadily harder to keep track of this swelling flock. They can no longer move without attracting attention. But something astonishing happens as they reach this critical mass. A family of farmers offers them shelter inside a *basse-cour* and sends them off the next morning laden with goods. The same implausible transaction repeats itself the following evening. People ask for nothing but to be remembered along the pilgrimage route.

They lie in such a courtyard one night, four dozen children from eight to sixteen, decked out happily amid the animal stalls. They have already reached the woods that ring the royal domains. They will enter the capital in just days. Stephen lies quietly in the stall next to his angel girl. One of the older boys, a monastery runaway, finds him there.

"What does the letter say, Stephen?"

Stephen smiles inwardly and recites the passage the Pilgrim told him. The whole band knows the message by heart, and the runaway novitiate asks for it much the way that the youngest asks for the same story about the cock, the hare, and the cow each night before she can fall asleep.

"Is it in French?"

"How should I know?" Stephen shrugs. "Is that important?"

"The words allude to those of Saint John, describing his vision on the island of Patmos."

"A-allude?" Stephen stutters suspiciously.

"Do you know what the note means? It means our parents have failed us."

Stephen rubs the back of his head, still smarting from the punishment his mother never suspected would be his send-off.

"And not just our own parents." The older boy employs all the rhetorical skill the monks imparted to him. "The entire older generation. They have lost sight of God's desires." In quick pastel flashback, he tells Stephen of the four great campaigns to retrieve the Holy City, narrating the sad degradation of the blessed quest over a century and a quarter—from the first inspired flame to the sack of the Church's Eastern capital.

A change works its way over Stephen as he considers the message he has been entrusted with. Suddenly, its import is clear. The king they must serve as messenger is not the corrupted, human one. They, this band of a few dozen children, are meant to satisfy the Creator's will all by themselves. They will succeed where their parents failed. They must convert the unbeliever, recover the Holy Sepulcher, besiege the city of Jerusalem by love, doing what force of arms could not.

Yes—this was the Pilgrim's intention from the start. *I choose one who follows my profession.* By morning, Stephen finds a new strength and gentleness. He addresses his collected charges after breakfast with a mix of love and fervor. "We are not on our way to Paris after all."

Not? Where then?

To the sea, by the most expedient route. Over the water to the towers of Civitas Dei. Let anyone who cannot aspire to reach there in perfect love turn back now, to France, to the world of things.

Not a child does. The band reconnoiters momentarily at St.-Denis, where a flaming sermon by the boy contrasts the conditions of the two sepulchers, this one flourishing, while the Lord's decays in pagan hands. The ranks of infant infantry swell with all those young enough to hear. Parents cannot reduce the stream of volunteers. The French king, as Stephen feared, bans the crusade, and professors at the earthly university declare it satanic. This is all the confirmation he needs: they must brave this alone.

The children swing south, where their cascading march gains a grip on the rural mind. By the time they reach Dijon, where they muster at the basilica, they number in the thousands. "And yet," the text interlude asks, "can even ten thousand children go against the warriors of Islam? One child would suffice to succeed where the compromise of adulthood failed. One little child once did far more."

Aching with resolution, Stephen turns away all petitioners over sixteen. The cause must be pure this time, untainted by anything past the first stages of innocence. The angel, his first recruit, infected by his seriousness, shaves her radiant hair and takes up walking in the rear, with the baggage train. Stephen continues to think of her at night, despite fasting, flagellation, and prayer.

They walk along in immense double file, a thread so long the middle can't see the end. A mélange of dialects fills the air, translated by magic. Here and there, children adopt a uniform—gray shift, palmer's staff, scraps of cloth sewn into a cross on the breast. Nights are steeped in fireside telling: fables, tales, legends, gests, sparked inventions to link each life to the great contour. But none of these asides can match the allegory they make now. By days, marching, they sing, several thousand voices in monodic unison, "O Lord, restore us to the True Cross."

The year is strange beyond interpreting. Overland reports tell of epochal animal convocations—fish, fowl, frogs, insects—massing for deciding diets. Dogs from all France and beyond assemble to fight their civil war. The beasts, in their spotlessness, *know*.

Deeper into Burgundy, on the road, in the brightness of midsummer, a voice near Stephen calls out a surprised "Hello!" Stephen spins around to greet it, but the caller is nowhere.

He has walked too far; he's begun hearing things. But he must walk many times farther still, before reaching home. "Hello?" Stephen murmurs, more to himself than to the phantom.

"That's the way!" The voice comes back, no more than twelve inches from Stephen's ears. "That's it. It's working!"

A close-up catches the alarm on Stephen's features. But his skin, in its silver youth, still proclaims the blessedness of those who believe without yet having seen. "Who are you? *Where* are you?"

A burst of giggle betrays that the hidden speaker is even younger than Stephen, ten years old at the most. "My name is Nicolas. I come from Cologne." (An insert shows the spire-line of the city, with a blowup of its greatest treasure—the fabulous golden Magi reliquary, containing Barbarossa's three crusade-booty skeletons, one a milk-toothed boy.) "At the moment we're camped outside Koblenz." As Nicolas speaks, his visage shimmers, solidifying in the air above the French band's vanguard.

"Cologne?" Stephen throws his tunic-draped arms up in provincial panic. "But I speak no German!"

"Don't let that worry you," Nicolas giggles. "I don't know a lick of French, neither."

The colored drawings clarify, in wonderful split-framing: a ghostly Nicolas hovering above the Rhône Valley, a disembodied Stephen, inverse fata morgana, over the Rhine. The children who walk nearest Stephen in the snaking column can neither see

nor hear anything; their road to Provence is brilliantly Mediterranean, vacant. In half an hour, word ripples through the French
ranks that their leader has begun to traffic in miracles.

The boys feel one another out, unsure whether to wrestle for
top spot or swear blood brotherhood. At last Nicolas pouts, "We
heard of what you are doing over there, and we want to meet you
in the Middle East."

"We? How many are you?"

The German has been waiting for this question. "At present,
eleven thousand three hundred and forty-seven. But the lieutenant in cadre six is still counting. We form a six-and-a-half-mile
file when flat out." A little proudly, the kid challenges, "How
many are *you?*"

Stephen shrugs Gallically over the private, invisible airways.
Nicolas mutters the Low German equivalent of *"Vive la dif-
férence."* Stephen can hear, in the murmuring background, several
thousand treble voices raising the chorale "Schönster Herr Jesu,
Herrscher aller Erden."

The boys stay in constant contact, tying in at least once each
evening. Nicolas enjoys charging into Stephen's ear throughout
the day, issuing communiqués about his swelling numbers. Stephen, his own force growing absurdly, gently cautions the boy
from time to time. "Remember, if we win the day at Acre and
beyond, it will be through love and love only."

This sweet upbraiding always results in grumbles. "All right.
But love can use a bit of muscle, can't it?"

Stephen comes to love the younger boy, however impetuous.
They have wonderful theological arguments over whether the
kingdom they are preparing will arise, at last, on this earth or on
the far side of the heavenly bridge. Stephen encourages Nicolas
to try his hand at healing the sick in his company, rather than
leaving them along the route. Nicolas in turn endlessly suggests
ways that Stephen might coordinate the movements of a migrating band now beyond all counting.

Nicolas becomes Stephen's confidant, the repository of hopes and the bulwark against night's doubt. "How am I to ferry an army of tens of thousands of children safely across the Mediterranean?" Stephen whispers to the ten-year-old, late, from a campsite a week away from that shore.

"Ha! That'll be easy. The waters will part in front of our faith, like the sea in front of Moses." This answer passes confidently up and down Stephen's column. "I, on the other hand," counters Nicolas, "have *real* problems. How am I supposed to port twenty thousand children over the Alps?"

Nicolas's logistical difficulties are soon taken out of his hands. He brings his immaculate enterprise as far as Mont Cenis monastery pass. There, Revelation's field trip begins to break up. His angelically impatient first and second cadres head by shortest route to the sea, via the Ampezzo Valley. Cadres three through five choose less devastating terrain, following the Adige River via Trento and Verona. Nicolas convinces the others that they must cross Lombardy and head toward Genoa to rendezvous with Saint Stephen and the French.

By the time Stephen reaches Marseilles, all Europe knows what is happening. The continental passage of guiltless children in pursuit of the millennium inflames imaginations from England to Hungary. People throng the roads to meet the crusade, walking for days just to see the battalions pass. Faith renews the dying world with a storming force of naïveté, a little child leading them.

As they approach the sea, the columns openly chant faith's refrain. *The waters will part, make a land bridge for us to pass. God has taken us this far. All the earth's oceans will dry; the world will be one, without divisions.*

They parade in confidence up to the shore. But the sea, it stuns them to discover, stays sadistically the sea. Callous water stretching to the limits of vision makes the youngest in the vanguard break down in bitter tears. "It cannot be!" Foretaste of failure fills thirty thousand mouths, failure on a scale humankind can neither know nor survive.

But a miracle awaits Stephen's crusaders in the harbor. A whole fleet assembles there, as if divinely arranged. Merchants stand ready to take the holy army to its history-ending destination. *Causa Dei, absque pretio.* (*No!* the flashlight reader shouts. *Look out! These men are evil; you can tell by their finery, the folds of their faces.* But the view from above—prophetic periscope of two mirrors tilting a perpendicular to everything—fails to inform pilgrim level.)

Stephen oversees the delicate boarding. A steady, incredulous joy spreads through him to see the force distributed among the dromonds, buzas, gulafres, cats—the agent vessels of an expanding world. One day he catches sight of the girl, in all her head-shaved beauty, high up in one galleon's perilous castle poop deck. He calls to her, forgetting himself, their cub chastity. "We will meet in front of the Dome of the Rock," she calls back, beaming at her saint.

Keeping Nicolas abreast of the boarding, Stephen knows that his thousands cannot wait for the arrival of the Germans on the coast. Nicolas, beside himself trying to keep track of his forces now scattering themselves through Lombard towns, waves his joint commander on ahead. "Carry on. We're right behind you. Just leave us a dusky brute or two to baptize."

Stephen boards the last ship out of safe haven. Overjoyed, he looks back on the disappearing continent. All around him, the child-manned fleet sings "Veni Creator Spiritus." He tries to contact Nicolas to let him listen in. But for the first time, no apparition appears on the empty air.

The German child at that moment stumbles lost through the Po Valley. His splinter group has been whittled by attrition to a few thousands. Rumor—in vague watercolor washes—drifts in from the other factions: stories of children robbed by peasants, their various virgin orifices despoiled by Tuscan aristocrats. Weary ten-year-olds give in to acquired vices, then take to them willingly in quick addiction. The pursuit of the True Cross becomes a struggle to ward off utter chaos.

Nicolas's western cadres struggle on. A few thousand assemble in Genoa. Some stay to found famous patrician families, in a brief flash-forward. Others press on to the Holy See. Every set of walls and towers, every pathetic handyman's castle even on this, the wrong side of the divided world, touches off the excited cry "Is that Jerusalem? Is *that* Jerusalem?"

In Rome, much later, the pope welcomes them, shaming Christian Europe by pronouncing, "See how these innocents busy themselves with preparations for recovery while we drowse?" Taking pity on pink limbs that have seen more than a life's worth of sacrifice, he absolves them of their vows. He promises that each has already achieved a foothold in paradise. He tells them to return as adults if they still desire to be pilgrims. But he forbids the expedition to proceed.

The way back is colder, more harrowing, less likely, darker than can be painted. Each one of them travels alone. The innocents that do reach North come back corrupted beyond recovery. And the land they return to is not home. Nothing more is heard from the boy Nicolas, who preached the end of history. He is stranded somewhere between Genoa and St. Gotthard, Gog and Magog.

Europe waits anxiously for word of Stephen's venture. The crusade has been so long under way it seems to have existed from the very launch of time. The home front half expects that any month must bring the account of conquest. They grill all travelers for word of the promised conflagration, this time bloodless and pure, the one that will transform threadbare creation.

But word fails to come. Waiting shades seamlessly into neglect. Some months after everyone has given up on hearing, an account works its way back to the mainland. Two child ships were caught in a freak storm and cracked open on the rocks off of San Pietro, southwest of Sardinia. The thousand children's bodies, washed up on the surf, collected in a modest crypt, miraculously fail to decompose.

The site of this Sign begins drawing pilgrims from many lands. It is hastily marked with a chapel built by order of the pope, a new Holy Sepulcher inscribed ECCLESIA NOVORUM INNOCENTIUM.

Twelve prebends tend it with perpetual prayer. The shrine, drawn in time lapse, vanishes over the centuries, to be rediscovered half a millennium later by Grand Tourists struck with uncomprehending wonder.

Eighteen years after the mass departure, a man gnarled by torture-accelerated age returns to the Christian North, claiming to have been a child crusader. The flotilla has already passed into myth, and this wandering priest's story—picked up in Albericus, de Champré, Bacon, the era's *Classics Illustrateds*—is a curiosity at best. Well into the waning century, travelers returning from the Middle East tell of light-skinned Muslim slaves in Algeria and Alexandria who speak a strange pidgin of Arabic and Romance. This is the fabled end of that child cargo: traded on the international spot market, sold to the Saracens by creedless merchants, martyred to this round of teleology, but passing on to their own children the remembered vow "Our feet shall stand within thy walls, O Jerusalem."

An estimated hundred thousand innocents are lost, sold, killed, betrayed, evacuated from this world by faith. Nor do the picture portals leave off there. They open onto a few more spots of scattered continuance: the Erfurt exodus. A mass child migration to St. Michel. The Kinderzeche. Dancing manias, disappearances, and sovereign successions over subsequent centuries are each given detailed treatment in a much-subdivided pane, as complex and effulgent as the best leaded glass, its Gothic model. But of the shepherd child, of Stephen himself, no more caption. He is shown, ghostly, staring leeward from a floating castle deck, looking out onto the last days that again circle overhead.

The final colored frame—the last, the very last—is a radical departure for the artist's pen. It leaps from archaic Treasure Chest style into UPI Wire Photo: boy soldiers in another epochal year once more marching through the Lion's Gate into God's Foundation, while other boy soldiers flee the sacred city through secular back streets. The mother of all battles. Above them, overhead, fly Armageddon's radar-evading Stealth engines of destruction, assembled by the same Angel City industries whose cost overruns buy their pauperized crusader state this little margin of imaginary time.

"Could it be," the text box asks a reader who has long since fallen asleep or started on something more vivid—say a *Sergeant Shrapnel* or his high-tech, laser-guided reincarnation—"could it be that the seed of the Thousand-Year Kingdom, that troubled dream toward which the world still falters, was sown in a place possessed long ago and lost, forgotten except to fable?" In comic boyhood, history's cartoon.

Well, *yes it could,* the once-boy concedes, his hands surgically returning the tract to the therapist's stack of night reading. It could. All predictions are perverted remembrance. They'll have to come back, after long wandering. No place else to go. They're here already, all around him. Every day, the law's brutal blue shock troops drag them into his hospital, those they haven't emptied their clips into. Disease coaxes them to him. He steps over them in their gutter-ambush just outside the tony retail Alhambras, the mushroom towers, the high-security parking garages, there being no more open places where innocence might encamp. *Ad mare stultorum, Tendebat iter puerorum.* The sea will part for them. It will have to. No other place large enough to hold them all.

Yes; how could he have failed to see it? The place is breaking up. Isn't that what has been flashing across all channels, pissing out of late-night talk radio rumblings, putting in cameo appearances on *Showdown Tonight,* left as live correspondents' reports on his answering machine while he was out? The narrow space he came from has already ended, been burned off, refined away. It capitulated in the same moment, in the time it has taken the boy to think this thought, to consume this illuminated manuscript, to page, to leaf through, to see, to believe, to receive the old list of infinitives, to lip-read the traditional closing, *this* one: Next Year in Angel City.

The boy grows manic, racing out of control. He wants everything, all at once. He demands a continuous barrage of milspec mayhem. When that's not forthcoming, he manufactures it. C'mon: new game. Scale-model Grand Prix down the emergency stairwell. Multiplayer stock market speculation with real quotes and Monopoly money. Murder in the dark, the hushed hysterics too soft for the night nurses to hear. Helicopter spotting on the roof, gawking at today's incoming wounded. He must live through those sixty years he has acquired without experiencing, all in the space of the next three weeks. He plunges the ward into a hopped-up nonstop campaign of chaos, and only the knowledge that it will all stop suddenly and soon prevents the pros from cuffing him.

Linda foresaw the whole reaction the day Nico checked in. Patently transparent—an old man's textbook *love me, look past my rhinoceros hideousness*. All the same, she finds herself locking horns with the little beast more and more frequently. Some days she just doesn't care what motivates his constant, vindictive disruption. She'd like to whack him one first and do the social worker stuff later. As for his wider subversion of hospital life—"You call this food? Lemme in that kitchen. Hey, how's about a movie theater in this dump? Casino. Dancing girls"—more power to him. But when he busts in on her Duchenne's support group, hysterically trying to shame them out of their progressive muscle wastage by threatening to use the four of them as a baseball diamond, she and Nicolino have their first shouting showdown.

Problem is, three of her four disintegrating dystrophy boys side with their tormentor. Leave him be. Nico's okay. He's our Main Mind, our man with a plan to take command. (We, after all, may live to see the extreme old age of thirty.) It's a sympathy vote for a kid picked off in a way even grimmer than their own. But there's something more than mere sympathy in this deference to Nico's new ward order. The others have been just waiting for a knee-high Boss Tweed to come along and tell them what to do next. Not just any newcomer; *this* one.

Anyone who has exploited prepubescence for any campaign, however well meaning, anybody who has ever trotted out pasteurized, freckled, fairybook simperers to pitch their wholesome radiance, has forgotten the lay of this land. Traveled too far in the interim. *Remember the children. What of the children? Doesn't anyone care about the children?* Rubbish, all of it. For Linda's money, these sales reps confuse innocence with a lack of opportunity. Been too long since they've gotten down on their shins to consider the turf. It's desperate down here at half-pint level. They're clutching and mean, and they take no prisoners.

Childhood is not that parade of vibrant kids teaching the world to sing. That's a new one: as far as Espera has read, the product of the last fifty years. She knows the histories from school. Time was when domestic theory wrote the whole batch off as changeling babies, perversely truculent sub- and semihumans. The prescribed treatment was to beat the devils out of their tiny, ripe habitations. No wonder childhood is just waiting for her to turn around and leave the room so it can retaliate for the running lancet sores inflicted on it by ages of adulthood.

Purity is an adult bills of goods. The sweet-meaning child is just an icon, a tool in this power struggle, *the* power struggle, the first, original, quintessential holy war between supreme exploiter and victim. Real children—the pet mutilators, the medicine cabinet moles, the ones that refuse to pee until their bladders burst—have all lost their innocence long before they learned to speak. They had it drilled out of them at the first vindictive parental backhand.

Small wonder. Her kids are an *ad hoc* delegation of oppressed, low-income, minority, viciously sick, festering, powerless, disenfranchised, and condescended-to culprits. They know in their intuitively subterfuging hearts that they are the test rats, scapegoats, and pack animals of the entitled—their mature dominators, the holders of vested interests, those of the despotic head start.

Hence their incredible attraction to an *adult* kid. Only that can explain how Nico charges in and takes over in a matter of days. His packaging says it all. The guy's *old,* and consequently brings out the natural submission to one's elders. Yet at the same time, he's this double agent, a traitor to his class. Here's this adult chucking it all in and coming *back.* And there's no champion like one that's just crossed over from enemy lines.

The last thing Linda wants to do is tangle with him, to pull rank. But what are you supposed to do when the monster calls his quadriplegic buddy a beanbag? When he threatens to attach a friend's catheter to the wheelchair motor if the malingerer doesn't at least *try* to stand? When, trying out his own remedy on Ben's suicidal depression, he gives the double amputee a highly prized board and orders him to skate or die?

Linda's charges refuse to protect themselves from this self-appointed terrorist therapist. Nor do they want her protection. They rush, instead, to that universal tendency of the oppressed, the victim's eternal willingness to exchange one cruelty for the other on symbolic grounds. He may be a tyrant, but he's our tyrant. Better him than one of you.

And the real adults, who have all read his chart, are just as disposed to let him run amok. The mere thought of telling him not to run in the corridors paralyzes them with shame. Nico, still possessed of boyhood's thought tap, knows he can get away with just about anything. He's unopposable, a berserk Mickey Rooney–Freddie Bartholomew mutant cross gone rampant, just before the boxer priest comes to straighten him out.

ONLY, THERE'S NOT going to be any reforming priest popping up this time. Nico's parents have been preparing their only man-child for his impending kiss-off by assuring him that whatever he says is holy law. The one potential surrogate dad that Linda tries to trick into assisting with Nico moans at her softly from his side of the suddenly Siberian bed. "I said, leave me *off* this one. It's. Not. A. Surgical. Case."

She wants to hit him. Slap his impassive face for treating her like, well, like a willful child. She would in a second, if she thought it might help. In the man's current condition, it wouldn't even arouse him. At least he's talking again, and all she can do is let him.

"Not my rotation. I shouldn't even know of this kid's exis-tence." He lashes the words with a ferocity that shifts her concern from the man-boy to the boy-man. One thing is clear, whatever other creeping etiologies come to bear here. Ricky too is spooked out of his composure by this freak visitor.

Her resident-in-absentia lies on his back in the dark, in her bed. Even his spending the night here is a major concession. His arms stay folded over unremoved surgical scrubs. He lies stiff, a magician's hypnotized assistant or Gothic knight posing for the sculptured upper deck of his terminal stone bunk. Gross miscal-culation on her part, to have brought up the Nico thing. They are back to the friction of their first tête-à-tête, without the erotic charge. She feels the slow spit of nebulous theories churning in him, where she had meant to forestall them. *I know,* she can feel his forcibly relaxed muscles thinking. I know who this creature *is.*

She dare not even ask him what he thinks he knows. He would dissolve in an ironic laugh at his own expense, pull back into a deeper pillbox, even as he turned to play with her. Play more perfunctory, with their every successive foray. Fondling as sop. She cannot even say anymore—*already? just three weeks this time?*— what she most requires from him. What she knows better than to want or say. To tell him how, with each new separation, she grows ever more frantic to have him up inside her, alive and covered and safe, would rush the day when he goes impotent at the mere sight of her eager need.

She refrains from the impulse to touch his chest, already feeling the obligatory, patterned echo from him. A quick panic fills her here in her own bed, invaded by this *invité*. She must have chosen him for this, singled him out before she knew him. But she *did* know already. Knew his reputation for Dial-a-Nurse. Knew the brutal occupation, the sardonic "Your patient, Doctor." Knew he was the very man who could replay her private nightmare scenario, the repeat foreclosure she seems intent on engineering.

She can ask him for nothing. Any request at all would be fatal for them both. The last thing she wants is confrontation. Just knowing that she dare not ask makes her a slave, sick with the irresistible question. She tries his shoulder, tentatively, feels it tense in feigned relaxation. She slithers in toward his ear. And what form will compulsion take tonight, what surrogate truce? Talk to the boy. Straighten him out, break him of cruelty's bafflement. Take him under your wing. Take care of this helplessness. Give it the protection only you can give.

Or she might speak to him for real. Might unleash at last the whispered accusations against her betrayer in age. This man, so much her senior, a decade: Was that the secret appeal? Old enough to be her grubby little uncle. He lies there across the minefield of acrylic blend, already a casualty in this single-elimination, sudden-death tournament. He lies cross-armed, denying, refusing the explanation she needs from him. She needs him to say, just once, what lies behind the pudgy, glowing, poster faces' pretended innocence. Don't you see why the boy runs manic? The dependent's bewilderment, the dazed, mislaid trust.

She closes the gap and cozies up against him, knowing how much this contact will deplete whatever stockpile of touch he might have left for her. But she needs the thing so much that she will take even sex again in its stead, since he can give nothing else. Friction—attenuating, static, distracting, ridding the minute of old injuries. It is the lesser of two requests. A way to avoid wondering when the private batterings—the cloaked secrecies, violations, and covert hurt-mes—will start again this time.

MORE WRONGS TO redress than there are hours in the day. The only answer, of course, is unflagging industry, the same ceaseless dedication and energy that enabled him, from essentially zero capitalization, to assemble the complete *Riders at the End of Time*, volume 3, numbers 1 through 161. Not that he makes the mistake of trying to pull off this whole scam single-handedly. He allows himself the luxury of delegating authority on labor-intensive matters. He's assigned his corps of engineers the task of building a little lookout nest on the roof next to the chopper pad, from which they hope soon to be launching bottle rockets, currently under development by Chuckie and the brain trust according to proprietary specs of his own design: various supply-closet combustibles set alight in one-liter IV bags.

Okay, everything they've mounted so far is just piddling stuff compared to the major campaign. But he refuses, on grounds of project security, to discuss future operations. Also, he's kind of winging it. Not really sure what he's after himself. The girl Joy seems somehow instrumental to the master plan. He doubles back to her on repeated, suck-up visits, cementing their wary truce with miscalculated small gifts: dried dough he swears will come back to life if soaked, half of a sundered walkie-talkie set, worthless books washed up in the tidal pools of trade, titles only she would read. *Decisive Sieges of the Sixteenth Century,* or *Our Friends on the Pacific Rim.*

"So are you getting any better?"

"I don't know," she answers gravely, unwilling to lie. He kicks at her crutches, toppling her in treachery. She emits a bleat, a "Hail" of surprised pain.

"Sorry. Just conducting a little experiment." She stares at him in incomprehension, a retriever whose hindquarters are crushed under its careless owner's recliner. "Look, I said I'm sorry. Here." He doffs the cap. "Go ahead. Pull my hair. What's left of it, anyway."

She covers her smirk with the back of an autumn-leaf hand. She forgets the pointless cruelty faster than anything can explain. Pain passes from her face without residuals, replaced by another, iodine hurt each time she steals a look at him. Something inside her cells would match his instant age, decade for decade. Something in her is crying, "Little girl, little girl, let go of me."

Sorties with the Stepaneevong female leave Nico's senior lieutenants more than a little nervous. What's the point? How's she gonna help us any? Come on; let's go steal some tubing and make a Comm Device. Or or or: let's say that the third floor is M-31 and the fifth floor is Heliotria. The Cyclogeneron's about 90 percent finished, but we need just one more trigawatt-hour of juice. . . .

But the guy they vie for is worlds away. Sometimes he's morose with preoccupation, and will snap, "Grow up, will you? The hell is this, Peeweeland?"

His crushing rebukes demoralize the upper echelons of Command and Control. The only encouraging spin to Nico's enigmatic insistence on parlay with this foreign element is that the more the two of them talk, the less they seem to need to.

He brings her a plastic soccer ball, half of a cruel carrot-and-stick cure. Astonishingly, she can keep it in the air with just her knees, elbows, head, and shoulders, even while propped up over her leg struts.

"Jeez. Where'd you learn how to do that?" But she cannot talk while the ball is aloft.

And he cannot wait for her to miss, which could be never. "Look," he blusters. "Joyless. They're probably not telling you everything, right?" She executes an especially skillful lob with the inside arch of her good foot. "I mean, you could be Xed off the charts as dead meat already, without even knowing it." If she gives a reply, he's the only one who hears it.

"Okay. So suppose you gotta go down," he postulates, watching her, wagging his head in admiration. She counts softly, out loud, her successive aerial taps, somewhere in the high eighties. "With all due respect, Joyless, I'd like to suggest to you that the only thing worth doing, if that's the case, is to try going down in the record books."

She giggles, and it breaks her concentration. The ball rolls down the hall, and she limps along after it. "I'm not that good," she says, the giggles still softly issuing from her like shy, unsigned, dime preemie valentines. A twinge of conscience nags at her. The books are waiting; she's been remiss. She shouldn't stand here playing all day. "I'm only so-so. Where I come from, they can keep a ball in the air all . . ."

"Not that record. I'm talking something truly grabbing. Totally new project. Wait a minute. Got it. This is a great one. Classic! What we got to do is write TV-25 Action Corps and tell them there's this little Asian girl lavishing in the charity hospital and she probably's not going to make it, and the only thing that keeps her holding on fighting for sweet life is her driving dream to go down in *Guinness* as the recipient of the most get-well cards of all time. What do you say?"

"Languishing."

"Whatever. Come on. They love this kind of pathetic kiddie crap. Capture the regional imagination. Feel-gooder campaign. Courage in the face of keeling over. Vote with your stamps. The whole bullshit waterworks. What d'ya think?"

She smiles like she hasn't yet smiled in this lifetime, and starts the ball up in the air again. Eight, nine, ten, eleven. "Clap your hands," she says suddenly.

"Say what?"

"Clap your hands. Don't let Tink die."

He plays dumb until she explains. That book I lent you? He makes out that he hasn't read it yet. Not enough time. Hospital's been going to serious hell in a handbag, and has been for years before his arrival. Consequently, it takes every hour in his agenda just to stabilize the situation. Reading's a luxury, strictly for those with time to burn.

"KNOW WHAT'S WRONG with this place?" Nicolino declares to a rumpled Linda. The lady is losing it; she looks like she's slept in that cute little physio getup of hers. "I said, 'Know what's wrong . . . ?' You're supposed to say, 'No, Nico. What?' "

"Do I have to? Okay, okay. Tell me what's wrong with this place."

"Everybody's so twigging *sick*. We gotta git outta here before we all go rabid. I've seen it happen. *Trailblazer,* number twenty-three. Whole pioneer colony just ups and goes completely stir crazy with cabin fever. Hey. A ball game. There's yer ticket. How 'bout it, Doll-face? You can swing a Dodger home bill for us?"

" 'Doll-face'? Let me see those comics of yours."

"Ha! You and the Navy SEALs, maybe. Come on. Get that so-called surgeon guy of yours to take us. You two are doing it, aren't you?"

"Doing *what?*"

"Oh, excuse me. I thought you were old enough to know about these things."

"You little *braguillas!*"

To which, he replies in a language she doesn't even want to identify.

"Not that getting you long-termers out of here is such a bad idea. But baseball? Kind of sedate, isn't it? No Amorphicoms? No Grid? No Galactic Heat Death?"

"You only need that shit when nothing's breaking."

"Nico. I'm not going to tell you again."

"Promise? Sor-ry. I meant to say 'that shirt.' "

"How are you going to keep a whole patrol of your contemporaries in one place in the bleachers for nine complete innings?"

"We'll only take the crips. You know; the ones who can't move."

"What a little fiend we are. All right, let's call the so-called surgeon. But I can't believe I'm doing this for you."

Kraft is ready with the subterranean-bunker, I'm-busy-for-the-rest-of-my-life-and-beyond, blanket refusals. "Wrong guy for the wrong job. First off, when am I ever going to have the time to . . . ?"

"You're off next Friday and Saturday," she tells him gently. "I checked the call schedule."

"You did what?" Checked on him, on his reliability. She has been out early, cutting off his lines of retreat. He is suddenly far away, indifferent, invulnerable, slack. Even the deadening silence between them feels luxurious, something one might thrive on.

"It doesn't have to be torture, you know. You might even enjoy it."

"Right. Herding a disease-ridden Halloween parade through an aggressive, beer-swilling, sweltering mass of demi-humanity? Set this group loose on Dodger Stadium? Let them out of the lockup? They'll have committed felonies in a dozen different states by half time."

"Half time?" She snickers, despite the chorus of early warning signals. "Maybe you're right. I do have the wrong guy." The joke settles between them in sad, wide ripples radiating outward in all directions.

He holds her at receiver's distance, fending off the One Good Thing, his near brush with salvation. Wasteful, deliberate, self-inflicted. "I, uh, went to a game once," he tries to blurt out. He would explain how the best course in life consists of avoiding the repeat of certain debilitating early scenarios. But he has lost the cadence of humor. He cannot even bring himself to think of that grandstand debacle, in the company of a father who taught him every survival skill but steals and bunts, everything about the complex international order except for where he belonged in it.

Softly, through the apparatus, Linda offers him redemption. "I'll go with you, if you let me." He wants to tell her she must get away from him, quickly and cleanly. That he has not yet driven her away already incriminates him. He sees it all at once. They will sink into one of those mutual balances of terror, where neither can escape the collateral damage caused by the other's tenderness.

His no, she assumes from his repeated objections, is a yes in other words. Over his increasingly ritualized objections, she books him for the Saturday twin bill against the intensely colorful but eternally hapless Cubbies.

"Pushover opponents. Couple of home victories should at least keep the beer-bottle frag bombs to a minimum."

"Oh, great," he capitulates. "Do I at least get to ogle the cheerleaders?"

"Hopeless. Hopeless." The sliver of good-bye in her voice as she hangs up suggests that she already anticipates all the ways he will abandon her.

Kraft tries to get Plummer to sub for him. Carver's emergency Lesionnaire is holing up in the residents' bathroom, perched in front of the urinals. As he tucks himself back into his khaki scrubs, he sings, "Nothing could be finer than to be in some vaginer in the morning."

"Very nice, Thomas. You compose that one all by yourself?"

"You kidding? Do I look like a genius?"

"At the moment, no."

"Such gems are not 'composed.' They erupt from a thousand simultaneous springs at the right moment. Overnight, they become part of the English-speaking heritage."

"Speaking of which. Know anything about baseball?" He lays out the request. "I'll cover ER for you."

"Do I get the girl thrown in too?"

"The girl? Oh God." Wouldn't that be a massacre. "Come on, Thomas. I thought you were onto Nurse Spiegel these days."

"Ancient history. Chalk her off. Confirmed kill. Notch on the old barrel. I thought I explained this to you already, buddy: I plan to follow you around, nibbling on your undigested scraps. You're my mentor, man. I mean, if you want to talk natural genius . . ."

The world, as is widely known, is divided into two sorts of

people. Exactly what those two sorts are is a matter of continuous speculation. No matter; wherever the division, Plummer falls into neither camp. He is beyond good and evil, freedom and dignity, sorrow and pity—in short, the perfect surgeon-in-training.

Which Kraft is not, as witnessed by the fact that as he enters the park, climbs into the funneled sunlight surrounded by a home crowd of 55,878 who lose themselves in an excitement as synesthetic as it is random, he feels inexplicably good. He and Linda shepherd a dozen kids, or rather, the kids suffer the pretense of authority as they break for the open air. The youngest of the group is a heavily urban-matured eight years old. The oldest—well, the oldest has been dead for decades.

Chuck, head now wrapped up tighter than the Mummy's, sports a batter's helmet several sizes too big for him, thereby succeeding in obscuring the bulk of his face. Joleene has been temporarily persuaded to swap the Chatty Cathy for a stuffed outfielder totem. "So that's what a Dodger is," Kraft murmurs to Linda; "I was wondering." The girl pulls incessantly at the mute thing's neck threads, threatening to yank its head off.

The Fiddler Crab cracks jokes about a left hand like his not needing a mitt. Ali, a recent admittance with a plate-sized creature in his gut, who's learned to tell everybody he comes from Persia so he won't get beaten up, nasals, "Play ball, play ball!" like some muezzin up in a box-seat minaret. The Hernandez brothers keep looking around nervously, afraid they're going to bump into one of their prehospital business associates. A mute, cotton-wadded Rapparition—shouldn't even be out of bed yet—scribbles his alexandrines down on the insides of a popcorn box and passes them for public enunciation to Kyle, whose larynx is about the last part of him still functioning.

Nicolino acquires a program through judicious swapping of a rare *Captain America* back issue. He alternates between kicking verbal lime on the leather uppers of the collective umpiring staff and making arcane marks on the scorecard, improving on the already Byzantine official scoring system. He attempts to fix forever in recorded memory the whole game down to the trajectory of every foul ball and the bleacher location of each lucky scab who snagged one.

He keeps up a running statistician's patter. When the good guys' three-for-three hitters come up, he yells out, "All right, he's hot, he's hot." For the oh-for-three guys, this becomes, "All right, he's due, he's due." The folks in the nearby seats, after their initial, shocked whiplash, go out of their way to not give the senescent heckler a second look.

Joy sits between Kraft and Linda, an aluminum half-brace leaned up on each of her idols' knees. She studies the game furiously for its meaning, waiting, as late as the seventh-inning stretch, for things to begin. She asks in a constant but decorous undertone for help toward a hermeneutics, and when Kraft doesn't know the answer to her question he makes something up. He makes up a lot.

"Dr. Kraft, how many teams are there?"

"Two." He steals a look at Linda. "Two, right?"

"Well, what about those black men?"

"Black— Oh, in the black suits, you mean. Well, they switch back and forth, depending on who's winning. Evens things up."

"And those? The white suits?"

"Those? They're beer sellers. Not official protagonists, as far as I know."

He is nervous next to the girl, jumpy, edgier than the terrain's bad associations can account for. He can feel Linda giving him the professional second-guess, and she's right. How's he supposed to explicate this, to tell her? You see, I've this growing proof, well, not proof, this conviction, okay, suspicion, hunch . . . These kids, this service, this pede tour of duty: they are—what are they? *Consolidating*. Converging on him. And everything depends upon his finding out why. What they are after. Where they are headed.

In between Joy's questions—"Why do they put that man in the middle up on that little hill? How many points does the little boy get for picking up the discarded sticks?"—he slips in a few cross-examinations of his own. He asks her if she remembers anything at all about her old home, the village, the river basin she was driven from.

"A little. My mother's twig broom. Our dog, with only one eye. The market. The smell of certain fruit. Dr. Kraft, how come they all have those big lumps on the side of their mouths?"

"Right. Those are plugs of chewing tobacco. You win if you can spit yours over one of those '330' signs while nobody's looking. The smell of fruit," he prompts her. "Durian? Mangosteen? *Luk ngoh?*"

She pulls her eyes from the all-fascinating field and stares at him. He receives it full in the face, this awful, searching look that would conceal itself even while flagging down the impossible rescue. It shoots out at him, both oblique and dead on, a summons and a bolt. How much do you know? And in the next instant, she relaxes. Not enough to worry about. Nothing of the atrocity's specifics, no real hold on the nightmare locale. Harmless superficials, she decides, because her look goes congenial, her ready-to-run bite loosens into a smile. "You ate a durian once?"

"Many." And to prove it, he does an imitation, reasonably good, given the intervening years, of a street vendor's call. The peanut peddlers flash him a dirty look: What's yer racket, jerk-off? A couple of militantly fecund families at the end of the row overcome their good breeding long enough to stare at the motley child band and their howling leader. No, Kraft decides, listening to his residual, perfectly pitched cries drift down to the nearer bullpen. It is too far, too incommensurate, too implausibly split. The gap between here and there will kill him just to gaze out over.

Linda practically falls out of her wooden folding slats. "Where in the world did that come from?"

How is he supposed to tell her? *From a place called Angel City, Land of the Free.*

Joy examines him again, fear creeping back into her instruments. "Say that again, please, Dr. Kraft." He repeats his strophe of fruit names, softly now, so as not to violate the national pastime. Then, in a tonal dialect he can almost understand, she says, "That is almost what we call them."

They must step no nearer. They already wander too near the shared, partitioned province. Neither wants to come any closer to where their paths cross, the tangents to earlier extraditions. Suddenly, it's all baseball between them, furious Twenty Questions about runs, hits, errors, pick offs, sign stealings—the whole semiotic flood. They scatter from any suggestion of common childhood geography, the one from guilt, the other shame. They backpedal from overlap like a fielder badly misjudging a deep fly to center.

"Can they both win?" she frets out loud.

"Uh, Linda?"

"Well, in a word, no."

"No?" Kraft echoes. "There's your answer, then. Peculiarly American, wouldn't you say? Better to fight on forever than to tie, apparently."

Joy smiles at the diction, his goofing for her benefit. This man will never be capable of wrong, no matter what he might choose to do. He is the one adult on earth who does not talk down to her. She takes his hand, a gesture universally understood among old fellow durian eaters. "How long does one game last?"

"Easy one. Until it's over. Kind of a nineteenth-century, determinist thing."

"Where's the Mighty Casey?"

Bits of Cracker Jack explode from both choking adults. The girl is devastated by her gaffe. She clearly has no idea what she's said. The recitation, out of one of her pauperized school district's obsolete, nineteenth-century, determinist texts that she has blindly committed to memory, could mean anything to her, passed through the filters of continuous dislocation. Mighty Casey as position name, like shortstop or first base? Mighty Casey as deciding machinery, deus ex apparatus rolled to the plate at the all-important juncture? Honorary title, rank, life achievement? In any event, to her, as essential to each staging of the genre as a sailor to the epic or a floozy to the lawsuit.

"Dr. Kraft, I don't understand this stupid game." This soul that did not flinch when the ER physician shattered her ankle, that awoke from the agony of excision to write the surgeon a thank-you note, now begins soundlessly to cry. A hundred ministrations and apologies from Kraft and Linda cannot convince her that she's done no wrong.

"I don't understand it either," he says, taking her hand back after she wiggles it free. "It's apparently some kind of ritual drama," he explains to her. "National salve. Expectation. History, allegory, fable, dream." He could be bluffing his way through the Chief's latest unread book assignment, those opaque, impenetrable predictions of the upheavals and reverses in store as we go guttering into the dark.

"It's a twigging ball game," Nico yells through a megaphone he has made of his rolled-up scorecard. "What the hell are you guys blathering about?" Now how did he hear them, above this crowd, from the other end of this screaming murderers' row?

The boy is taking his own emotional plunge, as a result of the Dodgers' deliberate, malicious betrayal. "Pitiful," he says, shaking his balding braincase, hiding it in his hands. "These guys couldn't reach base on an error even if they'd publicly promised homers to a dozen dying kids." The Hernandez brothers emit wicked, appreciative snorts in stereo. In fact, the local boys give it their best but go down twice in splendid paralysis to the normally hapless Second City conscripts, who this day look like world beaters.

Everybody is pretty bummed, but fandom's remorse cannot completely doom this day of reprieve and freedom. Kyle, who has brought along his Walkman, keeps repeating for the others, in astonished tones, "The kids from Carver are here today," exactly the way the beery announcer said it, between rollcall mentions of Rotary chapters and nursing home brigade minuses. The Hernandez brothers light out for the territory on the way back to the bus, but Kraft is still fit enough to chase down and snag their lazy, city-vitiated pop-foul arc across the parking lot.

He sees the girl board the bus and tries to help her up the awkward steps. He is mortified when she shrugs him off. She swings along determinedly, keeping up an impressive clip down the constricted aisle. She sheds the struts in the back of the bus and lowers herself into the seat behind the two old-timers with the L.A. caps pulled down over their wasted beaks.

" 'There is no joy in Mudville,' " Joy recites in ingenue singsong for no one, the words she once performed in front of a now-forgotten class, on a twin bill with the Gettysburg Address.

"Shut yer face," Nico manages.

"Please," Chuck adds.

Kraft pulls Linda down into the seat next to him, before she can slip away to join the children. He holds her hand, ribboning the fingers of the nearest girl, the only available one. He whispers to her what he's just seen—the small-arms exchange of first flirtation. Linda steals a look over one shoulder to see this stabbing thing for herself. But all she can make out is the boys in the back, already scheming the details of the next expedition.

WHEN THE NEXT one is launched, it's the last thing in the world any adult could have anticipated. Weeks of dilated child life pass; years click off Nico's accelerated body clock. That is to say a day, maybe a day and a half, real time. Nico shows up at his next scheduled Doll-face session and demands, "You gotta teach us to dance."

"Dance! You mean—?"

"What do you think I mean?" He is surly with compromise. "Dancing. Dancing. You've heard the word, haven't you? 'Blue Danube.' Shake yer bootie. Get up and get down. What do you want from me?"

"Is this a dare? Somebody's put you up to this."

"Nobody puts me up to nothing."

"Okay, all right. Calm down. Just tell me how in the world you came up with . . ."

"I don't know," he says, as preoccupied as she's ever seen him. He takes off the ball cap and runs a hand over his parchment-papered crown. The gesture is perfect, something he must have seen bald men do in some ancient cartoon. "I just have this . . . feeling we gotta learn some steps. That we'll need it if . . ."

"If what? Who's we?"

He tenses his gray temples and grits those teeth that have not yet fallen out. "The girls'll be thrilled to their ditsy little anklets. And the guys will do it and like it."

Why not? A group movement lesson is just one two-step away from her own therapies. She gets away with half her rehabilitating sashays only because the hardened, proto-criminal street toughs, in their sick and wounded conditions, can't believe she comes from this planet. But even she would never dare suggest something like this without Nico's bankrolling.

Beyond all credibility, he gets his minions to turn out for a class in the Virginia reel. Clumsy, hulking, umber gang members barrel down the chute of the longways set like bombs pouring out of a carpeting bay. She gives them folk weaves and figure eights, kicks and turns that aren't "too femmy," keeping bodily contact to a fleeting minimum. She rolls out all sorts of pieces— Hopi, Mexican, Ashanti. Best are the enchaînements and positional formations that even the crutches and wheelchairs can roll through.

They rapidly outpace Linda's passing competence. The best of them *began* beyond her. The Rapparition, recovering, concocts this elaborate triple-level, supersyncopated, free-falling gymnastic routine like nothing Espera has ever seen a body do. Its nearest living relatives are those dim, almost-forgotten jumprope choreographies, the bastard inheritances of her confused, crosstown shuffle-up. Double Dutch, Double Irishes, Red-hot Peppers, here mutated, further displaced until nothing but the skipping fear, the shaky shake breakdown is still recognizable.

Last night, night before,
Twenty-four robbers at my door . . .
I was born in a frying pan;

Can you guess how old I am . . . ?
Little Miss P, dressed in blue,
Died last night at quarter of two.
'Fore she died, told me this:
You better run or you gonna get hit. . . .
Call the doctor, call the nurse.
Call the lady with the alligator purse. . . .

Grandpa, Grandma, you ain't sick. All you gotta do is the Sea-side Six.

Everything she can give them is not enough. Not anywhere near what they need. Nico comes to her after a workout, vaguely distressed. "Hey, you're okay and all. But we gotta call in the pros."

She phones around, she herself now suckered into believing lessons to be necessary for their collective next step. The last of her calls is to the one she's been avoiding by mutual consent these however many generations. "Want to take a girl out dancing?"

Dancing? Girl? Capillary action works its sap into Kraft, un-welcome but irresistible. Bits of his skin crinkle like new clothes at the sound of her invitation. Take a girl dancing: template words that elicit images all over the cortex map. They promise the long-abandoned hope of heart-stopping prom night. Rustles of sweet silk delay, even here, the abrasive apotheosis of the land of instant gratification, where the pinnacle of sexiness is to lightly goose the twin cams at every stoplight, blasé behind double-polarizing wraparounds, blister-packed into phosphorescent sweats inscribed all over with slogans and retail insignia. (Why, Kraft has won-dered since coming to this state, must one pay double for the kind of legible ads that they used to hire sandwich-board men to peddle?)

But: take a girl dancing. A girl, she says, offering up to him the regressive, politically objectionable term as decadent conces-sion, crepe wrapped, shameless for an evening. Who would have thought a night of dance-floor romance was still possible, here, of all the world's sprawls? Who would have suspected there were dance floors left anywhere in these hundred and thirty incorporated hacienda nightmares, slipped in somewhere along the split fault-lip, wedged between the million-dollar, ranch-house historical destinies of capitalist revengineers and the *noir*-punk, cut-you-for-fucking-me-over disinherited who drift through downtown in a state of perpetual pre-aftermath?

But take a girl dancing. Yes. Oh yes; anywhere you lead. Yes, even the—*where?*—Pasadena Women's Club. Well, so be it, if that's the last bastion of fox-trot in this fifteen-million-souled nation flying point for westward expansion's cliff-dive into the Pacific.

Come Beginners' Night, Kraft hops behind the wheel and lets the vehicle do its thing. He's come to use the car more or less like a laser-guided toilet seat these days. Just slide in, snap down, plug into the man-machine interface, think the coordinates, and watch them come up like magic on the old plasma display pasted over the former windshield. Worktime playtime mealtime snacktime anytime. Sometimes he just likes to corkscrew up and down the parking garage ramp for relaxation. Last week he drove around the corporate limits for a good hour or two, trying to find a place to drop off his empties for recycling.

He pulls into the Women's Club parking lot with five minutes to spare before the departure of the first batch of box-steppers. He's got his best shoes on. They're oiled up and ready for anything short of jitterbugging.

She's waiting for him, swaying softly to herself on the steps. O beautiful for spacious! She's wearing the lightest conceivable summer cotton dress, embroidered all over in magenta and cyan mythical foliage, a weightless drape that hugs her perfect hips, clinging up and down her like a train of little-boy puppy-lovers on market day in some fairy fiesta town from the southerly extremes of magic realist fiction. This woman is half from another, completely foreign *country*. What does he know about her, about any alien land, let alone his own?

He rests his hands on her cottoned waist, too ephemerally thin. She curls like desert vegetation, the feathered tip of a talipot palm in bloom. What must he do—light a candle, leave a handwritten *gracias recibido* to the little unwed mother of God, cast a bit of homemade ceramic to hang by the altar in the shape of the revitalized part? She kisses him, takes him by the elbow and leads him inside, where he pays his two-fifty and she shows her receipt. They enter the meeting-turned-dance-hall, and before he can register, turn, and run, they ambush him. *Dr. Kraft. Dr. Kraft. We knew you would come.*

It's most of the baseball consortium, plus a new cadre of recruits. Some of the tenderfeet, to put it bluntly, will do no dancing tonight. A few are beyond motor maneuvering, beyond torso control at all. Ben, for one, a case Kraft helped on, is beyond a lower torso altogether. But each is grim and determined, demanding lessons to prepare them for some unspecified ballroom showdown.

"We had a spot of trouble at the door, let me tell you," Linda tells him. "Soon as they saw us coming up the walk, they were going to call the police for one of those discreet little arrests, like they slap on folks who heckle the president while he's addressing the Junior Chamber of Commerce?"

She's racing, trying to forestall his mouth from spilling its cries of treachery. "If they could have arrested a dozen kids without attracting attention, they would have. Tried to shag us off, but this is Beginners' Night. There's no other time we could come, and I paid full price for everybody, and isn't it illegal to discriminate by age? Huh? Somewhere?" Linda tugs at his sleeve while lovingly grinding his toe beneath hers. Isn't it, you cradle robber? She cops a feel, smiling like she hasn't had so much fun since college, t.p.-ing the rival sorority house.

The dancing teacher, redder than Moira Shearer's pumps, and her Korean step-modeling partner are both still in the throes of major-league embarrassment at the army of child cripples who have come for the Arthur Murray treatment. Teacher opens with one of those effusively flustered protests of liberal tolerance.

"As I'm sure you've noticed, we have a number of little visitors tonight. . . ." Place is at least packed, which reduces the vulnerability. "And *everyone,* as always, is very welcome. So will all those who want to dance and who need partners form two lines and pair off." Then to the portable tape player, where the first of tonight's soundtracks lies in wait.

And the first song? A great big American lunar crooner, Bingle or Johnny Fontane, sliding around on "Stalag by Starlight." She plays it to accompany the somber, stricken threading together of the two partner-seeking lines. Kraft, still stunned by the subterfuge, falls into line behind the last male. He watches the mating gears mesh—man in eye patch falling to woman with Parkinson's, man with heavy loop of keys hanging from his belt going to tiny, terrified Filipina who came to dance class seeking the one social activity in this newfound land that she thought would require no English.

He notices how the kids have rigged the line, counting off furiously in tandem, then weaseling into position so as to draw each other as opposites, the lesser of available humiliations. Yeah, it's starting to come back to him. All that lunch-line, recess, sports-field, field-trip, bus-stop practice in positional long division. Numbering backward by fours. Converting hours to the final bell into minutes and seconds and heartbeats. Turning margin inches into inch-and-a-quarters. Figuring necessary goals or runs per period, minimum final exam scores for a passing GPA. Around-the-world flash card drills—the countless calculations of departure. How many miles to Babylon?

All but the most incapacitated join in, grab a partner, spread themselves dubiously across the makeshift dance floor. Joy, who could limp through the calls better than a few of those who grimly but gamely take part, sits out the first set. She takes a seat next to the carved-up Ben, where they whisper and giggle to each other behind cupped hands, pointing out mismatches and clunky practice turns. Across the improvised ballroom, like munchkin cadres infiltrating the Emerald City *Residenz,* the urban disinherited prepare to stage a naturalist production of *Rosenkavalier*.

Something more than fear of Nico's wrath compels them, although a few well-timed glares from the boss do their bit to keep the ranks in file. The dance-capable among them pair off with a minimum of foot dragging, with only the Rapparition being dealt to an adult, a blue-rinsed lady in snugly tummy-tucking sequins, completely dazed by the consort that fate's conga line has assigned her tonight.

Kraft reaches the head of the snaking cue, only then discovering that another once-child has remembered the lingering, line-rigging trick of early education. "Hi there, hunk," Linda baits him, taking him by the stethoscope skitcher and hauling him to a corner up near the stage, where they can get a good view of the terpsichorean demo just now getting under way.

God knows how these folks justify billing festivities as Beginners' Night. The pedagogical Ginger, outfitted with a wireless throat mike, begins by chirping, "You all remember last week when we learned . . ." Well, Kraft doesn't remember last week. He has trouble remembering this afternoon. And trying to isolate the beautiful, liquid steps that she and her Asian Astaire float upon is like trying to parse flowing Arabic script. "Come on, Ahab," Linda implores him. "Shake a leg."

It's either that or become a spectacle, gawked at, even shown up by the same shabby underage irregulars he himself sewed together. You all remember the fox-trot, don't you? The bit from last week? The pogo stick, the frug? Teacher sets the tape machine turning again, heads sensing, speakers singing out a simulation of "Night and Day," a tune that dispels the nonballroom world, consigns its latest flash points to somnambulist thrashings. The song, the woman swaying gently up against him, the kids stumbling through instructed motions on all sides, the pathetic Women's Club two-hundred-watt spot standing in for a harvest moon seduce him, like the beat beat beat of the tom-tom. Okay, let's have at it then. Hum a few bars and I'll fake it.

The songs queue up in what quickly becomes a full-color his-

torical atlas of the dance academy at large. The complete curriculum, fiendishly arranged to lead them from fox-trot to tango
to don't-mean-a-thing-if-you-ain't-got-that-swing. A step for
everything, and *everything* its step. They dance to "Blue Skies,"
to "Stormy Weather," to "Misty," to "Paper Moon," to "April
Showers," to "I Can See Clearly Now (the Rain Has Gone)." Oh,
how they dance to "The Anniversary Waltz." They samba their
way through show numbers of those good, God-fearing, nativer-
than-thous, Friml and Romberg. They do these mongrel North
American polkas to tunes half Protestant hymnody, half "The
Yellow Rose of Texas."

They do a slogging "Tramp, Tramp, Tramp," a passel of barn
dances, a reconditioned "Foggy Mountain Breakdown," a "When
the Saints" packed with imminent expectation, and a resigned
boxcar deportation of "Hobo's Blues." As a hat-tip to the Mother
Country, they get a buttered-up rumba version of that pseudo-
franglaised Fab Four hit (one of Kraft's least favorite of his childhood's Top Forty). This being the Unided Snakes, the tape bears
a fair share of ballistics motif, from "Fired Our Guns (but Those
Whoosits Kept A-Comin')" to "Pistol Packin' Mama." Kraft
watches his recent small-caliber facial-trauma cases prancing to
"Put it down before you hurt someone."

They do wild shimmy-Charlestons not approved by any tango-
tea ever sponsored by the Official Board of Ballroom Dancing.
Their steps whisper of suppressed or denied covert influences—
Iberian, Cuban, black, black, black. Alongside the handgun hop,
they do the walkaway, the stamp-and-go shanty, the old Chisolm
trailblaze. We're homeward bound, I hear them say. Good-bye,
fare you well, good-bye, fare you well. We are coming, Father
Abraham, three hundred thousand more.

When they can't quite control the proper heel-toe, they make
up a sequence of their own. It hobbles Kraft to see, peripherally,
just what naturals they are. Teacher goes around the room privately tutoring each clinch. That's it; you've got it. And out . . .
two . . . three-and-now-sweep-*through,* two . . . three-and-come-

back-home, two . . . Some of the band are more than competent. Even good. And only the periodic "Get off my bloody foot, you *Homo sapiens;* your epidermis is showing" betrays the fact that tonight's class is packed to breaking with third-age quarter-sized fifth columnists.

The regulars—who are these people? If they come, as their packaging advertises, from the right side of the tracks, they are still living testimony that even the better berm is everywhere shard-strewn. The twosome just tangent to Linda's twirl exchange bios. She is a thrice-singled mother whose last husband has recently kidnapped her youngest girl and disappeared into the invisible consumer ratlands between Sherman Oaks and Van Nuys. Her dancing companion for this first set has recently been convicted of drunken driving manslaughter and sentenced to pay the parents of the victim a dollar a month for each of the eighteen years of the victim's life.

Everyone: Arabs in black glasses, would-be aerobiots with legs like stovepipes, homeowners destined for a hotel death, *mestizos* of every conceivable blood-cocktail concoction, timid souls who've done time in the self's prison for removing manufacturers' stickers from mattresses. A powerfully built man, Karok or Modoc or Yurok, turns the prescribed box step into a sad stenographer's account of the ghost dance, shuffling, dragging left foot, humming *hu-hu-hu* in hope of a return to aboriginal safety away from this place where promise and threat both push to breakpoint.

Across the crowded hall, Kraft thinks he sees Dr. Burgess thumping away obediently at the lesson assignment. Now how the hell? Here? This? Repeated stolen cowering looks, and Kraft still can't decide whether it's really the Chief or somebody else borrowing the man's body, taking the hackysack of digesting flesh out for an evening spin while Burgess himself stays home reading Dead White Male Classics.

The density of the dance floor, the sampler of tunes listing out of the cheap speakers—a checklist history of the country's sins as rich as a Puritan's embroidered alphabet—the golf shirts, the Mary Richards toreador pants, the endangered species shoes all shuffle-ball-changing for whatever the moves might still be worth wring Kraft's ribs, pound him, pump on him like scouts on a CPR dummy. Pathetic, pitiful, insistent, begging for scraps of social club love, each mass that he narrowly maneuvers past, the colostomy bags, the mastectomy implants, the bungled tummy tucks all but rubbing up against him, ravish his chest and lay him open.

Linda laughs, forced to step on his gunboats to keep them from keelhauling her. "Whoa there. Get along, little doggies. Left. *Left.* Right hand over your heart. Yes, even when you're facing south."

All he can do is hold this woman tighter to him, follow her as if she were his advance probe through this explosive field. This woman, who thought it productive to haul half the ambulatory pede ward here, and a third of the inerts. This girl, a tube of selflessness running through her as unfillable as those empty Torricellian columns pleading for the United Way. Teacher comes by to try to straighten out his ambling shambles. Yeah, smack in the middle of "Stompin' at the Savoy," the entire junior element stops in its tracks to enjoy a good yuck at his expense.

At break, as their carrion flock swoops down and devours the entire folding-table spread of Tang and spritz cookies before the forty-plussers can even get close, Kraft asks Linder, "Time to call it a night?"

"What, are you crazy? We haven't learned the lindy hop yet."
A four-foot person of color at Kraft's elbow mutters,

"So *these* the moves that the White Ruling Nation
Take to when they do their White Station gyration.
Lindy hop don't put *me* no closer to elation."

The Rapparition's companion from the first set, grown fond of the poet, his street metric—although she can't understand a word of it—apparently taking her back to her glory days as

Marie Louise's governess, embarks on matching him recitation for recitation. "Blake's 'Little Boy Lost,' " she says, in a spectral whippoorwill. " 'The mire was deep and the child did weep and away the vapor flew.' 'Little Girl Lost,' from *Songs of Experience.* 'Children of the future age, reading this indignant page, know that in a former time . . .' " Limbs as frail and thin as an ultra-fine pen point on onionskin reach down to take the Rapparition's hand, and he low-fives her.

Just as these two impossibly inimical hues slap startlingly together, the four Mills Brothers break out of nowhere. You're nobody. Till somebody. Loves you. It's a call to fall in, line up for new partners. A song, a performance in debt to every indigenous ditty ever tried out in these parts.

In quick planar section, Kraft takes in the whole converted hall at once. The guy with the huge loop of keys; the frightened Pacific woman, *Kon Tiki* on the return leg; the drunk driver carrying his unbearable penance; the mud-masqueing, ion-corrected, thirtyish professionals in their air-cushion shoes; the Parkinson's patient holding one shaking claw in the other; the vet trying to hide the fact; the off-duty cops and their split-shift robber opposition; the movers and movees and shakers and shook; longshoremen and short shrifters; palefaces and redskins; the old folks at home; the fast crowd that stomped at the wood-pile a half century before, here tonight only pretending to be beginners all over again: too much for him. How can he live? This place, this heartbreaking, magnificent, annihilating, imperialist, insecure, conscience-stricken, anarcho-puritanical, smart-bombing, sheet-tinned, Monroe Doctrined place . . . The searing, seductive, all-palliating, caramel curative of the been-through-the-Mills Brothers (sure, who else? you always hurt the ones you love) do their patented, slowed-down, lip-simulated, bastard-son-of-Dixieland instrumental interlude, returning only to insist that you're nobody. Till somebody. Cares.

Come on, join in, kick up your heels. "OK, ladies and gents. Are you ready for more of what you came here for?" Kraft, ter-

rified at the prospect of going back through the unforgiving
partnering line, swings around looking for Linda. His escort protection has wandered off to visit Joy and Ben, demonstrating, up
close and contagious, all the subtle foot movements that those
on the sidelines are missing. Kraft comes over to snare her for
the next round. As Linda laughs good-bye to the two wallflow-
ers, Ben calls out something to her. What? Anything, nothing.
Nobody till somebody. You look great out there. I like this tune.
Enjoy yourself! I'm glad I'm around to watch. Can you get my
cost of admission back?

Kraft loses the message in the general hilarity of regrouping.
Whatever Ben says, it stops the woman, bruises her, knocks the
breath from her plexus. Espera turns, fighting with her lip, twists
from Kraft's grip, and runs back to pick the boy up. She lifts him
up bodily, the upper half remaining of him anyway, the brutal
living stump, pruned back to nothing, to the nib, the stubborn
nub, the germ. Flushed with pleasure, Ben breaks into a shamed-
puppy grin. The band box strikes up a sleek, sexy "Satin Doll,"
and Linda, in perfect time with the teacher's "Ad-vance, and
together, and glide, and back," travels across the parquet for both
of them.

The Cheese stands alone. Or not alone; worse. Kraft stands
five feet away from the one soul whose presence most upset him
on arrival, the one girl he would avoid with all the power of a
pubescent crush. He can feel Joy appraising him from her seat in
the empty chairs pushed against the wall. Her silence is articulate,
more oppressive than ever. He hears himself, how he might yet
have to tell her, to administer her hero worship a lethal injection. How he has perhaps wrecked her, killed her, or worse. Your
ankle—I . . . The incursion could spread. All the way up your leg,
beyond. She stares passively at him, already knowing everything.

He half-steps over to her, and he must tell her now. You tell me
your dream, and I'll . . . Tell her the odds against her. Tell her what
she will never live to hear any adult male tell her. Tell her in that
almost common language she can half-understand and he, despite

an adulthood of effort, cannot more than half-forget. He takes
her by the hand, hers held out for his before he even extends. She
looks at him, adoring, waiting politely. Dr. Kraft? Looking away,
he asks, in his child's Thai dialect, "Care for a spin?"

BUT SHE BELONGS to someone else. The dancing expedition does
little to placate Nicolino or stave off the next maniacal enterprise.
He begs broken parts from the tech equipment jockeys, and he
and the inner circle set to work on a Wellsian apparatus whose
function they refuse to disclose. He institutes a strict regimen of
daily exercise, combat-readiness stuff. He casts about frantically
to answer the summons nagging at him.

The thing, the revelation, is so close that he goes gradually
bananas with the jitters. It looks, from the outside, like a burst
of senile activity. From the inside, he is cranked up worse than
a teen, a year before the flood of gonadotrophin that might account for it.

"Son of a Bisquick. This place is *so, mind-alteringly,* boring. We
gotta get something going. Quick. While it's still possible."

He sits splayed under a pull-up bedside table, scribbling furious letters abroad, guarding the texts with a sheltering arm. He
struggles with the pen-driven alphabet the way a first-year French
horn player might fight through the valved scale. Certain of his
letters get sealed TOP SECRET. Others he actually mails, Linda
picking up the postage.

One of those pathetic local television news-drink-spread shows
picks up on the story Nicolino feeds it. "There's a little girl lying
in Carver Hospital tonight who hasn't been on our shores for very
long. But even where she comes from, they know what get-well
cards are. Her name is Joy, and nothing would bring this Joy more
of the same than to go down in the record books as the greatest
recipient of . . ."

They send out a camera team fronted by a snitty little media
witch who tries not to touch anything in the children's ward except during those few seconds when the take goes "live." Then,

in front of the opened lens, she rests her hands affectionately on Joy's passive head. Pulling away as soon as the cameras stop, the newscaster checks her palms for shed hanks "My God," she whispers audibly to her crew, as if discovering rat feces in the coils of her electric range. "It's hair-loss city in here."

No sooner does the story run than the cards begin to pour in. Surreal get-well wishes from a sick world. Wishes in eleven languages, including her own, plus all manner of grammarless dialects. Some with no words at all, just pictures, little Crayola comic strips purporting to relate her own story back to her, tracing a narrow escape from murderous nondemocratic forces all the way to ultimate techno-cure and consignment to happy, waiting ranch family. Boutique-bought three-dollar cards with no signature. Mass-mailed photocopies. Delicate, church-circle, hand-maid handmades. Sympathy and condolence scrawled on the backs of cold-tablet packets. Long, rambling teeny-tiny-print letters about the loss of daughters to the same, never-mentioned disease. About daughters who are not their real daughters, about real ones swapped or disguised or hidden. Real daughters who think they are adopted. Adopteds, abandoneds, who never in a million years suspected. Mothers who are sure Joy is theirs.

Nico sits on the foot of her bed as the crates of communiqués pour in. He demands first dibs, as if the cards are really his and he has just been forced to use Stepaneevong because she's convenient. He devours the cartoons and drawings, passing them on with a low chuckle of having pulled a fast one. The hard letters, from the crackpot adults, he makes her read to him. Then the two of them set up a routing system whereby the bushels of mail are passed around for public consumption before they are turned back in for official record-book tallying. At least it's something to do.

But it's morbid, and it only serves to feed the ward's dancing mania. Each get-well is an acupuncturing coffin pin, rotated and tweaked in the suppurating wound until the subjects feel nothing except bewilderment at being held here against their will.

Aware of the risk, Linda shows up at bedside one afternoon

while an on-duty card-reading shift plows bleakly through the day's mail, no longer even grinning. "What do you say to a little amateur theatrics?" she says, to no one in particular.

No one responds, until Joy stares openly at the tyrant who has taken control of operations.

"You mean, like a play?" Nico asks. "Make me heave, why don't you? Like, little froufrou costumes and makeup and that? Of all the infantile . . ."

She is ready for him. "Bunny hopping at the Pasadena Women's Club?"

"That's different. That was . . . preparation." Even in midsentence, you can see him realize that this stray message brought by unwitting courier is preparation too. Exactly the thing he's been after. "What do you got?"

Linda removes from its hiding place in her pouch the old anthology, *A Country a Day for a Year,* the promised term of time now an impossible luxury. Nico emits a groan, beyond repugnance.

" 'The Goose-Child.' "

"Wrench my neck."

" 'The Wolf-Child.' 'The Lizard-Child.' "

"Three strikes. Blow off this animal kingdom thing."

" 'Jam on Jerry's Rock.' "

"Pardon me?"

"That's the name. 'Jam on . . .' "

Nico voices a loud fart, followed by universal oos of disgust. But Linda knows she has them now.

" 'Aladdin.' 'Sinbad.' 'The Magic Caldron.' 'Trickster Plays the False Bridegroom.' 'Hanuman's Burning Tail.' 'The Borrowed Feathers.' 'The Magnetic Islands.' "

"Oh, sure, right. I'm not dressing up as anything smaller than a minor landmass."

" 'The Three Golden Sons.' 'The Seven-League Boots.' 'The Frog That Made Milk.' "

"I *said,* bag the animals already."

" 'Beezaholi and the Cyclogeneron'?" a frightened voice from among the backbenchers suggests.

"Sure," Linda says. "Why not? Couple of diodes, some tinfoil . . ."

"No friggin' way. José. Full stop. Keep reading."

Linda sighs, a languorous Lillie Langtry, and returns to the table of contents. " 'The Wati Kutjara.' 'The Fake Beauty Doctor.' 'The Stone Eskimo Child.' 'The Mayor of . . .' "

Joy twists acrobatically under Linda's arm, her weight on her knuckles, as supple as a crippled beggar. Her fingers slide down the list of potential scripts at twice the speed that the false mother can pronounce them out loud. She sieves through the titles, moving her lips silently, looking for one in particular. When she finds it, as she never doubted she would, she calls it out in foregone-conclusion monotone, for the first and last time in her life interrupting another human being.

It is that spooky name, the old familiar, the last tale Linda would have thought children of this city would sit through, let alone dress up and perform this late in time's day. But the effect on Nicolino, and by association his entranced clan of republican guard, is enough to goose her flesh. "Lemme see that. Gimme that book."

He flips to the story in question and assaults it with the viciousness of the functionally illiterate. Here it is. The point of all the endless, agitated prep. The explanation, the need for dancing lessons. "Okay," he decides with producer's finality, "this is the story we're doing. You direct. We double-cast all us gimps to play both sets of teaming masses." Now: where're we going to find four dozen rat suits, a high dive, and a pipe?

How does this one go again? The ubiquitous, uninvited out-of-towner shows up on the city outskirts one morning to make a comprehensive survey. Comparing the checklists of the real against the ideal upward spiral, he concludes to himself with masterful, mumbled understatement, "Serious infrastructure problems here.

"Bad shape," he elaborates, a pleasant euphemism. One quick spin around the city-wall circuit confirms the obvious. From any perimeter tower, anyone paying attention can make out the state of affairs. Were the problem just cosmetic, it would already be unsolvable: the house plaster going shabby, the shoddy half-timbering rotting no sooner than it is rigged together. The open sewers back up into putrid pools, exceeding all stopgap attempts to sluice off the stinking sludge. The slum quarter spreads like desert into the heart of town, but the vitiated commercial sector cannot afford to pull the sinkhole down and do the required rebuilding.

The glittering Rathaus is a mammoth travesty, its obscene overhead bleeding the tax base dry. The guild buildings are down on their heels, held up by subsidy, levitation, and the magic of deficit spending. The centuries-old overhaul of the basilica has halted in mid–flying buttress. Quintessential urban nightmare, arrived at by what the grade schools will one of these once-upon-a-times take to calling civics: pauperize the past and mortgage the future to pay for an unsustainable, Pollyanna present. "An easy mark," the self-employed surveyor says, shaking his head with a grin.

The man descends from the ramparts and heads toward the diseased downtown retail plaza. It is market day, and he settles down between a fishtail vendor, a blood sausage emporium, and a rottingly ripe cheese stall. The out-of-towner has not eaten for days, and he takes whatever sustenance he can through inhalation.

He sits down unceremoniously, cross-legged on the bare ground. He pulls open a soft leather satchel from which he draws writing materials. Spreading a piece of parchment awkwardly in front of him, he begins to print, "Fore-year 1284, Anno D. Have arrived. Find it a flea-bitten burrow with big-league pretensions, well into the predicted collapse." A woman who has slowed to gawk at this bizarre act of mall performance art edges off suspiciously as he looks up. Another, holding a hank of carrots by the hair, mistakes him for a beggar or a pope's emissary collecting for some worthy ground offensive and drops a few pennies on his parchment. The stranger politely returns them.

He settles back to his writing, and to the fine art of underplaying. A knot of children stands at a distance, giggling. "Intractable physical plant problems," the man pens, with some freedom in orthography. "Situation hopeless, but not urgent. Nothing that can't be wished away for another overdraft day or two."

Two appointed luminaries reconnoiter at the end of the writer's row of stalls. They pretend to be part of a crowd engrossed in a cleaning fluid demonstration, but give themselves away by sneaking glances in the intruder's direction. A third undersecretary slinks over to reinforce them. "It's the suit," the stranger grimaces to himself, brushing an imaginary piece of lint from his multicolored threads. "Motley gets them every time."

The suit, however flashy, is mere window dressing for the real five-alarm. Simple literacy, just kicking back and taking down travel notes, and in public at that, is a prosecutable violation of the status quo. Still, the visitor goes on annotating methodically, deliberately failing to notice the *pro forma* town meeting taking place on his behalf.

After another few minutes, the display of blatant public scribbling becomes too much for the assembled officials. They sidle up to where the threat sits, stopping first along the cheeses to sniff nonchalantly at some Limburger. They halt abruptly in front of the scribbler, faking an afterthought. "Good morning," the senior among them manages, in a reasonable facsimile of surprise.

"Good morning to *you*," the stranger replies, the soul of enigma.

"Yes, well. Quite," the official sputters like a schoolboy. "We see that you are . . ." He gestures helplessly at the point and parchment.

"Writing?" supplies the stranger.

"Yes. Exactly. Are you from the Abbey?"

The stranger examines his own clothes, as if trying to solve the conundrum himself. "Have the brothers here shed the traditional brown?"

"No, of course not." The interrogator passes the reprimand along to his underlings with a shriveling look. "Perhaps you are selling something, then?"

The stranger smiles indulgently. Getting warmer. He leans forward. "I'm here to help you."

"Sshht!" one of the worthies silences him, casting around violently to see if anyone's heard. Everyone has, but the *ad hoc* steering committee nevertheless stifles the stranger with furtive vigor. They hustle him off the Marktplatz into the Rathaus cellar by a back entrance. They shuffle him into a side chamber and forcibly sit him down, interrogation style. The chief politico, searching the faces of the others to see if they disclose too much just by asking, pales and demands, "Who told you we needed help?"

Instantly, the interrogatee falls into his natural cadence. "Friends, your problems are apparent from as far away as the spires of Hildesheim."

This bit of cheek produces an outburst from the officials. Libel, lies, slander, discovery: Who told? The buzz goes internecine; they carp at each other in low local dialect. After several bursts of mutual recrimination, one of the number is dispatched to fetch the *Bürgermeister*. During the wait, the stranger removes from his leather satchel a telescoping tripod easel, which he proceeds to assemble.

When the *Bürgermeister* and the rest of the hurriedly summoned town council arrive, they prove shrewd enough politicians to let the visitor handle the interview on his own terms. For this, the man in motley has come eminently prepared. He places several brightly illuminated, stiffened sheets of parchment on the easel and begins. "Gentlemen, let us not deceive ourselves any longer. Your beloved town is nursing some serious infrastructure problems here."

Joachim the Stone Dresser—the power brokers' put-up sop to the laboring classes, increasingly unmanageable of late—interrupts. "What's an infrastructure?" The other councillors shout at him that it means roads.

"Yes, roads," the stranger elaborates. "And bridges. And walls and buildings and plumbing. Retail strip, industrial base, residential. It's all shot. Slum. Gone to hell in a hay wain." Joachim asks for an explanation of the figure of speech but is shouted down.

The stranger begins flipping his parchment diagrams, egg tempera graphs as gaudily colored as the man's outrageous outfit. "Here we see the per capita weighted performance of your town plotted against Goslar, Paderborn, and Lemgo, over the last forty quarters." The curves are snappily plotted against a cutaway view of a half-finished Romanesque cathedral. Goslar, Paderborn, and Lemgo all hang comfortably ensconced somewhere around the triforium.

The local boys, however, are headed for the crypt. Collapsing productivity, crippling trade imbalance, noncompetitiveness, voracious and untenable consumption. "And here, the figures for unemployment, infant mortality, and emigration." Each set of numbers elicits a groan of recognition from the captive and unmasked council.

"I don't need to spell out to you, gentlemen, that the general state of affairs is trending toward the iffy." The stranger possesses graphs for everything. He has pie charts for falling food yields, balloon inserts for inflation, bar graphs for increased alcohol intake and prison confinements, line graphs for bread handouts to the poor. In fact, between negative balance of payments, debt servicing, capital depreciation, investment failure, population increase, water poisoning, field exhaustion and erosion, diminishing revenue returns, graft, tax evasion, currency softening, brain drain, corporate flight, disease, defense burden, and mushrooming social service costs, the town is clearly racing toward a condition of Infinite Sink.

The lecture points out to the local brokers what they have long known in denying: each year, the town borrows increasingly more against principal to pay for the previous year's emergency borrowing. Consumption is biting into production and getting hungrier as the take gets leaner. Quite simply, the town is burning itself out, chasing its own decline. All the graphs converge on that one bankrupt point, a few years down the pike, when there will be no squanderable resources left, nothing at all.

"What we need here, gentlemen, is to implement a program of strict Structural Adjustment." The stranger flips to a sheet showing simply those two words, initial letters embroidered in luxurious vegetation, monastery-dense with devils and demiangels. This time, Joachim the Stone Dresser doesn't even bother asking for a definition.

"But we've tried everything," the *Bürgermeister* moans. "Believe me. Capital injections. Tax incentives. 'Buy Native' campaign. Urban development zones. Belt tightening." His face looks as though the last-mentioned measure is about to herniate him.

"What we need," the head of the exchequer interrupts excitedly, "is to hang in with the infant Hanseatic League."

"Will you shut up with the Hanseatic League already?" the *Bürgermeister* shouts. "The Hanseatic League hasn't don't shit for us lately."

The head of the exchequer whimpers, feelings deeply hurt. "The Hansa is going to be big someday."

"Thing's not going to amount to diddly."

"Polish Corridor!" shouts the head of the Archers' Guild.

"What we need is to substantially reduce the pressures from over-population," contributes the abbot's man.

"But population growth never comes down until well after the standard of living has started to rise." And the stranger has another graph to prove it.

This observation releases a flurry of competing theories and prescriptions in the room, all strident, each sickeningly familiar, and every one feckless and futile. Throughout the fray, the motley lecturer waits patiently, leaning on his improvised podium. At last, the room falls into an exhausted lull. The *Bürgermeister* asks the man, this unwashed illegal immigrant whom not one of them knows from Adam, "Tell us, then. We beg you. What's our problem?"

The stranger smiles, savoring the served-up moment. He flips another piece of parchment on the easel, and pronounces the flamboyantly displayed word. "Rats."

The council is too stunned at first to respond. Then they produce the obligatory, derisive laughter. "Rats?"

"Rats. Any of the diverse, murine species of rodent . . ."

The *Bürgermeister* snickers nervously. "How can rats be the problem? Paderborn has rats."

"And Goslar!" an indignant Joachim snaps, secretly pleased with following the syllogism.

"Yes," the stranger concedes. "But neither of them has rats quite like Hamelin."

Quickly, before he loses shock's initiative, he produces a slew of explanatory graphics. Vermin population's impact on food reserve depletion. On depreciation of real estate—sewers, cellars, road bed, new housing starts. Increase in disease; costs to health, education, and welfare. Loss to tourist income and investment from abroad. "None of the effects, taken separately, is disastrous. But taken together, they create a threshold effect, preventing the town from reaching economic takeoff."

The leading lights of Hamelin confer among themselves. In

the absence of any more-likely explanation, they are inclined to except the causal mechanism. Besides, the stranger has all the figures at his disposal, and who at this late a date would dare to be so medieval as to dispute statistics?

Discussion wheels from cause to countermeasures. The commander of the Archers' Guild says to leave it to his troops. With a systematic program of superior firepower, smart targeting, and will, they can have the little brown problem licked by fall of '89.

"But do we *have* until fall of '89?" the *Bürgermeister* asks. The stranger only shrugs.

The head of the exchequer comes down for a massive importation of cats, picked up in bulk quantities on the spot market. Others object, pointing out: (A) The unlikelihood of being able to secure sufficient felines to turn the trick. (B) The unavailability of foreign exchange credits sufficient to foot such a venture. (C) The subsequent expense of securing a similar consignment of corrective and compensatory canines.

Local ingenuity is soon exhausted. The council has no other recourse but to turn again to the stranger and ask for his recommendation. "Genus *Rattus*," the stranger carefully explains, "is a perverse animal. It's no good reasoning with him. He will go on proliferating until the bottom drops out of the entire self-supporting system. He will extend his success until it buries all competition and pulls down his hosts on top of him. He possesses too much native smarts for most traps. Poison is too good for him. Nor is he sufficiently God-fearing to respond to religious urging. In fact, there is only one thing the rat will listen to."

He waits until begged. Then he discloses the word with the perfect timing of a free-marketeer. "Music."

One half of the council explodes with cries of fraud and nonsense. The other remains skeptically purse-lipped. The abbot's man alone corroborates: he once saw his aunt Agatha sing a trio of baby-gnawers into contrite squeaklessness for the length of three antiphonal treatments of the Kyrie.

The stranger withdraws from his satchel the strangest-looking *flûte à bec* ever to appear along the Weser. It is tiny, more of a narrow ocarina than a pipe, its cylinder a slight, silversmithed figure with finger holes running the length of its gown. "I'm afraid this is all I have by way of résumé. But I guarantee that I will rid you of all problems with it, or you will owe me nothing."

"And how much will we owe you if you succeed?" the shrewd *Bürgermeister* asks. The piper grins at him strangely and names a figure just slightly below the total hard-currency reserves of the entire Northern Marches. Said fee provokes all manner of sneaky sidelong council looks. They couldn't possibly pay anything near that amount; it is fiscally unrealizable, as the quarterly reports put it.

And yet, they will pay that much now, or they will pay a good deal more over the long haul. The council bows its collective head with the helplessness of a public official caught over a pork barrel. The *Bürgermeister* coughs casually. "Fine. No problem. Your terms. Plus a healthy bonus for finishing the job quickly."

Only the blundering Stone Dresser, thickheaded with integrity, holds out. "But we were saving our money. We need it to finish the basilica."

The *Bürgermeister* takes a deep breath and adopts his best patronizing campaign voice, saved for idiots, children, and the obstinately underprivileged. "We've been working on that church for the last two centuries, son. It'll keep for another couple lifetimes." In the casual tones of all weak-hand negotiators, the mayor reiterates that the piper will not get paid a single pfennig until the town has been demonstrated rat-free by an objective, third-party fact-finding commission. The piper agrees, again eerily amused.

On the day of the promised purge, the piper requests that all the bells in town tear off an absurdly long peal. Colliding carillons of all colors and creeds bang away blithely on teeth-freezing, diabolical sevenths. A first, tentative, pioneering rat-beak peeks cautiously from out of its cellar bunker. Others follow the lead, appearing from between wattle holes and out of drainpipes, curious to learn how long that leading-tone agony can persist before resolving to tonic. When the bells break off abruptly without resolution, the exposed rodents reel as if hit over the head with an unlicensed glockenspiel mallet.

The piper then takes up a strategic stand in the middle of the Marktplatz and produces his seraphic, silversmithed tube. He announces the first piece on his program—an onomatopoeic pan-pipe idyll by some Frenchman that not a single one of the beasts has ever heard of. But from the first plaintive, impossible modal tones, they are done for. The mimetic ditty, swelling like rapids in a rising river, foamy and expectant with near-narrative, soul-ravishing ripples, builds to a perpetually postponed, eternally almost announcement of new arrival, that long-awaited descent of formal ecstasy.

It visits again, for every creature that has ears to hear. How big the place is, how strangely familiar beyond saying. The interval field fills with drumlins and rifts, chord-catches that flare free of politics' darkening penumbra. The piece hints of cross-border calls for help, the membrane embrace, a fate that these notes, like dutiful parents, refuse to do more than allude to in front of the offspring, the underaged. Music—the choking scold of closeness, the basilica at funds' end—again sounds its insistence that soul is headed somewhere, forever caught in midpassage, in leap's parabola as it pitches from the burning structure, abandoned to the airy apotheosis it was fixed upon from the first, no matter what temporary and transient panic snags it on its way back to ground level.

One fat brown rat, suckered by the rabbit punch of that sweet outpouring of tones, creeps halfway from safety, the better to hear explanation's up-close whisper. Her next of kin—squeaking in holy terror, *Get back, you fool; don't be insane*—stop in midsqueal and cock their own conical little heads, puzzled by a poignant, dimly recognized, still-discernible invitation that nestles in the notes. Belong and be lost. The tune reads like one of those misplaced love letters at last delivered to the forgetting door just up the avenue, generations after its intended has died.

The piper follows up the French pentatonics by embarking on a solo sonata by a Thuringian provincial, hailing from somewhat closer to home, but still a virtual unknown to the local music-loving rodents. At the first arpeggiated tracings of A minor, the rats begin milling, rumoring among themselves. What *is* this? Here, at last, something one might learn from: the comprehensive architectural drawing, the crib sheet, the answer to the ancient question of *whence evil,* the touch that sense hungers for, quieting angst, reconciling crisis, finger-painting with balm the crests of industrial madness.

After a few measures, the rat hordes discover that they want nothing else but to be forsaken, to throw themselves away, to make love to their destiny, however awful the chapter and verse held in ambush for them. They ask only that the blow be swift and unmitigated, that completion come now, that it consume them in the beating forge, ravish them with answers.

The townsfolk, instructed in advance to stay behind doors, witness this epic theater of the absurd unfold outside their front windows. Rats begin slithering out into the open, assembling in groups of desperately adoring listeners across the town square. They push down into the expensive front-row seats that even the scalpers scrap for—anything to close the gap, press flush against the piper as he stands winding his inspiration. An adult human or two sneak out of their cottages with a grain scoop or meal mallet, sick with excitement to seize the weird occasion and bash in as many congregated rat skulls as possible before the encores. But a sidelong look from the piper is enough to send these forays scurrying back indoors.

Rats: Mammalia's abandoned and abused underclass, products of broken rodent homes, ladle lickers, cat killers, baby biters, pillagers and gnawers at civilization's tuck-pointing, mobile incisored havoc, random terrorists, surprise packages of plague. A parish of pestilence, a veritable national bank run of blind mouths! Who in Saxony would have thought rathood had undone so many? Each one an arrested psychohistory of criminal disfigurement, they pour out of hidden tunnels, shimmy down off roofs, come clean from hideouts of honor in church chancels to hear this: the sound of healing deliverance, delayed for so long, forever, the diminuendo clink of the tumblers aligning in the lock of divine plan.

They pack into the central square as if for an all-star, super-band, gala charity extravaganza performance of the heavenly host's hall-of-famers: Live Revelation Relief; Apocalypse Aid. When all available standing room disappears, the vermin swarm the mezzanines and upper decks, buckling the balconies facing the market, clinging to the rotting timbers and gutters of the Rathaus. Overhangs and ledges fill with rats dangling precari-ously from shop signs and gables. Rats crawl over one another's shoulders, assembling in rat ziggurats, laying down a continuous, plush living shag four or five pelts high in places.

Sound rushes from their collective, forgotten past, music that spells out everything that will still befall their race, all races. A few of the more impressionable ones burst into tears at all that the modulations dredge up in them. Others shiver in rat-somatic eu-phoria, preening their reptilian tails, pointing their bristly snouts toward heaven in thanksgiving simply for having been alive for this moment. The astonished townsfolk cannot tell just what shared vision this carpet of cubic rat is granted. The solo flute transports them en masse into a promised place, a vantage point granting that privileged glimpse of blissful, universal design. Rat rhapsodic rapture: the vast, scattering sugar-and-grain mill of creation.

Seeing revealed tonal teleology play across a million pointy little snouts, several townspeople want to cry out to spare the creatures. Others are filled with desire to rush out and join the doomed beasts, kneel down beside the enthralled throng. But no one does. The town's contract with expediency has been struck; it is too late to revoke, in any case. The piper turns his back on the assembled audience, producing a rumbling, aggregate rat-roar of protest. But he does not take the flute from his lips. The music persists, a constant circuit of peace passing all understanding locked into this endless circle of fifths.

The piper edges himself infinitesimally down the Osterstrasse, step by step toward the Weser. The crowd—no, the nation, the global confederation of rats—refusing to surrender what is here so excruciatingly close to deliverance once and for all, presses along after him in cold delight. Fortunately the streets have been cleared, roadblocked and flag-routed for this parade catharsis. The waves of wee timorous cowering beasts flow down the street-sluice toward the city walls, lower mammals molded into a molten flood, rats tumbling over rats, surging surflike in curlers and cleansing eddies. But the living flood admits to no shoving, no panic, no collapse of societal mores. Not a stampede at all; more of a dense, euphoric dance, cobbles pounded in time to the soaring tune, each figurant in the formation as certain of its precise measure as it is of this glorious, fading daylight.

They glut the length of the eastern avenue, packed tighter than dead leaves in autumn or mud in spring. The road becomes a single, continuous file of suppliants on their way to some unimaginable rat holy site. When it dawns on the front ranks of entranced dancers just what potter's field they are posting off to, only the slightest momentary objection ripples through the column. Distress passes; courage revives. Flute lilt reveals just how untenable their rattish existence had been until the covenant hidden in this little turn of phrase came to release them. Sarabande assures each quivering whisker that they are now linked to a destiny far preferable to any softer, safer end.

All the way up to the very banks of the Weser, even when the piper stands aside and nothing but the murderous flow of rapids remains between the avant-garde and their arrival, hesitation is briefer than thought and more easily dispatched. The lead rats expand into the watery sacrifice required of them. No bill too great to pay, and, with a gnawing smile, given the payoff. They rear up, plunge into the waters like, well, like lemmings. Happy, even, to go down, half in love with a resonant death, provided they can still hear the promissory sounds and sweet airs buzzing about their tiny ears until the moment when the current closes above them.

Realization at last ricochets through the ranks of animal caravan. No word travels quicker than fulfillment. Alarm backtracks through the flow faster than the flow can advance on it. Thus the rats at the back of the queue, not so much pushing as happily piling on, out of earshot of the fatal tune, could easily call upon innate survival instincts and save themselves. It would take no effort at all to break off, turn back from disaster, return to town and begin the difficult work of restoring the decimated pest populace.

But not one rat does. An even greater urge keeps them promenading almost gratefully, for three quarters of an hour, into a river from which not a single forepaw reemerges. Yes, a mother pauses here or there along the bank, thick with plunging bodies brown, and an occasional old retiree breaks into uncomprehending tears as he takes to the drink. But all choose this moment of crystalline clarity, receiving it willingly as opportune, a godsend really, far preferable to a return to the quotidian misery and ignorance that have marked their lot until that moment. It takes no bravery to listen to the soul-stilling music and make peace, put an end to experience. No courage, no strength at all aside from joy.

The last corpulent rat in the miles-long parade plunges into the water with a sort of snappy salute of thanks to the piper, who only then stops playing. No sooner does the primordial musical lure break off than the sole survivor recovers his sapped equanimity. Reviving at the last possible instant, he surfaces, rights himself in the current, and with his last full measure of devotion pilots his battered body downstream to Ratland, where—the reason he was spared—he prepares a manuscript account, this firsthand report on the proximity of ecstasy to horror.

Ghastly shepherding accomplished, the piper at last lifts the flute from his lips. Satisfied that he has done the deed as mercifully as possible, he stares at the site of the rat waterfall, seeing them still, in phosphene tracers as he pinches closed his lids. What's the point, he wonders, the purpose of wisdom's chill deliverance? He smiles grimly and turns back to town, already knowing the furtive, grubby little coda of accounting awaiting him there.

Per expectation, no grateful town lines up to douse him in ticker tape back inside Hamelin's circumvallation. He is met under the eastern gate by an ensemble of dazed gazes and several of those questions that resent having to be answered. "What the hell you put *in* that music? Packs a kick, don't it?" "Say, yer not from around these parts, are ya?" And instantly, without an interval for decent shame, the community reneges. "You see that? Those varmints plumb up and spontaneously offed themselves. Just like they knew what they had coming."

The piper shakes his head sadly, having anticipated this expedience. No sooner does the well water stop festering with floating carcasses, the wattle holes cease breeding disease, the stored grain quit transubstantiating into hard little feces, no sooner is the town snatched from the incisors of hell, once again spared what is known locally as the Youngest Day, than folks habituate to believing that destiny meant all along to lift the curse of damnation before it became a real hassle.

The scope of salvation is too great for gratitude. By the time its savior reaches the packhouse district, Hamelin has revamped the eyewitness histories. The town is now, has always been, and ever shall be no less than steadily, appropriately blessed.

The thought flits idly through him: he should go into another line of work, one that makes more allotment for the moral caliber of his trading partners. Say, highwayman or molten lead wholesaler. But he puts aside the consolations of philosophy and heads to his doomed date with the town exchequer.

"We want you to know how deeply the council appreciates what you have done for the citizens of this town as well as the environs as a whole. The necessary paperwork on your disbursement will take a while to process. In the meantime, we'd like to present you with this token of Hamelin's sincerest recognition. . . ."

The piper takes a room, *mit Frühstück,* above the Meat Hall. Once a week, during the open grievance hour, he petitions the council for his back pay. Each week they beg him to be patient; one needs to understand that all the town funds are not in ready asserts. For a sum as enormous as the one they must pay the piper, certain long-term indemnities have to be called in. No business on earth can pay out 90 percent of its net worth overnight. Why, that would be liquidating to the point of evaporation.

After a spell of outrageous deference, the piper comes to the officers with a vague ultimatum. The exchequer, paranoid that the man might jeopardize Hamelin's standing with the infant Hansa, assures him that they will have the amount ready, in full, by the beginning of the next fiscal quarter. But come the appointed date, there is yet another unforeseeable delay. The piper stands at the back of the town council chamber and lowers his head. "I see," he says politely. "No, really. I fully understand." He takes his leave of the Rathaus, certain he has done everything in his power to act in good faith.

The next Sunday, when most of the town's adults are still in church, the piper settles his *Gastzimmer* bill and packs his satchel. Then, for the last time in this locale, in this lifetime, he takes up his post in the Marktplatz—a monklike figure in motley, legs together, pipe to his lips—and begins to concertize. The very first air from under the mouthpiece, waves of compression and release, maps a country, a republic of staggering rightness. For those only recently banished from the place, the music loosens a visceral, recollected purpose. Children out knee-deep, wet in spring's games, stumbling by gradual intervals and small mother-may-I steps, suddenly luck onto the one universal chord, up close, tangent to everything.

His long, self-spinning line is sleet against a windowsill, the seduction of tree-branch rustles interrogating the pane, luring one out of doors. Implied interior harmonies are fraught with hunger, parched. Old friends whom you yet remember—everything about them except their names—stand rhyming in the dark, haunting the half-timbered alleyways. They gather under the overhangs, too late at night, refusing to come in when called for bed. The sound is birdsong, batsong, angel, extinct pterosaur. It is the shush of an envelope slit open, the pulse from breath half a pillow distant. Brass bands in the gazebo, martial melancholy airs, high sopranos up in the choir loft, a scream of pain from the next hospital bed, stubborn harmonicas on both sides of a violence-stilled front, a beast trapped under a bushel, the tick of the second hand, the abiding shouts of an emptying city heard from miles off, the overtone series of night silence.

The flute does the work of a light dawn dew, revealing that every square foot of the familiar, commerce-stunted world is, in fact, covered in florid web. The tune's contour traces no less than that rapture that recourseless minors are told to wait for in all bedtime tales. And at its first teasing ear-stroke, everyone who is yet ill-advisedly a child spills out the front door, cocks a curious head, then breaks out laughing in recognition. Oh! *This* old guy. What took you so long?

The cadre of adults, however, are universally frozen in place. Churchgoing, field-mowing, crockery-stowing, they hear nothing, least of all their young skipping clandestinely away to see who else in this world can possibly know the melody that has been plaguing their heads since—when?—last night, the life before, twenty-four centuries at my door. Every battered, conscripted day laborer, the devil nightly bled out of him, every manhandled mug under the magical cutoff age, takes to this melody like a new soul to the amniotic bath.

The youngest of them follow it more clearly than they as yet follow speech. A tiny blond girl with bruises down the length of each tubeworm thigh begins to sing a descant. Another, perhaps twelve, her flesh harder, her father-inflicted running sores more secret and circumspect, starts to twirl *a tempo*. She sets off others, mad bodies spinning reckless Ptolemaic epicycles through a market that fills with children aligning to the sound like filings to lodestone's invisible rose.

The whole carnival consolidates in a subslice of time, in the moment between one frozen adult's footstep and the next. Children march into the square banging and blowing and beating on makeshift drums and fifes of their own devising. In those where music has been stillborn, strangled blue in the bloody birthing sheets, the cord of melody twisted around the infant neck, song now frantically roughhouses free in the open. Rhythms race the way little dead sibs do, making up for lost time on their one released night of the year.

Solo flute sparks a tremendous tagalong chorus counted out in rope skipping, beam swinging, seesawing, clacker clapping, acrobating: all the manic, oscillating metronomes of native idiom. Voices from all corners—calls and responses in the highest registers—take up the tune, improvise lyrics, lay down an obbligato above the piper's air:

How many miles must we go?
Hush, baby; play on. No one knows.
Will we make it there by candlelight?
Maybe one day; never tonight.

A boy who celebrated his seventh birthday underground, in salt passages no wider than his emaciated body, reverts to a game of fighting tops with a boy who last year had to kill his crazed father with a backhand bottle gash. Girl slaves kneel down to jackstones or rummy bones. Others gavotte about with tiny babies on their hips, real mothers playing with last year's dolls. A half-Mongol mongrel tribe ride imaginary hobbyhorses, battle on piggyback, cross stick weapons, everywhere singing. Some dress up in tablecloths and shawls. Others tug rope or tag or hide. The market erupts in celebration of every child's pastime yet devised, and several still waiting their invention. Each one is a step in a vast, improvised, composite dance.

Though fewer now, nose for nose, than at the piper's previous gig, the mammals filling the square for this reprise are more ecstatic and numinous. More certain. Their eyes, their hands, their open voices, their shared heart iambics are already transported. They know this song the way they knew to start breathing with the midwife's first abusive slap. Three sweet notes and the hope that has kept them alive is at last delivered. They are leaving at long last, today, now. This frozen instant. This time, there will be no delays. Wrapped in these supernatural pitches, subdividing them, pushing up against the vein of tone, inside the ambient candle globe of the sonic glow, the quickest, brightest children are already across to the other shore, the far face. Through. Over. Sky-blue.

On an alley cutting across the town's axis, the one band not yet tune-transformed makes its way agonizingly toward the square. The children of the house of desolation, confined just outside the city walls: no one has thought to alert them, and only the carrying power of summer air and the acuity of hearing when there is nothing to listen to tip them off. The plague house adults, too far from the sound to be frozen by it, do not bother to lift a hand against the exodus.

The band of sick ones clips along toward the market. The faster they rush, the farther the goal disappears in front of them. Their anxious skipping is disciplined, kept in check by the self-appointed child kapos in charge of this march. A boy of twelve, his injury not immediately visible, waves his arms in front of him like palm fronds, or those little national flags that liberators pass out to spruce up their reception.

"Faster," he whimpers. "Hur-ree! They'll leave any minute." His foot scuffs clumsily against a cobble, but he does not look down.

"Shut your face!" the oldest boy commands; actually, *Hold your head,* as they say in that time and region. He is older by too many years to be possible. Wrinkled, sagging with a disease that made his parents turn him out without provision. His head is unholdable, sleek, slippery, stripped of hair. He holds one hand on a blind boy's collarbone, roughly guiding him, and the other underneath the armpit of a girl whose leg has been taken off above the knee by a crescent of Romanesque iron. "We're going as fast as we can."

"I can go faster," the girl hisses. She tries to move her tree-stump crutch at cut time across the cobbles. But while she takes twice as many steps as before, they are only half as long.

"Easy," the bald boy says. "We'll make it." The panpipe and its pickup chorus carry in the air over their heads. The roll of that sung rhyme immobilizes them with desire, the need to melt the last mile with mere will. "We'll make it, or I'll slaughter you all," he adds cheerfully. "They'll wait for us." He spits out a bit of tooth grit. "They gotta."

But the group's advance cadres already shear off. The band loses its front-runners to the melody. The lead invalids sprint marketward, laughing like imbeciles. All those unimpaired by their sickness are off, accelerating, casting a reluctant look back over a shoulder, shrugging, apologetic but vindicated.

"Hey, wait up. Stick together."

But the sound is too close now to hold out against. Its appeal, brook-clear and incomparably more refreshing, is greater than loyalty, debt, the bonds of the plague house. Betrayal is a crime in this world only. The notes they hear forgive everything.

Of the last, teetering stragglers, the girl is fiercest. She is first to return to walking's brutal pragmatics. Pushing herself forward painfully, she crinkles her nose in thought. "Will it be another town, there, do you think?"

Her features are dark, gracefully rounded, from nowhere near here. Her father was a Horseman. That explains her eyes and ear whorls, and perhaps even what God did to her leg, although His instrument was a fireplace andiron. "Will it be a city?"

The question falls on a dwindling gang of lag-behinds. Her human crutch, the boy with the tortoise-neck folds, picks it up. "Jesus. Who knows? Whatever you want. Who *cares?*" He wants to shake her, kick her existing knee out from underneath her. "Can't you feel it yet? You're getting your leg back there. Me, reprieve from freakhood. We'll all walk for our damn selves, from here on."

The cries of collective delight in the distance insist that they, all of them, will emigrate, today, to a place where they will not be tied down or caged, sent off to strangers, hung up in trees or exposed on the roadside to die, whipped naked in cellars for their parents' sins, shown corpses and executions as moral instruction, locked in closets for having nightmares, seared on their softest parts, groped out in sport, strangled for saying yes, put up as collateral for debt, traded, sold at seven, sentenced to life apprenticeship. The tune piping in the distance is deliverance from evil, the end of that torture, childhood.

"But nobody's going anywhere if we don't get a move on." The two that he hustles down the road exhale exasperated affection. The last delinquent band is down to a frayed thread, pulling itself on in urgency. The freak boy lifts the blind one and runs with him, carrying him like a root sack for several paces. The girl laughs and tries to crutch along quickly enough to catch them up.

They take the last twist of serpentine street. The cluttered, cobbled-up plaster buildings tumble away from one another and the townscape falls off into the open expanse of plain. The two who can see suck in their breath, slapped violently by the sight in front of them.

The one without eyes shouts, "What is it? Tell me!"

The girl hobbles slowly into the healing scene. She fights to say, "I can't. I can't describe. It's wonderful. Children everywhere. It is really happening."

"Where are the parents?"

"They're all . . . stopped."

"Stopped? What do you mean *stopped*?" The blind boy screams for description, his terrified rage giving way to a sobbed giggle of disbelief, of joy at the thing he thought would never happen, yet believed in since before birth, before blindness. The girl's incoherence overloads his blacked-out imagination. "No! Wait. Don't say anything more!"

At that cue, on the downbeat of that "more," the figure at scene center turns. Unlike the rats at his earlier matinee, the mass of playing children issues no protest. Rather, the dancing, rope skipping, and hobbyhorse cantering simply step up a notch. Children tack toward the moving music like comets lassoed by the sun. The entire canvass migrates gradually outward from the market, down a discreet street, forming a carpet deeper, denser than the one the rats made.

"Come on!" the blind boy screams. "They're starting, they're starting!"

The sickling trio stumble along after the trailing edge of celebration. But bliss recedes from them swifter than an ebb sneaking out of the Baltic. The speed of the getaway—a crowd racing at the pace of a messenger charged with averting catastrophe—gives them a foretaste of the trip's distance, the miles they are headed.

A town of frozen adults falls away behind. They pass a parent or two along the road, enameled in midstride. A duchy of children, in a world where half of all human beings are under fifteen, is about to escape murderous adulthood, slip past intact without attracting notice. Cast away from it in mid-Sunday, down the main thoroughfare, in brilliant June.

By the time the impaired three pass through the North Gate, the flute, farthest beacon, is seven leagues beyond them. The mobile boy tries to yank his companions along more briskly, berating them, shoving, cajoling. He curses under his breath, "Oh Christ. Christ. Move it." He sprints ahead a few hundred paces, to map how quickly the vanguard pulls away from them. The mass dancing mania seems to suck stamina from its own punishing cadence. The tempo, the traveling speed of this reel, is too great to sustain. Those without the right steps haven't a prayer.

Another instant, and even the blind boy panics. He can hear how soft the nearest rhyme-skipping child has become. "Hey! Wait up. Not so fast." Each syllable, screamed by a hysteric caller in the world's last round of kick-the-can. They can barely hear the flute at all, so the flutist surely can't hear them. Disaster, here, at arm's distance from the end: Can this be the way the story was *meant* to go? Just thinking the word brings it on them, and they are lost.

The intact child throws up his arms, crucified, a gesture invisible to the blind and too clear to the crippled. Furious, the girl digs into the dirt road, and, for a few moments, actually manages to match pace with the child rear guard, keep it within striking distance. But before she can summon the strength to make the impossible next burst, she looks up and stops in place.

"What? What is it?" the blind one cries.

The old child has stopped too, just looking. Neither will answer the shouts of the littlest. What could they say? Who could call up the journalistic will to report that the sky has thrown wide a portal of blue, the north wall of the Koppelberg has split open like the slats of a secret bookcase, and that all the long-suffering children of Hamelin are pouring in?

"You two run," the girl snaps grimly. She doesn't even allow a wasteful minute of protest. "Go!" The two boys struggle forward a few steps, at a ghost-of-a-chance gait. But a few steps confirm the worst. They will never catch it together, not with one of them needing leading. The last child will vanish, the impossible opening will have sealed before they reach it. The compensation promised since before time, one greater than anything life in this place has ever offered, will be lost to them as they watch from a stone's throw away.

The little-boy-lost stops dead in his tracks and refuses to move. "Get out of here, you son of a bitch," he chants, a forsaken smile playing at the corners of his lips. He and the girl will turn back to a town death, companionless, never to know, the only ones left of an entire generation of once-playmates wiped out by epidemic euphoria. "Get! I never want to see you again."

His guide—skin smoothing, head tufts growing back; the effects, even from this distance, of the opening in the earth's side— runs ahead stuttering, in anguish. Ten paces, then back five. The blind boy points a harsh finger, not quite in the right direction, condemning the deserter to a miserable gallop. With a bitter little cry of triumph, the abandoned one calls out, "Nicolai!" He loosens a noose of string around his neck, where he had attached a packed lunch for the road. He throws the sack violently, wildly forward. The freakish one scurries to retrieve it, shooting back a look of stricken joy that the boy cannot see and the girl cannot reach. Then he too vanishes down the road and into the riven-open mountain wall, the hole gaping wide in the naked air.

The lame girl drags herself abreast of the last remaining human her age. From this moment, loneliness will be the most merciful thing life has to offer them. Her little one has fallen into the gravel, face down. She lifts him, dusts him off. "Come," she says, taking him under her arm, as much for her sake as his. They can at least grope their way to the spot where the others disappeared, fix in memory the portal that has slammed in their faces, narrowly denying them the cure for innocence.

But the frame, the hinges, the jambs of the impossible passage have already faded, fused back into blank hillside even as the town of tune-drugged adults revives. The firsthand accounts from these shrill, unfossiled ones will not outlast the horror of their having survived. This version of events—piper, rats—is all the smudged variorum left, a bastard compromise script lying somewhere between what really happened and what can bear admission. For the blind and lame left-behinds—the trace memory of evacuation.

Joachim the Stone Dresser, the first out of the sleeping spell, stands on the North Gate parapet, watching a column, a whole eastern front of children disappear into legend. Three of his own vanish along with them, infants for whom—precociously—he has just begun to learn to feel affection. He stands watching two forgotten forms helping each other along the road. He hopes for a wild moment that they might be his. Then, seeing the devastation in their steps, he hopes guiltily that his have gone.

He thinks: *This has all happened already. When have I seen this before?* But he could not possibly have seen it. He is not old enough. The template end-time exercise left town long before. Colonial expansion, offshoot of stripling volunteers, or that crazed campaign naïveté, accounts unfolding nowhere but in his mother's singsong, recorded in no other archives than the base of his brain. But in that old story Stone Dresser recognizes the day's annihilation, as if recognition, remembrance, were never more than dry runs for the close.

The children have gone east, crossing that little letter-juggle from *Liebestraum* to *Lebensraum,* leaving Hamelin more living room than it will ever be able to fill. Joachim descends the capped ramparts, stands stiffly, insensate in the street that swallowed them. The two last children will be invested with every privilege the city has to offer. He personally will see to it. And free sweets on demand, for life.

HOW DOES THIS one go again? A green-clothed figure . . . Get the account, the one written, as they all are, as medicinal compensation for an ill, confined child, to ease the time remaining to him. Get the lines, forgotten for so long, skipped over at the time in favor of the lavish illustrations. That fabulous, inexhaustibly elaborate, foreshortened, piled-up street scene, deep with winding columns of those music-soothed animals. Get the poem, the spotty transcript lying on its shelf in the literary canon, the cult artifice, like those primitive plane-totems carved from logs and laid in waiting along faked jungle runways.

"For he led us, he said, to a joyous land, joining the town and just at hand."

Joining the town? Yes; the next brutal high-rise institution over. Just at hand? As near as the artery in an open neck. As near as that nerve cable, slipping its way down through the tunnel of spine.

It occurs to the sleepy listener, for the last time, stalling for more escapism before bed. Comes on him with a clap, like the mountain closing over him: the chill of suddenly realizing, *this really happened,* on a specifiable day, in a well-documented year. The magic musician is based crudely on some bizarre original, an occurrence now lost in too many transmissions. Lost, except for the general contour, one standing up to existing fact. A sizable band of children gone off in a group, at the end of time, as they've

been doing repeatedly at all hours, down odd years at steady intervals, through the shimmering, unstable portal, gauzy at best in
both picture and caption iambs.

In the last tragic, accidental lockout, the sleepy staller, now
jolted upright, catches a glimpse of the places you can't get to in
stories. *All of them right here, within walking distance.* Joining the
town. Just at hand.

And there, in the least corrupt of remaining transcripts, is a
coda exactly the opposite of the one that frozen adulthood remembers. How in some Transylvania there's a tribe

> Of alien people who ascribe
> The outlandish ways and dress
> On which their neighbors lay such stress
> To their fathers and mothers having risen
> Out of some subterraneous prison
> Into which they were trepanned
> Long time ago in a mighty band . . .

A prison from which only a reverse trepanation can spring
them. A surgical strike: the bore of story through the braincase,
into the firing core. The local cast of cripples picking it out for
their amateur theatrics recognize in dim silhouette their own dis-
pensation, the disaster that repeatedly leaves them here. And—
good God—the trepanner, the first drowsy surgeon adult they
chose to do the dirty cutting, to sink the cranial post holes for
the soul's release, sees it in a sick flash: that's it. That's where this
group comes from. Their strangeness, their dress, their slew of
alien languages. They've sprung up subsurface into this Angel
Transylvania, drawn irresistibly to this vaguely familiar kiss-off
rhyme. Only this time, they cannot keep from uncovering where
it has taken them.

THE STREETS IN town are a bloodbath of crisis. Slaves and whipping beasts in life, the children, in disappearance, drive their col-

lected parents to mass remorse. Shrieks and torn clothes form the Marktplatz's new airs. The time for self-indulgence is forever past, but no one who should realize that does.

The town council mounts an emergency session in the Ratskeller. "I swear to you," a panicked *Bürgermeister* calls into the screaming chamber, "we can make more of them."

Joachim's entrance accuses worse than the condemned Christ whispering, *Not ten minutes more with me?* His sorrow slams the room into silence. The illiterate puppet councillor, the merchants' sop to the artisan class, walks stonily up to the town rolls, lowers his palm onto the leaves, and commands, "Write it down." On this specific day, through our own common failure of imagination, our inability to project . . .

Stone Dresser dictates the precise message that will carry down through fixed myth to alert future sicklings, invoke them to rise up, retrace their dazed return. "On June 26, 1284, through stupidity and a mass tin ear, we killed our children."

As for casting: no need to trek across town to those studio lots, the instant vistas of belief shot on dislocation. No call to solicit in the film set cafeterias where centurions lunch with storm troopers, senators with psychopaths, fake doctors with would-be children. They are self-sufficient, cast-ready, right here within their own institution.

Nico knows, from the moment he decrees which of Linda's therapy performances they're going to mount. The withered sideshow boy, age disengaged, has it all blocked out already. There's not a chart on the ward who couldn't become a shortsighted, self-serving adult politico, by modeling the role on a favorite probation officer. To play the paralyzed townies, they need only ape the service nurses and orderlies. After all, they have only to stand there, stony accessories after the fact. For the well-meaning, big-hearted, but ultimately fumbling indentured public servant—what the hell; how about everybody's favorite Minnesota Mexicali, in her first cross-dressing role? Nico will even let Ms. MinneMex take producer's credit, providing she remembers who's calling the aesthetic shots.

Rats they possess, in their usual superabundance on this, the wrong side of what were once upon a time the tracks. You can hear them scuttling around behind the plaster, see them sunbathing up on the roof or surfing the stagnant parking-garage pools. Casts of rat thousands are no problem, and if there's any labor dispute, some gnawing Actors Equity thing, they always have the cockroach under-studies—the ones the size of a child's fist—to fall back on. And for a lead, Nico has his eye on this guy, a latent messianic, as ready-made a piper as fate could pitch in your path.

No; casting presents only one insurmountable snag. They have no children.

Dwarfs, maybe. Midgets, mites, pygmies, Lilliputians—chopped up, scaled down, wasted, disenfranchised. Shriveled, hypernecrotic baby elders nodding off on the toilet with a milk-shake-straw hypodermic spiked into whatever limb is still soft enough to break and enter. Eleven-year-old mothers of their own little half nieces and half sisters. Self-mutilating infants. Housing project survivors. Teen mob operatives and operatees, test cases and trial recipients for unbearable hardware. Million-dollar-a-week underground business middlemen. Those who will go directly from their treatment here to prison terms for murder or worse. They have a steady supply of underage, balloon-letter, sponge-bread breeders and bed wetters. But not one child.

Tag? Tops? Piggyback? That would strain the suspension of disbelief to breaking point, even among the Playhouse playhouse set. They haven't even so much as a single credible summer-stock juvenile. Intensive care just turfed a little girl, left her lying on Linda's doorstep after a few weeks of "Hail Marys" during which they hung her up strapped to the sustaining meter-taps. She is the size and shape of a dachshund thorax, with two smashed ribs, fissured head, and torso smeared all over with a shiny, blue-green oil slick, like a fungus colonizing the skin of a faltering Bartlett pear.

"Wreck of the Hesperus," Plummer called her—anesthetized pros' parlance. "Peanut sittin' on a railroad track. The tyke had pelvic inflammatory disease so bad we had to do a double egg-beater on her." One year old. The man responsible—Mama's current beau, looking for diversion during her latest delivery—wound up getting fifteen years. The kid, as always, got life. Linda is to treat the baby for lingering limb impairment and pass her on to the social worker, who is left, in turn, to thrash things out forever with the assistance of the anatomically correct Raggedy Anns and Andys.

These are their choice for young ones.

But Nico knows they will need even this maimed creature. They must dress her in peasant rags and deed her to some surrogate big sister, herself rustically keloided from neck to nether parts. Offer the baby up to be chucked into the air in time to the delivering ditty. That, on second look at the synopsis, is exactly the point, the secret of this story's draw. The day on which their bruised, abused, futureless ancient counterparts skipped town seven hundred years before is the same day that will freeze facts in their pragmatic tracks, finally freeing these chart-condemned to do the tag thing. Go piggyback. Believe in amateur theatrics. Act out the child's play.

Nico takes over the idea as if it had been his from the start. He launches a massive promotional blitz to sell the story to the others. Persuading the boys consists of the usual bribes and blood threats: debts canceled for cooperation, crucial comic sequels withheld for failure to comply. Most of the street savants, with some grounds, consider the entire project yet another load of Eurocentric, racist, imperialist, hegemonistic, queer-ball, degrading eco-exploitation. Why the fuck should they dress up as a bunch of doomed little Kraut goombas? And nary a martial arts sequence in the whole script.

Nicolino, inspired, co-opts these holdouts. "You: we need you for the Rat King, Mr. Rat Heavy Heself. Big, ugly beefalo muffa, and *chillin'* like nobody's B. And you, you can be that Julius Caesar rat, the one who lives to write home about it. You, we're going to let be the principal baby-brutalizer. Strip you to your waist, give you a hockey mask. Think how awesome your tattoo will look under the footlights."

They're sold the instant they start bargaining for plum parts. This frees up Nico to concentrate on the females. In practice, he needs the blessing of only one of them: the boat princess, that Stepaneevong. The one who chose the fable in the first place. Through no effort of her own—she's either out in the halls learning how to limp without a crutch, or tucked in bed, booking for an imaginary final exam—she's become the revered senior states-girl. Fagging unfair, but go figure. It's as if all the other mindless rope skippers, the guaranteed survivors of this ward, have wind of what's up, and defer to her in shame.

He pays a bedside visit, this time with no sidekicks, no seconds in tow. He stands at her elbow, Dodger cap in hand, maybe thinking that the last lone tufts of eiderdown on his evacuated skull might win him some sympathy points. "Yo, Joyless! What is it now? Trig? Bio? Nuclear physics? Spelling?"

"History," she replies, concealing the edges of her widening mouth behind two fingers. She has learned to hide her excitement like winter seed under snow.

"*Again?* Stuff never ends, does it? I ever show you this great *Treasure Chest Illustrated Classic,* the one where this whole army of kids—I mean, like we'd be the oldest ones in the entire outfit—storm off to whip the Musclemen? Really happened. That's the unbelievable part."

"What happened?" she asks, all hushed urgency.

"I ransomed it to the adults."

She means the crusade, not the comic, but does not correct the confusion. Nico picks up and flips nervously through her stack of books, picking at her paper-snipped place markers. Rome, Münster, London, Roanoke, Vientiane: each slip marks another adjacent subterranean prison, points of arrival and departure. The scraps slip from his palsied fingers and scatter across the floor like tails on a paper donkey. "Criminetly. You read some weird stuff, I'm here to tell you."

She stares at him, her eyes huge, relentless, and black. "What part?" she says to him, softer than the sweetest confession. "What part do you want me to play?"

The question pops his clutch, but big time. Here she is, coming out both feet, as it were, in favor of the plan. That's it, then; cake. Wrapped up. History. No fight, no hard sell necessary. She'll bring the femmes into the fold, wagging their tails behind them. Slight shift of the bargaining chips, and he ought to be out of suppliant mode, well clear of the proverbial woods. The tough part should be over with, all but put to bed. But in fact, they just now slink up alongside it.

Of course she already knows. Knows it the way she knew he could be depended on to kidnap her choice of tales and take over the production. Knows it the way she knew, on first thumbing through the picture book, that Hamelin was already in the itinerary, a scheduled stop for history's through-service deportation trains.

He spins around defensively, unnerved. "I mean, what the hell, eh? Somebody's gotta take charge. Who do we have capable of pulling something like this off? Floor full of target dummies. Sickos, freaks, and illegals. You: okay. So you're our supreme genius. Everybody knows that. But you're handicapped. You don't understand this country. This place. They think they can buy us off with toxic canned peaches and Jell-O cubes. If that doesn't work, they cram a tube down all available holes, park us in front of the vid, and threaten to send us home if we get better. I swear on my last sheet of toilet paper, they're trying to deep-six us."

"Deep . . . ?" Joy casts about for the translating dictionary among her hopeless references.

"Deep-six, eighty-six. 'Za matta? You no speekee? Out. Off. Posthole us. Cash in our chips. Cancel our receipts."

"You mean kill us?" Her eyes widen impossibly. This is the truth they have been waiting to whisper to one another. *This* one. "Why?"

"Well, aren't you the little angel choir? They don't like our kind, case you haven't noticed. Screws up their bookkeeping, jerks around the bed count. And it's a whole lot cheaper to kill us than to give us our own little jungle kingdom."

"But they take care of us."

"Will you listen to this! I don't know whether to laugh or barf. 'Take care of us' is right. Okay, so they stop short of lethal injections. But they bust their royal butane to make this place about as survivable as a slow boat to . . . Oh, shitski, Joyless. Sorry. Just an expression, huh?"

A slipup ugly enough to bungle this whole transaction, to condemn it to Sudden Infant Death. But Miss South China Sea punishes him with nothing worse than a serene smirk. You *boy,* the look says. You harmless boy; how I'd love to rouge your sagging cheek pouches, lipstick that chapped mouth red, tie silk bows through the few remaining sprigs of your hair!

Their complicity infuriates Nico. She'd be frog bait by now, nightcrawler in another world, were she not essential to his plan. And in one quick shudder, he receives the even creepier realization: he is essential to hers. Her legs, perhaps? Her mobility. She uses him as executor, someone manic enough to enact the story she, for her own private reasons, has selected.

Point blank between them, they come to terms: *We must play this thing or die.* Repeat the fading incantation and pass through, rush the crawl-sized slit or be rubbed out, deep-sixed, three baby steps away from the tear they reopen in the seamless cell wall. In the lost boys' world he would cackle at her, threaten her with something sharp, leap through the window and escape on the pulleys and spy wires sketched in by this issue's artist. But in this world, he only chews on his bleeding cuticles, pushes back his nonexistent locks, and hisses. "So. How's about it?"

Her turn for appalling compromise now. "What part?" she asks again, head down. Having bestowed him with executive powers, she must bend to whatever role those powers assign her. "I could make the costumes," she bleats. "I could whisper the lines. I could look up the different versions of the story. There must be an awful lot." Stress scatters her cantering accents wildly through the syllables. "I could print the programs. I'm a very careful printer." Better than any of her peers born into twenty-six letters. The advantage of the late starter.

"Well, yeah, fine. I'm sure you print just great. Only, you see, we've got that base covered already. What we really need now is . . ." He frets at the row of plastic sizing holes at the back of his cap band. He cannot bring himself to spell it out. It. What we really need.

"What part do you make me play?" The words rustle like raw silk, that raw silk that refuses to burn. Her voice, doubling back ever softer, sounds like a refrain to one of those eternal rounds common to every culture. She tugs at the vowels as at a female fighting kite, one caught in a bright, parti-colored quarrel high up in the sky, far away, beyond eyesight. "Nico?"

He will not tell her what she already knows.

"I'm the lame one, aren't I?"

"You're the crip," he agrees tersely. "You're the gimp." He flares his beak of a nose at her, flashes the *so sue me* look. Showdown slides off into a shrug.

She tries on the idea of never making it, of being the one eternally left behind. Their entire breakaway child republic will make it out, all escape on the virtue of her story, her sacrifice, all arrive safely except her. The knowledge plays like a cold, focused, close-up gel spot on her. She half-expected this, from the start of her concerted studies. But now, a working pact between them transforms all hideous kiddieland, and departure is real.

As the pair fall to arrangements, the details of set and stage-craft, the boy's gravelly, senescent voice goes low, half sympathetic. His subdued countenance turns away from her over their daring plans. Perhaps he even feels, just this once in his compressed, accelerated life, the shape of guilt, the pitiless cameo he places in her hands.

SO MOTLEY'S THE only wear. And motley is the only crew capable of carrying the plan off with this ferocity. Mickey and Judy, transcribed to the earth's marked races, the planet's disinherited—*Andy Hardy Goes to the Pen; Andy in the Big House*—take over Linda's office. They fill the corridor back behind Neonatal, spill into the Theraplay Room, turn the halls into their private pickup rehearsal barn.

Everyone's in. The littlest are put to work learning forward rolls and cartwheels and whatever other traveling acrobatics they

can negotiate. Suicidal eight-year-olds who only last week tried
to seal themselves up in the industrial-strength Husky bags for
rubbish removal paint backdrops, towns and mountains and sky,
open air such as their fume-stunted lungs have never inhaled.
The Rapparition, the Fiddler Crab, the No-Face, the Hernandez
brothers—each already a character actor in his own urgent one-
act—take to this collaboration as if joining the supreme, platonic
street gang, the enterprise that all of Angel City's other five hundred rumble clubs strive for. *La marea de Dios.* God's attack rabble,
in their theatrical debut.

From the first, preparations are out of Linda's hands. Her
coaching consists of getting out of the moving violation's way.
Any further suggestions from her would be as welcome as a lap-
dog at a nude beach. Her each schoolmarmy stutter of "Maybe
flaming torches aren't such a hot idea" sounds, even to her, like
a fetid little check of death. Her every shouted encouragement
comes off condescending, a reprimand in disguise, one more governor slapped on innocence's wild turbine.

Yet nothing she could do would more than momentarily muck
things up. They are stronger than she is now, for the simple reason
that they know where they have been. They come from poverty's
every proliferating precinct in this balkanizing city, a state-sized
political sprawl pulling its unassimilatable self apart piecemeal.
Theirs is the nation's flagship, the Western vanguard, the index
of leading things-to-come, the fast track into the next eternity.
They were born knowing it isn't home. And all the fledging
comic tragedians, calling out cues to one another in three dozen
native languages, act with the natural flair of those who know
where they must be going.

Just watching them cuts her with recovery. Oh God: these
little girls, singing that a cappella road jingle they've collectively
made up. It's her all over. That dark-eyed little spitfire *girl* tugging at the hem of her dress in the front row of the yearly class
photo. What's happened to her? What bottomless hole did she

tumble down? What noxious DRINK ME vial swelled her up so grotesquely that she cannot even fit into one of their pygmy chairs at the back of the rehearsal room?

Some insidious, viral, sexually transmitted, colossal failing of nerve she's caught from her Kraft sinks in, and she can't take it. Can't look at them anymore, much less call out prompts. She sees in them all the babies she and Richard know better than ever to have together. Here are the souls of the infants they would pillow-smother at birth through overcaution. Every performing child becomes a prodigy too painful to clap for. The parental terror that paralyzes her and her mismatched mate drives her from the rehearsal room with teeth marks on her fingers. Creeping back in, she tells herself: Playact a virtue if you have it not.

These, her shock cases, ham it up in those pathetic paper hats as if they have only this staged moment seen: this life, this life we missed, the one we were stripped of? Here it is at last, restored to us in dress-ups. My spot. My cue. My line.

Onstage, their ravaged lineup reveals the telling symptom. A solid chunk of the revue is bald or balding. Not just peach-fuzzed Nico or the kitchen-match look-alikes waiting for their locks to grow back. Not just the radiation club or the Kemo Kids, grinning at their overnight transformation into a skinhead mob. The makeshift footlights pick up a glare on every other pate in the chorus. Does the hospital stand on a seething East Angel landfill dosing us all, accumulating fastest in the tissues of the very young? Have the building's lab machines sprung a leak, sloshing the halls with a child-specific spray of rays?

Something wider, Linda concludes. The theme runs through her story almanac—the shocking hair of the very young. Feather-crested Hopi infants. Baby Zaal in the *Shah-nameh,* white-cropped as an ermine in winter. It shows up, always an advance signal, the Now about to announce itself. And here it is in droves, massed regiments of hairless rats returning in Act Two to double as themselves: a troupe of shedding, expectant deprivees fresh from ballroom dance lessons. Those who don't bald by symptom or side effect join along in an act of reverse protective coloration, the leaf willing itself to blend in with the rare animal hovering on its surface. They all cover for the ones already singled out. *Take me too.*

The industry they lavish on this venture outstrips the sum of Linda's every other cure. Pure energy. Each djinn takes to its specific task without being told. They fan the hospital, scavenge it for usable bits. They assemble costumes and backdrops from pilfered bedpans, gauze, linen, and tubing. They inspect each other's handiwork, block out scenes together, write one another's lines. The *auteur* urge runs through these illiterates like mumps through kindergarten nap hour.

And the place they construct in the forced-pastel dayroom: infirm Angel City hasn't seen its like since the last large-scale emigration. Shipping-box battlements draped in rayon raiment project a proscenium that leaves almost no room for audience, whoever that might be. The sham city walls are stuccoed all over with wild child heraldry. The streets are a tumbled maze, the lace of evacuation's ancient follow-routes.

This surreal Hansastadt is enhanced by Nico's strange frame-tale staging. In his plan—an intuitive masterstroke—a poet reads to two kids in sickbed. The rhymester informs the sufferers, *mutatis mutandis,* about their looming cure by another name. (It's the Rapparition, perching on a TV stand, chanting the bit of lame Browning that only he could get to *sing,* "It's as if my great-grandsire, starting up at the Trump of Doom's tone, had walked this way from his painted tombstone.")

The story takes literal shape in front of the two chronics, joining the town and just at hand, a play in which both poet and sicklings take part, trade places. The players who join them to flesh out the tale cycle round-robin through analogy's available profiles—all participant presences, teller, tellee, told.

Linda, watching in knots, begins to wonder if the piece is meant for public performance at all. It feels to her more like a fierce group training exercise, a dry run. Perhaps a drill: learn by heart these seven warning signs, the portents of nearing disappearance. The more they memorize their lines, the more they improvise.

All the while, the pace picks up, pitching toward frantic. The physiatrist can only sit by, riffling through her worthless cue cards. They keep her on for no other reason than that she has not yet secured them their leading man.

Consequently, the children must do their acting around an empty spot upstage. They work the negative space, falling in behind a piper present only by implication. The pied stranger grows even more convincing *in absentia*. The performing trees, the rocks, rats, river, and town politicos, the magic mountain backdrop, the featured children masquerading as their own missing selves, all play off the truant soloist.

One role in particular drives herself savagely in prep for the lead's delayed arrival. Clinical Linda must bench the girl a half dozen times, precautions for which Joy rewards her with almost resentful sulks, were this girl capable of resentment. The little lame cameo rehearses furiously, forgetting that it doesn't have to be perfect until there's an audience. Or maybe not forgetting, maybe just deciding that Now is always its own public. After all, no one knows opening night's hour. She calls out her lines, flails to her masking-taped mark with inexhaustible amateur zeal.

Nico, doing his militant DeMillenarian tyrant bit, barks at everyone but her. Two against one. Actually, it's the whole lot of them against the lone authority. Everyone in the cast conspires to keep Linda from butting in with Your Own Good.

Joy's own good is only this: to draw near, in dress run-through at least, the place she is denied in the master script. A glimpse now will make the last lockout more bearable. When it comes time for her to hobble across the stage, a Method-acted cripple more lifelike than life, she pushes her ulcerated bone beyond capacity. She crumples and sheers. Linda watches the girl go down in slow motion. It is the old moment of maternal horror: in the end, the best parent must let them all fall.

And fall they all will, beginning with the boat girl, who snaps and spills to the floor. Omnivorous eternal booker, assimilation-intent A student, she is nevertheless stunned by this pop quiz. She balls up on the Theraplay Room rug, screaming so violently that not even Linda dares take a step toward her. Silent at every step of the deportation, stoic all during her cells' savage trans-pacific drift, she screams now, on arrival. At her bloodcurdling magic shriek, every onstage freak in waif's clothing reverts to the real thing. Referred pain convulses through the faces of the entire cast. Not this. Not Joy, the quiet one. The one beyond pain, spasming in torture on the floor.

Her limb twists backward, withers like the ashes of a self-immolating monk. But her anguish is out of proportion to the pain, even this nerve razored open and limed. Her writhing is more than bone-based. Unbearable implication flashes through her even before she hits the ground. Stunted syllables work up from her throat. "No. Not yet!"

Not *again,* she means, immune to her own anguish but grieving for that doomed, near-miss girl she is *playing.* From hysterics she fades to soft mewling, then level-voiced, rapid reasoning with anyone who tries to touch her. Everything is okay. Just one second, please. Let's finish this rehearsal and then they can have a look at the leg.

After several minutes of frenzied standoff, Linda sends for the parameds. These conclude that a little judicious pharmacology is the persuasion of choice. Persuaded despite herself, the girl falls asleep and is lost.

Espera tries to alert Kraft, but he seems to have finally achieved his beloved nowhere. He is not in the call room or at home or at any known transmitter extension.

Turns out he is down in the ER, having responded to an assist request, Plummer's tired old time-honored line: "Say hey, Dr. Kraft. There's a consult down here with your name tooled all over it." Power-tooled, to be precise. A seven-year-old who has discovered the difference between a hand and a bandsaw. As Kraft finally emerges from the cutting room, uncountable incarnations later, a vaguely familiar woman is waiting to waylay him.

"It's Joy," Linda tells him.

Kraft nods at her intelligently, as if he can almost place this woman's face, or the words issuing from it.

A BAND OF children wander into the suite where their colleague is being readied for the inevitable. They come not so much for her as to dampen their own terror, assure themselves that the creature they saw curled up in anguish on the stage floor was a trick of the lighting.

All the show's principals are present and accounted for. They are led, as always, by time's toy, the principals' principal. Nico plays with the traction bed's counterweights. He assures her, "We're holding up the production until you can make it back."

She gives him a forlorn look: It's dull in our town since my playmates left. She has calmed since her flailing fall, but something in her busily turns over a distant phrase that the others haven't gotten wind of yet. She pulls herself away sufficiently to answer, "You can't wait. Not possible, Nico." You knew when you assigned me the part.

A little looking around, a quick, pragmatic show of hands. "No, you're right." The offer was only for show. Caught in the idle kindness like a fly's wing under a cover slip, he glances around the room. His eyes dart about for a change of topic. Something wants to insist that there is still a route out, a path, perpendicular to every other, that they might still take. And, suddenly grinning as broadly as on the day of his admission, he sees one.

"Well, for the love of Jiminy Cricket's dick. Look at these." He slogs into the burlap sacks in the corner, each filled with several thousand get-well cards. His pet project for the helpless crip, back when he was still your basic greenhorn progeriac casting about for a new game. Back when getting well was still a competitive sport. He kicks one of the sacks, grabs his toe, and hops about to mugged laughs. "We've got that record sewed up, anyway."

But Joy roots quietly about in the three-ringed binders that have never left her side since she beached her open craft here in this hemisphere. She searches through her communiqués from message-mad America. She extracts a clipping about a Brit boy with brain tumors, evacuated to this continent of medical mavericks and sometime miracle workers, where you can always find someone who will operate on anything. This boy, capturing the imagination not only of the local media but of World News, has already scavenged enough well-wishes to beat her haul by several orders of magnitude. Thirty-three million cards, and he continues to solicit internationally for more. Worse, to add insult to injury, the winner is getting better.

"Oh Jesus. Joyless." Nicolino turns the piece over, desperately reading the bisected horoscopes on the flip side. His claws shake under the weight of the disastrous scrap. Disease's impeccable timing destroys the protection racket he tacitly promised her. He balls up the newsprint, crushing along with it the long list of coordinated lies that childhood has tried to hand them from the start.

Even the most cross-language remedial among them sees through the fairy narrative now. That old crone who tricks the charmed early readers into believing she is their mother spits them out four paragraphs before the ever after, stranding them in wildest nowhere. Or a place worse than nowhere, sicker, wider with not, with never: this Emerald City blazing away all its nonrenewable futures at this instant, there, outside Pediatrics' window.

FINDING THE FATHER proves easier the second time. Despite the hospital's promises of good faith, Wisat's signature on his daughter's release alerted the governmental wide-network trawlers. Immigration picked him up and has been holding the guy in a state of blind bewilderment since Joy's first trip under the knife. He is so desperate to see the girl and learn of her fate that he even agrees to return to the scene of his betrayal.

The only hitch to securing this new round of permissions lies in words. They leave it to Kraft, the scutboy, to break it to the victims. "Extent of femoral incursion indicates immediate aggressive invasive proc . . ." The girl, again serving as translator, just stares charitably at her doctor. She wonders how the two men who have come to mean the most to her in her two lives can inhabit the same room, albeit unable to speak to one another.

Kraft notices the hush, the hang time where her translation should follow. He looks up from his scribbled chart and catches her staring. He stares back, at the eyes he has been avoiding for reasons more numerous than the mistakes he has made along the length of her treatment. Twelve-year-old eyes, black as the lacquer on a ceremonial barge, black as the silk pajamas that a generation of high schoolers just a grade or two older than he were told to empty their clips into.

He calculates back to the year when he first saw these eyes, had them burned into his own retinas. He was, at most, two years older than she is at this pre-op hour. And the girl: the girl, in '69 . . . Why bother pretending to do the math? The girl was what she always will be. The girl, already, even then, was twelve.

He freezes in her gaze, the defense that night animals fall back on when astonished by light. Locked in her continuous pupil and iris, he tilts his head in a dissociative shrug of pain, as if he refuses to make out who she is. Dictaphone-steady, he repeats her prognosis. "The patient is dead animal mass unless we radically hack her back."

She blinks at him, neither wince nor recoil. The glance is that of a village girl—too young by a year yet for the silk coils that will couple her hair to another's—getting her first glimpse of her arranged lifemate. Her look inquires curiously, a dressup, a play-money look. She turns to her father and performs a near-faithful transcript of the sentence. "The patient" remains "the patient," "dead" stays "dead." But "radically hack her back," to protect her doctor, she renders as "operate."

Only: the sounds she makes, the shadow puppet epic her syllables throw against the scrim of her father's face. Kraft shrugs off the standing wave of sleep. He shakes himself like a dog shivering from the surf. The dialect's five tones reach him from a listening post inside his cochlea. He watches the old man absorb his daughter's condemnation. The judgment is just one more isolated blow in the familiar serial assault, this week's flood, famine, or mass genocide writ small. What has become second nature cannot shock. The pitch-language report of his baby's fate is already an old friend, an ancient poem trotted out again around the expiring fire.

The girl's recommencing hell is just a footnote of an appendix in this wallpaper roll register of continuous death. The girl will go the way of her mother? She'll join her brothers and sisters, the small army of offspring that was to protect the professional healer in his final infirmity? So she too will vanish, like country, land, crops, animals, favorite sticks of furniture. The family bo tree consists entirely of dead descendants and ancestors, the still- and the unborn and those dragged horribly back to birth. Life exists for no other reason than to dull the persistence of the living, to deaden them by degrees each time another of its branches is lopped back, slashed and burned.

The father holds out the backs of his hands for obscure study. He shrugs absolvingly: *These things happen.* It's a professional gesture, the move of the accredited Mawkhan. He knows, already, what the Cycle has in mind for his daughter's errant vital stuff, and he asks only to facilitate it.

He asks only one thing, a thing his polyglot international girl would be powerless to translate, even into her own tongue. Yet Kraft somehow intuits this simplest request, *recovers* it. The other medical man would like to do a brief procedure of his own, and then he will put the leg—the femoral incursion, his life's life's blood, his little girl—into the hands of the current dominant culture. One technique, then leave things to the state of the healing art.

Parent and child exchange a few hurried necessities in their private language. Kraft—coming to, coming back, his brain, numbed by several sleepless years of Human Service, condensing around the lost range of the five pitches—finds he can follow them. Not the content; individual words blow past him in a blur. But the *shape,* the inflected sense, insinuates itself, snuggles up willy-nilly under his arm, embraces him, shouting, "Ricky!" The words lie just next to a language he once spoke, one he can force up now only in ungrammatical museum shards.

But fluency, like all childhood diseases, carries a germ of the first contagion. He concentrates on the swift word flow until one phonetic swirl breaks over him: *farang.* The foreigner. The albino. You, my friend; they're talking about you. And this word, shared over so many regions from Morocco to beyond Mandalay, the common term for otherness, springs him loose. The thing that defies his spastic grasp wanders back into him, intact.

And now he needs to—how do you say?—say something about it. He blurts out, interrupting the blood pair in their emergency preparation. With no particular program more pressing than this first urgency, he starts to sing:

Chahng, chahng, chahng, chahng, chahng,
Nang kuay hen chahng rue prow?

(Tell me, little one: Have you ever seen an elephant?)

Wisat jerks up, his placidity scattered. Although his daughter told him she has exchanged a few nonwhite words with this *farang,* she has said nothing about his possession by spirits. The old man cannot figure out from what world this outburst comes.

"It's Thai, Pa," his daughter prompts in the same language, calling him by one of the few terms shared in root as widely as "foreigner."

Of course it is. What else could it be, here on the far, shadowed side of the world, in this city of a thousand languages, half of them invented here?

"The elephant is a great creature, and not very light at all," Father Wisat sings, changing tongues as easily as he used to for clients on the far side of his river valley border.

This version is slightly different from the one the once-Ricky remembers. But the tune is the same, and the line scans.

"His nose is *really* long," Kraft rhymes the man. "It's frequently called a trunk."

Both men giggle at the overlap of their outside knowledge. They finish the song together, while the girl for whom they ostensibly sing looks on, smiling painfully, knowing that the grown-ups can't trouble themselves so long as they are thus occupied.

By song's end, Kraft can talk, really talk again, after half a life deprived of words. He can say anything either part of him needs. And the Laotians' Thai is equal to his own. Can this instant recovery of speech mean that the Farsi is still in there, the Urdu, the Arabic prayers? He and his new near-neighbor speak of nothing—of geography and kinships and favorite fruits you cannot get on this side, even in the most exotic Angel City bazaar. Of places you cannot find your way back to, even with the best of maps.

"*Dee,*" Wisat pronounces, sounding to Kraft's ears like a near-native. "*Dee maak.* Excellent! We have nothing to worry about then."

"How so?" Kraft asks, finding the words without pause. "What is good?"

"It's good that you come from somewhere else. Like us, only, maybe you stayed dry during the voyage? Maybe you made it over in one hop?" His epithelial folds glint at Kraft; the relatively favored are always fair game. Kraft wonders how old the man is. Granted, he has this twelve-year-old kid. But he is a hundred and forty-four at the youngest.

He should correct the man. He should announce: I'm not from somewhere else. I come from here. Only I left at an early age. Then came back, then left, then . . . He would explain, only the chronology eludes him, and he cannot say exactly *where* he is from.

Wisat, oblivious, elaborates. "The trouble with Americans is they think everything begins and ends here, this time. No return, no earth. Imagine: no ancestors! How can one live? It must be terrible. Even their smallest action dies right after the deed is done!"

"A nation of oversteerers," Kraft mumbles in English. The phrase would not translate, even if he had the words. It is intelligible only to those with no beginnings or ends but their own. No time around but this one.

Wisat declares that no one who thinks deeds are their own consequences should be allowed to saw into the spirit house of another's marrow. They should be outlawed from healing, not so much for the sake of the patient's karma as for the surgeon's.

Kraft drifts from the argument. Just the perfume in these clipped syllables returns him to a moment when each sound and scent queueing for experience, when all the sensory boutique whispered of preknowledge, when the new seemed full of nearby, culminating explanation. First etudes, Handel or Haydn, the Hagia Sophia, jasmine, burned peanuts, *gong wong yai,* black-market currency exchanges, handworked bullwhips, iguanodon skeletons, a swing south: these, the multiplicity, the range, surrendered to culpable adulthood. Faintly familiar already, nodes on the scheme of things already inside you. Now they are back, insisting you've been here before, calling out both question and command: *Remember?* Remember. Little one, have you ever seen an elephant?

Commotion calls Kraft back, a noise in the street. A ghetto-blasted popping sound issues over the crunching glass, the assorted squealings, the general yell of background noise. Even before its envelope parts from the white sound waterfall, every dog within a two-mile perimeter of Carver begins baying. Exactly why the grunts used to slip in and poison these beasts in advance.

Crazed cacophony, but quotidian enough that Kraft would not even cringe except for what happens to the girl. Violently, she repeats her stage swan dive. As the trigger sound becomes audible to humans, a quick-quick-quick scimitar subdividing the aqueous air, she throws herself at her father, shouting a single word, the surname of dread.

Her movement is more astonishing given that, below the waist, she is little more than two moist streamers of crepe paper. She reverts in fear to her native tongue. Wisat must translate now, baring his remaining teeth in parental embarrassment.

"Dragonflies."

Kraft hears it home in, a small rotor-blade flotilla, Plummer on the helplessly receiving end. Then it hits him: How old is this bean sprout? He checks the chart, verifies that she was not even born until years after the last Huey was swept from the continent's edge. Even granting that her war was the lingering one, dragging on in unpublished secret, beyond the limits of American attention span: Dragonflies? If the gunships were even around past the child's birth, who was flying and maintaining them? And to what ends, in that pathetic, valueless valley, except to drive out this old medicine man, annul his wife, excise all his offspring but the one remaining infant, and scar this one permanently with a monstrous metal mother's quick-quick call, a Lorenzian imprint gone mad?

That question sets off a dozen others in Kraft's head, questions that should have occurred to him long before. How did these two reach here anyway, rural refuges of permanent war? How could they have gotten out, met the exit fees? Whom could they have paid? They had no possible means of escape. Therefore, Kraft concludes, they cannot possibly be here.

The girl cowers from a conditioning she could not have picked up firsthand. *Acquired* chopper terror, learned from old footage, her father's accounts, or daily proximity to heavenly herbicide recipients. There are enough of them, in this city filled with escapees from all the burning jungles this city has torched. She lives alongside Hmong who cannot lift a fork without family consultation. She goes to school with the grandchildren of Nisei internees. She eats with Asians who have never seen real peppers. She studies with Asians who cannot find China in an encyclopedia. She plays with the children of potassium flashes, several hundred thousand let in over a few-year span. Half-children of fathers who thought they'd never be found. Mothers who never stopped searching. Asians who blew free of their necropolis home, smuggled out for the market's going fee or shipped to Oahu and Guam in empty American caskets, surviving by impersonating death. Asians who came here long before the first European, before the invention of the word "Asia." Asians who will never have the slightest grasp on what passes for sanity here on this side of the rim. She might have contracted the sky-burn terror from any one of them.

Kraft looks away from her panicked embrace, so as not to humiliate the child even more. He picks up the top book on her study stack, placed conspicuously for his benefit over the *Let's Learn About Stars and Planets!* and the *Electricity and You.* A slender pastel paperback called *Through the Looking Glass:* it takes him until the invocation to remember that he bought it for her, in a luckless attempt to get the girl to read beneath her level, below herself.

Child of the pure, unclouded brow
And dreaming eyes of wonder!
Though time be fleet, and I and thou
Are half a life asunder,
Thy lowing smile will surely hail
The love-gift of a fairy tale.

It takes him until sestet's end to remember the place he bought it, the city, the day, the woman he was with, the woman's name, why he has avoided her. Too close for memory. Memory lies half a life asunder now, in Krung Thep, that other City of Angels where *he* was the resident immigrant.

A gnarled hand grips his, covers it as it flips pages. Wisat, pointing to the slight volume, chuckles. Addressing the *farang* in the old imperial language of occupation, he says, *"Vous êtes un bon homme."*

Kraft looks up. The girl is back, hiding her sheepish face. In the five tones, the most musical language ever invented to say human things, Kraft sings to her, "We're going to have to take your whole leg off. And it may not be enough."

Father and daughter look surprised that he makes the pronouncement public. They give him the look of the medically indigent, the look of those who know wider beginnings and ends.

Wisat asks Joy something in an undertone Kraft cannot catch. The girl fishes about in her school supplies bag, emblazoned this year with Japanese crime-fighting robots that change into F-15s. The satchel is full of flat-ended number twos, edible paste, and carefully preserved if worthlessly smushy steel protractors. She extracts a flash of silver that she passes to her dad.

He in turn hands it to Kraft with the verbal gift-giving formula of a land belonging to neither of them. Kraft takes the present, mumbling the thank-you phrase once second nature, yet never his. At first, he mistakes the gift for a small Buddha. It is, in fact, a metal, Western-winged trinket.

"What is this?" he asks, his skin going voltaic.

But Kraft already knows what the thing *is*. It is the necklace angel hanging around the surplice in the sole portrait he possesses of his choirboy father.

"It's a good-luck . . . a good-luck . . ."

"Charm?" To wear while he cuts away her parts, so that things might go well with them on their way from her hip socket to the incinerator.

She flashes her eager thanks for the term and copies it industriously into her notebook.

"Where did it come from?"

Once again, dismay at this doctor's New World need to make questions overt. Joy shrugs. It came from the place all good-luck charms come from. She points vaguely at the roof, where the emergency medical dragonflies have just landed.

"It fell out of the sky."

Out of the sky: of course. The place from which all charms fall. The first word, the formula invocation, the once-upon, anomalous and abandoned, comes back to him. Now he can give her the missing bit of her fallen angel, the key. *More than your lifetime before you were born,* he owes her, his half of the child hostage swap, *a boy your age fell out of the same blue.*

That was how he always arrived. And left the same way, a year or two later, when his father went on to another part of what was then still called the developing world. They followed Foreign Service's Coriolis, their country's crusaderism with a human face. One day the boy fell from the sky and landed in the City of Angels, capital of the Land of the Free.

His first snatch of Free speech—from an armed, khaki passport-controller in the improvised airport—was more melodious than any song he'd ever heard. He would have asked the officer to chant the phrase again, had he known how. No need; the whole city was pitched in a singing school of spoken tones.

He had lived in cities that had been sacked a dozen times before the City of Angels had built its first wall. Yet this seemed the most ancient place he had ever seen, the least concerned with the passage of time. It was built in a bend of a senile river meandering down to the South China Sea in switchbacks as lazy as the sutures in a baby's skull. The city perched on this floodplain like a water strider, a floating reed mat that had rooted into an island. What roads there were had been canals until a few years before.

Planless, Krung Thep sprawled away from the river, its watery network spreading like ant trails through sugar. The house his father took them to fronted on a vegetated street and backed onto a canal served by water taxis and buses. Like every other building in the city, the house bobbed on shallow piles.

The walled compound of his new home contained the same servants' quarters, outdoor laundry, rain jar full of mosquito larvae, and copse of rotting aromatic fruit trees he had grown up knowing. But it had one distinctly local touch. Where the shard-tipped wall adjoined the canal, under a tree of wax-pink, edible Liberty Bells sat a tiny house. Doll-sized, its piers supported a triple-tiered, sharply gabled roof in orange and green ceramic. Flame finials shot out from each apex, gracing the encrusted eaves.

Ricky asked the cook, his confidant, about this tiny domicile. In a patois that became his bootstrap into Free, Som told him it housed all the essences that had been displaced when the big house was built. The boy liked to leave jasmine and burning joss sticks by the diminutive front door, an act between veneration and apology.

The floating city consisted of countless life-size, real-world spirit houses. Banks, arcades, bars, Turkish baths, whorehouses, markets, polo clubs, slums, schools, embassies, and dark mazes of hovel stalls all proliferated unzoned. Yet there was only one decisive industry in the Free capital: propitiation.

The city existed to build monasteries. The bulk of Free will had been channeled into them. There was one just up the street from the compound, and one a hundred meters down the canal. One stood across from Ricky's international school. An enormous temple complex, a walled city within the city, occupied the bow-bend of the river, the kernel of the old town. Most of the three hundred monasteries, from sprawling communities to single sheds, were classical in style: bell-shaped stupas flanked colonnaded halls with terraced roofs flamed in finials and topped with tapering spires.

The city was on a centuries-long project to convert itself into an immense way house for the spirit world's indigent. Even those desperately poor without drinking water—two million Angel inhabitants lived and died by milliliters—contributed to building. A week's income went to replace a roof tile, signed on the underside before being slipped into position. Free heaven, the boy learned, was not a place but release from place, an escape of the turns of the Wheel. A celestial New York, a mendicant Tokyo, an incorporeal Paris, the City of Angels constructed itself in an architecture beyond desire.

The neighborhoods forgoing enlightenment ran in two-story, poured concrete shanties. Shops at ground level were topped by a combination office, warehouse, and family living cube. In these shops the boy learned to bargain. Even a hundred grams of candy had a concealed price that had to be discovered jointly by vendor and customer. Ricky could fake shock at suggested retail, feign indifference over an item he burned for more than all the pocket change in existence. He perfected the art of walking away, then turning at the right, world-weary moment to suggest, in the most resigned tonal speech, a compromise. Shopkeepers baited him with inflated prices, just to see this miserable excuse for an albino roll out his repertoire.

His vocabulary grew rapidly. His ear, at thirteen, was still liquid. There were sounds in the massive alphabet that his parents could not distinguish, let alone produce: an intermediate between *b* and *p;* a vicious initial *ng* that came from a place in the back of the throat missing in white adults. Impaired, his parents employed Ricky to negotiate with tradesmen or placate Som's anxieties over the invasion of the evening's *pallo* by winged hordes.

A barrier more intractable than pronunciation prevented his parents from ever becoming Free speakers. In Free, a word's meaning hinged on a proper deployment of the five tones. His mother, an amateur musician, could hear something wonderful happening in every spoken syllable. But neither she nor Kraft Sr. could hear, let alone enunciate, the difference between "color" and "four."

The boy, on the other hand, knew the tone of a word before he'd even learned it. He knew the tone *was* the word. Thus he could make, from what sounded to his parents like five equivalent syllables, the brilliant if rhetorical question, "New silk doesn't burn, does it?"

He studied Free at the International Institute of the City of Angels. The school housed the city's foreign children, a monastery complex without the finials. The school mascot—racist joke on all *farangs,* whatever their melanin—was Hanuman, the white monkey general from the national poetic epic.

Ricky soon studied Free with the oldest, even learning the elaborate script. He learned to name two dozen banana varieties from dealings with the canal boats. Som taught him how to sing in a seven-pitch musical scale, twisting each note with the word's inflection. But his real language lab took place in the streets, where he quickly learned everything from "corner kick" to "bugger your mother."

Time thrived not in the verb but in context. Yesterday it rains. This afternoon, it rains. Cool centuries from now, when you at long last graduate from bodily history, it rains. The subtle colorations of tenseless time seeped deeper into him. He slowly understood it, or, in the Free for "understand," it heart-entered him.

It heart-entered him until he felt nowhere but where he was, a white ghost in an inland port on the Gulf of Free, in a street overrun by pedicabs and tone-haggling merchants, laced with jasmine and temple bells, bells rung by pilgrims' staves in the same intervals as the seven-pitch songs Som taught him. He sang the songs at thirteen, hearing in advance what the pitches would sound like at second hand, when the one place on earth he ever belonged to was reduced to this exotic travelogue, dim cartoon.

His parents were resigned to let him assimilate. He could wander the city at random. For two and a half cents, he took one of the hundred color-coded buses, hanging out the open back door even when crowding did not compel it. He clung to the Sunday Market, where he watched limbs thick with elephantiasis shrink at the application of fluid distilled from rare barks. There too he could buy fish and birds for the merit of releasing them. Fruit could be had that he had seen nowhere else on the planet, tastes that had no equivalent in any other language but this, the one he now tasted in.

The Sunday Market attested to fields and rivers a little more forthcoming than most of the places he had lived. But even this relatively affluent emporium had its extensive subdivisions where the deformed laid out mats, where mothers solicited for their hydrocephalic infants—heads huge, smooth, and shiny as museum vases. Here, the boy invested his bargaining proceeds. At thirteen, he still felt the ludicrous hope of making a dent, although somewhere he already knew that all the coins in the world would never release even an insignificant fraction of the agony locked in this one illusory turn of the Wheel.

The southeast of town was a slum so vast and desperate that no philosophy could reduce it to illusion. Ricky traveled there one day, one of the few city corners he hadn't yet seen. The bus conductor punched his ticket using a six-inch, coiled little fingernail, and asked where the boy thought he has going. Ricky responded, "I *live* in this city." I live yesterday, now, in another hundred centuries.

But he was not ready to see just where he lived. In Squatter Town, houses for displaced spirits were irrelevant. The living there displaced nothing; they had never taken possession of the lease. Fathers defecated and mothers listlessly washed dishes in the same fetid film where their children still found the energy to swim. The diet here could not even sustain the hope of religious escape. Days were no perpetual Wheel to be ridden until history released the day's residents. There was no passage of days here. Days were an inconceivable luxury for the privileged and already sprung.

The squatter boys in the streets did not even bother to mob Ricky as he handed out dimes. They took the coins and looked away, weary. One older tough, a spark in the swallowing dark, at least summoned up enough irony to push palms together in front of his bowed nose, a parody of the gesture of thanks and departure.

Squatter Town graduated the boy forever from temperament. The size of the floating ghetto, the rotting slackness of life scavenging its own dead, defeated any scheme human history might invent to justify itself. Ricky discovered, at the moment his body was everywhere tufting, losing its pink larvahood, that the Sunday Market sufferers were not confined to a few, licensed begging stalls. They proliferated in whole, autonomous free-trade cities of their own, outstripping in per capita growth anything the upward world could hope to offset.

He could make no sense of the slum's exploding compass. The image followed him around fastidiously wherever he went. He asked his Free friend, the Institute gate guard, how a slum that size could consume a city so gifted. The man darkened and pronounced his explanation.

"Do you know Hitler?" the guard asked.

Ricky confessed to having heard of him.

"I want to do for our Chinese what Hitler did for your Jews."

The boy could not even cough out "Why?"

"Chinese take all the business. They marry Free women. They hoard currency in rice sacks and make us pay double to get it back."

Ricky took the question to church—a Lutheran outfit that met in the attic of a Catholic school. Ricky asked his confirmation teacher, an Air Force captain, who quietly informed him. The war was sucking the entire subcontinent dry. And all unnecessarily, because stay-at-home lawmakers had never come out for a look. Only one step could halt the hideous drain: permission to saturate the Yangtze, every hundred kilometers. The captain tapped the palm of a spotted hand, tracing a precision pattern up his lifeline. He claimed his Free colleagues at the leased bases all agreed. Ricky sensed how soon he would have to put away childish things.

The boy tried to lose himself in diversions. He attended ceremonial combats—kites, fish, cocks, kick-boxers. He bought
numbing doses of sugarcane and iced coffee from vendors, smudgy
newsprint scandal magazines, spirit-restoring roots from the canal boat flotillas. The International Institute was good for killing
thirty hours a week, his classes serenely unaware of the watershed
crisis he had just unearthed. After school he took refuge in Indian films where heroes leaped ten meters into the air and landed
while simultaneously twirling a machete and completing a tight
end rhyme. But by the end of the film, as he stood at attention in
front of a projection of the king while a *pipat* band insinuated itself
into a facsimile of the royal anthem, small Kraft's desire to efface
himself demanded, more than ever, its obvious out.

The boy told his parents he would enter the monastery at the
onset of that rainy season.

"Time-honored response," his father chuckled, as if he had the
early teen mind pegged. "Too bad you're not legal age. We could
use you in the Foreign Legion."

Ricky had no idea what the man was talking about. Between
the boy and his father lay every kilometer they had ever logged.
His parents had brought him up without cruelty, with all the
amenities. But their attempts at understanding him were, like his
belated exposure to his national sport, doomed to enthusiastic
blundering. How could they think he wanted to forget something? Completely wrong. There was something he needed badly
to remember.

Most Free males spent some time as monks. His parents, who
had delighted in his language study, taken him throughout the
country, and set him loose in the capital, could not object. Fourteen was ripe for a novice; some boys entered the monastery as
early as eight. Some stayed for three weeks; others found themselves still in the temple year after year, finally dying in the abbey
of their original petition.

The postulant went for religious instruction. They started with
the story of the Enlightened. A rich prince undergoes a spiritual

crisis, realizing that he can expect nothing at the end except sickness, suffering, and death. The prince renounces the world and goes into seclusion. He undertakes a search for absolute truth, discarding a variety of paths, even starving until bones pierce his skin and hair falls out at the roots.

One day under a bo tree he wrestles with the Tempter, who tells him to choose life. He defeats desire, thereby gaining knowledge of his prior existences and seeing the flux of creation's constant rebirth. He wakes to the nature of suffering, feeling, and eternal migration: the universe as lotus pond.

The child learned of the three planes, the shape of time's cycle, and the names of many fixed points in the spinning sphere. He learned the stages leading to awareness and memorized those scraps of scripture he would need to recite at his ordination. He was accepted by a small temple on the other side of the river. A senior monk took a straight razor to every hair on his head, including eyebrows. Glimpsing the result, Ricky was shocked at the deformed terrain, its lumps and crevasses. Derogatory street slang was right: he was an albino, a freak. His bared skull was whiter than the bleached onion skin through which he had once traced the countries of the world.

Wrapped in cloth as white as his virgin scalp, he was carried three times around the temple under a parasol. Inside, seated cross-legged in front of the abbot and a dozen monks, he was examined and had all the answers ready. At the end of the questioning, the abbot—an old man in perpetual danger of disappearing into his orange robe—peered through his glasses and asked, out of nowhere, "Where are you headed?"

Panic rushed on Ricky like a monsoon. But just the way day's rain, for a minute as opaque as sheet tin, can vanish more rapidly than it blows in, his confusion cleared onto equatorial blue. He gave the first reply that came into his head: a colloquial phrase something like "I've already been." The abbot's slight smile implied that, if Ricky hadn't entirely passed the exam, he would be taken on as a promising exception.

Alone in the community, he was shown his cell—an open teak cube draped in mosquito netting, with a low prayer dais and a water barrel shared with three others. The youngest novices flocked around him until a senior monk chased the boys away. Ricky was taught how to put on and fold his robes. Then he was left to himself.

Right speech, right gesture, right countenance. No possessions. No food after noon. No singing, no music, no pictures, no broadcast. No leaving the compound except for barefoot dawn alms, receiving the day's food from merit seekers, out on the streets. He knew these rules but did not yet know what, aside from the common meal and the several chants, he was expected to do all day.

Nothing, everything. He could go for instruction with the senior monks. He could think or write. He could talk softly with the other boys during certain hours. He could meditate. The abbot gave him an English book on the subject from the monastery library. None of the other monks could read it, and the abbot was eager for a report on the contents.

This book—*An Awareness of Air*—started out as clear as the moon in a still water barrel, yet grew infinitely infolded with each rereading. Every line undid and rewove the previous opaline paradox. The plot was all about how to sit quietly and grow so mindful of breathing that you were once again oblivious. It said how to hold the hands, the neck, the body. But when the text described how to hold the thoughts, things grew slippery.

Meditation ascended by stages, like the tiers on his processional parasol. Align the spine, close eyes, focus on the thread passing through the lungs. Ricky reached detachment with a little effort, then went back to reading. Next came intense concentration. He breathed for a long time but was never sure whether he achieved the state or just thought he had. He returned to the book to learn that this was just a stage on the way to a more intense indifference. As the white light approached, he was supposed neither to shut it out nor give in, but to go *through,* to yet more things falling away.

After days lost in the various positions, he drew close to the white light, but the excitement of approach dispersed the condition.

On the book's last page, he read how everything he had just read was worthless. Study and words were the worst enemy of the thing that all the study and words meant to nurture. He brought the book back to the abbot and reported how the work counseled its own destruction. Grinning and shaking his head, the abbot placed the volume back in its space on the shelves.

The boy breathed on in silence, now without trying for anything except respiration. His days were so free from distraction that he could not recall the urgency that had forced him here. An hour became fuzzy; the interval between two temple bell peals gaped grotesquely. In the silence of his cell, one day's tidal sine of light traced the rise and subsidence of whole existences. Once, in an afternoon lasting longer than belonging, he thought he was about to receive knowledge of his previous lives.

After a while, time ceased. Kraft Sr. came to check on the boy. Returning to conversation enough to anticipate how excruciating time would again be for several days after his father left, Ricky begged the man to stay overnight. But his father had work to attend to, the exploits of world political will.

Ricky enjoyed going into the abbot's study to stare at an image of the Enlightened, a dark ceramic of the man reclining full length, light with deliverance, resting his head on the crook of one arm. This statue was nothing like the thousands of Free treatments of the pose. Its was alien, other. The abbot told him the statue came from far away.

"How far?" the novice asked.

"Farther than you could walk in your life. And it is as old as it is distant."

"Older than I could walk to?" Ricky giggled, against the precepts. But the abbot quietly joined him.

"It is one of the earliest likenesses of the Enlightened in human form. Before that, artists only traced his emblems—his footprint, the tree."

"Why is it so strange?"

The abbot's lips tightened. "The first images were under the spell of the West. Half Hindu, half Roman."

"Is that true?" Ricky touched the reclining figure, finding in it another dislocated, crosstown soul.

"I don't lie to you! What do you like most about him?"

Ricky answered instantly. "The face."

"*Heu.*" A sound that meant anything. "What about the face?"

"It's all opposites. He is smiling deeply, but . . ." The face of a thousand-year-old boy.

The abbot completed the unreachable thought. "But there is nothing in the world to smile about."

Ricky stared at the face's hurt bliss. "Is it valuable?" He hated the question as soon as it left him. The Blue Book value—its rarity—was more than the monastery buildings put together. He had meant to ask: *Do others need this image as much as I do?* But the idea had gotten lost on its way to the air.

The abbot did not reprimand him. "We use it."

The boy reached out to—what?—pet the statue, console it. But in a freak impulse, his hand shuddered. He tried to clip the flinch, but will was one step behind muscle. Even before the figure slipped from its shelf to pieces on the floor, the boy saw the irreversible and wished himself dead, floating lifeless above the earth's atmosphere.

The abbot, twenty years renouncing the illusion of things, cried out at the senseless shards, his shaved head blanching as pale as the white novice's. He said nothing, and the harshness of that silence cut the boy worse than the disaster.

Just months before Ricky had arrived, in a cell near his, an old monk had hanged himself. But the boy could find no place in the desert of ceiling to attach the end of a robe. He sat on the bare floor, refusing meals, forgoing prayers, unable even to close his eyes and listen to his breathing. All he allowed himself was to re-play the event: Had the figure slipped before his hand twitched?

No; he would not rewrite chronology. Had he wished to destroy the thing? Why?

Nothing made sense, least of all the impression that his spasm had responded to some summons from the childlike wrinkles of that face. In the instant just before he sent the figure crashing to the ground, he had heard someone—not the abbot, and certainly not the Enlightened—someone stretched out on the human cordwood pile, violently shouting from out of the hand-lit oven, "Come away!" And those words had burned a serial number into his arm, jerking it in fatal reflex.

The memory of the statue shattering dragged him around his room like a chained fighting cock. He confined himself in the cell until that afternoon when it became a choice of leave or asphyxiate. When he finally threw his door open, the force of sun blinded him like the bare bulb of an interrogation. He took an awkward step over the stoop into the forgotten place and almost tripped over a mass on his doorstep. He dropped to his knees and toyed with the thing as a caveman with first flint. It was the largest shard from the shattered statue.

Ricky took the fragment inside. Not the whole pile of permanent shame. Just this long, pristine surface, undulant as a sensuous seashell. He looked at the simple curve—once the swell of a reclining man's side as he awaited the last migration. After long looking, he made a decision. With a small knife blade and sewing needle lent him to mend his orange robe, he began working the stone surface. He searched below it for artifacts, brushing the pin tip back and forth like an archaeologist's whisk.

Ricky carved for three days. He discovered that his hands, alone of all his willful body, would do what he told them. He could think an arc almost too small to see, then duplicate it on the stone skin. When he put in place the last delineation between tiny vertebrae, the magic intaglio replica blood vessels, he knew he was finished, that he had done what he needed with the shattered waste.

He took the shard back to the abbot and handed it to him. The abbot stared at it through his thick black frames, his face clouding over.

"What is this?" the abbot softly demanded.

Ricky could say nothing. He could add no description to the thing that the thing didn't already contain.

The abbot squinted, running his nail over the startling internal detail. "Do you know what this is?" the abbot asked again.

Ricky did not dare tilt his neck.

"This is the voice box of the last child to leave the Wheel." He put his fingernail inside a striation. "The place where the final farewell shout will appear." He chuckled softly to himself, thanked the boy for the gift, and set it on the shelf the priceless statue had once occupied.

The day arrived when the boy would leave the monastery. And on that day he made his last rounds, taking leave of the monks—the abbot, the senior who had shaved his head, the new crop of novices. As he was given back his lay clothes, Ricky found himself, to his horror, wondering what he'd gotten out of the experience.

That he still asked meant he had gotten nothing. He would forever remain the offspring of his upbringing. Beating through his pallid skin was the sick bias of his home island: we must be *headed* somewhere. Somewhere unprecedented. He would never escape the need to unravel, extend, be *off.* The question itself, the desire to arrive, prohibited passage. He had gained nothing but the ability to chant in Pali, to survive mind-numbing tedium, and to hold his hand steady enough to carve.

He was stunned to learn that he had been in the monastery just under a month. The new school year was still weeks away. Four steps into the world, his whole head was thrown open. He stood on the front edge of outside, frozen like a cave creature blinded by the outside. Eyes, ears, throat, nose, and pores all dilated, back-pedaling to accommodate the exchange threatening on all sides to swamp them.

Four weeks of deprivation had damped down his senses to

exist on thinnest impulse. Now the city erupted around him in a Water Festival, a New Year's of obscene scale. From all sides, people shouted at him to hurry up, buy something from them, save their child, get out of their way. Each word was a firework exploding next to his ear. He was jostled by brushes, bumps, casual collisions, the mercenary seductive assaults of endless unfed cats arching against his ankles.

And smell: a wall of overpowering durian, jasmine, charcoal, animal feces, now vined over with pungent parasites. Quinine barks, mosquito repellent, sandalwood from a second-story window, frying banana oil, the inks of cheap romance magazines, starch from schoolgirls' uniforms, fear in its many street varieties, beetles exhuming the soil, smoke from minidragon industries, lotus leaves rotting in a canal, rice paper, powdered-over fever blisters of infants, cot sores on the old—heat, fever, ecstasy, survival, melting ice. The *scent* of ice melting.

Food everywhere, indecent in its variety. Fried shrimp crackers, *saté,* boiled fish, teas, peanuts sugared or sopped; sesames, rice-flour gels, meats whose awful origin Ricky only now calculated. He stopped a vendor and bought a slivered mango. Crouching by the curb, he held dollops of it to his tongue. Sweet venoms shot straight to his cerebral cortex and blasted across that synapse map like purest Golden Triangle opiate. He had never—he knew now; would never forget (although the sensation was already vanishing, unarrestable)—he had never *tasted.*

Across the spider's web of paved canals, unable to keep to a bearing, a bantam who'd taken too many kicks to the head, he mazed his way through a city that, in his month away, had changed beyond recognition. How could he have missed this all? Just over the river, in a back alley not far from the palace, he was jerked around so violently that he started to run. Something alive, complex, a pulsing, globular disorder tumbled over itself, like Rama's monkey army rampaging in the overgrown forest. He knew the thing from ancient history. Sound filled him, and would not all fit. The attack inflated his veins like a surgical balloon.

It came from no one source. The air itself generated a coordinated agreement of particles, a sonic sphere. At last recognizing it, Ricky yelled the word "Music!" into a crowd that went about sweeping stoops or hanging out carcasses. Someone somewhere had the radio on; that was all. But extended aural abstinence made it seem as if all the molecules of earth had converted themselves into one steel-gong philharmonic. He had learned the song a life or more ago:

Tell, me, little one: Have you ever seen an elephant?

He relearned the folk song in Free class the next semester, almost before his ears had readjusted to the outside. Hair growing back, he sat among chums grown prematurely sophisticated on the two-year circuit, the child elite of four dozen countries—offspring of UN relief agencies, intercontinental traders, lifer servicemen, or covert advisers; children who, like Kraft, claimed they didn't know what their parents did—all linked by the shame of their privileged sahib-ships, each child damp with the friction, misery, and exquisite alarm of awakening urges, each feverishly pursuing fluid formations of allegiance and taste, each of them struggling to get through this toddler's tune, banal in the extreme, singing in half-earnest for the last time before falling into jaded, self-conscious silence.

His face grew hot and his giveaway, traitor albino eyes began to flush themselves from their rims. Ricky sang along in quavering full voice, even while classmates around him openly laughed. His arms and emaciated upper chest shook as if naked in the arctic, but he laughed too, to realize it: he had gained nothing at all. Nothing that he hadn't always, from the start of time, already had.

He sang forte, to drown out that searing, tiny treble vocal cord of accompaniment, that appeal beyond bearing. But he could not outsing memory. At song's end, before they went on to plane geometry, he raised his hand and, in his most pristine Free, in that soft, insistent forensic of children (that planetwide Stone Age tribe still lumped together in one clan), he said what he had learned while gone.

He told how there were children their age, alongside town, just at hand, wasting away hideously, calling out to this international class—this *us*—to come away. Come save them.

Her rubbery resistance, sensuous in the stretch of its catenaries, spectacularly miniatured even by Oriental standards, is so uncannily perfect that it forgoes a navel, bears no hint of that dimple where the mold took its molten feed. What in creation *is* this thing? Smooth, slick, rippled, striated, zoomable to full complexity at every magnification. His textbook snip sneaks through the slippery veneer, revealing whole structures folded within structure. Up here, at organ level, it seems a stash-stuffed haversack, an elastic, single-sheet hyperbolic solid lashing with surface tension a vitreous humor that would otherwise spew jelly all over the cavity.

Press any part, push this subassembly with the blade, that doorstop wedge so narrowed that it becomes lethal. Interrogate the clayey marbling with that oldest simple machine on mankind's curriculum vitae. Separate and split, part the red corpuscular sea until the thing unsheathes, cleaves back into a Rothko cross section that did not exist discretely until this clean trough vectored it.

But do not—God—think who this is. Not a body, not life, not that little girl who—not. Just these forty centimeters, here to here. Heuristic. Virtual reality. The live-in flight simulator. Dr . . . er, Kraft. Twelve-year-old Asian female presents with insidious, edematous living shit creeping up toward . . . Your choice of clubs, and a mock-up fairway. YOU make the call.

Boyhood trains for this, with its pancultural small-animal torture. Species-wide, in every country he ever barnstormed. All its mini-Mengele enterprises, the How-What-Why kits,

"101 Electrochemical Things You Can Do with Grasshoppers."
Ornamental firefly-abdomen rings. Lanyards of sparrow ligament. Enraged rhinoceros beetles, whipped into welterweight
frenzies. Low-voltage lizard pithing, combing back fish scales.
Fruit bats twined to a stake—the poor boy's remote-controlled
helicopter.

All these clandestine recreations mean to retrieve by violence
the thing that violence denies them. And the hardest harrowed,
the most disconsolate, wander into professional sadism.

And this rubbery, slittable resistance, midway between failed
tapioca and a chewed-up gum eraser: here is the prime pornogra-
phy, the stuff of all prurient fascination. Tender obscenity spreads
itself just a micron of latex away from his fingers. He must wade
into lewdness up to the hip. Send out the search-and-destroys.
Isolate the evil empire of spreading microblasts, envelop and excise. Create strategically safe hamlets, your free-fire zones, and
work outward from there.

But wasn't that what the child inside him had in mind? Ease
back the unbearable, extend into the light. *We must head upcountry.*
We. Our whole rainbow coalition. The infant international community. The brilliant Mickey Li, trading pictograph lessons for
jump shot tips. Gopal, whose government already had plans for
him after education. Tati, batik by adoption and grace. Claudio,
with his legendary chocolate sandwiches. Ali, whose feel for market vicissitudes promoted a series of wildly successful commercial
ventures on the lunch hour steps. All off, on foot if necessary, to
answer the call of a sister village, the town of misery beyond explanation's event horizon. Can we get there by candlelight?

Get *where?*

To the core of the blossoming tumor.

He hears the Millstone wind-tunneling in his ear, doing his
geriatric Driver's Ed teacher a month before retirement thing.
Working in close, fistfighting the nodes, Kraft torches them by
fractional degrees, whisking them away with tiny tempered-
steel sliver pickers while the hypertensed attending spits through

his surgical mask, "Wa-wa-watch it! That's the goddamn artery you're slinging around there."

The knee-length formal gown shimmies a bit as the Millstone's foot pumps away at the imaginary safety brake. The man is intermittently unstable at best. A word-salading zealot. Precisely as Kraft lifts the edge of adhesion and begins to shear the disease from where it cleaves to the end of acceptable tissue, the man starts to hyperventilate. "What are you trying to do, serve this girl up as Hamburger Helper?"

Kraft is, in fact, having some trouble self-actualizing here. The Millstone just stares at him, along with the rest of the veiled team. Anesthesiologist keeps pumping the magic punching bag, calling out stock ticker numbers that slip steadily toward debit. Millstone shouts, "Come on. Calm down. Clean things up or we're going to get some vicious scarring."

Scarring? A pretty scar the length of this girl's body would be the luckiest outcome she could hope for. Kraft rejoins the dark assault SWAT forces macheteing their way inland, upriver, deeper inside her.

He sweeps low, near the knots of growth he must defoliate. Blades whirring, like the fairy dragonflies that fly these phantom criticals in. Like the ones he rode in. The hive of bugs that flew their mercy platoon on its last leg into the triple canopy, the schoolchildren strapped in between stacks of charity goods. He saw another swarm of the things the other night on the tube, zoned out again on nonfiction footage, horrific public education stuff, the only shows he has patience for in his unusably few free hours. Trance, daydream, daze, stupor, coma while waiting for the wrap-up, the big—what's the undoer of bang?

These TV choppers: the same make, same breed, same *machines* that, between unlisted missions, airlifted their prefab schoolhouse upcountry to the jungle village he himself had picked out on the map and insisted upon. The one that had called out to him.

Millstone does not flutter now, does not even breathe. He is waiting for Kraft to finish the delicate stuff before cuffing and

booking him. Wouldn't be so quiet in here if it weren't an ambush. Somebody's even turned off the radio, the vid, the eternal
ubiquitous soundtrack. It's silent, anacoustic, surf-in-the-ear-
vessels time. Somewhere outside the operating theater—where?
adjacent? just above this room? have they gotten loose, taken over
the institution?—he can hear the familiar sounds of his ward,
children of daily abuse, voices in the undergrowth, singing the
latest in a continuous descent of jingles that propagate out of wed-
lock, ignorant of their parentage:

> Ching, Chang, Chinaman chopped at a rat,
> Snarfed it back like a ginger snap.

And then *sucked it down,* and then *slurped it up.* Every restless per-
mutation along the way back to suckling innocence. Chop, Chow,
Chang, Chinaman, and then it comes to Kraft, in a ginger snap: the
disguised anxiety hidden in this verse enchantment. How are we
going to beat back the rat-eating Asian armada from our already
wretchedly refused shores?

The world, as seen nightly, in increasing doses of nonfiction
TV used to drug himself unconscious, is awash in open boats.
Moroccans landing on the casinoed beaches of southern France.
Cubans punting to Miami. Albanian fishing craft listing to Italy.
The Kurds, targeted by all takers, beached, landlocked in dry
mountain seas. Asia flooded, dammed behind chain-link pens in
Hong Kong, Formosa, Nippon.

The favored ones are put through the holding camps' full interrogation. Are you a *real* political refugee, or just starving? (As if
indigence weren't oppression by its maiden name.) This sieve sorts
life into Right, Left, the same old two deciding queues, quintessential camp winnowings. Mass mockeries of the Last Ordeal,
only none is ever the last. You: through. You, you, and you: one
giant step back.

Escape this deluge by turning a handful of rat gourmets back to
their so-called dominions? Pitiful, pointless, like the little blond

lowlands kid with his digit in the dike. The Leg-ups' worst, concerted nightmare scenario: the wages of empire, brown foster
foundlings returning with a vengeance. They trawl in solid con-
voys, every serviceable craft commandeered, skulling away from
the mass quarries of bone and lime. Rivulets of humanity trickle
into unbailable flood, a tidal surge coursing across privilege's
topographic contours. They wash away the sparse island respites,
leveling them in one swell of instant erosion.

The whole South is cut loose, fleeing by any means the positive
feedback loop of privation, a step in front of the aerial canister and
tracer. The very air is ignited behind their spree, the shock wave
lifting them along, flinging them flying-monkey style toward that
figment of deliverance. Driven out, and by whom? By the eminent domaineers, the same squatters to whose blessed destinations
they bail out.

Driven out by dragonflies, the agents provocateurs he saw
again last night in blue phosphor simulacrum, that cozy, flick-
ering glow the color of a patio bug-zapper. The hum of one
too, but more curdlingly eerie, without soundtrack. Only the
sober, clinical voice-over, "In the rainy season of sixty-*buzz*,
combined Special Forces of *buzz* . . ." Hit upon the surreal little
fairy plan . . . But *fact*. As in, actually happened. And there, on
factual film, while the factual narrator mediated the escapade,
was Operation Wandering Soul. One of the roster of colorfully
named undertakings: Operation Flaming Dart. Mayflower.
Royal Phoenix. Rolling Thunder. Niagara. Junction City. Sea
Swallow. Linebacker Two.

Because he could not hope for sleep, he chose numb distraction, nonfiction Wandering Soul, the sinister lace-wing roundup.
The voice-over explained it in teacherly tones, described the sick
side-junket, more literary than military. Dragonflies at night
swarm above unsuspecting villages, high enough to be indistinct
from the season's background locust whirr, the night's dark radiation. On cue, spectral voices cut in, lighting up the night like
aural phosphor flares. "Our babies," native collaborators call out,

translating the names to regional variants. "Our offspring! *Have you forgotten us?*"

Disembodied chill semaphores, piped through megaphones at three A.M., a crude and bizarre attempt at demoralization howled down from haunted heaven into the animist jungle. A monsoon of invisible, amplified voices from out of an unreal parallel. The point was simply to ply digestion's pits, to curdle skin, to play terror off of shame by leveling the claim these villagers would be most inclined to believe in. We are your ancestors, expelled from your frag-shattered pantry altars, exiled by your bad karma and evil politics. Give up, capitulate, come over. Do this, our last bidding.

The whole project might have been pure theater, cinematic American weirdness in the jungle. But the account was too outrageously surreal for Kraft to be anything else than the recognizable exploits of the Foreign Service's fighting wing. Film didn't register the ground panic, or say whether the hot stick shoved down the anthill bore results. It's all inference, aerial recon, a grainy, underexposed, handheld frame from on high, inside the chopper, the innuendo of mayhem.

But the *effects* of the operation, its results, were never at issue. All the instigators wanted was all they ever want: a gold star, extra credit for inventive derangement. Look what we made. Our program, our play, our restless, destined superiority. Take that. Hit me back. Tell me what happens next. Love me.

The camera panned too much to make out the protagonists. And the voices calling out directives to one another were drowned out by the amplifiers doing the grandparent souls, and the omniscient narrator turning the whole crazed event back into fable. Kraft stared up close, his nose to the monitor like a kid pressed to mall glass. Couldn't see a thing. But he knew who was flying the beasts before the show even aired. The same ones who dreamed up the scheme to saturation-bomb the countryside with transistor radios, so the rice farmers could listen to agitprop. (They took the batteries out to build bombs.) The endlessly inventive crew, the fecund fathers of the same meandering band just then heading upcountry, two dominoes over. Air America by all its multinational names.

Then, briefly caught on his private mental celluloid, leaning out of the open cage to peer down into impenetrable blackness: it's Kraft Sr. Leans too far, too curiously, and the charm, at gravity's first callow come-on, slips the man's neck. The silver bauble Dad has had forever, the one that's protected him from pitching into utter, pragmatic corruption, is lost. Takes a decade or more to float down the air current parfait. Winds bat it about gently for years, like seals with a beachball. It traverses the sealed border on its long paradrop down and lies in a river valley, awaiting the next child.

This glimpse of darkness's raiding party cut neatly to a pledge break where the pain-o-meter declared how few degrees shy we were of need's complete pacification. The association condemns him to dredge up that contemporaneous Operation Mayflower— junior high musical, lyrics to tunes pinched from a smash hit based on a cheery little Dickens book about the criminally destitute. The production was set at that posh Chao Phraya River hotel where Maugham liked to luxuriate. A Thanksgiving show, a holiday that half the student body had never heard of. Act One, Pilgrims land by *klong* boat, meet Native Americans, and come to culturally relative understanding with same. Act Two, contemporaries repeat same maneuver, landing upriver in modern-day City of Angels (now cleverly playing itself), assuring the Native Free there to greet them that

We'd give an-y-thing
To keep peace flour-ish-ing,
'Cause it means ev-ry-thing (ev-ry-thing?)
Ev-ry-thing to us!

God: What had they been thinking? Same thought that's still dressed up in every night's news serial. Assist history, by any protection racket necessary, to its unbridled outcome. Push it along its path, civilization's two-stroke engine, condensing out of cold, cosmic dust the raw swaps and consolidations of power that are its only end. The stuff of every school musical.

It blazes into his head as he curls over Operation Operation, the Millstone ready to restrain him should Kraft give him cause. Atonement. Everything in his innocent suggestion—let us fortunate ones go upcountry and build a school—every word in this selfless reversal of "Please, sir, I want some more," already smacked of a child's compensation. At-one-ment for adulthood's sins. Somewhere in this history-ravaged place, they might make up for the outrage to dead ancestors.

What can he hack at next? Here, something slashable. A fix, a small blow, a nickel in the drum for the old meliorist dream. He circles and slipknots the hideous foreign bits, cuts them off and kills them. He drops the insidious nodules, pellet by pellet, into the waiting pan. It's one of those saint's offering plates full of detached teeth, deflated eyes, severed digits. The emblems, the means of continuous martyrdom. Tainted nipples on a dish. "Want to know a secret?" the girl's foster mother asked him one night, early on, when all their secrets had already been taken hostage. "For some reason, my breasts . . ."

"Wait, wait. You aren't going to make me do anything kinky?" He could still talk like that. How long ago? Only a *week*? Dissimulating monster. Where had he gotten the strength for such bravura pretense?

"Shh. I'm trying to tell you something." Something you will always be able to hold over me. "For some reason, my breasts . . ."

"These here?"

"Quit. Mm. For some reason, my breasts . . . aren't *sensitive*? Usually, I can't feel anything at all from here to here. But when I'm with you . . . ?"

It seemed the announcement of a small victory, a further invitation to dine out. They had been young once, insouciant with each other. For all of fifteen minutes, one Saturday night, before they shed the respective pseudonyms.

"What do you mean, usually?"

This woman was not even Linda by looks anymore. Ready to bolt or bail, or some combination. "I meant, previously."

"You just need an older man is all." Still up to the joke, still thinking it *was* one, failing to see how irony fizzles into fact. Because yes, he made them pucker and yearn, stand and be counted. He alone, but only because the others had never discovered the secret to insanely upbeat females. They have this craving they don't like to admit. Hate in themselves, in fact. The sinister flip side to blissful Do-Bee-dom. They like to be vised, pinched on a neck nerve and held at attention, unsheathed, paralyzed with incisors, bitten.

Vulgar intimacy—the sick equivalent of his fingerwork now, pawing every nude, chalk-scored sector of this comatose pubescent. Little girl and an older man who knows her more privately than any lover she might live long enough to meet. A thigh is a thigh, its soft, femoral vee made more suggestive by the wax-pear color of her incised epidermis, the blood sluicing away from the suction, the smell of the cautery. Were it not for this gang of hired hit men around him, he would talk to her, soothe her though this shattering foreplay for which she only fakes anesthesia.

Talk to her. Softly, in that language, the one he rushes back inside himself to rescue from the burning structure. Softly now, when one might say anything, anything at all. Broach the account he just now reconstructs, tell her while she sleeps, when the weirdest fears slip out like wild things gliding across night's closet threshold, stupidly left ajar. As he works the appallingly sharp scissors, his hands detach from him. They carry on working, as discrete and sovereign as the Invisible Man's white gloves. He looks on, fear blotting out his receptor sites, the primal, convulsive stuff, like those waking dreams when he imagines reaching for the phone in pitch blackness and touching a human hand. Terror not of the imagined threat, but of *imagining*.

The parade he himself devised passes in review under his autonomous fingers. After two inert decades, the details of that end run on suffering come back to him. Two dozen kids from ten different countries—the oldest, sixteen; the youngest, nine. Not one had prior building experience. Traveling under the Institute flag—the White Monkey General—they represented no government and followed no program but care. Of course they had to have an operational name for the thing. Every human action needed its cover. They took their tag from the dominant culture hiding behind its rainbow front, the one this fantastic fifth column meant to atone for: Operation Santa Claus.

Those fourteen days rise up out of the girl's cracked-open hip as he chases infection up her obliterated leg. The specifics of that old disaster hatch like malarial larvae in this aseptic room. He must tell someone, or be pulled apart in memory's undertow. Tell who? Linda is out, impossible. She would guess in a minute, hear in the first syllable the reason why he ever even remotely loved her once. She would see in a flash just how she first appeared to him—her hint of strangeness, the half-brown, half-breed tone that he clung to while running from.

He can tell her nothing. Not after the reciprocal awfulness she has already signed over to him. Not after her airy courage—anesthesia, he now sees—in entrusting him with her worst, even while searching out his to treat it.

He replays these mangled mental tapes while his knuckles bang up against the clamps and retractors keeping Joy's invaded layers out of his hands' way. He anchors his thumb against her pulped tibia to steady himself. Recovering the lost event is beyond him. Anything that happened less than four weeks ago, the start of this rotation, eternity's internship, is hopeless. Pre-pre-med is a rococo blur. Details, names and dates, the blinding clarities, the sidebar precision bombs from off the front page of his life's morning paper of record: gone.

Some muscle gasp refusing the irreversible gash he was just about to make in this pelvis retrieves him. He looks up to a room of cackling masks. With mouth and nose blanked, laughter and horror collapse into identical slits. He's covered; he can fall in as if he never left. Can triangulate by the key-word method.

"Did you read about the five-year-old girl found guilty of inciting her molestation? Judge said she was behaving in a flirtatious manner."

The era's hot topic. Team banter, doing its best to hold off the horror of the interior. Who's speaking? Impossible to tell one from the other. Identical covey of cloaked desperadoes, green skullcaps, white bandanas pulled up over their faces, waylaying the living stage. Just throw yer limbs down and nobody will get hurt. He looks from one to the other, squints. Can't tell who is talking; wouldn't know who it was even if he could trace the source. He doesn't know any of these people.

"Brazen little tramp. Got what she was asking for."

Fiend. No one could make that joke without meaning it. But why fault the man for repeating what the judge actually *said*? Even if they overthrow the travesty on appeal, disbar the judge, sue the robes off the sucker, the thing still transpired. This country, this self-defiling race, its reeling, abused, psychotic, accusatory voiceprint conscience seeking relief by compounding outrage, is his home. A place thrashing about for release everywhere but at the source of absolution.

Memory, once it has been jettisoned as useless, turns whatever is left of social probity into whoopie-cushion comedy. Kraft, slack at the center of a shameless knot of grown-ups dressed like a bunch of budget summer-stock transvestite Klansmen guffawing at the apocalyptic tidbits and lascivious human-interest fillers that wrap up the thousand-year news broadcast, pros who have grown so enslaved with brain-inflaming spirochete that the words "moral decency" provoke a nervous ironic titter, thinks: Yes. Got what we asked for. Solicited our own bloody wholesale rape like the cheap little tush-swinging toddlers we are.

Sick insight opens to him like a shining flower. Another night's late interval, a lifetime after their film-hopping honeymoon. She had boxed him into the pillow and was turning him to face her, an insistence he easily deflected with some squirming familiarity, maybe nibbling a rib. She suddenly demanded, "Little boy! Where *are* you? Were you ever sexually abused as a child?"

He had his half snort already perfected. "Not to the best of my recollection." Recollection, of course, never any better than what experience can afford. "Why do you ask?"

He pieces together the answer only now, after the idiot's annihilating delayed reaction. *She* was. His hunch is immediately gang-raped by grotesque irrelevances. How old? How long? How badly? Who? Stranger? Family friend? *Family?* Suspicion's principal suspect—oh, awful—is always the victim.

"You show all the classic symptoms," she teased, tickling his ribs. The playful ebullience, the intimate, knowing tone.

Little Linda, molested? In a second, it swells to explain everything, as complete as it is unconfirmed. He wants to run from the cutting room, race up the four floors to her office, trailing the frail girl's soft tissue. Stand in the door and berate her. How dare you grin like that. How can you trust? How can you *live*?

Chill chases up his nape, the sudden snap of floorboard in the sealed pitch-dark. Her scar is this stupid optimism, never being able to feel, to admit how bleak we really are. . . . Her whole compulsively giving, holistic healer routine—the ultimate evasion, supreme crippling. Total anesthetic seal-off, cureless because never forgotten.

Sex, her expert damp abandonment, their freestyle, exquisite wrestling matches on his apartment floor: *Are we going to do some aerobics for a little bit, or what?* That she could even ask without retching, let alone implore so amply, so avid . . . Pleasure, wantonness like he has seen her take in the exchange is inconceivable, worse than obscene. Feverishly faking full recovery; flinging herself into the one thing her whole soul must cringe from, just to consider.

The operating banter has moved on to the junior high schooler who killed her baby because the courts wouldn't let her put it up for fostering. Silently, he closes what is left of the ruined girl. She is now indistinguishable from the Asian twelve-year-old from the other side of the river, the one his pilgrim party met on its tropical Christmas operation a half world ago. The little girl, driven from her village by voices, ancestors calling out of the sky. The one on film—too familiar for horror anymore; exactly why they keep reprinting it until it is threatless and limp—her clothes burned off in a pillar of flame, running down the road to the nearest help, the nearest *adult,* who is busy photographing this kiddie nude.

He sews shut the provocative one, who, after all her eager search for approval, would be best off mercy-pithed now. Nothing remains of her but macerated tissue. The salvaged pulp is probably still infiltrated, the search-and-destroys as worthless as they ever were. And he, Kraft, committed this atrocity, punished her worse than any crack-hopped, tremor-fingered, street-ganged, random serial murderer could. More unforgivable, what he's done, because more conscientious, more selfless, professional, deliberate, necessary: autoclaved mutilation of love.

LINDA LETS HERSELF in quietly, her loaner latchkey slithering through the Yale's tumbler tunnel. The elated raiding of a few days back now feels more like answering a summons. She never knows what to expect anymore, in the intervals when he is ostensibly off call. She stands in the forced door, listening for some clue in the dark. Just the sound of suppressed respiration from the far side of the threshold is enough to trigger ancient panic attacks, a rude head rush. The sotto voce threats emanating from his silent front hall fill her with desire to deny every attachment before it can be denied her. Her hands struggle to pull the knob forever shut while she forces them to push it open. There is no cure but hair of the dog.

His apartment is a pit, an abyss. Why did she get involved with this emotional leper in the first place, when all the signs cautioned her off, when he himself told her, with his last remnant of worldly charm, that he would one day go surgical on her? She must be the real sicko here, in this thing up to her hospital insignia. Trying to love the man, for no more reason than to prove everyone wrong. One little supportive smile, one recreational theraplay scenario and she hoped to strip the permanent, told-you-so, hardened finish from the boy's bleak, condemning H and P. Why try to plead the ludicrous case for recovery in this irrevocable place? Charity can be only a kind of belated revenge.

She recognized him instantly, the jokey verbal competence, trying to charm her while a host of betraying postures peeped out from behind his poise like live ordnance poking out of the living room wall. She thought to outmatch his evasion, hold out her arms to him—always her best feature. Unleash the entire arsenal of care. *I can make you whole. Rub your pulse back to beating.* Pathetic porta-box first aid, like sprinkling camphor on emphysema.

She needed little Ricky's infirmity for her own private ends. To overcome exactly this dread that swells thermostatically, filling her holding cavity, immobilizing with the worst that memory and imagination can conjure. His labored breathing breaks in waves around her in the black room, a sound she thought she could love but would run from now if she could.

One of these days I will come home and he . . . She rehearses the worst cases as she tentatively flicks on the light with her grocery-bent elbow. And before thought can shape itself around the image, she finds him just as the much-practiced terror predicts. Precisely the way she knew she would one day come home to find him. He is sitting in his makeshift, bachelor meal nook. He might be only waiting for his mate to come by, waiting to tell her, with a protracted shaggy-dog smile, of the day's surgical shoestring catches. But he is not.

He slumps at the counter, head down. In front of him, in fastidiously arranged ranks and columns, stretching out along the synthetic Formica plain in a kind of orchard-perfection, are more quart containers of milk than she can count. Enough to baby-shower a whole nursery of infant teethers, sufficient to slop down a day care's generous week's worth of cookies. And each of the perspiring cardboard towers bears a smudgy gray-scale portrait emblazoned with the caption: HAVE YOU SEEN THIS CHILD?

She sucks in sharply. Now comes that awful scraping, focus dulled by refusal. He just slumps there, languidly scouring the faces and disappearance data for the revealing pattern, unaware, even, of her presence. Should she call someone? Who? Certainly not those crazies down at the ER. Her clinical composure, she discovers, works only in the kingdom of pedes. She is less than helpless to help someone who was ten already when she was still wet with expelled placenta.

She steps toward him gingerly, careful not to startle. "Ricky? Low-fat, I hope?"

She steadily subdivides the distance between them, thinking that if she can just get a hand on his shoulder . . . She closes enough space to make out that the wax-coated photo-transfers he so intently stares down are close twins, stereoscopic. Then and now: age five, at time of abduction. Today, age nine. But if the child is missing, how . . . ?

The captions explain. The last known photo of the missing one on earth—some school portrait or candid birthday shot— has been computer-aged. The smiling, composite cartilage of the snatched-away has been fed through a fast transform that knows all about the way tissue bloats and widens and falls slack year by year, everything that even a face flush with the priceless unpredictability of love must inevitably become over the scatter run of time.

She's seen these three times a week for the last decade, and still flinches. She, Linda, who no longer even blinks at flailing spastics or livid purple human whetstones. The dairy industry's notorious public service spot. Why here, and not on Wonder bread wrappers or cheerful two-tone jars of Peter Pan? Something to do with the antagonistic effects of calcium on kidnapping. A way of shaming, over a bowl of Cocoa Charms, that most common of abductors, the estranged parent, into returning the paschal stolen goods. No, the reason for milk, like the cartons' malignant subjects, this brigade of the universally missing, lies buried deep in the North American bedrock, the Vishnu Schist.

The piper has been busy of late, logging overtime, capitalizing on the general spread of night, dragging his net across the subdivisions and condolands, the isolated farmhouses and condemned public projects, the sprawling, illegal squatter towns that compose the world's temporary housing. Has been everywhere, threading down the centuries of serpentine trail heads, spreading the hits across all continents so randomly that no international bureau could hope to trace so much as a backwater fraction of his route or modus.

She fights the urge to finger one of the wax dossiers, knowing that, as with litter on the street, the one who touched it last is responsible. She has already participated in this state's drive to register the children at greatest risk. She has watched the authorities create whole photo and fact portfolios of prospective kidnappees, take advance prints, with almost loving anticipation of the theft they mean to prevent.

All-points bulletins *in advance,* yet another Midas-like touch to the Golden State. The Binge-Purge State, the SIDS State. Even as she debates turning and fleeing, an empty billboard somewhere within a few miles of his flat is attracting nightly crowds of people who gather below it, seeing the ghostly apparition of a recently abducted nine-year-old Latina. It's been the "spot" for two weeks running now, scene of violent outbursts at the company's refusal to light the blank placard for each night's pilgrimage. The Portent State. The Unsustainable State. Give nothing else, but give good video.

Linda bends away from the quart-carton gallery, the yearbook of Annihilation Middle School, certain she will discover the little miracle girl's features among the lost graduating class if she but looks. "Planning a lactose binge, buddy?" she says, falling frail and flat, blindly fumbling for his arm. Their contact thuds neutrally. "Shakes? Malts? Frappes? Smoothies?" Repeat the weak gag until you get an anemic laugh, scold, scream—any response at all.

When he looks up, it stuns. His eyes swim with conspiracy, sparkling with theories so clear he need not even spell them out aloud. Look: the young everywhere are getting ready, rehearsing—children of the murderous projects, two-pound needle-preemies lighter than their mothers' controlled substance ingestion during term, gang killers, stick figures from the Southern nations, even these privileged princes, snatched out from under their kiddie kreative movement instructors' eyes—they are preparing, leaving at night on some vast, planetwide, still-obscure dress runthrough. . . .

Her eyes water at him, pleading, and he groans, deflated by her failure to grasp his flash of explication. He shies away from her, slips her grip and returns to reviewing the troops, a dejected ancient emperor of milk containers, lining up his glazed, ceramic cadres for a last muster preparatory to their mass live burial. Kidnapped, abducted, seized, carried away, *shanghaied*. Marco Poloed, the man who left shortly after the departure of the Children's Battalion and was still there when the second emigrant wave, the Ratcatcher Expedition, took off for ports unknown. Does she believe that her case load of historical ignorants chose theirs, of all five billion possible scripts for amateur physiotheatrics, simply because they liked the *plot*? She forces off his accusation before it congeals in her. One more incriminating motivic link and she will be down alongside him on emotional hands and knees, scraping her nails in attempt to excavate sense from the resistant cartons.

They multiply in front of her, these paired public service posters. On the left, Child at disappearance; on the right, Child computer-reared into the present. Each distinct case claims her, calling for undiscovered therapies, yet-to-be invented regimens of exercise that might break the loop. Each smiles, even mugs for the camera, *Get it right this time, 'cause I'm outta here.* Their impish grins of send-off sweetness hint dimly at the foreordained. But around the eyes, the way the cheeks crinkle in imitation mirth yet reel with bewildered trust, there, perched above the dollhouse frock collar or tiny blazer and clip-on tie, skin's swaddling linen already fights back a muscle tic, the twitch of some other, older, extradited once-child's pathetically misjudged attempt to out-smile horror.

Twelve dozen kiosks calling HAVE YOU SEEN THESE FACES? sprout up across Ricky's kitchen counter top, an orchard of shock. She will never have a chance at any of these cases. They are farther from reach than her most mangled cutting-room vets. She shuts her mind to the sea of stereo views, blots them out for her own safety. The only case she can still hope to influence here is him. The emperor.

She wants to rush the receptacles, hustle them all into available refrigerators before prolonged exposure to room temperature can lace them with toxins. Ricky's undergraduate, bite-sized appliance might save, say, six.

"What in the Blessed Nurser's name are we going to do with all this milk?" She holds him, and he submits to petting. "Haven't you heard that dairy is out?" Expelled from the Four Foods pantheon, she would go on, if she could find the will. They might give them away, dispense them door to door like promos for a hot new product. But in a land where even the tamperproof shrink-wrap is sewn with random malignancy, no one would accept such a compromised gift.

She cradles him, a man old enough to be her abuser uncle. After their first formal evening together—that moviethon, just weeks ago—she'd called her mother. "Look, I know I've been wrong about this in the past, but there's this guy. I just don't need anything anymore. All the anxiety's gone. It feels, I don't know, like arriving. Coming home."

She actually used the taboo word out loud, to one of the two people who shared her lifelong embrace of mutual blackmail, the tacit refusal to hand over the place's negatives. Her mother, who kept holy water in the fridge, who threw elaborate coloratura fits about far less, simply shrugged audibly over the wires and asked, "How do you know you love him? I haven't even met him yet."

Nobody ever meets anybody. Always a matter of equanimity and stealth, a match-up of missing parts under cover of deniable darkness. Once he joked about it: a furtive shuffle as she came in the room, and he would look up, saying, "Oh, nothing!" Now, when she kisses him for no reason except that they are both lost, both all-points material, he looks up the same way, only the terror, the furtiveness, is real.

She does not know the first thing about him. And she will leave him now, agree finally to be the abandoning one, the way he wanted from the start, knowing less than on the day they crossed paths on rounds. She begins taking the milk outdoors, four quarts at a time, to leave for whatever mange might run wild in this alley. Her eyes catch the open instrument case, the tarnished French horn sitting on the Formica table, it too slated to be taken out and interrogated, perhaps beaten. Has he actually been playing the ancient thing, diverting his auditorium of abductees with scales or remembered grade-school showpiece repertoire?

"Ricky? You had the horn out?" Of course, asking is no good. As always, the accumulated inconsequences, the trivia that make all the difference in this peopled world, go unanswered.

She picks up the twisted coil of brass and hands it to him. "Play me something." Up to your room and practice an hour before you even think of going outside.

She reverse computer-ages him, back to age eight. Or not him: another close-to-the-chest orphan DP, borrowing Ricky's face in order to blend in with these new surroundings, to mimic himself into inconspicuousness. A reborn half-Kraft, but done over in Linda's brown, tagged by her goofy earlobes and big teeth that will one day be, but only too late, after their attendant early trauma has hardened, beautiful. She sees the boy's features for an instant, and her lungs collapse in on themselves, as if the resentful child himself slugs her in the solar plexus. She must run from the apartment before just looking at the man kills her.

It will never happen now, the ending they were supposed to have. This one will run, instead, like some women's magazine fiction, the last column clipped out along a coupon silhouette from the flip side of the page. She tries to come about, console herself with fierce pragmatics. They would have made the worst kind of parents in any event. With their combined professional commitments, real children would have been impossible, except perhaps through some offspring time-sharing arrangement, two weeks out of the year, like a gulfside condominium. And the latest photos from the continuous news flash would thermal-fax themselves, register in their newborn's Play-Doh face, turning the least hint of growth unbearable.

Kraft, the adult version, grown up in every particular except the essential, looks at the musical instrument this woman places in his hands. He turns it over, inspecting the valves the way a dinner guest might sneak a discreet peek at the china mark. He sticks a cupped hand in the bell and makes that trademark pucker sound of brass players warming up their mouthpieces. She hopes dizzily for a moment that he'll play, bring the remaining carton mug shots to life again, singing in a long file behind him. Instead, he removes the horn from his lips before any real sound can slip out.

When he speaks, it is absolutely clinical. Competent, surgical, perfectly modulated, as if he has never been out on anybody's ledge, as if his soul has not just been caught strung out all over its dark night. "The girl will be legless, if grace allows her that much. At the hip. Mutilation. For my money, worse than the most senseless accident."

Worse, because antiseptic, deliberate. The girl's adopted society has marked her for life, the way some clans disfigure a sickly child, chop it up to prevent reinfestation of the next born.

Linda looks out his window, east toward the desert, where people once buried their young under the kitchen floor, to keep an eternal eye on them. The marks he has made on this girl, the skilled, high-tech dismemberments, were all for this: to keep her soul from coming back, raiding the world again in the form of *their* child, a child she has just glimpsed, but who will never, now, return.

She will break for the door as soon as he looks the other way. But Kraft just sits there, fiddling with the bits of detachable tubing, in the creepy calm of someone reconciled to being slated from the start for a rented death. He has already made giant strides toward arriving, in half the usual time, at that neighbor ward, the mirror service to their own, where an opposite incontinent band hangs around the TV room, staining the floor in a pony-show ring.

The hospital: she tries to remember how long Kraft's Carver rotation is to last. Can she avoid him in the halls between now and the day he's slated to go? She might sit tight and wait until his impending departure makes him the one responsible for leaving. She thinks what he has next. Intensive Care.

They are still colleagues a while longer, day laborers in the high-tech cathedral enterprise. She could avoid him for weeks in the huge monastic cloisters, the intricate, self-regulating, self-sustaining community of specialists from abusive phone receptionists to sicko plastic reconstructors whose idea of a conversation piece is a silicon implant on the coffee table.

In fact, the industry is so sprawling that it has managed to disguise its chief purpose even from her. They are deep in the process of setting up an underground railway, one that conducts the lost causes from here to the next nightmare halfway house as quickly as possible. That's what they do for a living, she and this man, her topical lover, this unstable, latex-faced anchorman whom she has just discovered sitting in the dark surrounded by a bright school assembly of faces on a hundred spoiling milks. The boy hornist's job is to cut up sick children—their legal and sanctified abductor.

What dying childhood needs—so obvious, she thinks, to anyone who's been paying attention—is not another swank kid-

killer like Carver, perfunctory holding tank for prepping the virtually dead. It needs a larger-than-life tree-fort resort where a
lifetime's transactions can take place faster than in the outside.
She knows the shape: an arcaded, terraced, gardened, courtyarded
children's pavilion, with ceramic and brocade, half timber and
gingerbread cupolas, a live-in architectural anthology of hospices
in the oldest sense. Everyone welcome; check your maturity at
the foyer. A multiweek, all-expenses-played vacation crawling
around the plasterboard moats and battlements with the shrinks
and muscle-unkinkers, everybody horsing around side by side
for a change. Solve society's spreading fester at the source, and
wouldn't half of all the day's intractables shrivel away? Break the
downward, dry-sucking cycle of indigence in one generation . . .

BUT THE COSTS, woman. Less than any other air castle, mall,
megamulti-theater, hardened silo, Stealth production facility, or toxic manufacturer's outlet park. She could campaign,
show with incontestable charts that we can pay now or pay a
lot more later. But to figure the figures would take *foresight,* an
increasingly fabulous commodity. Conventional wisdom, that
old oxymoron, cannot afford to destroy those monsters eating
our wealth alive. We'll carry on down the perpetual sinkhole
until the poor give up their debilitating poverty. It's that simple,
a simplicity consistent with life in the kingdom of once-obscene
wealth, where servicing the previous years' accumulated debt
will soon be enough to run up another year of deficit. The land
of the nationwide centrist cell, ready to backlash at anything
that hints at its real condition. A landmass-wide, inhospitable
hospital clutching a status quo that has already broken up . . .

   She sees again to the milk disposal. The flight reflex and its
strangled form, the need to rush to him with selfless assistance,
collide inside her like two thrill-romp first cousins in stolen cars,
each marine-screaming in her head, trying to outterrorize the
other right up to the moment of impact. She cannot bear to look
at him another second.

"Not to worry," his puffy lips issue, hissing. "We've put a little Tiger Balm on the stump, and we're keeping a sharp eye." Said almost sweetly, reassuringly, a sick reference to that mother of a new admission who for two months had used the Orient's popular smear-on cure-all to fix a vertebrae-dissolving nightstalker crawling up her baby's back.

"Tiger Balm Gardens, Hong Kong. World's gaudiest theme-park cure retreat and the transpacific's answer to Anaheim. Chinese kinderland. Been there, in my previous incarnation as Youth in Asia. I ever tell you that?"

You've never told me anything but "Shut your face," she would singsong back. She hates him now, like a spurned daughter, or closer. She wants to close his eyes for good with a quick fingernail gouge. But he jerks suddenly and forestalls her, swinging the horn's fluted crocus-cup up to his mouth and playing.

He is rusty and uncertain, stabbingly out of shape. He has not played this evening, or anytime this decade. But another awful warble subverts the sound. He is trying to bend tones through the tube that are too inflected to fit down a Western bore. Over-blowing, half-valving, he jury-rigs pitches that have long been expelled from the orchestral overtone series. Another scale, a further sound.

He pulls the instrument away without looking at her. "Thai song," he explains to her, apologetically. The two words, so gentle and awful and defenseless, slip into her chest and quietly bruise the place beyond healing. She will never get away now, never be able save herself or him. *Ricky, Ricky,* she wants to say, *put your head down, here, on my softness.* But her throat is coagulate, hopeless.

"Dear moon," he goes on, "give me rice. Give me curry. Give me a copper ring to tie around the little one's wrist. Give me an elephant for the little one to ride. Give me a lizard that will cry, 'Tokay!'"

She takes him outside, thinking back to when such a thing was therapeutic. Each trunk in the ratty stand of palms outside his apartment is emblazoned with a psychedelic cuneiform that, when read across like an acid-house Burma-Shave, announces: "Dope will cope with hope."

Linda walks him like one of her tensor-flexor train wrecks. She tries to tell him something distracting, something palpable he might hook back into. She tells him about the story theater project. Nicolino—

"Which one . . . ? Oh, right; Methuselah." Pretending he doesn't know the creature who has been menacing the expanse between them.

Nico has come up with a beautiful idea. She giggles just to think of it, almost recapturing her pretense of equanimity, the serenity that comes with being sweet-and-twenty and indiscriminately able to love. "They want to form a Hamelin traveling company. Isn't that great? Hel-*loo*. I'm asking you a question?"

He smiles rapidly and nods.

"One of them has found this weenie cartoon map of the city, and they're picking out venues. They want to bring it all over town, all their neighborhoods, put it on at . . ."

"Perform? In front of people?"

"Isn't that how plays usually go?"

"Where the hell do they think . . . ?"

An electrogram jitter spasms across Linda's temple. Gently, she reins him in. Astonishing, how easy it is to affect a convincing calm.

She falters a minute, studies him, then against all training fails to take appropriate action. "They have their pick of spots," she carries on. "Schools jump at this kind of thing, if it's free. Arts and crafts fairs, public parks, old people's homes—you could do one show an afternoon from now until you grew up. Well, maybe not until *you* grew up . . ."

He forces the expected grunt, but a beat too late.

"You're really old school, aren't you? Keep them in bed until they've got runny ulcers up the wazoo. Can't you see? Something like this will do more for them than our entire body-shop operation put together. Get out and see the place, playact. And it's not half bad for the audience either."

She drops all hope of pulling off her assignment—to tell Kraft about his role, recruit him for the main motley. "Oh, buddy," she veers again, too cheerily, "you *have* to come see the costumes they've made out of nothing. Rats! They really are. And the cuddliest vermin you can possibly . . ."

Rats: skateboarding, hoop-stuffing, switchblading, glue-sniffing, slam-dancing, card-collecting, video-vitiated, guiltless, impoverished, sinned-against, discriminated-against jungle-gym victims. They killed the cats and bit the babies in their cradles. *Rats.* A word all over the well-meaning popular press lately: the current euphemism for the dozen million disinherited minors on the street in the lush subtropics, down where "disappear" has long gone transitive. Where the police sooner murder a waif than work up the papers. Where the advance cities have already slipped, as theirs does now, into uncontrollable turf war, the vortex of street free market that squares off big business against urchins. Where whole abandoned countries consume steady supplies of diced-up lives on their determined hurtle downward.

Even here, in the North, on ground still a meter above flood, intact for another half decade, they have all gone precociously, sophisticatedly *rat,* superaged by witnessing ten hundred slow-mo deaths before puberty. Told that all the purchasable world is theirs, then unceremoniously strip-searched for grabbing it, they know their real birthright early, the transparency of the fables handed them.

Kraft is silent, thinking: She could not have gotten them back into these dated fairy suits—innocence's routed camp—if it didn't fit their own hidden purpose. Somehow, they're using her.

And yet she goes on touting the idea, blithely, unsuspecting. "Then they return, in the second act, dressed as . . ."

He tries to call it back, that pestilent poem, born of an older, even more pernicious myth, the one that refuses to let go. The verse version, composed, so he learned in school, in one hemisphere or another, for the invalid son of a friend. And suddenly Kraft has to know: What did that child have? Did it live?

"They want to," he starts, and can't at first recall the expression. "They want to take the show on the road?"

"Yes." She is crying now, unable to sacrifice anything more to him. Alkali seeps out of her, all the sulfureous backpressure of wanting to do right and missing, always missing, no matter what she tries. "Yes, goddammit. I just told you. Can't you . . . ? What the fuck is *wrong* with you?"

He doesn't even hear the inconceivable profanity pass out of her. "Without Joy?"

He races along some linked anxiety, the need to determine the full extent of what these band members are calculating before they hurt themselves, before they can pull off their elaborate plan. "No, it's impossible. You can't let them go out there. Haven't you read the papers? The casualty figures, the stats. Christ, you've seen the way they bring them in through the downstairs drive-up. Continuous Doppler relay race. Shriners' shoot-out circus. You're going to lead them out on this little field trip? So that you can send them *back* to me as massive crush avulsions?"

Timed to confirm him, a squad car sidles up alongside them. Officer rolls his window down just a crack, to ask whether there's some trouble. Has their vehicle broken down or something?

Kraft turns on them furiously. "Why don't you go beat up a couple welfare gorillas?" Only Linda's quick shoulder restraint keeps them from arrest or worse.

The relative peace of this neighborhood, the privileged quiet of their immediate surroundings, is all a distortion, a local fluke, a maraschino paid for on ingeniously overextended credit or stolen outright. And it's all coming down, being called in. She takes his elbow and turns him the long way home.

Waiting for them on the back stoop is that tribe of foundling milks they have just put out. He cannot even lift his head to whisper, "Don't you see it, where they want to go?" He threads his way over them, the lost boys, the ones who left when we were small.

"All my old kindergarten familiars," he says, turning in the threshold, too far past coherence for her to follow. He stands in the doorway, surrounded by this campfire ring. Stereo faces stare eagerly, smiling him down, waiting to hear tonight's installment, his firsthand account. Ancient friends, wised up, computer-aged, looking for all the world like the final heist's advance interference. Returned for a while, God knows why, to the here and now. Placed in his care, only to be snatched away again.

Listen my children, and you shall hear. Hear the remains of the unshed core that Once was once built upon. Here is the most, the closest you will ever know, the traces that stay with you when you can no longer even place the source. This is the text, the spooky grandparental ramblings in back rooms off kitchens stinking of toilet-flush conservation, those huddled alley debriefings, the day's last recap before lights-out.

Listen up, and forever go on listening to the eternal campfire replays. Commit to memory those night imperatives that will come to seem, lifetimes later, inconceivably strange sequels to prospects that never came to pass. Re-create, in spoken hologram, mental wire-frame model, the anachronistic singsong quatrains, and learn again how every account is itself the time hole mosaic it so minutely describes.

Words will return at livid intervals to haunt even you, the most hardened, back-of-the-class switchbladers. They will pop up unsponsored, unshakable, like old manslaughter charges. Harbor the last recounting, and repeat it to yourself, looking back, in the reflected light of telling, on that circle of scared, scrubbed faces, struck with the full horror of related events, sitting here listening, just listening, before the leap.

This is the stuff of final exams. Audible, even behind the reach for the conventional opening: Once upon a time, Once before this world. Once, long ago, they say. Never here. At Cottonwood. Over yonder. In a kingdom by the sea. You, of all people, must remember. Because Once has no other visible means of support. It will die for all time when you lose its least particular.

Storytime is over, and yet, the rustiest recitation will come claim you one day, when you least expect it. You are as ancient as the oldest *then*. All the word's shadow-puppet spectacles—the magic cabins, monkey armies, unrippable spinnakers, interlocking dreams, winter fruit trees, inscribed rings, insidious machines—can come to their appointed end only if you sit still, stop sniping for a minute, and listen.

Once, far away, there lived a boy who wanted to make things right. He would come to his mother after dinner, a dish towel in his hand, and she would shake her heard sadly and wonder how the world would end up killing him. When the obligatory three wishes came and ambushed him, he politely refused all but one. Just let me try to cure things. A simple enough request, and he himself volunteered to lead the way to the broken locale, the spot that needed fixing.

He had lived everywhere, belonged nowhere, and had already seen hopelessness huge enough to glut the most jaded famine tourist. Misery was the rule in the two-thirds of the earth the boy had visited. Eight of the best pickup starting eleven he ever played with died of deficiencies. His friends lived in cardboard and subsisted by selling jasmine ringlets to jammed motorists. He worked with a school service club, aiding at a state asylum where concrete cubicles swarmed with children—deformed, diseased, degeneratively crippled, industrially poisoned, lumped together and left to rock on their haunches all day on the bare floor. There, he had watched helplessly as a boy his age picked at ooze in the back of his head, trying to get to his brain and scoop his curse away by its roots the way a child from a luckier continent might crumble a honeycomb.

After a summer of monastic retreat, he saw the obvious: suffering was not a condition. It was a thing. Need, like wealth, its claim-jumping cousin (which the boy, one sad homecoming, had also seen), could be made and unmade. Poverty was an unfortunate detour, a world jerking too suddenly toward its one shot at well-being. Suffering had nothing to do with power and exploitation, good versus evil. It had to do with logistics, better delivering.

Generations of adults before him had overlooked the simple corrective. He would have missed it too, had an ancient boy not whispered it to him. Hold a bit of the miracle cash crop out for seed. Then send these shoots where nothing had yet rooted.

And there was such a spot, no farther away than his pointing finger. One day, when the moment was right, in the middle of class (you remember *classes,* those wards you worked in before this ward?), the boy raised his hand and asked, "What would it cost . . ." This was how he started the matter. He knew enough to speak the dialect of the person he was speaking to. "What would it cost"—although he suspected that no one had yet put the full price tag on our being here or not—"to build a school?"

This was his simple, inexorable idea. One school in the right place: all it would take. The most negligible null will unfold into all, if it has at its heart the self-propagating spark. Nail broth. Engines that could and estranged third sons that ascend all manner of glass mountains on sheer will. The goose that lays the golden eggs that *hatch.* He was no naïf, and knew that food would disappear in a week. Clothing too would stretch at best only into the next decade. But a school . . .

The boy's teacher made the fatal mistake of humoring the off-the-wall question. Build? Where? The boy was ready with his answer: upcountry. One of the hidden villages from which Squatter Town's most destitute continuously poured. He pointed out on the classroom map the spot he had selected, a tribal area near the border.

"Right here," he said, "Nam Chai." The easiest place to drain grief's ocean is up in the hills, where the flow is still a trickle.

The teacher juggled a few rough estimates, an improvised economics session. The boy's classmates took to the idea. Teacher then made a group project of writing up the proposal for the Institute's Headmaster, hoping thereby to vitiate the scheme with democracy's death sentence.

The boy's plan would have ended there, except for the ironies of design. In crumpling up the proposal, Headmaster gave himself a vicious paper cut. And when he put the bloody fingertip in his mouth to stanch it, the bubble tasted cold, like gold leaf patted on statue stone.

The taste brought to the man's mind the story of that plaster likeness of the Enlightened in one Angel monastery, pretty, but worthless. One day during handling, the plaster cracked. Deep in the fissure, something glistened. The plaster was stripped off, revealing a figure of pure gold. Only then did amnesia lift: the statue had been covered during one of the eternal incursions, to keep it from capture. As final safeguard, the city willed itself to forget, the last safety.

This had happened years ago, before the boy was born. But this letter, or rather the taste of the slit it made in Headmaster's finger, made the moral clear. The city itself was cracking. Its disguise of timeless compliance was forever compromised, stripped off in a pragmatic deal done at missile-point. The region was already lost, sacrificed *en passant* to historical destinies. Its fish runs and fecund fields had been redone in Air Force blue. The world was ending and about to begin again, and who could say what awful gold would appear beneath its plaster disguise?

The letter was opportune. The thin coalition, led by the country that once refused a Free king's offer of combat elephants for use in its own suicidal civil war, was in urgent need of PR. It was losing to its own self-incriminating conscience. If beaten prematurely, the *farangs* would never complete their reduction of the last sane stretch of the globe to total hell, a prerequisite for return to worldwide infancy. One good report on foreign philanthropy in the region, and the purge could go on a little longer. And yes, thought Headmaster, reading the petition. Why not the pupils of the International Institute?

In truth, the boy could not have cared less about the world. International interests were no more than the street gang refrain he knew in a half-dozen languages: Stay on your side of the line, or you die.

The world could rot with all the other unreachable mangoes on national interest's tree. It could incinerate itself, the goal of all governments, so long as it left this one innocent spot a chance to break into the still center of heaven's hub. The city's angel orders—the heavy smells of orchid and pedicab exhaust, sulfurous curries and feces-sweet durian, Som's saffron-flooded recipes, the timbre of temple bells, Sunday Market barter, the five tones— were too much to bear losing.

Yet the city had already started out on its own death march. Its venerable saving grace, a calculated accommodation, had been beaten at last. The lump was there, in a thousand and one Turkish baths, in the raw purchasing power of soldiers on R & R from the steady-state war, in cash that would trade this accommodating place into prosperity.

Against the Enlightened's advice, the floating city had chosen for growth, life, illusion. At dinner, the boy's father, baffled by the fact that attached itself more lovingly to him with his each covert business trip, said, "In ten years, the place will have launched itself into wealth or it will have burned up like cheap charcoal." Lotus pad pond, or cesspool. A mood came over the man, one that had never taken hold in any other of the far more miserable countries he had helped subvert.

The boy watched his father shake his head and exhale, "Serious infrastructure problems." At fourteen, the boy knew vaguely what infrastructure was—as much as he would ever know. It meant roads. Roads, telephones, depots, sewers: all as ethereal in the City of Angels as this trip around the rim of the Wheel.

This was the infrastructure he proposed to improve, beginning with an upcountry schoolhouse, that bootstrap, the capital required for lift-off. A bemused teacher relayed the message from Headmaster to cheering class that a school would cost almost nothing at all, providing you built it yourself.

In a rush of industry, they chartered buses, laid in supplies, requisitioned materials, and secured the state's approval. School books, chalk, pointers, and globes (some still proclaiming obsolete borders) miraculously began piling up from out of a fabulous caldron. The logistics were taken out of the initiators' hands. Yet, overwhelmed by success, the boy and his class hardly felt the coup, experience's autocratic take-over.

The unlikely project, theirs still in feeling if not in fact, was barraged with more student applicants than they needed. Headmaster culled them down to a final cut, as if picking the cast for the spring musical. The final mix had something calculated to it. Alongside the boy founder, Kraft, came a Security Council of upperclassmen: Elaine Chang (a compromise on the two Chinas question), Dimi Popovich, Gopal Patnaik, Eleni Katzourakis, Bandele K, and Jien Daishi. Fleshing out this core were a host of Tatis, Claudios, Yuans, Jacqueses, and Jills ranging from fourth-grader to near adult. The chaperons included Headmaster; Sampao, the Free art teacher, and old Springer, who had taught social studies at the Institute for so long he no longer had a nationality.

This careful cross-cultural balance was upended in one blow when it came to naming the project. Because it was December, because the build-it-yourself school would be a gift from the blue, and thinking, perhaps, to lend the whole enterprise an ironic disguise by giving it a paramilitary ring, Headmaster christened the expedition *Operation Santa Claus*. The name horrified the boy, and he nearly dropped out at the last minute. Only his friend Gopal's assurance that Santa was one of the officially recognized incarnations of Vishnu the Defender kept him in.

The expedition opened with a giddy field-trip feel. The caravan consisted of a busload of volunteers followed by ramshackle grain trucks filled with tools and donated supplies. Festivities on the bus ride up included manic, perpetual choruses of "Ninety-nine Bottles of Beer" and its anthropological equivalents from four continents.

Kraft joined the precocious Institute boys at the back of the bus. The moment's obsession was paper airplanes. For the previous two weeks, boys had stood on the roof during recess, struggling with the engineering problem of how best to fold a piece of paper to defy gravity. The ingenuity of the hundreds of experimental designs continued unabated in the cramped quarters of the child-mad vehicle, although test flights grew a little erratic. An Afro–Middle Eastern consortium worked on a tube-and-airfoil design to maximize distance and flight time. The Anglo-European alliance, feeling their competitive edge slipping, pursued showy climb rates and speed. Kraft worked for a group of independents who wanted to produce the most unlikely, unwieldy design that would still fly.

Near the first refueling stop, they visited the shrine of one of the Enlightened's most famous manifestations. The student travelers filed above a depression in the ground two meters deep. This hole, it took a moment to gather, was a footprint the length of two men. The toeprints radiated in perfect concentric circles. The foot itself was oval, pristine—as sinuously magnificent as a Siamese fighting fish. Most miraculous of all, the foot had left its impression not in soil but in something more resistant, metallic. Flecks of hammered-thin gold, no more than a handful of atoms thick, clung about the relic, like the ephemeral backing papers of toy tattoos.

That night, they pitched camp in a clearing in what seemed the gentlest of forests. Sampao, the art teacher, who had chosen the campsite, went around grinning until the children realized something was up. Kraft was the first to crack it; their forest was a single, all-over-arching tree. They were ensconced beneath a lone banyan, its every branch sending down air roots that turned into trunk and started the cycle all over again, its center spreading outward indefinitely, an enchanted wood large enough to swallow this entire student society, a thicket maze so extensive and dense that even the classic cartographic bread crumbs (lost, in this version, not to birds but to giant red fire ants) would be no help.

The stories around the campfire were inspired by the defense-less, unearthly adventure, by being out so late with no curfew, no home to return to in the morning. Gabi Lauter told of the Kinderzeche, an annual festival from her birthplace honoring the children who saved the town from destruction during a war that had lasted longer than a generation. Farouk Ali—one of those demonic, genius-grant-funded child wizards behind the world's seemingly spontaneous playground chants, the war cries of the paste- and eraser-eating set, the fear-enforced slanders that made even captains of industry, walking past playgrounds, lose their equanimity and assume the taunts were aimed at them—produced an Arabic rhyme that, freely translated, went something like "Cinderella, dressed in yella, went downtown to meet her fella. . . ."

Farouk good-naturedly supposed out loud that Guus Vandersteenhoven had been chosen to come because a mission like this needed at least one boy who would be willing to stick his finger in a dike. Guus swore nobody in his country had ever heard that story, or the one about the kid with the ice skates, either.

Claudio, a hopeless intellectual whose most vigorous sport was the crossruff, changed the topic to a fantastic tale of art treasures transported to England via Khartoum, where they had been brought from the collapsing East by that Messiah fighter, Chinese Gordon, of the Ever-Victorious Army. Dimi said that he'd read the same story somewhere, and Farouk asked him if he'd ever finished coloring the book in.

Quintessential cookout fare, in short, followed by ghost tales and toasted bananas over the night's last embers. Some played cards or pit-and-pebble while the light held. The youngest swapped things—plastic figures or little cast-iron cars—while the oldest grilled one another on the lyrics of the latest stateside songs to reach this place, by then pathetically dated.

Adulthood would reach them almost superfluously: the popular South Americans had their bank vice presidencies all but signed; the Chinese and Indians their elite if shabby governmental back offices. The junior Eurocrat brats saw in this trip invaluable résumé experience, while the offspring of international Asian cartels would remember these tropical forests years later as game board squares to be played to. The sons and daughters of lifer soldiers and PX personnel, the long lineage of crate-lifters, passing this once for socially acceptable on a disguised outing up from the underclass, already felt the knee-jerk exclusion from their school chums that even in these presophisticates went unnamed.

Kraft, who had already begun to dream at night of saving everyone he knew from Ganges-scale floods, saw in the flicker of the bug-drawing fire that he was destined for futile sandbag duty at the end. Surrounded by a circle of lit faces that suddenly seemed too impossibly young to be his contemporaries, he froze and could not deliver his piece when his turn came around. His national allegory—the wandering guy with the sack of apple seeds—had degraded along the way to the executive mercenary, Kraft Sr., leaning out of his machine in the pitch-black, calling down amplified confusion on lands too wayward to reform by any other means. The country of the universally displaced had somehow graduated to evil overlord, backing every backwater tyrant who owned a cattle prod. It had torn itself apart on cynical profit, gone debauched in a single step, and nobody could say how or why.

What national folk tale could he relate, he who had been home for all of six weeks in his life? He thought he might tell them of the child's "Come away!" that had inspired this field project. Instead, he made due by playing the *kluay* obbligato while Francisca Ng, daughter of a high-ranking international aid officer, sang:

Where are you off to, little girl, so late?
Are frogs calling, do owls keep you awake?
How far must you go yet, at this hour?
Can't it wait?

Where in the world the tune came from was anyone's guess. The girl, a grade older than Kraft, could sing the verse in any language, with no damage to the musical line. Her voice was spectral, beyond forgetting. All who heard her wanted to jump up and continue that night, to push to the boundless banyan's edge, into the threatened countryside.

On day two, stopping to stretch and bat about a *takraw,* one of mankind's few cooperative sports, they were met by a khakied American who came from nowhere out of the bush. The man asked for food and told an incredulous student council that he was walking home. He deserted them as quickly as he had appeared. The exchange made Headmaster remind them that they were nearing the shooting zone; the war that they had all seen broadcast was near, border violating, and real. Hill tribes in this region were routinely rounded up by the government and sent against the insurgents, local peasants who had suffered opposite recruitment.

Nam Chai, when they arrived, was not so much a village as a letter of intent. The government had made a colossal mistake in agreeing to let them see the place, let alone attempt philanthropy here. Not only was there no school, there was no market, no shop, no post office, no sewers, no garage, no clinic. The dwellings were no larger than Angel City spirit houses.

The bus discharged the legation, and all the living souls in that few square kilometers formed two queues of the mutually incredulous. In one glance, education as escape revealed itself to be wishful thinking. Something was wrong with this village, more wrong than any school could cure. Some antique curse—a troll extracting weekly blood tribute, some slow leach, a heavy-metal impurity lacing the all-purpose stream, a terrain inviting perpetual foreign invasion—hung over the place, turning assistance almost cruel.

The self-appointed international ambassadors of goodwill unloaded their trucks. They stacked the modular walls, the globes, chalkboards, and diminutive desks next to the foundation spot in the morass. Their heaps might have been more useful as firewood. The inventory seemed as pointless as a stockpile of thousand-watt ice shavers rotting in some outletless outback.

Over these confused caches flew the school flag with its Hanu-man silhouette.

Every other village child suffered some exotic jungle affliction. Faces swelled shut under parasite assault. Leeches laddered up legs. Wild defects bent fingers back like the brass nails of a classical dancer, or sprouted wing stumps between shoulder blades. These were the bastard UNICEF wraiths, those dirt-cripples that privilege was supposed to save with a couple pennies' worth of trick-or-treats.

What ruined Ricky, though, was the abject happiness of this monstrous pantheon. Even the sickest tore around in uncontrollable excitement. They spun through the village shouting in hill dialects how everything was at last coming true. The monkey army had arrived, fresh from the City of Angels.

On the whole, the assortment of internationals responded better than Kraft to the shock of these village children. Slight Janie Hawkins, whose teaspoon tits had recently begun debuting in the boy's nightly revue as he fell off to sleep, instinctively cradled in her white-fuzzed arms a limbless newborn the size and pallor of a bleached rugby ball. She sung the first song that came into her head, a lullaby from her long-forgotten Kentucky:

Every time the baby cries,
Stick my finger in the baby's eyes.
What'll we do with the ba-a-by?
What shall we do with the baby-o?

There is a patois known by everyone below the age of consent. A system of shouts and postures is enough; words would just confuse things. Within an afternoon, troops from opposite ends of the planetary playing field had formed a work force. They set to the improvisational plans as to a life-size mud castle. Boys who had never heard of a latrine pitched in to dig a bank of them on no instruction at all. Carters, haulers, trenchers, plumbers, joiners, carpenters, metalworkers, masons, sanders, water fetchers, day carers for the as yet too small to day-labor: everyone fell to a task without being assigned. The engineering feat fashioned itself out of nothing, memory.

Children who only grinned foolishly, as at a comic myth, at tales of seasons, the back-and-forth battle of summer and winter, children who wouldn't know the grim stomach-pit thrill of oranging September if it came up and rattled their lunch boxes, collaborated in their own undoing by erecting the edifice that would forever, for generations to come, stamp the school calendar upon them. Kraft began to wonder whether they had chosen the wrong place, whether he had somehow misinterpreted that distress call transmitted to him across the citizens band.

Work proceeded rapidly. The Institute candy stripers had not booked themselves much time—two weeks of winter break, a whirlwind gift-spattering run, even by Santa Claus standards. The floor plan called for a circular sala whose walls could be thrown open to the weather, extending the tent of learning like a processional umbrella or a catch-all sarong.

Once the ground had been readied and the pilings sunk, the skin went up with a speed that surprised everyone. Each set of pint-sized hands hammered in gearwork happiness, humming inside the dovetailing whole. Walls went up in half an afternoon, so smoothly was the effort shared. The heavenly pavement could be laid by this time next month; Cleveland, Djakarta, Addis Ababa could explode with great textured marble cylinders of learning, structures that would make New York and Tokyo seem botched hick towns if all adults worked as they once toyed.

One afternoon, midway through building, when the rapid rise of teak lintels sent waves of anticipation through the crew, the landscape began to throb softly as if the piece they had just inserted had set off an oscillation in the fabric of air. The children of the strategically meaningless hamlet placed the sound before the city sophisticates. They scattered into the undergrowth with barks of pleasure-threaded panic.

Farangs, as usual, failed to recognize their own handiwork until it swarmed them. Kraft's first thought was that Dad had tracked him down, sent out a pin-and-interdict against this Operation Claus, which, acting on its own initiative, was not in the best of coalition interests. The megaphones would start up, or they'd go gunship first and ask questions later. One well-placed shaped charge underneath the teacher's desk, or a ten-thousand-fléchette canister. Or, most ingenious of all, a camera rocket trailing a metal wire beaming back pictures, steered by some JD four years older than Ricky, parked up in his hovering air platform in front of a monitor as if watching *American Bandstand.* Any of history's current munitions and delivery systems would do.

The airships landed and Nam Chai came out from cover. The machines spit up a small team of pale, bellied men with film equipment. Endless hanks of cable and portable generators appeared from nowhere, glutting the makeshift landing area around the school. An albino dressed in the camouflage fatigues worn only by teenage heavy-metal fans and greener members of the press corps hit the turf asking who was in charge.

Headmaster's quiet news leaks as the group departed the city had, like a banyan branch, taken root. Word of the unlikely roving charity had reached the international media, message-in-bottle style. Temporarily sated with soldiers setting one another on fire, briefly glazed-eyed with the tedious predictability of horror, and always on the lookout for the latest curio, TV dispatched a mobile cell to get the take on this group of kids cheekily trying to work its own welfare.

Not your cheap feel-good, the producer rushed to assure. Not your toss-off geopolitical PR puff piece. "Just, like, you know: 'Out-of-the-mouths-of-babes'?"

Headmaster nodded in acquiescence, serving the turn of the Wheel.

Even the Northerners stood in awe at the unloading of equipment. The hardware was a cargo cult's fetish come true. Sampao executed a series of sketches on rice paper. The village kids, thinking it Stage Two of the incomprehensible project, served as native bearers.

"Can you give me a good cross section of *color*?" the producer requested. Headmaster selected a sample core of babes, out of whose mouths the world would learn just what it was up to. He chose one student from each of the lost continents, and Kraft, the trip's most colorful North American.

Ricky suggested that they include a hill tribe kid. He picked one, a boy named Lok whose hobby was gumming up the nostrils of domesticated animals with red clay. The film crew jumped at the novelty. They patted the boy on the head, violating a dozen cultural prohibitions, and asked his name. Lok replied, *"Yet ma,"* which Kraft refrained from translating.

The man they propped in front of the camera was a former pro athlete who seemed surprised that none of these children asked for his autograph. Kraft lied and said he thought he'd heard of him, and this settled the man enough to get him started.

"Deep in the jungles of Southeast Asia, just a few hours from the Mekong," he started, and Gopal ruined the take by snickering. ". . . is exactly the place," the ex-sports star continued, after the splice, "you might expect to find a guerrilla army. But *this* army will *surprise* you." His voice sashayed in pitch, as if he were about to rattle off the toll-free number you could call to place an order. *"This* is an *army* of *peace,"* he said, emphasizing the last word's outrageousness. "The guerrillas come from over a dozen different countries." Gopal nudged Kraft and asked if Americans could count that high. "And *every one* of them," enunciated the genial ex-jock, working up to his punch line, "is a *child*."

He gave the first question to Elaine Chang, who looked Oriental and had been pointed out to him as the Institute brain. "Can you tell us what you and your schoolmates are doing here?"

"A television interview?" Elaine replied tentatively. On the second take, she got the answer right: "We're building a school."

"And can you tell us why?" *Come on, you can do it,* his voice pleaded.

Kraft held his breath, but Elaine, eminently sensible, answered to perfection. "Because they didn't have one."

"Yes," the reporter granted, grinning at the home audience, like that show host whose book, *Kids Are the Wackiest Wonders,* was upstaged by his daughter's subsequent plunge from an upper-story window. "But do you think your choice to build a school *here* has anything to do with what is happening nearby?"

He waited expectantly, perhaps for a polite show of hands. "Can any of you tell us what is happening in this region?"

Gopal cleared his throat and took the plunge. "I'm afraid if you haven't figured it out by now . . ."

The reporter adroitly intercepted the boy. "Gopal, you're from . . . ?"

"India. It's a large country just through the center of the earth from . . ."

So the interview went, turning the simplest act of care into the usual broadcast circus. The reporter didn't want children building a schoolhouse upcountry. Not: I'm fifteen, and I rub myself off nightly and I've twice smoked ganja and my job is digging post holes. Not: I'm eight and I like melting dolls and I can't bring friends home when my mother's there. He wanted allegory, Little Eva or Nell, a two-minute twist-wrap in the manner that this rightless class has always been painted: perversely small, alien creatures, a delightful variety act in their Tinytown getup, dancing, prancing, romancing, just like homunculus adults. He kept rephrasing every question until it became an elaborate description to which the student had simply to answer yeah.

"This little boy's name is Luke. . . ."

"Lok," Kraft corrected, knowing that the reporter would stop and explain to him with increasing testiness that for American TV, only one person was allowed to talk at one time, and that person was him until he said so.

"This little boy actually *grew up* in this very village, a forgotten town lost in the crossfire, but one where his new friends from many countries are now building him a building that might change his life. Luke, can you tell us how the war has touched you?"

Kraft interpreted, and the cameras ate up the image of the two crew cuts jabbering at each other, the brown one shyly smirking as he spoke. Ricky turned back to the MC. "He wants to know whether you have any chewing gum."

Shielded by the omnipotent edit, the reporter hacked on. "How does it feel when you hear shooting in the distance? Are you worried that it's coming closer?"

Kraft dutifully relayed the question and Lok's answer: "He says he once saw a body spread across the river path. Lots of teeny creatures were making their home in it."

The reporter got excited; they could use that bit. Maybe they could take him to the spot for an image. "Luke, can you tell the boys and girls back in America what you most want to learn at your new school?"

A slight altercation followed, the boys barking at each other in their playing-field pidgin. The reporter gently reminded Kraft that he mustn't hold anything back.

"He wants to know if American girls have a furry patch between their legs."

Cheers broke out from all quarters, and Kraft was reprimanded for ruining expensive film.

"How about you?" the reporter turned on him when the fracas settled. "Are *you* frightened to be here?"

A whiff of future came across the clearing, and Kraft knew that the refuge was already lost. The miracle beans he had hoped to stash away in the soil would not take root until this patch of ground too had been flooded under a sea of asylum seekers. And he felt free to say anything he wanted, safe in the knowledge that any truth he might utter would never slip past the editors of this new continuous primer in illiteracy and evasion, the world's last will and testament.

Listen my children and you shall hear the sense of the words this boy spoke as adulthood has hung on to them. TV wanted the war in anecdote—this season's diversion for the stimulus stunned. Very well then. The boy began to speak softly, plumping the rhythms like a jump-rope rhyme. He spoke of all the hot spots he had put up in for a while and had been forced to evacuate. He told of a Caribbean island that sowed its fields with its own carcasses rather than share the land. He described half a billion subcontinentals massing in sacrificial machete waves over the shape of God's head. He painted a perfect white-tower-topped palace by the sea, then set it to the torch.

"Aren't *you* afraid? Isn't everyone?" he giggled. He tried to say how every place he had ever lived was an armed camp, swarming with shirtless, underaged adolescents toting lightweight grenade launchers. He said how he had read that there had been two wars a year, each costing an average quarter-million lives, since the start of history.

The war over the river, he said, mattered to the cameras only because home boys were dying. We were using wire-guided weapons and aerial defoliants. They were using children with spring-loaded shredded-tin-can bombs strapped to their chests. In a few years, the reporter's war that this school outing opposed would probably be turned into anonymous, stylish, prime-time violence, colorful punji combat for rating stakes. The kerchiefed, bare-chested, M-16–decked commando filmed in front of a stand of bamboo will turn the war into a small-bore lullaby.

He mumbled this prediction, accusing no one. Was he afraid? Anyone who wasn't was not paying attention. That was the point of this school: to teach the children of the village what was being done all around them to the children of Planet Earth. Just the Who, What, When, and Where, because the lone Why was too awful to bear. Ricky declared that the only solution to the crisis across the river, to the trauma racing through every country on unlimited tourist visas, was mandatory intermarriage at gunpoint for a hundred generations, until everybody looked exactly the same. As his sentences grew longer, he savored his first taste of cynicism along the sides of his tongue, right next to "Sour" and

"Salt" in the *Science and You* diagrams. And with that taste, he crossed a subterranean border into old age.

He finished his diatribe to dead silence. The cameras had long since shut off. The reporter was already gesturing for kids to go over by the school and move some teak trunks around. Kraft's impromptu parable was sucked up by a spinning dust devil into the vacant sky above Nam Chai. The wind carried off his words as it would a scuttled fighting kite. He watched the reporter film his prepared tag, khaki flapping in front of Kraft's classmates, each swinging languidly at a fake nail, guilty of betrayal but unable to help themselves.

"We've all heard the line 'A little child'll lead them'? The question is whether those of us old enough to remember have the courage to follow. This is . . ."

Kraft camped out that night in the roofless sala, all the shelter he wanted. He sat toying with a giant chalk protractor, convenient tool for projecting Euclidean circles into the arcless bush. The whole project felt suddenly cruel—laying this foundation, then retreating to the City of Angels without supplying the one thing needed to touch off the genesis: a teacher. He rummaged through the boxes of supplies looking for a fuse, but only came up with a stack of fraction-wedged pie pans, a thick-mounted jigsaw of the world ("Mideast," "Southeast Asia," each a single cartoon balloon, for easy assembly), and a softball-sized heart with cutaway flaps that he clapped together like the slack jaw of a ventriloquist's dummy.

A shuffle announced the arrival, in the dark, of a few other *ad hoc* Security Councillors. Jien, Bandele—he couldn't make them out. "They're looking for you, buster," someone who sounded like Eleni Katzourakis said. "The adults. Headmaster. Herr Springer."

Figures spread around the unfinished room, squeezing into the matrix of desks that had been shoved to the side to avoid construction damage. "Hey, Kraft." That was Farouk. "That little speech of yours . . ." He gave a half-whistle of admiration and disbelief.

"Yeah," a Janie shape and an Elaine voice said together. Then, again stereo: "Jinx!" As if it were easy, here in the unfinished dark, to pretend still to immaturity.

Gopal chuckled. "Not bad for a liberal lackey."

Whatever other votes of confidence the delegation had come to give him were drowned by the arrival of Lok, leading a pack of rabble who had managed to slip out of restraints under cover of darkness. The townies burst in, rollicking but stealthy, a sampler of deficiencies whose only revenge was a know-no-better amusement.

Lok tore over to Kraft, spitting in hill dialect delight, "Hey, do that again!" That bit of extended sass, mouthing off to the pod of helicopters that had come bringing nothing at all, not cigarettes, not opiates, not candy.

Nam Chai's future proceeded to parade about the room, rooting through the forbidden containers and demanding an explanation for every arcane item. They found and unspread a cartoon, room-encircling alphabet banner: *kh* as in bottle; *k* as in water buffalo. From the bottom of one eclectic crate came a book from the empire's sunset years, destined for Malaya or Burma but ending up here, in the one country that had never been anyone's colonial possession.

Kraft, folk hero of the hour, was made to read. He had to repeat Messrs. Rat and Toad a thousand times for the little ones, who hadn't a clue, even in hasty translation, what the words meant, but who knew a funny voice when they heard one. Calls of "Encore," even from the ironically amused anglophones, were punctuated by fanatical cries for "Bed-*jah*!" from Lok, for whom badgers and moles were monster fantasies as outrageous as monkey generals or demon kings. What was the appeal of a story that meandered, messing about in boats, going nowhere? Kraft went on doing the voices, the creatures' falsettos and growls, all the explanation ever granted.

Only waiting until the contingent had gathered, a face appeared at one of the unfinished openings. One look at her hushed the hilarity, confiscated it like an intercepted note. The stalk of body stood wrapped in a dress cut from an old rice sack, the stenciled brand still visible, swallowed up in a dart. The burlap makeshift lent the wearer the aura of escaped animal kingdom. The Northerners thought at first that she was a local, but she left the village children even more surprised.

Two Instituters undid the wall's hinges, but the creature wouldn't enter. Like a velvety automatic weapon, she repeated two singsong syllables. It was not Free, nor any language Kraft had ever heard. "What's she saying?" he asked Lok.

Lok answered in dialect, an aggressive but entranced "Who the hell knows?"

Just as suddenly, Kraft *heard,* although the syllables remained impenetrable. The rice sack girl was chanting, in some form of *Ur*-pali, the same words that had issued from the abbot's crabbed statue the instant before he'd smashed it to the floor: "Come away!" Come away.

Her furious gestures confirmed him. Asian, yet pale, luminous, she glowed like an impatient filament. She circled and yipped, dashing a few paces into the bush before doubling back to see what was keeping them. Every so often, she released explanatory bursts, pleas that might have meant anything: a parent prostrate on the path with snakebite, a house on fire, or a feast just one village over, replete with *pipat* band and unlimited roasted bananas. Her choreography proved the size of the prize, as a bee's dance spells out to the hive a massive find.

The children stared at the dancer, then at one another. Even the upper forms deferred to Kraft, as if his taboo-breaking incantation of that afternoon had summoned up this sprite. Kraft took a breath, although there was never any choice, not even briefly. "So. Who's up for it?" he asked in English. Then, once more, in the five tones: *"Bai mai?"*

It surprised no one that she led them toward the neighboring disaster. Even the Northerners began to realize that the trek wound them slowly down to the river, the imaginary buffer between the one country that until then had gone officially unscathed and the other, already smeared by the nightmare adjacent to it. But the specific destination Kraft could only imagine. It took the shape, in his sleep-heavy head, of an improvised emergency paradise, a forced regrouping along an itinerary of true amazement, a swelling river settlement full of the napalmed and claymored, driven from their lives.

A camp of children, he thought. She has come for the newest batch of recruits, new lives to boost the ones already assembled there. These thoughts contended with the rattan and fern, the shadowy plants scraping his face on the dark path. The girl knew the terrain, keeping to the best track, a packed mound both dry and open, yet not too exposed to bare moonlight. They walked long enough to lose track of time, and only the gibbon whoops from distant canopies convinced Kraft that they moved at all.

Although he was older than their guide, he felt like the little girl's infant. How many kilometers now? Are we there yet? It occurred to him that they might not make it there and back again before Nam Chai awoke to miss them.

A sound like twigs snapping underfoot grew gradually as they walked until he had to recognize it: sporadic small-arms fire. Then, pitching over a sharp rise, they saw it. She had led them right up to the river at its narrowest, the same river that meandered to the senile dowager city a thousand kilometers downstream, at its gum-diseased mouth. Here it was narrow enough to skip a lucky coin over. Before they had time to take in the sight, the girl, twenty meters in the vanguard, slipped her rice sack off and paddled into the current, her shift held over her head.

On the other side, she dressed hastily. Annoyed at the others' failure to follow, she made that odd hand gesture, palm downward and out, fingers curling repeatedly. To the Euro-offspring, the wave meant *good-bye, auf, au rev . . . ,* we will never see each other again. But in the region, the fingerpumping was fiercely unambiguous: *ma nee,* get a move on, what's keeping you? A cold, deadly Red Rover.

Lok was first in after her. He slipped into the water as if it were a buffalo patty pool. Kraft watched terrified as Janie Hawkins stripped and lowered herself in after. Then the other student shadows began to shed their shock, and the party became a filament of frog kick and dog paddle, as silent as tension permitted, a cortege of clothes held above bobbing heads under the angled and eerie moon.

Compulsion brushed away the risk. Swimmers peeled off one by one, the group crumbling like a heel of hard bread. Kraft stood with the group riveted on the Free side by their failure of nerve or inability to swim. They had been brought here for life's one classic examination: turn back to camp now, to a life of empty safety, or press on, on nothing, following an apparition that might just as easily be malicious as revealing.

Kraft, answerable for every life in the water-snaking conga line, gauged the instant. The girl, whose Oxfam face made her the perfect insurgent, had come to lead a unit of foreign imperialists into ambush. She had suffered some Special Forces Pentecost from the air and had wandered stunned for days until she found the only people she could trust, minors, whom she now led back to a scene of unimaginable hideousness. She was It in a trillion-hectare, multinational kick-the-can, the globewide game that every child knows is taking place without him, and finding them assembled late at night, she decided to cut them in. She was the recruiting arm of a child cartel intent on stopping the war where the adults had failed, and she took them now, untrained and flawless, to the front. She was a shape changer, a demon from the *Ramakien,* come to teach them what the tales really meant.

He knew what he needed to do. Break off, bring the contingent back. Instead, by the dark riverside, he began to undo his shirt. As he touched his collar, a sound wafted across the stilled air, the lightest of clicks. He knew, on the envelope's attack, what the snap was. The girl had just stepped on that kind of mine, pointlessly polite, that warned the victim by the cock of the firing pin.

In her excitement to keep the file moving, the girl had dropped her guard just long enough to miss the telltale artificial mound. Kraft had no moment to shout *stop,* nor did he know the word in her language. He didn't need to. She knew what she had triggered as soon as the click rippled up through her foot.

It caught her in her stride's downbeat. So drilled was she in stories of such a noise that she froze before the fatal follow-through. She stood, pinned to the spot, unable to so much as shift her body's weight.

Like a wet appliance that clamps a hand onto killing amperage, dread clamped the children electrically to the riverbed. Everything infancy suspects is true: there is no floor, no ceiling, no warmth, no reassuring voices from the next room, no bed but what hides under it. There is just one lullaby, waiting to detain you.

Every one of them was mature enough to panic. Those in the water swung in midcurrent for the Free shore. Those still on land braced or hit the earth. Ricky, ever the boy who shouts "Look out behind you!" at the Punch and Judy, ran *toward* her. He began to call out whatever commands came into his head. Hold still; we'll come and slip a rock onto the pin. Breathe imperceptibly, slow your heart, while someone runs back to the village. Keep calm. Keep your weight centered. Rub your leg if it stiffens. Tell us what you need and we'll bring it.

The words were gibberish. They unraveled in the air before reaching her. She heard nothing; so the boy had to tell himself in later years. She wavered a moment between sense and need. She knelt and clawed at the ground hiding the mine, mewling like a trapped animal. The others yelled at her to stop. She did not even look around. She began to whimper, looking off in the direction she had been taking them, at an invisible hole, some epochal, closing chance. She fidgeted, twitching her thighs as if confined at a desk in that new school prison. Children wailed at her, in every language they knew, not to bounce, not to jitter. Her agitation accumulated, and the demand to be off, *now,* while there was yet time, increased until simply holding still would have killed her as certainly as moving.

A faction was already tearing back through the undergrowth. Another group, coaxing, circled warily toward her, threading through death's bulb nursery, knowing their impotence even if they reached her. The best they could do was hold her to the mine, bring her food, carry away her waste for decades until she died of old age.

In the time it took to bounce a ball and sweep up a single jack, Kraft rejected all other choices. He broke for the river and in a few strides had topped his best fifty meters. He ran full out, silently. It seemed to him a searing slow motion. His eye worked faster than his legs could pump, and three paces from the river he saw that she was going to move. He stopped to yell, but could not force the air through his throat until she was already away.

She lit out for a spot in the clearing, flinging her whole body off the trigger as if safety depended on a further deadline. The sight on the near horizon compelled her to fly or be annihilated anyway. She knew, and never turned her back. The light that she touched off by leaving lit up the jungle canopy.

Even years later, there was never any sound. The first noise he could ever remember was the spatter of clods drizzling back onto the ground they had just failed to escape. But that came long after. First he had to witness, reflected like a shadow puppet epic against the scrim of indifferent air, the vision the girl was after. The explosion transfigured the girl in a sky-wall of visuals as fractured as a fly's convex eye. That endless interval of flash condensed in vivid, live coverage the campaign under way all over the globe.

The mine, planted in the sober calculation that it might well take such a girl, took along the soul of everyone in the blast perimeter. It opened up a hole in the night air into which they stood transfixed and looked. Poking through some warp in the firmament, on the biggest of big screens, lay the surprise destination of every child Gypsy ever rounded up and quicklimed.

Before Kraft could force himself to look away, he saw. The old story had been mangled in word of mouth. What had always been reported as an interdicted vision of bliss, a glimpse at child heaven sadistically denied those left behind, was really this: a first look at the staging ground where the worst afflicted gathered. And the locked-out grief of those left behind was the anguish of those whose enlistment is refused.

The sound and light show, the event rim of the burst, collapsed just as quickly back into the blast's confusion. The girl and Lok both fell to the far side of the explosion, allowing Kraft for an instant to believe the fiction that they had been blown clear, with just the stray limb lost, the disfigurement shared by a quarter of the population in these parts. In the space that it took the air's shock to settle, he had healed them already, frenziedly restored them to prosthetic life. Then compensation dissolved, and he hurled himself into the river, gulping water as he thrashed toward the crater.

When the adults arrived—Headmaster, chaperons, villagers, alerted by incoherent messengers—they set to their rehearsed worst-case procedures. By dawn, every child that had left Nam Chai the previous night was accounted for, except for the boy Lok and the foreign girl, whose existence the adults only half credited. The blasted ground bore no trace of bone or pulp. The mine had cleaned all implicating evidence. Hurried reparations were made in the Institute's name to the lost boy's parents, deeded over at the same time as the soccer balls, T-shirts, and streamed elementary readers.

The school building was deemed complete enough to be finished with local resources, appropriate technologies—whatever the current euphemism for abandonment. The Institute scholars were hustled onto the bus caravan back to the City of Angels, this time without layovers. For a year or two, those who had taken part were fed occasional accounts of the progress of the sister school they had helped found. Children were learning things, the reports agreed. Exactly what they learned went unsaid.

The boy: of course. You want to know what became of the boy with the beautiful idea. By the slightest of accidents, he slipped in between conscriptions, lived out his twenties in an anomalous interlude of what the North called peace. Sent back to a home he could not assimilate to, he was schooled there in the impossible art of putting bodies back together. After long banishment, he slowly came to think of the upcountry expedition, Operation Santa Claus, the Land of the Free, as bits of myth to be dealt with only on call-troubled nights.

As for the City of Angels, where he had lived out belonging's last years: he read about it in the papers now and then, when he read a paper. Bangkok had newly industrialized, paid passage into the dominant camp, gone Little Tokyo. By all accounts, it had grown into a skylined, sprawling, runaway, AIDS-infested needled nest. It had become a child-peddling shambles. Some hundred thousand juvenile whores of both sexes made a living in the place, the murder capital of the exotic East, the Golden Triangle's peddler, catamite to the slickest tourist classes, gutted by CarniCruze junkets and semiconductor sweat shops, glistening in fat postcolonialism, clear-cutting its irreplaceable upcountry forest to support its habit.

From his stateside confinement—the man *with* a country, the nightmare opposite of that morality tale they terrorize you with in these parts in the sixth grade, when you are most vulnerable—the boy read of Free students dying in bulk, their blood flushing the streets, sacrificed in trying to reclaim the old round of corruption and coup, dying, and for what? For politics, the Wheel's worst illusion.

The place became a figment of childhood, a site on an itinerary that from the first had been no more than an extension of authority's vocation, his parents' dream. They too revealed themselves to him in time. His mother acquired the status of a filed form, and he passed her by in age. And Kraft Sr., Wandering Soul's conductor if not engineer, entered the old age due him: a nursing home apartment full of Post-it notes to himself: "Stove top?" "Cigarette butts?" "Turn off lights?" Here and there across the walls, greeting the boy on his filial visits, mental jogs mapped a track of terror in the wake of the ephemeral words slipping away from the man: "mollify," "onus," "evensong."

Occasionally, a letter from Dad would arrive, overposted with a police lineup of stamps, addressed in a loopy handwriting that resembled the boy's earliest attempts at onion-skin tracing: "Dear Richie, The enclosed article beautifully explains the wonders of laser light. FYI. Thought you might like to know." Dragged back to the first condition, just prior to permanent exile.

So the boy grew older, simpler, sleepier, until one day the pupils of that forgotten jungle school came back for him. They returned, one for one, back from all those years held in some detainees' transit Westerbork (the murals of which, you must sooner or later learn, depicted a brightly colored, larger-than-life piper going about his eternal job description). He grew until waylaid by *you,* my old friends, tomorrow's casualties, today's belated show-and-tells.

Listen, my children, and *there,* as every story formula ever committed to memory puts it, *there you have a tale.* And here you come to the end of it.

They travel light, pare back the carrying weight. Essentials only. When the requisitioned gimp vans come to take them on the road, they bring along just the costumes on their backs and a few props—a tonette, a papier-mâché mountainside that splits down the middle to reveal a fleeting crevasse.

Angel City is not the place they left upon entering the magic maintenance hideout. They see for the first time the town that has passed itself off as home. They play tourists to their own back *barrios,* the ones the package junkets only buzz through with the tinted windows rolled up shut. They perform in Jorge and Roberto's alma mater, where the classes are led through the auditorium in controlled shifts, frisked by armed guards. One seventh-grader in the audience is rushed to Carver in mid-performance, when the smuggler's balloon he swallowed earlier that morning breaks inside him.

They play a gazebo in a once-park on the east side, where indigents of all ages crawl from their Masonite maisonettes to stare at the inscrutable proceedings as if at another unreadable eviction notice. A religious club where they do an afternoon show is raided two days later for sheltering a hive of illegals. Necrosis has taken hold everywhere. It's all coming due, extended credit's final statement. Privation now costs more than wealth, the old pyramiding scheme, can hope to generate.

They cross over to the happy Valley, where bad conscience has booked them at the Galleria for a matinee. There they play to a weekend mob of glazed children who call their parents by first names. Children with weekly Top Forty head-dos, two-hundred-dollar helium-injected shoes, color-coordinated spun-silk lip-shaped purses stuffed with supplementary credit cards slung around their want-not waists.

The Hamelin rats had no idea. This unspannable gulf accounts for the spreading partisan rumble, the GAS THE BASTARDS T-shirts, the collapse of the street economy into a single, exhausted, gag-gift boutique of hate and rage, as if future GNP depended on our continuing to buy fart cushions and SHUT THE FUCK UP coffee mugs for one another. It explains the six hundred autonomous Angel armies, now the city's chief employment for minors. It glosses the junior-chamber-of-commerce consortium of tax-free, million-dollar-a-week retailers, cataclysm's middlemen, scalpers at this ticket-holders-only mass send-off.

Travel works an awful mental broadening on them. They are toted downtown, where they have never been, past the Ray-Ban investment house towers and airline office blocks. Each one is a laundering of the architectural balance sheet, a pauper's hospital in disguise. Even here, the down curve has begun, steeper and more abrupt than the city planners suspect.

In the van, they amuse themselves with road games. A chunk of Nerf cinderblock and the newest rap lyric hold them beguiled for whole freeway jams. Nico bullies the group into leading Joleene to believe she's telepathic: "My God, you've guessed our secret object again. Quit . . . How in the . . . ? You're playing with our Innermost, girl."

"I don't know how I know. I just *know*. I think, and it comes to me. It just springs, like, into my head."

They switch between suppressed snickers and reverential awe at the girl's newly discovered power. But they never tell. The girl will die thinking she's psychic.

Nico is everywhere in the van aisles—cheerleader, voice coach, tour guide—working the sickos, most of whom should not have been allowed to step foot out of the plague house, even for these brief, homeopathic afternoons. He plays with the young ones. "Okay, punks. Huddle up. Let's go over the playbook."

He prepares them for the longer outing rapidly coming up. He waves a comic in front of them like a shiner lure, but the tykes just sit there on the knife-slashed vinyl, facing him, their very *instinct* to curl up on the right side of the page rendered cagey, extinguished by unspeakable early conditioning. It hurts to see how much it will take before these stunted crips will be ready.

"Criminy. You younger generation are frigging illiterates. Hey you: yeah, the one with the wet spot on your pants. Complete this rhyme. 'Simple Simon met a . . .' "

A sidelong look of suspicion gives way to a lagged but crescen-doing "Pimon!" of near-rapturous relief.

"Yeah, so ya got lucky. 'Going to the fair. Says Simple Simon to the . . .' "

"Pimon!"

" 'Let me taste your . . .' "

Agonized pause. Total exam panic. "Hair?"

"Hobbling God on a bloody crutch! Okay, okay. I'm sorry. Hair. Whatever you say. Just don't blither on me."

And why not? These infants, connoisseurs of every conceivable tang, have at least hung on to that primal impulse to pop everything into the mouth: paste, plastic, wrapping paper, cakes of hardened snot, a salad bar of gravels and soils, earthworm pies, pasty pastry scabs, lead paint peels. A hank of hair is among the more innocent of the thousand and thirty-one flavors left their lingering ability to savor. They will miss these taste buds dearly, this time next month.

"Well, I'd let you taste mine, guys, but . . ." He springs the arch grin that vampires always flash their victims. "Got no hair!" He flips his cap. His translucent, purple-pink, shriveled parchment map of bared veins sets off the desired shrieks of terrified delight.

Emboldened, one of the pitiful tinies asks Lieutenant Chuck if she can satisfy the shameless longing that's been nagging at her for weeks. She wants to put her fingers into the resounding hole that still plumbs deep into the lower left of his reconstructed face. Chuck clears away the clutter of removable prosthetic and stoically caters to the request not once but several times, while each little rat extra trills in fascinated disgust as she finger-probes the pit.

"Don't wiggle or you'll touch brain," Nico warns, causing a new round of diving for cover among the nightmares-in-training. Chuck holds still; anything for the cause. Each must be prepared to submit to whatever it takes to secure the trust for the impending Big One.

An altercation at one of their school stints temporarily grounds the road show while Linda clears up some legalities. Some fiendishly healthy, overaged fourth-grader insists at snub-nose-point on following the Hamelin children through the papier-mâché mountain to whatever offstage hidden prospect it opens on. The scare is no more than a routine, late-day urban heart murmur, but it is enough to keep them hospital-bound for a little longer. While the players wait for the incident to be settled, Nico continues to recruit for the standing cast.

His canvassing brings him even among the pre-young: he hovers over the incubator, the greenhouse glass palace of a six-hundred-gram, red sugar beet born four months too soon. He plagues the nurses with questions that they find cute for a while, until the obsessive grilling progresses toward the macabre. He asks about the catheters, pump primers jammed into the surfactant-stripped lungs to keep them from collapsing like a graft-riddled public housing project. He wants the tech specs on that hypo needle stuck through the umbilical into the heart, the standing kegger tap for injections and test draws. He wonders out loud what would happen if it were accidentally disconnected. He demands to know if these still-unshaped souls, the only humans coming up for air before they are even zero years old, might be close enough to eviction that their speechless brains still carry some trace of the original place.

"Hook them up to the CAT scanners," he urges, beginning almost winsomely, then waxing vulture-beaked when they laugh him off. He dares the authorities, gives them all the early warning they will need by muttering audibly, loud enough for even the packets of preexistence to hear. "Yeah," he says, his lips almost pressed to the Plexiglas, "you guys too."

BRING ME SOMETHING, Joy begs each time the troupe sets out for a new venue. She lies in Intensive Care, allowed no visitors, unconscious, swaddled from top to shortened tip, strapped to the electromechanical life assistants, without which not, nothing.

Staff has no idea that Gramps Jr. is sneaking visits to her. The IC nurses, if they came across him there, signing to the comatose girl in an unearthly semaphore, would not even know how he managed to break and enter.

What? Bring you what? He lifts one balding eyebrow as if to ask: *What souvenir of the death throes out of doors do you want for a keepsake?*

He needn't ask. The answer is obvious, lying uselessly all around her tube-thicketed bed. Books, of course: before she went under the knife, before she would agree to suffer the anesthetic, Joy made her doctors promise to stack her magic hoard alongside her in the IC, so that the pick-a-mix of printed spells would be there the moment she came to.

Still booking, cramming for the pop final that has already been slipped her. Nico picks up one volume after the other, flips through the stack, shaking his head. *How can you read these things, Joyless? They got no pictures.*

The ones that do have illustrations are the bleakest. Smeary black-and-white negatives from the written-off countries populate that pathetic social studies text, groundlessly optimistic even back when it was printed, sometime around the year of their birth. Previous borrowers' Crayola do-it-yourselfers lay down illicit tracks in her heavily bookmarked history. Bright tempera washes explicate the book that Linda has placed on the top of this stack—advance pastel flowers on a granite grave. The swirly romantic maroons and silvers of the legend of Saint George, who, it says right here, had to slay a dragon that had developed an unfortunate taste for human calf, child veal cutlet. Wouldn't even get him six months' probation in most states these days.

He picks up an intimidating reader, gauging by the tiny type that ordinary kids wouldn't be hassled by it for another four grades at the earliest, if they still troubled with reading at all by then. The collection's carefully cracked spine falls open to a short story about kids being sold door to door during some war. Houses on fire, Krauts doing their Space Invaders number again. He prefers the Pacific Theater. Still, it'd make a great comic: Cosmic Quester gets dimension-shifted into this place where they're shipping all their kids . . .

At the end, underneath those "Questions for Further Study"—he can't believe this—she has actually scribbled in a whole dollhouse-sized bible of answers, printed in teensy longhand, spidery, like she's still writing Whoositskrit. For the very last question, "Interview a contemporary . . . ," she has patiently printed a whole case history too tiny to read.

He snaps the book shut, to trap the answers inside. *Fine, Joyless. We'll bring you back whatever you want. Name the title. We'll liberate it for you from the very next school library we play.*

He does not mention that the touring theatrics may be over for good. He gives her IV sack a shake, the practical equivalent of shoving her down on the foursquare asphalt, and makes ready to sneak back through enemy lines.

Nico, wait. Don't go yet. I'm afraid.

Deep breath, slowing for stamina. We almost got away without having to do this. *Get outta here. What's to be afraid of?*

It's not going to work. We are going to miss it again, aren't we?

Grow up, huh? He nudges her traction set, grinning. *We're about to pull this sucker off, once and for all. Exactly the way I told you.*

Nico, I've been reading.

No duh.

Shh. What's happening to us, it's—farther along than you know. Wider. There's a lot more to it than we thought. That story. They . . . made a mistake remembering what really happened. They got confused,

*in the time it took to write everything down. That place they escape to,
the childrens?*

Children, you DP.

*It's not what we think it is. The way you perform it is . . . wrong.
Don't you remember? Don't you? It's not about escape. Not about leaving at all. The hole in the mountain is just where they are held, caged up
together before being shipped back.*

Shipped back? Why?

Can't you see? They still need us for something. Here. *Nobody can go
until everybody . . .*

He has never heard her so talkative, certainly not while she still
had the use of her voice. She is no longer herself, but a convert
frantic to make her single point. And tugging at his thoughts, she
insists, *Look here, Nico. And here. All over, everywhere.*

She flails at her texts, rooting around in ones that even adults
should need notes from their mothers before being allowed to
check out. She selects telltale passages, forces them on him from
her comatose horizontal. *Look here: three thousand new refugees, every day. And doubling in less than ten years.*

She rolls out the sick ciphers, like a UNESCO bean counter gone stark, staring prayerless. Here: the soft parts of homeless
street swervers, collected in plastic garbage bags for the per-pound
cartilage bounty. Just down this hall: crack and HIV little sibs arriving and dispatched again at a nationwide rate of one beltway
suburb a month. One child in five, born below the subsistence
line. And this, she lectures to him, eyes clamped shut in her liq-
uidy, shinered sockets, all this without taking a step out of the
world's richest nation.

The times table she forces on him is just another tired catalog,
impenetrable text in a world grown senile on images. But she has
her own visual proof to bring the journey's contour home. She
leads him to a baroque, fine-line Magic Marker chart, several
loose-leaf pages Scotch taped together. Scores of different-colored
marks stand for the spectrum of evacuations, the scope and scale
of each assorted outrage. He finds the treasure map by telepathy,

tucked carefully in the flyleaf of a book called *Waiting for 2000: A Grade School Guide for Millennium Straddlers.*

The scatter pattern of her careful connect-the-dots historical atlas leaves no territory for doubt. Graduation Day is already upon them, and their study group has been cribbing with an obsolete, fractured-fairyland flat-earth projection of the turf.

She smiles at him, weakly but warmly, from under the massive sedative, letting him on to her last secret.

You know what they taught you, early on, when you still attended classes? How the surface of the earth was mostly water?

He says nothing. He can already complete her argument, the example left for the student as an exercise. The thing teachers everywhere neglect to add. The thing that every kid from the newer neighborhoods now knows first hand: the people of the earth are mostly afloat.

Hey: not to worry, JS. I'm telling you, dudette. We have our moment picked, and as soon as it arrives . . .

You will slip through the crack without me. And when you come back—that is the worst part. You will all be in another place, without knowing how you came there. You won't remember why you talk or dress the way you do, the way no one else does for thousands of miles around. You won't even be able to say what you were escaping.

Leave without you, Joyless? What kind of monsters do you take us for?

The monster in question makes a last, bored flip through the stack of scare-tactic facts. His smirk pretends not to know that it is under scrutiny.

Besides, he tacks on, straightening his Dodger cap in the reflection of her life support apparatus, *these little picnics we're doing now are just reconnaissance. Chill out, huh? On the day when we tweak the ending, you'll be along for the ride.*

He stands a second time to sneak out, but still she won't let him. The cold sweats shiver her limbs. Her whole torso quakes quietly, as if the traction bed hid a Magic Fingers. The tremors are on her, the wind-up ones. Now he must run, or give in too to hypothermia. To knowing.

Nico, Nico, Nico, she says, just to be saying, to keep the alternative at bay. *Here,* she indicates. *No, the other stack, just underneath.* She leads him to the thinnest volume, the belated song for the nursery, the one still wrapping her in original sight. The marker suggests there are a few pages left yet in this one.

Its tenacious cradle-grip on the girl is as strong as the first clasp, the instinct to grapple at giant index fingers, to clutch at rattles, to latch on to any probe that the immense creatures from above extend to hook us with. He picks it up, groaning.

Nico, she pleads. *Nico? Read to me?*

WEEK'S LAST CLINIC wrings the woman out. She comes from it like a doily from a lye bath. Her final half-hour session of the afternoon expanded into a life term: a couple who, despite the prenatal tests, chose to keep and care for what the chart calls a severe mental handicap. As if any couple from these parts were not sufficiently handicapped already. The child seems set to stretch the terrible twos into a decade, and Linda's simple assignment is to keep him from biting his tongue off every time he moves.

Only the couple's infinitely uncomprehending hurt keeps her going. It never crosses their mind that the daily, unbearable confusion of routine might be less had the child been different. Love, it seems, is past choice, past examining. It is a severe handicap all its own.

She comes from the punching bag session dripping wet, gritty, foul to herself. She will not go home, a place that has lately taken on the appearance of a giant but empty shoe, filled with silent, sacrificed shouts. She might just be able to make it to a shower downstairs, in the staff stalls, to find some provisional hideout here, an unoccupied call cubicle where handicapped humanity will let her curl up and fall asleep for a hundred years.

Ah, now—for that she must slink unseen past the same monk's cell where she once tried to seduce him: *Come on, come on. Old Dr. Kraft in there, bashing the bishop.* Who was that girl? Where is she gone? Dead, deported. He has embalmed me, shot me full of the pharaohs' eleven secret herbs and spices. Done me over, rehabbed me in his own image. Rightly so; the Clara Barton thing never did any lasting good. More of them every afternoon, more brutally clipped and bewildered. Better off like him, carapaced at least, killingly efficient, steering by the self-conscious voice-over in my own head.

The scalding shower dilates only her superficial vessels. She could go out somewhere, cleaned, slicked up, and get a man. It might help, tonight, unsnag her from the immediate brambles. But the man would be him, all over again, and his microbial Registered Delivery would remain every bit as fatal. Besides, she'd botch the cosmetic doll job, slap the silks and scents on too desperately. Overt and vigorous never works, not even on the most unsuspecting of meat club marks. It lacks the necessary self-delusion. She will never be able to dumb her nerves back down again for romance. Right now, she hasn't even the energy for a token soap job.

She dries methodically, every hidden part; the building is a hotbed of sepsis and fungi. She just about jumps through her baby-powdered skin to turn and find another presence in the room. Only after seeing the other body does she hear, in backward time, the door open and Nurse Spiegel enter. The pretty little number, Kraft's squeeze before, before *her*. Linda will ask her how she can still live, having crawled up close to the airless mine shaft inside the man.

But Spiegel gets her question in first, a question whose sunny Golden State affect wouldn't know nausea if it spit up on her. "Hey, Lin. You making it, babe? Wanted to ask you something. You guys working on another dress-up thing?"

Espera has to think: You guys. Dress-ups. "No," she says, wanting something more friendly than the monosyllable, but helpless to expand on it. The forms of kindness are gone, buried under slag. "No," she whispers again. The outing is over; her shot at renewal is lost. "Why?"

"You *sure*?" Friendly, insinuating suspicion, annoying elbow-nudge. "Those aren't your half-pint getups the nurses have been seeing?"

Linda is the last to hear. Spiegel, who has only the most theoretically vindictive reasons to mislead her, tells her an outrageous, corroborated fable. An epidemic of vague reports, figures appearing around corners, impossible posses at the ends of long corridors. All airy gossip: Spiegel has no other register. "It's not just the nurses, sweetmeats. Dr. Kean, who you know is as Drug-Free America as they come, was telling us he saw a band of tiny coal miners, the Seven Dwarfs, smeared in black dust and wearing these canvas overalls? And a bunch of, you know, millworker girls . . ."

Linda checks by reflex her calendar watch. Old vaudeville routine. Teacher: How long ago was the Industrial Revolution? Smarty: What time is it now? Well, it is not Halloween. Not even fall. She thinks: her group has learned how to contact their sister cells, union locals from all over the timeline.

Tipped off, Espera watches the ward, keeping a continuous eye on who is supposed to be where, when. But it's like slapping a guard on the dancing princesses. She can't trap them. A dozen will vanish at a pop, no place traceable in the building labyrinth. They come back an hour later with transparent fabrications: We were in the cafeteria. *I checked the cafeteria.* Oh, right after that we were hanging out in that storeroom on Eight.

"You needn't lie to me," she tells them in her gentlest read-aloud voice, trying to restring some thread of trust that has sickeningly snapped. But betrayal is deep, deeper than pity. They deny everything. Not even her most painfully smitten little suitors will tell.

Not that she needs telling. She set it up; now the idea she germinated in them has rooted like so many small science projects, those lines of lima beans in moistened paper towel. The children are leaving in secret. Her terminals and unworkables have begun making their own forays into a city sealed off from them. They are budding off into age villages, all the under-sixteens once more seasonally leaving to establish new settlements all their own. Other loose bands come to claim them, orient them to the general gathering so long in accumulation. They are joining up, taking their place in the circuit, the Grid whose completion awaits them.

On no evidence at all, the whole plot occurs to her, the clear-out in miniature. She hears its secret promise all over, as if she weren't hard now, hideously pituitary. They mean to flee in one brief wingbeat the sick entanglement that slits innocence, the offer that forever flooded all that was left of the real neverland, hers, leaving no take-backs.

It has come back, the gaping escape clause, as she knew it would one day, if she but positioned herself lifelong in the company of children, if she just waited patiently long enough to be overlooked. And though they refuse to bring her along—*her!*—Espera can still win her vicarious redemption by being the one who could stop them this time, but defers.

As it is, she isn't given much chance for deference. The plague hits the hospital's full grown before even those expecting it are ready. On the Wednesday after she learns they are leaving in secret, Linda confronts the presumed ringleader.

"You can trust me, Nico," she tells him, knowing full well that to speak the words out loud is to lie.

He answers with a curt "Sober up, Doll-face."

At two the next afternoon, as if she has panicked the plan's instigators by almost guessing, all childhood hell breaks loose.

He has not slept now for, oh, call it an even Week for One. He's finally managed to donate his body to medical science, one of those West Coast investigations into how many days of deprivation it takes before you start conversing with hatchet-wielding gremlins on the foot of your bed.

Funny thing is, this stay-awake dance-marathon-cum-firewalk-ritual is no longer forced on him by the apprentice system, the National Board–certified schedule winnowing the men from the boys, the true sadomasts from the mere zombie wannabes. Sleeplessness has become a matter of personal choice. He gets off on how the tracers solidify, stalactite style, into palpable tableaux. Strangest of all is the image that memory, like an obliging mother gull, has spit up all over him, predigested for his nourishment. He screens again, in his skull, that jerky home movie about how he was young once, but got lost deep in the jungles of experience.

Driving is a particular trip. A bit like sailing, if you think about it, the eight lanes of traffic scudding off in front of him, glinting like sun on foamy surf that stands as stiff as the peaks of beaten egg. He finds he can control the half ton of metal by passively feeling out what the wheel wants to do—exactly how the other million and a half freeway-loaders have been navigating all along. He snickers over the stick, to think it took this crushing fatigue for him to catch the drift of his fellow Angel flotsam.

And while driving to Carver (he forgets from where exactly), he gets his first signal from deep space. He's moored in the vehicle backwash, bobbing against the fender of the Cressida in front of him like a yacht bumper thumping the dock, when he sees from the oversold freeway shoulder's Yellow Pages three giant crosses and a sign reading NOAH'S ARK BEING REBUILT HERE.

The second signal arrives late that evening, or perhaps the day after. Kraft comes momentarily to, staring at a monitor where toddlers in a roll-your-own shelter in a hill country in the process of conscientiously shelling itself out of existence are sitting at mock-up desks. For his private viewing pleasure, they stage a song, in world English, attentive to the video cameras, disburser of all curse and benefit: "Stap de woor," *two, three,* "fur de shilderin . . ." Kraft's been away, lost track of just what war the catchy chorus alludes to. Some damn fool thing in the Balkans, or wherever they've set the venue this season. The kids obviously love it, because they get to bang on the desks on the offbeats.

The videotape laps it up. Entertainment, this nation's number two net export. Modular script number 38-A. Cue the mellow tenor (how does he make his voice *do* that?) to intone the lead-in, "Every war is a child's war." Same mellifluous, brain-lesioning ad copy tone they use for the fabricated dramas, that theater standing in for sense of historical purpose: "This Sunday, as the world watches, two ancient rivals meet head on to decide once and for all . . ."

Crisis has grown so adroit that it auditions its hostages exclusively from these choice offerings. They sing for the cameras, caught in the violence of progress that overhauls everything and changes less than nil. The plea is all mediated, packaged as escapist newsreel, because if it ever really crept out of the rubble of the bazookaed day-care center calling Mama, no one who heard it could live. All the lethargic hyperactivity that waiting consists of at this moment would go still, lucid.

One badly pounded-over sopranino continues to trill to him, even as its life's blood trickles over the cinders of the alley where it has been jumped. He hears it at night, his eyelids toothpicked open, counting the Champagne poppers going off outside his window, hoping the roll into upper exponents might make him drowsy. It's the slim but marginally possible suggestion that this sexy romp in the run-up to mass offing, where even ladies' magazines ask "What to Say If Mr. Right Asks You to a Snuff Film," might yet be no more than a massive market correction on the way toward lasting fulfillment and VCRs for all.

The voice says, *Ricky, clap your hands.* What are the odds that the chorale prelude is so vast that each note of the cantus firmus, a whole lifetime resonating in the dark, swamps our mayfly ears with a sound like blood-soaked nails on a chalkboard? But *clap your hands,* the hope begs him; don't let the sadistic little sprite die. She didn't mean anybody any harm. And it's either clap or give in to the prime-time abyss lovingly opening up underneath him.

He tries it on for feel: *Things are about to turn.* The phrase is his national myth, the dream of that flag-waving, fallen-laurel country on whom God once shed His grace like a rattler sheds his skin. His entire autobiography awaits that plot twist. Solar breakthrough. Cold fusion. Gene therapy. Cryo-seedbanks undoing willed mass extinction in the nick of time. An uptick at the UN. Newly industrializing nirvanas. Three hundred fifty million free-market consumers in the former East. The sixteen-megabit chip. Retrieval TV, the death of broadcast.

Hope's whole checklist is wiped out by one night of the ER's demographic evidence. Every bit of well-being this life has achieved depends on perpetually eating alive the recourseless and exposed. The truth consists of amorously embroidered erectile lanyard nooses, the party tricks with splintered shot glasses that Plummer and company cannot stanch. These are the times' frilly, split-crotch *fin de siècle* unmentionables, inscribed with undying valentine "Maim Me's." Each victim is trained to carry on her own earliest abuse in the names of the fathers. The crippling acquired gene will not stop spreading until everyone has been mishandled, everyone's psychic icebox stuffed with frozen child.

That fact, surging through his carotid, leaves him two choices. He can take his sleeping roll into the outer darkness and lie awake there, tallying the screams. Or he can change the channel. He squeezes the remote control as if popping a painful, watery cyst.

Next over, a fast-breaking advertorial proclaims how secret carrot extract smeared hourly over your face in ruinously expensive gobfuls will keep your skin young, presumably with you still in it, until the end of time. In the supreme, feeble-headed culture, being born later is a moral virtue.

This puff is interrupted by a genuine ad, for a real product, the station itself: "Our uncompromising four-part series on media sensationalizing." Sunday, just after the video version of the novelization of that runaway mega-reprint, *Profiting from Total Collapse.*

A storm of endorphins, and his mother comes to sit down beside him. He scribbles a note on a canary legal pad to remind himself, should he ever stabilize, to look up her date and cause of death. Meanwhile, Mom, who never had much to say while alive, is deep in one of her favorite reminiscences.

"You just wouldn't hold still," she says. "That happens with colicky babies, especially when they have other things wrong with them. Well, we—the nurses and I—tried everything. We propped you up; we wedged you in place with stuffed animals. You just would not stay put." Kraft smiles wanly at the specter's account, knowing the punch line hundreds of times over. "This was in Seoul, in 'fifty-seven . . ."

" 'Fifty-six," he says.

"Don't correct your mother. Where were you raised, in a barn? This was in Korea; not state-of-the-art by any stretch. God knows where they got their radiation from. Our old castoffs, probably. Anyway, there was no other way you were going to take the doses unless I held you myself, in my own arms, the two of us, standing together in front of that awful machine. . . ."

This, the first sacrificial bond he will never shake off. Her moist, swallowed "Oh, Ricky" identifies the larger hurt. She never loved him more than at that infant moment, because he could not harm her yet by loving back.

By traceless association, he is again on the western leg of that disastrous homecoming tour. He is in some national park just up the road from that phantom hitchhiker. He and his mother perch over a display case on "The Winning of the West," reading in embarrassed silence:

BLABS
These metal spikes were placed in the noses of calves, to
wean . . .

Accomplished in humans, he remembers thinking, without resort to hardware. The stab grows in lockstep with the calf. No parent loves as fiercely—he's seen it here, in the assiduous death camps of the destitute—as one who loses a child at birth. Proof is up on the call room prickboard, a poem-laced card distributed to the Obstetrics staff, commemorating a named, fully invested baby, dead after one day. And loved horribly, worse than one lost in the flush of age. A haunted, coupleted, last-century thing, translated from a vanished original: Permit your little one to come; I will conduct it home.

All these muffled hits that strangle him by inches, iatrogenic events, injuries caused by medical care. A public hospital, a chop shop to scare off ghetto death? Jesus God, it's the present's quintessential scheme to borrow itself out of debt. A reflex squeeze on the remote, and he shuts down the set. This sends Mother, as well, temporarily back to the spooks' anteroom.

He is half a life late for rounds. The question is no longer whether he can face the prospect. The question is *will* he, and the debate migrates down into his arms and legs.

When he arrives today, she is awake for the first time since going under. Father Wisat, dislodger of locked migratory spirits, is gone, his own traveling soul retrieved by Immigration, which, while sensitive to the situation, has the country to protect.

The girl's smile, once automatic, fails to break through the layers of apparatus strapped to her face. The covers flatten at her south, two feet before they should, an absence, an obscene vanishing trick. Her torso is caught in the act of sliding off to another world. He can still smell on her the aromas that bore and bone rasp released from her.

"Hey, sweet stuff," he greets her, gagging on the steel wool words. "How are we feeling today?"

The plural pronoun is poison. Her face is impassive under its morass of black and blue, the record of the various blunt implements shoved down it. Maybe her English is gone, systematically beaten out of her. Or perhaps the answer is too obvious for words. We hurt. Nothing else is.

He turns her, probing, fastidiously recording all measurements in his write-up. The hacked-apart schoolgirl, who once wrote him shy thank-you letters, looking up the spelling of every other word, holds still throughout. Except for her labored gasping, she plies him with silence. He cannot bear it. He'll go write himself the magic prescription. It would be easy. Kindergarten.

Her eyes are cold panes. They give no hint of anything but indifference to the attentions of her betrayer. She is so shocked by her internal mauling that she cannot even cry for help, let alone want to.

He must hear her speak, even the word that would make her hatred unambiguous, the accusation he would refuse to defend himself against. He must tell her, *Weekly Reader* style, how the operation went, what they found, what they tried, what they gave up on. A lunch-meat-on-balloon-bread synopsis (the mustard the precise color of those pots of yellow reserved for affixing the blazing sun to newsprint) of what she can expect from the life remaining to her.

You may have noticed that your body drops off a bit sooner than it did. Something in her refusal to speak says she has a better sense of where she is, more profound, more real than his chart can hope to lay out.

He could cut through, lay the mutual knowledge out on the traction bed between them like a hand of crazy eights. You know;

you know. My baby, Joy, don't make me say it. But a sense of impending disaster worse than disease leaves him staring at his clipboard. The real disclosure must come from her.

He considers a full frontal bluff: I know what brought you to this hospital, the reason you are all assembling here. I know, in rough outline, at least, what you and that pal of yours are planning. But that gambit could lead only to the same grisly cul-de-sac: his untethering in front of her. Rocking, lathering, sobbing uncontrollably like the special residents five floors above.

He hunts, hypertensing, for something to sound out aloud. Talk, jabber anything, only make it fast. "All right, Ms. Stepaneevong." His accent is tone-perfect, if shaky beyond recognition. "Time for the end-of-year review."

That brief quiz you've been waiting for from the start. A crucial, last-minute check on her preparation in all disciplines. States and capitals. Planets of the solar system. Periodic table. Content does not matter one atom, so long as she'll talk. The work she has in front of her expands like a crazed zoom fisheye, and suddenly, the fact is as plain as the bruise that was her face. Talk, extemporizing, is the only skill that she will require in school's next annihilating grade.

Material for the promised pop test lies everywhere at hand. She has stacked all around her, for the moment when she would be ready to use them, the collected texts of her private library, an anthology of telling. He grabs at a loose bit on the nearest pile and sits down on the end of her bed, amply vacated now, as if amputation were expecting him.

One box of the newsprint scrap has been heavily outlined in Magic Marker script, not hers. Arrows flank-attack the article's lead, and clumsy balloon print asks, "This one?!" His eyes run over the piece. His lips moving silently in sync, as if still reading with training wheels:

James says that when the Rebel troops set fire to his village, he ran one way and his parents ran the other. He has not seen them since that moment of confusion. "They are not dead," he insists, not even pausing as he grinds grain for tonight's communal dinner. "I just don't know where they are. If I knew, I would go to them. But I don't, so I stay here."

"Here" is a refugee camp on the Akobo River, the border between two stricken African republics. In its misery, the camp is like any of the thousands of shanty cities that proliferate throughout the world. But the residents of Akobo Camp are victims twice over. They fled the Sudanese civil war to the one place where they would be safe from slavery, mutilation, or death. Reaching the haven of Ethiopia, they walked straight into the upheaval now ravaging that land. . . .

Akobo Camp is remarkable for another reason: of all the twice-displaced who have found their way here, after trips of several hundred miles that led from one shell-torn front into the other, not one is older than sixteen. . . .

"No fair," she says, the two breaths costing her brutally. "No fair reading to yourself."

Her tone neither forgives nor accuses. But the sound pumps him full of something dangerously like hope. "No sass, or I'll put a frowning face right here next to your case write-up."

He slips the account back in the stack, so deep she will never have to read it. He swaps it for the top book, more appropriate for adolescent girls, judging by this gawky, goofy-looking, little raven-faced Nancy Drew in barrettes on the cover. Closer to the ticket. Some kind of girlhood diary, written long enough ago to become otherworldly romance. He starts to read, uncomprehending, then starts again at the line break, the way he reads in bed when he has fallen asleep and refuses to admit it, backtracking at every period, plowing every sentence over again until he realizes that he catches nothing, and still more nothing on the retry.

He scans once more in force, thinking, as the words refuse to come clean, *Here we go, then. Ricky-boy, hold on tight.* He focuses by sheer will an attention that, like a stage spot, narrows down from babbling sentence to faltering phrase to blurry word. He turns over this deranged but familiar orthography, strange resemblance, an idiom like a secret brother you visit only once a year, shut away in that tacit, untalked-about home.

Explanation hits him without the appropriate relief: a foreign language. But what is she doing . . . ? She might perhaps have French, a few words, from the residual colonial ghost. But she couldn't know this one. This one was—where?—Indonesia at the nearest. Dutch East Indies.

"Okay," he settles in, choosing desperately to ignore everything, all incoherence, all emergency broadcast, all advance notification, to go on pretending to a semblance of sense. The persistence short of dying. "Here's your question. Who is . . ." He browses the lines near the opening. *"Lieve Kitty?"* Answer carefully, and in complete sentences.

Before she can scold him, Kraft realizes. Kitty has gone, made the leap, slipped back into fantasy from whence she came. That grackle-haired Anne on the cover invented her, conjured Kitty up, retrieved her from the holding room of hidden friends, sculpted her from scratch to keep Anne company up in night's false-walled attic, during that last, lonely few-month stretch before deportation.

Kitty is this book. The secret pen pal that the little Frank girl created, because one always needs to write *to* someone. *Because paper is more patient than people.* Dear Kitty is the figment of that photo, the girl in the desk in front of you in fourth grade, whose eyes, a season before the finish line, smile weakly in advance at the worst that human ingenuity can dream up to put her through.

Joy, what is left of her, brings up a noise from the back of her throat, midway between giggle and gurgle. "There is no Kitty." Exasperated with grown-up silliness, the adult refusal to accept the real.

Journalism and journal: Kraft should have known. These two

late-day narrative styles round out the brief but comprehensive sampler, the trading-card sets of story that Joy and her accomplices have been busy collecting. Treasures on the scavenger hunt handout: find these somewhere in the city at large, and don't come back until you have them all. Now they have them. She can return, like an ethnographer at the end of her field trip year. *Dear Kitty: I grow hopeful now; finally, everything will turn out for the good. Really, good!*

That's it. The list is complete. Or almost. The collection crew now must mount a massive sweep, the scale of which Kraft only vaguely makes out. A drag search for the missing read-alouds, the concluding *Lieve Kittys* from Bergen Belsen and its blood descendants, the notes from the civic-minded citizens tipping off the authorities to the secret room.

It would not be bluff now, to stare her down. He places his hand on her gauzed-over stump and thinks, I know what you are up to. All of you.

But the words he speaks out loud, to the witness air, evade the insight. Lie low, something tells him, and go on living. Out loud, all he says is "Beauty, can I do anything for you?"

She blossoms at the nickname, enough to incline her head. "Yes. Please." She would smile, were it not for the pads of subcutaneous rupture weighing down her cheeks.

"Dr. Kraft." So soft, maybe he makes it up. "Dr. Kraft. I don't know how to do this."

Seven in one blow, a burst of staccato words in a slight, Asian clip. She admits the obvious, the thing his cowardice empowers by running from. The leg alone—the whole lower body—will not be enough. Its childish sacrifice has appeased no one. *Tell me how,* her capillary-spattered eyes plead with him. Give me the next step.

Now, unlike the first time he watched her die, no portal opens. The view out the window of Intensive Care is blank except for a ratty palm, a bank of hospital Dumpsters, and a hummus vendor across the street. The moment grows unendurable in knowing how little chance it has of surviving. He dares not say *Hold out,* or she might.

He could tell her of his own deportation from the place, a record only recently recovered from long live burial. But her evacuation is more extensive, more complete, taking her beyond all preparation. He fumbles for the one deficient revenge ever offered.

"I don't know how either." He brushes a hank of limp hair from her mouth, where it has snagged. And goes on to give her, in as many words as the telling takes, the point of starting out on any once upon a time. The surgeon's sense of an ending.

HE CRAWLS UP from the call room bed, fully dressed, his lids never having touched. A hot shower, and he realizes he is drowning, going under for the third count. Even with the spray squelched, he cannot get his breath in the foaming turbulence of air. He must call her. *Her,* the borderline jailbait, the one whose parts he but recently stroked, avoiding the more awful amplitude lying between them. Her name will come to him in a second. Linda, who has at last left him, as he advised her at their earliest flirtation.

He could drag upstairs, wash his hair, get a fresh change of clothes (his scrubs beginning to golemize on grunge and blood) and charm her back with a "Lady, you owe me lunch." Insouciant, with just the right smidgen of vulnerability, just a hint that he's fifteen minutes from complete, deep-end, isolation-tank psychotic breakdown if she doesn't dose him down and tuck him in.

A hello wouldn't hurt, basic kindness, and he could even come clean, tell her everything he has only now told himself. He makes to leave the cell, but is prevented by a knot of menacing Third Worlders with electric whips. What's your hurry, mister? Go on, have a lie-down. They shove him back onto the bed, where he is jolted—the downed tablets kicking in—across the alkaline flats of his pores. A thousand simultaneous spring-loaded disasters erupt inside his gut.

He sinks in time lapse into the bed. He flails at the bedstead for reading material to steady him and comes up with that May issue of *Rifle & Handgun Illustrated*. It's all weirdly familiar. He has lived this before, but where? Just such an era of accumulating, societywide, sedated, nostril-flaring panic. It's crucial he remember. Yet the patient's chart is riddled with these missing episodes. One continuous archipelago-hopping campaign from *fin de* to *fin de,* torching itself on the conviction, the absolute certainty of impending mayhem, always waiting for the last word.

But never like this before. There has never been the means, the raw megatonnage, the window of opportunity that a city like Angel, a country like the one on his passport, commands. Fear has never been so slickly institutionalized, marketed on such a mind-fogging scale, sold on such favorable terms, nothing down. And to fear something resourcefully enough is to bring it off, wholesale, well before the magic date.

Ten years, and they'll be hooking generators up to bicycles to listen to emergency radio. Cutting up railroad ties for fuel. Licking the lids off trash cans. Rodeo Drive will be a vast black market, like the one in the streets outside Carver. A slow, exaggerated drift toward videoclip, mass multiple-personality self-homicide: the perfect end for a world that has achieved the ultimate aim of being both great tasting and less filling.

And Kraft alone is left to tie apocalypse to vanishing children. Scarred tree rings, ancient internal hemorrhages, origin myths of the bewilderedly trepanned. Abuse is the seed money. Banishment sets the *Bildungsroman* rolling, and every page thereafter is the kid in the backseat saying, "Are we there yet?" "What happens next?"

Where *happens* is not a thing but a place, a remembered premonition cathartic enough to close the opening's rip.

This is Kraft's insight as he goes under. *No one* this side of childhood exile, not a single memoir or condescending picture book, has ever gotten it right. But no one has ever lost it either: that first house, where want and terror, the toy soldiers of self itself, have not yet split off and solidified on contact with air. He's seen it up close, under the loupes. From their ringleader, that Weight Watchers Khrushchev, to the martyred *Lieve Kitty,* each is a raw umbilical stump, a residual direct tap into placenta, the subterranean world.

Enough sleep narcotic now syrups through Kraft's forebrain to bring him almost back as well. The lost tumbler contour: September, racing home in the rain, the runny-soaked page of oppressive sums due tomorrow, the stink of ubiquitous earthworm in the nose's lining. Get it back, returned to the viscera—the car antennas maliciously snapped off for no reason, the lessons on saturation bombing picked up in Sunday School at no spiritual cost, the crack-of-dawn smell of oatmeal equivalent from the squatters' quarter, the trinket bought for the beautiful half-Japanese girl next door (the one who will leave you longing inadequately after halves, forever), thrown into a canal when nerve collapsed—get that back, and you have it. The bead, the cross-locus for the *there* where they now abduct themselves. The locale of sickening, defenseless, permanent fragility, the one that growing up consists of more or less unsuccessfully denying.

And then it hovers over him, forgiveness in the form of a class reunion. They have come back, those two foreigners, just to give him another look, to lift the hole in the fabric for a follow-up, now that he is grown, responsible, ostensibly aware. Second shot, in a stronger body. Now he might do something about things as they are, now, when the worst has been done, when he's lost all and nothing can hurt him further. And thinking, *I will remember this when I wake up; I need only the trigger, the call-back,* he falls into the first recuperative peace he has known since the incurable Hansel and Gretel checked into his ward.

PLUMMER WAKES HIM. The maniac breaks into Kraft's call room, scrubbed, giggling crazily. "You're not gonna, you won't *fawking* believe this. Buddy boy, buddy boy, have we got a celebrity body lineup for you."

Kraft comes out of his coma far enough to sample the distur-
bance. An extended adolescent stands above him, eyes watering
in a colloid of shock and excitement. Thomas—unthinkably—is
crying. And he won't tell, but in his manic elation over something
finally happening, an event, definitive, coming home to roost at
last, he merely hustles Kraft out of bed and shoehorns him down
the hall for the denouement.

It starts in the ER and splays, like a family Labor Day, down
the adjacent halls and foyers. If it is not precisely the scenario
Kraft has been anticipating, it is its next of kin. He feels almost
relieved that it has arrived, taken shape, capped imagination.

But imagination could never have managed *this* without assistance. Plummer does his sugar-rush, play-by-play patter. "Tried
to beep you, Dr. Krafty, but yer number was not in service. Suite
phone bungied up too, suspiciously enough. But what the hey,
hey? Now that we got you, the gang's all here. Father Kino, Dr.
Purgative, Miss Peach . . ."

Plummer starts to sound just like the throbbing bass of a dash
radio in a distant Mazda playing acid house on volume 12 while
idling at a stoplight. What a civilizing cleverness, how they always put the ER on ground level, right by the parking-lot receiving dock. Ideal for bulk shipments.

The halls fill with disembodied spectral wails, paramedical
commands in Pilipino, the shouts of admission nurses whose bureaucracy has broken down under the weight of the penultimate.
A kaleidoscopic aural chaos. Kraft looks out over the event just as
the infotainment folks bust in through the sliding doors with the
Minicams.

The thing that has come over to play, exceeding Kraft's still-
narcotized ability to take it in, is just your consummate, postur-
ban, median mass murder. Atrocity, like art, attends to the flavor
of the age. It sinks vast sums into R & D, to produce an imagery
tailor-made for the sensibility that has habituated to every horror
imaginable except itself. "Hey," Plummer twitters away by Kraft's
side, "it's not much, but we call it home.

"Guess," Thomas keeps nattering. "Just guess. You'll never, not in a million, not in a coon's, not in a dead man's . . ."

Guess *what*? Even that much evades Kraft. The identity of the monster who did this? The Herod behind today's installment could be any hopped-up, factory-outlet counter helper with fifty bucks for a gun, that party favor easier to purchase than alcohol in some states. He wouldn't even need the fifty bucks, because there's always financing.

Once again, the bullet sprayer is just another sleepless burn-baby one degree worse than the rest of us, turned by ubiquitous, state-sponsored terrorism, the housing-project prison on all sides of him, into trying to out-horror horror. Butcher, baker, ex-war criminal sponsored by the NSA, short-order loner, Veteran of Foreign Police Action, Secretary of Health, Education, and Welfare, crazed chemmed-out cardboard apartment dweller. How high would you like to point the finger? Who do you want for your guilty party?

"What's your hunch on this one, Krafty? Jets versus Sharks? Tong war? Fast-food shoot-up? Get a life, bro; that was *last* year. Football stadium spree? Please, leave that to the effete Europeans. Airport terrorist strike by Oregon Ecotopian separatists? Indiscriminate mall-walker mow-down?"

They pick their way through a litter of stretchers. Seeping bodies line the corridors because there is no room at emergency's inn. They drift listlessly in the direction of the operating theater, with some vague notion of assisting in the red tide bailout with their plastic beach pails.

In Kraft's doped silence, Plummer loses it. "Mother fucking Mary!" he screams. In the general frenzy, no one even turns a head. "Look around you, shit-for-brains. *Look!*"

The order is so violent that Kraft does, pushing back the sheets from one upward-staring face, then another. He cannot see the common denominator in this sea of victims, so salient is it, so long expected, so presupposed.

"You're fucking kidding me. Are you blind, or what? Helen

pissing Kell—" Kraft looks for something deeper, subtler, more insidious. When Plummer shouts the patent axiom, it's only the givenness of the observation that shocks him. "A *grade school*, Peewee."

At last, Kraft panics. "What school?"

"Oh Christ. Martin Luther King Junior High. Bobbie Franks Elementary. The Little Girl Down the Well Montessori School. Who fucking cares?"

Kraft would kick him in the face, Free style, but has no time. He skids around, thinking to race the half-dozen flights up to Pediatrics to find where the piper was playing today. But he remembers the tour's cancellation. Then the sickening backwash, the shame at mouthing the parental refrain: Thank God it wasn't *my* child.

Plummer looks about, grinning. "Hang on, kids. It's Chinese assault rifle time. One-one-thousand, two-one-thousand . . . ready or not, here I come."

At this outburst, crazed as celadon glaze, Kraft takes the man's wrist and tries for a steady tone. "Thomas."

"What? 'Get a grip,' right? 'We're doctors, goddammit.' Ever notice how much these scrubs resemble the traditional restraining jacket?"

Plummer begins to trill "Whistle While You Work," complete with late-'thirties warbling. The sweet dwarf-tremolo serves only to conduct the shape of revelation deeper into the fibrillating heart.

Kraft bathes in iodine wash, up to his biceps. He listens to the sea of voices around him. The operating room is ablaze in the high-frequency flicker of fluorescences, a cozy home version of the seductive Christmas tree star, Shinto devotional candle, menorah stem, the burning White Light at the tip of civilization's long bushmaster black fiber-optic cable.

Kraft's eyes must dilate, stop down to the sight of the banquet spread for them. His own organs have never been particularly good at depth perception, especially under such light. But the slaughtered softball teams, the choir groups and secret note-passers still being wheeled in, their IVs bobbing above them like golf cart pennants—these are unmistakable. He need not even sponge off their features to confirm the ID. Schoolmates. His all-star backfield from twenty years ago. Old neighborhood friends.

Work begins without prelim. It proceeds, with only the smallest verbal dispatches, into time beyond telling. They make the first-pass sort, splitting the stretchers into two camps, red blankets and blue, those that might yet be addressable and those for whom injection and deliberate oversight is now the kindest remaining treatment. Decision is quick and concise, applied to each new batch. The sieve is axiomatic. Care for the still savable is relegated to stopgap. Gross clinical movements, close enough, timeshare between points of impact, with vague hopes of getting back to stabilize.

Kraft's hands go autonomous; their overlearned skill runs on ahead of him. From time to time he stops to say certain procedures by name: RUQ abdominal wound requires immediate hemostasis by application of . . . But even these speak-aloud bits are a kind of Latin liturgy, mumbled by heart with no feel for the meaning of the words. He drags, a deep-sea diver, through the reef-encrusted deep.

After a while—no saying how long, now that time has formally ended—activity in the room accumulates. It condenses into concerted efforts like planets congealing out of stellar dust. The luxury of study, the idea of a worked-out operative plan, takes on a laughable Club Med quality—decadent contrivance of primary care givers still living the dream of sustainability shattered here.

They operate, seat of the pants, improvisation night, open stage. He nods out along someone's splattered linea alba and comes to, still working efficiently, hovering out-of-body over a half-sized left anterior aspect, retracting the gaping hole by hand as Dr. Brache crams the loose party favors back into the split *pi-ñata*. Habituation is a marvelous thing. The annihilating assault Technicolor lasts only until it becomes familiar. Then standard emergency procedure sets up its own counter-rhythm. A little movement, a little breeze in the face of the unlivable. Endurability is simply a rate function.

The uses of childhood exceed human count. What he wades through is this year's quota compressed into an hour. They apply the same tourniquets, thread the same running locked sutures, ligate the same living tissue with their 2-0 chromic. So where is the threshold point, the place where what remains is no longer life but contorted burlesque? Well, in a word, *here*. Even the attempt to make sense of it is obscene. It's over, over. There's nothing for it except the stylized *as-if*, the subjunctive, the reflex motions of *would* and *were*. Call, as always.

While Kraft holds his finger in the blood-spewing hole, a little melody of contrived naïveté loops infinitely through his head. It's a phrase out of some expectant cartoon picaresque, but lovely, dark, escapist beyond telling. The words go: "Don't leave just yet. Don't fall." The tune is lullaby incarnate. He fishes for a piece of lead that has molded itself against what were once vertebrae, humming to himself. He times the drop of the lead into waiting stainless pan to spank on the cadence.

Although time has ended, something keeps changing out there in the space beyond the theater. The kids must have gotten shot sometime before three in the afternoon, when school let out. Last he stepped out for air, it was dark. But whatever change persists outside the hospital is just a leftover, inertial going-through-the-motions, a hysterectomy case on hormones, a midlifer returned to the singles circuit for reasons that escape him. Night falls, as always. The cut-faceted flares come on all over Emerald City. A lovely petrochemical astigmatic glow enchants the sprawl, holds out the flirting promise that society's postindustrial theme park is nearing its eternally imminent completion.

All done with back projection, of course, double exposure, soft focus, the industry's proficient visual con. The addiction to hope is no surprise, in a creature whose soul is a complex kludge, imagination's overlay superimposed upon superfluous animal circuitry.

Mind is a sucker for its aboriginal entrapment. *Then what happened?* What happened is *this,* narrative's two-minute drill. These lacerated trick-or-treaters left at Kraft's door.

News covers it all night, while the story is hot, between "Dates of the Stars" and tangled tales of accidental incest. Tonight, anyway, this one is the lead. Collective schoolyard death—this ring of real-life Riverdales and Sweet Valley Highs, assembled like a crop of eager Presidential Achievement Medal winners to deliver the valedictorian address. Its plot feeds the country a night's full course of the Gothic frolic it has come to require.

The ER staff and their temporary conscripts—sworn in under the crisis clause—stay glued to half-hourly accounts of the shooting that has landed in their laps. They follow the story on huge TV monitors mounted in strategic spots about the lounges. They leave the apparatuses open, bloodletting them for the glossless glaze they offer on the event. They watch the Minicams come into this same ER, pan the room, point at the monitors, which disappear down a White Rabbit hole of video regress.

They see in slight variation, half a dozen times, each abdomen gaping underneath them. "Updates," the wire vendors call the repeating hook. Yet the only new data, aside from the killer's high school yearbook photo, a glimpse at his underground cache, and some revised stats from the assault rifle technical manual, are the updates that everyone in this room already knows: the count increment, a charity-drive target gone mad.

Reporters start relaying as news the bits all the other news media say. Panels of experts pick at the thing listlessly, like hostages to the Clean Plate Club toying with their asparagus. The stats sprout their privately suspected proofs: one in five American schoolchildren has possessed a gun. On any given day, one hundred thousand come to school armed.

Internationally, vicarious glee sets the dominant tone. Iran, Syria, South Africa—the usual pariahs—have a field day. World Service dubs the solo corral gunfight "this peculiarly American crime." Yet if it is at all peculiar, Kraft thinks, it is only to show

how the States is still, for a last short gasp at least, the world's innovator, the flagging standard bearer in trade's westward migration, as first formulated by one of those Adams boys.

News drags the standard surreal figures back and forth into the
viewing plane. Its sick traffic is matched only by the continuous
crowd tiding in and out of the frantically composed operating
theater. It's pure opera, a lavish *Medea* in modern dress mounted
by artists in exile's holding camps. One alderman makes the point
that most of our annual firearm homicides are caused by unregistered weapons. Thus, what we really need to discourage the
illegal trade is easier registration. The city could even liquidate
some of its crippling debt by selling portions of its massive seized
arsenal. . . .

Surgical nurses palm Kraft the requested blades as in that old
game, pass the shoe from me to you to you. Their heads bob like
toy water-sipping ducks, peering up to gape at the monitors while
they clamp and cauterize, listening, as if the clue to the next incision, the mystery they hold braced under their latex, is out there.
In the floodlit close-ups of hysterical mothers. In the filler human
interest about the kid whose life was spared by a truant afternoon
in the video arcade. In the pastel artwork pinned to the corkboard
of the decimated classroom.

Bodies and delayed broadcast: the team members watch both
images at once, needing only the colored glasses to go 3-D. They
watch in the stunned peace that settles in after event passes all
understanding.

On the dozenth repeat of the simpering anchor's "Topping
the stories this hour," somebody snaps. It's Kean, raving, "Do we
have to . . . can't we get a shade less grotesque soundtrack?" His
tone is puerile, an I-didn't-ask-to-be-here-you-know. Even here,
disaster is, de facto, every man for himself.

"Whatcha want, Father Kino?" a mask-muffled voice heckles him. "Mozart symphony?" In a world where such things still
mattered, Thomas would live to regret the outburst. Kean would
ensure that he never got certified. The thought is an idle curi-

osity. It has gone hypothetical, scattered among the dozens of schoolchildren strewn all over Carver's cutting room floors.

One of the scuts obliges by shutting off the media. The decibel level drops so precipitously that Kraft cannot at first place the crash of surf that swooshes in to replace the news. Then physiology returns: the bruits in the capillaries shaking his tympanic membrane. By concentrating, he can mold the sound into the aural hallucination of his choice. He tries his hand at contemporary avant-garde, a piece of pitch equivalents pulled from the points on a random medical chart.

The aleatoric stuff is a piece of cake. Emboldened, he allows it to adhere into the *Kindertotenlieder:* a little light has gone out in my tent. From there he works massively backward, fashioning the pulse into the censered thrill of Renaissance polyphony, that paltry little *Glory to God* issuing out of a host of fist-sized boys' choir lungs, the organs he holds now cupped in his hands. *Et in terra,* the high, hanging resonators soar off, the lines below launching them vaultward with complex but concerted churning, heartsick with courage and perseverance, releasing a plainsong whiff of the place all leading tones lead.

Music issues from inside his skull marrow, an automatic writing like the one his hands obey. The sense is punctured when the notes begin to take their madrigal dictation from another source. He hears the choir above him before he even looks up. There, in the observation mezzanine, a line of children stare down from on high, pressing their palms to the gallery glass.

They gape slowly, like baffled, landed bass, silent except for the soaring twelve-part Stabat Mater sluicing through Kraft's ears. Their motet starts to partake of this grisly Christmas, Saint Nick, their patron, revealed as the all-seeing prep for the Last Judgment. He barely recognizes them, so spruced up, surpliced, tricked out like this, high altos at the very lowest, launching effortlessly into the piece they have been rehearsing all these many weeks. They sound their stunned bit of praise, steeped in the requiem service

that assembles them, wringing whole-toned *in paradisum* from catastrophe's loft.

He has been waiting for them. Chuck the No-Face; Joleene,
falsettoing through her Chatty Cathy; the High Latin Hernandez brothers, radiant as altar boys; the Rapparition, springing the
hymnal's Index of Meters with his freer syncopations. Today's
front line, brought together in his ward for a purpose, have only
been awaiting the arrival of these cadres, through the old portals
of disappearance, to begin the mop-up evensong, the consolidating tutti heave.

They converge through all history's holes. The child miners
are there, the factory fire victims, the bands incarcerated to reduce indigence. The ones converted, over generations of shame,
to fable and fairy tale. They ring the observation platform, staring
at Kraft's handiwork. On an unseen cue, they break from their
antiphony and await orders from the commander of the hour, his
face more beaked and wizened, head balder, nervous energy more
premeditated when seen from a story below.

Little Father Time in his Dodger cap counts casualties, scouring the bloodbath for the expected sign. His eyes, from this distance, dart around the shredded scraps like sparrows after lunch
crumbs. The inventory of his gaze courses over the head wounds
and exploded chests. His own face absorbs the features of those
that are food-processed beyond recognition, no longer identifi-
able as human.

That look settles on the pieces of disintegrating sponge Kraft
pretends to sew together. Kraft follows the glance down, sees the
girl under his instruments for the first time. He traces with his
gloved hand the still-gushing projectile gash. He places his finger
in the ruptured esophagus, the severed tendons relaxing what's left
of her mouth into a Quattrocento smile radiating peace. She will
be spared, at least, reaching comprehension. The age of consent.

He looks up at the loft, helplessly. What? What do you want
me to do? The answer is impossible; the girl steps from behind

Nico, comes from the shadow where she has hidden. He almost tears from the operating team, breaks for the mezzanine stairs to grab her, carry her back to Intensive Care. But the measured, appraising stare she levels at him fixes him in place. Something is different about her, a change he cannot quite name. Then it comes to him. She is upright. Whole. Her legs restored.

All at once they are beckoning, bailing scoops of air over their shoulders. They turn, point, gesture down a path that won't wait. Kraft's eyes well with salt. He pleads with them to stay just a minute longer. I can't. Not now. I can't abandon this in the middle.

It takes him only one stopped heartbeat to realize, humiliated: the *come away* is not meant for him. What would they want with a traitor, a grotesque, repulsive giant, a freak who would smash any clubhouse he tried to squeeze into, a sellout double agent in the pay of age? He snickers at his mistake, the arrogance of it, the pitiful decrepit who cannot recognize his own wrinkles in the mirror. Not him: they have come to whisk off their slaughtered school friends.

The a cappella *Knabenchor* resumes. Their ravishing high notes launch a pathetic prayer at the clerestory, a help message holding at bay, for one more hemiola, the floodgate crossing. *All sick persons, and young children. The fatherless children, and widows. All that travel by land or by water. Give peace in our time. Defend us from all the perils and dangers of this night.* The tune flies up, flushed like a suicidal game bird. It keeps going, up past the atmosphere, eternal as tempered alloy, as awful and permanent as a satellite plowing the black vacuum, pointlessly rehearsing its greeting, millennia after the message senders have all gone.

Kraft sinks back into the pointless exercise, just short of salvage and past salvation. He works head down, endlessly steeped in bodily punishment, an automaton in darkness. He does not look up again at the observation glass or at the faces of the mauled meat packings under his hands.

Tempo imperceptibly shades off. It would be possible to stop and count bodies now, if one were inclined. The field lies, if not cleared, at least preliminarily shoveled. A portion of the mown-down children have been rerouted, airlifted to "more appropriate area facilities," as Admin informs the press. Another portion, steadily rising, are lost in post-op, give up languidly on the table, or fulfill the prognostic leveled at them on arrival.

He cannot say how his colleagues hold out. All but the most manic one or two have long since stopped talking except to call for the occasional clamp. A round robin of catnaps takes over when the rush of violence no longer suffices to kill fatigue. Chief comes and taps you on the shoulder; it's your turn to dive into oblivion a while. As Kraft goes down, the darkness is so thick and sticky that it coos at him.

Needless to say, he goes on cutting and sewing in sleep. Creatures spring out of cracked kid chests at him; whole bodies disappear down holes that open up in the operating table. They die on him even faster here.

Reports filter in, litter his dreamscape with the everyday surreal. With the whole surgical staff overwhelmed by this brilliant diversion, the guerrillas move in and the nightmare evacuation begins in earnest. In the chaos created by the assault, the preemies disappear into thin smog, along with their Plexiglas incubators. In their wake, the second wave—the severe handicaps and defects—disperse as one. They were just waiting; he might have pieced it together. Camped, quartered until the arrival of this go-ahead.

He wakens violently just before the last dance step. He is cutting again, alongside Kean and a stringer he can't recognize. Kean is rambling. "Well, kiddies, we've saved this one. This one, and maybe that head wound thing from yesterday. But these here are turfed."

The man dusts his gloved hands into the open chest. "Still: two out of a couple dozen ain't bad, given the conditions. Should be good for a certificate from the mayor's office." The man turns to address Kraft. "You'll be set for the advance residency of your choice."

Kraft surveys what is left of the room. Torsos in every con-

tortion lie live in their fresh cornerstones, the latest act of ancient sacrifice. He fiddles with his gloved hand for compassion's
trinket. Nothing else signifies. He stops in front of a school kid
whom Kean gives no hope. They are easy to find, those about
to take off. He skims the chart to verify; yes: irreparable. Then
he hangs the tin angel, septic with time, around the slender and
severed neck.

With no link, he is out in the anteroom, on breather perhaps,
with nothing more recuperative to do than stand in front of the
plate glass and look back in on the emergency still under way.
Someone fastens a blood-pressure cuff to Kraft's biceps, pumps it
to tourniquet tightness.

He turns to find a green alien, masked and gloved, tugging at
his arm. It is one of those creatures from far away, accumulating
energy for aeons, assembling a machine the size of imagination's
galaxy, a particle smasher that will break the bonds of memory
and deliver life from forever by the simple expedient of splitting
time. All those still young enough to learn a foreign language
have been conscripted. Because Kraft alone of adults has accidentally gotten wind, they come now to abduct him.

It takes him some moments to realize. "God, Espera. You've
come. Listen. Where did you take that show? What schools?"

She dissolves into hysteric, giggle-soaked sobs, the witch in
water. It flashes into his mind, just what she is trying to cover up:
the itinerary, the venues of tomorrow's mass murder, and the day
after's.

He starts to level the accusation, but her snorting, out of control, enrages him. "Listen. This is important. Who did they have
playing . . . ?"

She comes to with a crack. She rolls her head limply back and
forth on her shoulders, in disbelief at him, at his theories in this
theory-killing place. "I can't . . . It's not happening. It's not. For
the love of . . ."

The punctuating profanity is lost to a language he doesn't
know. "You sick animal," she whispers. "Look at you. Look

around." She is throatless, on the verge of slapping him, throwing the worst, most vicious thing she could say to another human scaldingly into his face: Grow up. Grow up, won't you? She stares at him as if his hands were sharp instruments. "Oh, Ricky. Ricky." You boy.

"She left this," Linda says dully. "In the tablet by her bed." She holds out a notebook scrap. Joy's *Lieve Kitty*. Kraft is terrified to take it. When he refuses the scrap, Linda, practiced, reads it to him aloud.

Of course you are mine! Otherwise I wouldn't kiss you, would I? Buuut . . . you are my best friend, huh? Are we going to get married and live together in a big house? I saw a beautiful white house with blue shutters. Right by a playground. And then my mom and dad can come stay, yes/no?

love Joy

Only a love note, then. He is destroyed, abandoned, as promised at the very start. Linda stops, her voice hanging in allegation.

"This is not to me," he objects. "I never kissed her. It's the other, the old guy . . ."

A choking laugh rips out of the woman. She removes mask and gloves. Once more it is briefly her, the radiance that almost saved him. She is shaking her head, biting back her lip, trembling *hopeless, hopeless,* as if he has just come home, his new coat torn, after she warned him.

Disclosure hits him, a kind of delayed confirmation, one more closeless closure. The numbers now make grief a deplorable indulgence. He gives himself five seconds of denial. He is beyond pretense, past anesthesia.

But the pain is duller if you don't stop all at once. "What about the other?" he asks. That Methuselah kid?

A look comes over her, a stunned confusion of disgust and fear: You knew, then? Everything? "They've come for him. The researchers." Her tone suggests accessory, smuggling, assisted betrayal, parental profiteering. "Oh Christ," she sobs. "How long did he have left, anyway?"

"And the others?"

She returns his matte stare, uncomprehending. Hallucination reaches a pitch where he can't remember if the carnage has really happened or he has fabricated it. He catches on to a dull ironstone finish to her eyes and realizes that she too is drugged. Has been for a while.

She leans to take him, wrap him, punish, revenge, and absolve everything. But as she gathers to correct him from above, she crumples, hands balling at his clothing for a hold. She grips whatever she can cling to, the infant's reflex fist. To release would be to slip endlessly. She mumbles something into his sternum, words that bite their way through his cartilage. *Te necesito. Me sofoco. Cuando no estás, no tengo aire.*

Saturated in death, she lapses into her real language. In less time than it takes her suction fingers to gouge into Kraft's neck, empathy undoes him. He never once asked this woman the first thing about her life. He sees it now, more real than his own. At last he makes the leap to why she searched him out. How she located him. What they are both doing here, hip-deep in baby genocide. All done to rewind the film's opening frames, rework them. Another shot.

Lit in this flash, he sees the assailant that reality arranged for her. Not Mama's wholesome, milk-headed brother, smuggling her into the closet and pounding away at her for years, terrifying her into a pact of intimacy from which she would never emerge except in obsessive giving. Her smotherer is more sinister, darker, southern. Every hour of her life, each time she moaned in hurt pleasure at Kraft's touch, it was in the fantasy that she might open her eyes and see *him,* her destroyer, might spit in his face or fall bleating into his arms. Love: the abuser's name she swore at knifepoint never to reveal, paying its nightly visits, refusing to kill and deliver her, however old she grew.

Refusing until this instant. Kraft looks at her for the first time, infected, condemned. Nothing is left him but her, and simply loving her back is worse than all imagining. She tears away from their crutch embrace. She darts a look over her shoulder at the insanity around them, fleeing it down blackness's alley. He searches her face—Linda?—but she stares back wildly.

"Let it die then," she pronounces. Let us all suffocate. Be snuffed out along with these babies—the best release anyone can hope for. She whips her head back and forth, screaming soundless acceptance, flush up against the sick proximity infusing every instant until the last.

He tries to close the gap between them, to sedate her somehow. But she pulls back from his hand as from a brand. "You touched me," she tells him, lapsing back to a numb scold. "You'll have to rescrub."

Cataclysm spreads in front of him, all but complete. He reads the report already, the way it will appear in the arch piece the Chief will assign him for next month's book club. How we murdered our children. What form will explanation take this time? The one the times demand. Corrupt survival fable, deranged beyond recall. Based, as always, on actual event, but garbled in desperate retelling.

Unless *he* tells her. For once, a firsthand account, a transcript beyond the journals, the papers, the nighttime anthologies. He will say what all eyewitnesses have, since the first fireside. He will tell her: I saw them. I know now where they are off to. I know where they *came* from. They have left us behind, with nothing but this thin plot to live on. To keep alive another sentence longer.

"Linda," he says. How does it go again? Clap your hands. "Linda. Listen."

A white-clothed male, mid-thirties, climbs to the top of a public hospital in a terminally ill Angel City neighborhood on Wednesday night of the world's week. Children, abducted at dusk from their rooms in front of a thousand witnesses, excitedly ring him. Up through the lobby they've come, past the receptionists and nurses' stations, avoiding the banks of public elevators shuttling like scythes, keeping instead to the stairs, taking these at a clip remarkable for so impaired a band.

They rise as a mass, up, always up, scaling the sealed escape shafts. They make their way airward, bubbles on a hull. In shifts, slung over his shoulder, the man carries, fireman style, a girl dying on the edge of puberty, an amputee, an earnest sailor-suited youth with suitcase, a wound victim whose lungs would not last one flight unaided.

They reach the roof long after last visiting hours. On this stand-in sod of tar and pebbles, under a forest of vent excrescences, cooling ducts, pipes, and wiring that make meshes beyond all power to trace, they group and take a sounding. If one saw . . .

No one sees. But *if*—that neverword, the home to all meaning: if you could see, it would all seem perfectly to scale, a school fire drill, except for the giant Christopher in their midst.

The air is unexpectedly harsh, the children not properly dressed, the city exhausted, packed to pointlessness with traffic, more meandering than any of them imagined. The tales spell out their route, like charms on a bracelet that must be read in order. But what if they've gotten the stories wrong, misread them?

Over the edge of this roof, all the way out to the olive-obscure horizon, no sign of the place they must head toward tonight. The chance of their arriving intact shrinks to nothing in these sterile extensions of poured stone. They waver now, while the helicopters home in, following the flood beams like shepherds tracking their nova.

But hesitation, however real, lasts no longer than their condensing breath. At a single syllable from the man they are off, stepping across the hedge, passing disembodiedly over the building's barrier through that pale, acidified, solidifying Angelino smog wall, taking the Imperial Highway in a few leaps. They set a new direction, one that has been hiding in orientation's rose until this moment, mimicking the other compass lines, now revealing itself as perpendicular to everything.

Drop the medicines and accoutrements, the intern commands. Reduce our carrying weight. Keep a change of clothes, a toothbrush if necessary. One luxury—that bedtime book, common property, with the lavish illustrations. Lightness is all in such ventures. Already we're too near the limits, the threshold of the opaque. We will never arrive at the place until we've stripped back to the core.

Empty-handed then, awake, they track the freeway for a while along a hidden frontage. They look for that familiar parlor door left open, the gaping frame inviting them softly into body-warmed dam-ask, conversation's paneled room.

Landmarks fall away below: City Hall. The Observatory. The immigrant's triple hand-built towers. The Archangel Gabriel. And beyond—those banked windmills milking the desert crevasses, pan-handling energy from the air. The evidence of migration's rest mass recedes beneath their feet: basalt heads leaning back into the island. Pacific missionaries adrift in an open boat. A stone fence the length of a continent. Golden mountains tapering to single points. A road spreading from Persia to Spain. Fifty-ton rocks rounded up into standing circles. Glass fragments clustered in cool frequencies, opening their transept apertures onto heaven.

They sleep in the open. Talk around their temporary camps

is always the same: the nature of the scavenger hunt itself, where they are headed, how close the trailing police and hospital authorities might be to catching up with them.

Tell us one, the children plea-bargain, before they'll go to bed. And the lone adult must improvise this evening, from memory, a story of origins, having misplaced the picture book somewhere in transit.

A duchess, riding in style along a dusty road, stopped to dispense charity to a woman who was nursing in the dirt, mourning last year's laughter. The beggar's twin infants, helpless, hungry, crusted with stale infection, incited the duchess's indignation. "Woman, where is your husband? How is it that you are left alone with two mouths to feed?" The beggar had no answer, so her wealthy sister generously supplied one. "This is what comes from lying with two men."

The beggar filled with an outrage as pure as poverty. She cursed the duchess: If twins were the price of bigamy, then let the lady bear as many children as days in the year. This the duchess promptly did on Good Friday, Id al-Qurban, the Holi, Chinese New Year, Liberation Day in the year X. Three hundred and sixty-five at once, and all the boys were named John and all the girls Elizabeth, in the language of whatever land each one wandered into from out of the open womb.

A bastard a day? What became of them?

In the space of their first evening they were gone. Half walked into central Asia. Two fashioned a dugout and island-hopped across Oceania. Three or four dozen learned that cancer-baffling skin trick and stayed in Africa. Almost as many turned ghostly white, plowing the inhospitable North. Fifty fanned out across the Americas. One child joined a scientific expedition to both poles.

And their lives? Did they reach where they were going?

Twenty-three were shelled out of their villages. Eleven stood up in front of tanks with bricks. Another twelve drove the tanks. Ten percent were sent to camps, and relocation, for half these, was consummated. One little girl became a child star, touring the world under an assumed name. A hundred and one had to interrupt their lessons to set up in business prematurely. Several made the hajj, sauntered to Compostela, ascended to the Forbidden City. Six performed as prodigies. Five joined the circus. Four served as illegal couriers. Two more were State Department plants. Seventeen succumbed directly to curiosity, and the remaining majority died in doorways, puffed with poisons and ingested antidotes.

Not one stopped here for any length of time. Kilometer logging started at once, although the motive for mass exit may have been nothing but the search for a meal or a pair of good long-distance shoes.

The story makes due for the moment, scares even the oldest obediently to sleep. But in the morning, some of the smaller children are sorry they ever came. The littlest fade first, the heavily hurt, the limbless, the ones with the fractional hearts. Children who would have died tomorrow in bed have been made to travel distances that would cripple the fittest adult. Enchantment frays at the end, and the whispers begin.

The hospital beds look better at this distance, their diseases less inevitable. Giving themselves up would be as easy now as standing still and waiting to be found. After the additional distance of this day, even the longer-legged among them begin to fade. Are we there yet? How much farther?

An old question, older than anyone alive. Desk-disciplined, sepia ten-year-olds in Meerut, the week before the Sepoy Mutiny, thumbing their dog-eared, half-century-old copies of *Songs for the Nursery,* were expected to acquire it by heart, recite in perfect imperial accents:

How many miles to Babylon?
Threescore miles and ten.
Can I get there by candle-light?
Yes, and back again.

The Children of God, threescore and ten years under Babylonian captivity, made discreet inquiries into their own evacuation. *What are we after?* That convention hall where all the planet's hidden children congregate. Some other place that might clarify what has happened here. *Almost there?* asked the Saxon schoolchildren on the Rattenfänger expedition, and once again on those night transport trains six and a half centuries later. *How much longer?*

If your heels are nimble and light, you may get there by candle-light.

But where? Get where?

This short list of escaped pediatrics is not the only band out and about, skirting the shoulders, the back alleys along the interstate lanes, tonight. The place is awash in child villages, from Nebraska to Dinkaland. Solitary adolescents walk across the outback, threading the way to the scattered Places of Dreaming. A school full of Welsh miners' children vanishes under a mountain. Ge youths seclude themselves upriver for decades. Whole divisions of preteens wander the Vakhan toting guided missiles. A class of Bolivian villagers follows an odd child to the Land of the Grandfather. Pubescent refugee males form autonomous boy-nations that drift through the sub-Sahara. Several thousand children for whom adulthood would have been an unnecessary elaboration put themselves at the service of causes, hungry for martyrdom, a massacre the equal of their innocence.

They are leaving now in all epochs, all regions, packing off by candlelight. Stories continue to pour in. Myth shades off into reportage, fact into invention. If, tomorrow around the fire, to seed the needed child-courage, the one leading this group God-knows-where were to make a diagram on a strip stranger than a Möbius, dotting every place a child has ever disappeared, would a revealing curve take shape? A tendency, a table of tides, extrapolating to reveal that one spot, the Babylon that whole schools strike off to at all hours, losing everything to reach?

So many are adrift, out of doors late tonight, too far from home, migrating, campaigning, colonizing, on pilgrimage, dis-placed, dispersed, tortured loose, running for their lives—so many interrogate the miles there and back that any myth that need might invent to map their progress will somewhere, in time, be born out. Even this one. *This* one.

Their movements are as plentiful as the places in the world they cannot get to. The paths they take are more fractured, less predictable than the weather on this late-summer night that sets them loose. "Tomorrow," the lone adult promises them, "we'll be home."

It is a loving enough lie, omitting only to add that home too is a way of leaving. It is *about* leaving, a departure as certain as any urge, longer even than the sense of having come from there. The pleasant clapboard, the kitchen table, so perfect for late-night re-unions, waits patiently for its occupants to come back. But there will be no stopping. Their return will be brief: two nights, a long weekend at most, over the holidays.

Whatever the house this band might at last locate, the smell locked in its furniture, piping through the radiators, ungluing from under the wallpaper will be the smell of people who have long since disappeared. In through the open front window will come the scent of meadows, burning woods, rain forest, tundra, jungle, sea floor, nitrogens resting a minute in skeins of soil on their way back through the cycle. The first hint of open evening will be too much; they'll be off again, kitchen tables carrying notes of summer flights. At most a way station along the route, home will be less than the lightest touch, long outlasted by the desire to reach it.

But just the mention of the word leaves the runaways, some who would not have lasted out the week in care of the anesthe-tizing State, ready to resume the first program of childhood: the command to quiz the world. For a day longer, they are certain of forever, and the night is theirs. They can see in the dark; their eyes are yet that mint.

The tour leader removes his coat, hospital issue, insignia indict-ing, and places it under his head here in the grass. Perfect roadside pillow. On all sides of him these new lives curl up, still proof in the recall of a longing longer than belonging. They have not been around sufficient years yet to believe in any myth so transparent as permanence. They want tonight's installment before dropping off. Those three hundred and sixty-five siblings: How did they end? Did they ever meet again?

Oh, perhaps. Over the years. They get together every so often, what is left of them, to celebrate their birthday. They compare notes, the layouts of the place, all the secret excuses to push on, to navigate. They talk about open land, doors left unlatched, places where they might build cities or ways they might tear down their earlier, terrible mistakes.

They study economics, they write long books, always lavishly illustrated. They fill walls with murals of overgrown, forgotten, impossible lands of Cockaigne. They formulate a history longer even than the hope of its imminence. They send a deep-space packet-boat probe straying in the muted vacuum for millennia, seeking, searching for a place it might finally touch down, carrying as interplanetary barter a parcel of stories, pictures, messages in threescore and ten globe-bound languages all unintelligible to any being the Voyager might one day come across, each reading, "Greetings from the children of Planet Earth."

This is one that my older brother the surgeon gave me, his little brother the storyteller. No more than the slightest *Just So,* about how the once-monk came to own a framed letter of appreciation thanking him for saving two child lives out of a hideous many.

He was trauma surgical resident in Watts when the recurring nightmare happened on his shift. The papers have all the details, if you want to read them.

I sent him my draft, to see if he might somehow be able to save it too from its inevitable end. My best intentions had failed to disperse the bleakness of the real.

He said, "Call the woman up. Linda." The one I'd once danced clumsily with at the Pasadena Women's Club. "She's still in L.A. She has a story for you."

She did. From her hospital office, Linda told me of life eavesdropping again, exceeding the worst make-believe, horror for horror, joy for joy. She described a little girl whose life had just replayed the one I had invented. For better or worse, this one was saved.

The story meant nothing, except that it had happened.

I asked her about the boy.

"Which boy? Oh, him. He'll be back." They always come back. Next year, next class.

"How do you live?" I asked.

I could hear her shrug. "*I* live just fine. But a child dies of poverty every two and a half seconds." One at her every fourth word.

She, like my big brother, is unmarried and childless, though neither is old yet, except in soul. Maybe they are too bound by all these lost histories and physicals to make more hostages.

If it were possible, I would tell them how, under a different binding, they live another, open book. Someone else's narrowly rescued life story. Yours.

"Does it have a happy ending?" Linda asked. "I want a happy ending. Make someone donate their organs, at least."

Someone donates their organs, all of them. You.

REMEMBERING SOME OLD pain, forestalled until now beyond all the odds, you wrap up this tale. "That's enough for tonight. Go to bed."

These words sound out loud, as if spoken to a child, sitting on the top landing in the dark.

The child is dazed. "Dad! You promised."

You make no response, not even objection. Growing bolder, as oldest children do (this one even older than the man he pleads with), the boy pushes his luck. "Tell that spooky one again." You know. You, Mom, those sick kids. Wandering at random.

He wants a scare that will dispel his worst fear.

The memory comes back, intact as original violence. It cuts into you, insurgent, deep as the first urge, the desire to strangle in the crib this thing that will destroy you if so little as one of its perfect cuticles is cut back.

You hate the boy for how he has forced you to love, to love him like, yes, like a child. The first, the most sickening: a love so awful that you must watch the creature go down, calling you, stunned that you do not step in with the effortless rescue. You know now how you will watch him fall, fall forever, a fall that will not stop with skinned knee or broken arm, a cast the school friends can sign in pastel. The end of all falls is impact without end.

You cuff him, ruffle the baseball cap, run your hands through the luxurious hair. "Tomorrow. Remind me." With appropriate groans, he stomps up—always up—to his room at rooftop.

In the kitchen, you ask this woman—this other with whom you share this house, these offspring, this life—whether perhaps we have been assembled here in safekeeping, awaiting some return.

What do you mean? *she asks, although she knows what you mean. It always comes down to this. Every night.*

You tell her again of that spacecraft, launched back when you were both too young to know you were young. The one with the pictures and recordings, the message in all those languages. One day the rest will trace it back to us from where they have vanished, drop by, ask us to come out and play. But all they will know how to say will be the only words we've taught them: "Greetings from the children of Planet Earth . . ."

She laughs at the idea, and hurt, you defend. You follow her up to bed again, in the dark.

On the way, you find the blanketed shape huddling at the top of the stairs. The woman, your wife, handles it this time. The killing responsibility of care, split down the middle between you.

"What are you doing here?" *she demands, in the playacted voice of authority.* "Get back up. . . . You're supposed to be asleep. Didn't your father just tell you . . . ?"

But it's the little one this time, the girl, and her eyes are burning, wet, incredulous, on fire. There is a look to them, such a look it scares you both.

It can be only one thing, one discovery painful enough to rate that gauge. Remember? Remember it? And yes, she blurts out, confesses, each word catching, tearing into her with the merciless beauty of the thing. "I finished it. That book you gave me? Your old favorite? I just finished it."

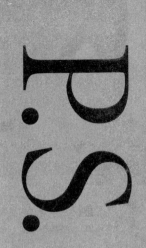

About the author

Read on

Insights,
Interviews
& More . . .

Meet Richard Powers

RICHARD POWERS is the author of
thirteen novels. His most recent,
The Overstory, won the Pulitzer Prize
in Fiction. He is also the recipient
of a MacArthur Fellowship and the
National Book Award, and he has
been a four-time National Book
Critics Circle Award finalist. He lives
in the foothills of the Great Smoky
Mountains. ∾

About the author

More by
Richard Powers

THREE FARMERS ON THEIR WAY TO A DANCE

"Dazzling and audacious. . . . Nothing short of astounding."
—*Philadelphia Inquirer*

In the spring of 1914, renowned photographer August Sander took a photograph of three young men on their way to a country dance. This haunting image, capturing the last moments of innocence on the brink of World War I, provides the central focus of Powers's brilliant and compelling novel.

As the fate of the three farmers is chronicled, two contemporary stories unfold. The young narrator becomes obsessed with the photo, while Peter Mays, a computer writer in Boston, discovers he has a personal link with it. The three stories connect in a surprising way and offer the reader a glimpse into a mystery that spans a century of brutality and progress. ▶

More by Richard Powers *(continued)*

PRISONER'S DILEMMA

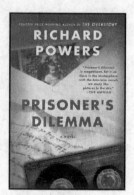

"*Prisoner's Dilemma* is magnificent. Set it up there in the stratosphere with the American novels we study like pictures in the sky." —*The Nation*

Something is wrong with Eddie Hobson Sr., father of four, sometime history teacher, quiz master, black humorist, and virtuoso invalid. His recurring fainting spells have worsened, and knowing his ingrained aversion to doctors, his worried family tries to discover the nature of his sickness. Meanwhile, in private, Eddie puts the finishing touches on a secret project he calls Hobbstown, a place that he promises will save him, the world, and everything that's in it.

A dazzling novel of compassion and imagination, *Prisoner's Dilemma* is a story of the power of individual experience.

National Book Critics Circle Award Finalist

"The most lavishly ambitious American novel since *Gravity's Rainbow*. . . . An outright marvel." **—*Washington Post***

Stuart Ressler, a brilliant young molecular biologist, sets out in 1957 to crack the genetic code. His efforts are sidetracked by other, more intractable codes—social, moral, musical, spiritual—and he falls in love with a member of his research team.

Years later, another young man and woman team up to investigate a different scientific mystery—why did the eminently promising Ressler suddenly disappear from the world of science? Strand by strand, these two love stories twist about each other in a double helix of desire. ∿

Excerpt from
Three Farmers on Their Way to a Dance

Chapter One

For a third of a century, I got by nicely without Detroit. First off, I don't do well in cars and have never owned one. The smell of anything faintly resembling car seats gives me motion sickness. That alone had always ranked Motor City a solid third from bottom of American Cities I'd Like to See. I always rely on scenery to deaden the inconvenience of travel, and "Detroit scenery" seemed as self-contradictory as "movie actress," "benign cancer," "gentlemen of the press," or "American Diplomacy." For my entire conscious life I'd successfully ignored the city. But one day two years ago, Detroit ambushed me before I could get out of its way.

The Early Riser out of Chicago dropped me off alongside Grand Trunk Station, a magnificent building baptized in marble but now lying buried in plywood. I lugged my bag-and-a-half into the terminal, a public semidarkness stinking of urine and history. Subpoenaed relatives met their arriving parties under the glow of a loudspeaker that issued familiar, reassuring tunes.

One hundred years ago, the Grand Trunk must have quickened pulses. Pillars of American Municipal balanced a fifty-foot vault on elaborate Corinthian capitals: America copying England copying France copying Rome copying the Greeks. A copper dome with ceramic floral trim bore the obligatory inscriptions from Cicero and Bill Taft. Now the station's opulence left it a mausoleum, empty except for the Early Riser executives who threaded the rotunda in single file.

I fell automatically into line, sensing the station's layout. The soaring ceiling seemed out of proportion to the size of the hall. When my eyes adjusted to Detroit's industrial-grade light, I received a shock, the same shock I had felt as a child when, at a public swimming pool, I saw an old vet unstrap and remove his leg before taking a dip. The antique terminal had been similarly amputated: the corridor I walked down was not the station's length but only its width. The Grand Trunk had been sent packing: plywood sheets boarded off palatial wings and multiple gates, leaving only this reduced chicken run between a lone arrival platform and the main exit.

Transferring trains in Detroit was the cheapest if not the most expedient way of getting from Chicago to Boston. Drastically cut fares promoted a new route, the Technoliner, for the first month of its run. The line subsequently folded, the technolinees long ago forsaking Detroit for Houston and northern California, and even longer ago forsaking trains for planes. Another case of our railway being behind schedule. Nevertheless, I sank as low as Toledo to take advantage of the reduced fare.

When I'm in money, I can leave half-eaten meals in restaurants along with the best. I've worked hard at overcoming a natural ▶

stinginess. But when I'm out of money—a cyclical occurrence paralleling America's boom/bust economy of the last century— I easily fall back on old habits. This trip found me once again short, having just spent a year in the Illinois backwoods on a small business project that did not pan out. "Pan out" comes, I assume, from the prospectors' days. Flash in the pan. I spent my early thirties in isolation, chasing flashes in the pan.

With my technical background, I knew that I could find work in Boston providing I could put down a security deposit on an efficiency and still have enough cash left over to dry-clean my interview suit. My money margin, marginalia in this case, did not worry me so much as the immediate problem of how to spend the six hours between the Early Riser and the Technoliner in a city I had, until then, celebrated by avoiding. It was me against motion sickness in the city autos built.

But as sometimes happens when killing time, I would come across something in my brief Detroit layover that would kill not just six hours but the next year and more before I came to terms with it. Sifting the downtown for novelties that might deaden ten minutes, I did not imagine that the next ten months would find me obsessed with everything I could learn about Motor City and the fifth-grade farmer who put it on the map.

When I made my stopover, Detroit had already been undergoing a manufactured and heavily publicized rebirth for some time. The emblem of this new era, the Renaissance Center, may be the single most ambitious building project of recent times. Its five black towers outscale the rest of the city the way Chartres Cathedral dwarfs its surrounding town. Four cylinders flank a central, massive pillar, each hanging black glass over girders in disguised International Style.

But if the city were not already dead, would it need a rebirth? The name "Renaissance Center" resembles an ad campaign declaring Sudso "All the cleaner you'll ever need," or a restaurant assuring, "What we serve is really a meal." And just as when telling an old widower that he looks well we mean he ought not to push his luck, the leading citizens of Detroit, in naming the Renaissance Center, implied that they would be pleased if the city could, at this point, break even.

The size and opulence of the center meant to attract tourists and conventioneers into double-A, self-contained luxury. The palace executed its purpose too well. It drew people (read money) up and away from the surrounding businesses, and because the towers were so self-sufficient a village, the people never came back out. The area surrounding the Renaissance Center showed the signs of a hasty evacuation and rout. Gravitating toward the towers, I passed row on row of brick, triple-decked residences standing vacant, their windows and doors broken open to reveal nothing inside.

I figured that the Renaissance Center (dubbed the Ren Cen by those who make a living truncating all words into monosyllables) would be good for a half hour. The inside was a contemporary version of the Grand Trunk—the multileveled, involuted architecture that had delighted me as a boy of six, when I still believed in Tom Swift and urban renewal. I ordered a meal, reading the menu right to left, in a disk-shaped restaurant floating on a moat in the central tower, spinning, gradually but perceptibly, driven no doubt by a thousand Asian coolies chained to a mill-track on a hidden lower level.

My training in physics made the huge spinning plate seem an unintentional homage to the last, great empirical experiment of the nineteenth century. In 1887, the physicists Michelson and Morley set out to measure the absolute velocity of the earth through the ether field. The two scientists floated a gigantic slab on a sea of mercury, on the same scale and setup as the slab I now rode. They shone a beam of light through a prism in the center and back to mirrors on the perimeter, reasoning that ▶

light flowing in the direction of the ether stream would travel faster than light flowing upriver. But Michelson and Morley found no difference in light speeds, regardless of orientation. An international calamity followed in 1905, when Einstein, a Bern patent clerk with no reputation to lose, suggested preserving the velocity of light at the expense of the concept of absolute measure. The century was off to a quick jump out of the gate.

I came across an account of this experiment again much later, after pursuing the Henry Ford hoax through the infant century. But at the time, I drew the comparison casually. I waited until the disk completed one full rotation before disembarking. Since I don't smoke or drink and swear unconvincingly, symmetry is my only vice. Escaping from the Ren Cen, I walked counterclockwise for a few blocks to reverse my dizziness. I sat down on the nearest set of steps. A bum approached from across the piazza and requested a quarter for some suntan oil. I explained that I needed it to dry-clean my interview suit and he left me in peace.

Nearby, a vintage '50s statue depicted a green, cupreous titan hefting a petite, state-of-the-art, Waspish couple in one hand and either a globe or an automobile—I can't remember which—in the other: Spirit of Detroit. Two lawyers fist-fought over a parking space. A woman sold clods of earth out of a shoe box. A man with a ventriloquist's dummy explained to an indifferent crowd that the present secretary of state was the Antichrist. A prominent clock harped on the fact that I was doing a rotten job marking time. If I was going to make it to the Technoliner intact, I'd need better diversion.

I bused to the Detroit Institute of Arts. Now the finest of this century's paintings will never make up for our concurrent botch of everything else. Art can only hope to be an anaesthetic, a placebo. The best artists know that patients always fake their symptoms and must be tricked into diagnosis before treatment can take place. The last thing I expected to find at the Institute was a mystery, a work of art demanding to be tracked down, a trail unfolding indefinitely, approximately, the way memory tries "recoil," or "recommend," or "record," coming as close as "recoup," but never alighting on its real object, "recover."

The foyer of the Detroit museum opens onto yet another Grand Hall, a high-vaulted, Euro-sick, stone rectangle entirely unfit for displaying works of art. Rococo satyrs and curlicues alternate with heat-duct grills in a confused architectural legacy. In 1931, in the depths of the Depression, the Institute's Arts Commission, backed by Edsel Ford, asked the Mexican muralist Diego Rivera to use the room for a fresco commemorating the greatness of Detroit.

It was an odd marriage: Edsel Ford, whose father was the first among capitalists, in cahoots with Rivera, the notorious revolutionary who secured Trotsky's political asylum in Mexico. Rivera, the Third World champion, praising the city whose chief icon is an enormous electric sign tallying new autos as they come off the assembly ramp. Diego, who once incorporated a wall fuse box into a mural, working in a room the gaudy copy of Bourbon splendor. But Detroit and Diego shared something critical: both were in love with machines.

The Institute put up ten thousand dollars of Edsel's cash, embarrassed to offer "the only man now living who adequately represents the world we live in—wars, tumult, struggling peoples" such a meager sum. They suggested he limit his work to fifty square yards on each of the two larger walls, one hundred dollars per square yard, by some esoteric formula, considered fair for a man of Diego's stature. Thus the Fords, standing in for Michelangelo's papal patrons, might have suggested the fellow not do the whole ceiling, but just a little bit above the altar. Rivera grew increasingly ambitious in guilty compensation for ▶

Excerpt from *Three Farmers on Their Way to a Dance* *(continued)*

the gringos' liberality. Edsel, finding out that Diego meant to cover all four walls, upped the ante to twenty-five thousand.

The Institute told Diego that they "would be pleased if [he] could possibly find something out of the history of Detroit, or some motive suggesting the development of industry in this town." They did not suspect that the huge man would cart his bulk through all the factories of Detroit, holing up for over three months at Ford's, Chrysler's, and Edison's plants, sketching thousands of preliminaries. Rather than appease the room's rococo anachronisms, he blitzed them with a vision swept up off the factory floor. And in the final work, the curlicues and satyrs go unnoticed, lost in Diego's mechanical vision.

Rivera worked behind a screen for two years, an hourly laborer painting sometimes sixteen hours a day, in a room whose glass roof created greenhouse temperatures of over 100 degrees. Journalists, glimpsing the work in progress, declared that the murals, far from praising the city, would "knock Detroit's head off." The unveiling provided plenty for all those who secretly love a thunderstorm. The crowd stood baffled by the revealed work, seeing no historical allusions or civic allegories, no lineup of leading Detroit power brokers. The public flocked all the way out to the museum to see what they were forced to see every other day of the week: ordinary, characterless people chained to endless, sensual machines.

Diego had committed the principal subversive act: he painted the spirit of Detroit in all its unretouched particulars. Strings of interchangeable human forms stroked the assembly line—a sinuous, almost functional machine—stamping, welding, and finally producing the finished product—an auto engine. Men in asbestos suits and goggled gas masks metamorphosed into green insects. Languorous allegorical nudes mimicked the conveyor. The frescoed room showed the spirit of Detroit from a much closer distance than the comfortable, corporate copper titan

12

I had passed on the street outside. Viewers at the unveiling found themselves inside Detroit, just as the mural-men crawled in, around, and over their creation, striking a mutually parasitic relationship with metal. Diego had painted a chapel to the ultimate social accomplishment, the assembly line, a self-reproducing work of art, precise, brilliant, and hard as steel.

Bishops and businessmen instantly mobilized to destroy the frescoes. It is not hard to read subversion and heresy into the average work of a person's hands. The task becomes easier when the work is ambitious, joyful, and revolutionary. Rivera's was a duck shoot. Even those who had not yet visited the museum found a garden variety of blasphemies in the work. People saw a ridiculous Saint Anthony tempted away from his foreman's plans by an allegory nude's legs. Depression-sensitive capitalists saw in the figures communist-inspired proto-humans. A panel showing the inoculation of a child burlesqued the Nativity.

Diego's compliment—that Detroit reveled in the vitality of the machine age—became, in the mouths of its interpreters, an insult. Edsel, the people declared, had been taken in by a piece of dangerously populist propaganda. An organized outcry of radio broadcasts and written petitions culminated in the *Detroit News* saying that "the best thing to do would be to whitewash the entire work completely."

The work stood. Those cooler minds in the opposition knew that whitewashing turns an ambiguous work decidedly subversive, whereas a busy and ambitious mural was its own death kiss. Left alone, it would date itself more and more each year, playing to an increasingly disinterested house until one day, with the roots of civilization still intact, it would pass a magic milestone and become that perfectly harmless, even socializing item, the historical artifact.

I knew nothing of all this as I stood in the mural room between trains, nor did I suspect that I would be caught up in ▶

finding out. Viewed from inside the factory, the self-reproducing machine demanded allegiance or resentment, but denied the possibility of indifference. Technology could feed dreams of progress or kill dreams of nostalgia. The old debate came alive in Rivera's work with a new strangeness. The machine was our child, defective, but with remarkable survival value. Rivera had painted the baptismal portrait of a mutant offspring, demanding love, resentment, pity, even hope, but refusing to be disowned.

With new eyes, I noticed a minor panel on one of the small walls, off to the side of the conveyor murals. In front of a sculpted dynamo more erotically contoured than any nude, a white-haired man sat at a monolithic desk, face pinched into an amalgam of benevolence and greed—Ford or Edison or De Forest or any of a dozen crabbed industrialists and innovators.

In this face, the face of our times, lay all the evidence I would need to break the hoax, to crack the mystery. Had I recognized the composite face for what it was, I might have saved a year spent tracking down the other leads: Detroit, Rivera, Ford, the auto, mechanical reproduction, portraiture, ether, relativity. When we don't know what we are after, we risk passing it over in the dark. The Chinese played with fireworks for hundreds of years without inventing the gun. Edison thought his moving pictures were just toys. The physician who first set out to discover appropriate anaesthetic dosages discovered, instead, addiction. And I, thinking the clues to my discomfort lay elsewhere, turned my back on this crabbed face and left the hall.

By the time I reached the far end of the adjoining hallway, I was in an extreme state of agitation. I had forgotten all about my connector. To calm myself, I began repeating an old nursery rhyme: While I was going to Saint Ives, I met a man with seven wives. Rivera's murals had upset me deeply and I thought only of getting away from them. Putting one last corner between myself and the factory, I wheeled smack into a mounted photograph:

three young men from the turn of the century stand in a muddy road, looking out over their right shoulders. I knew it at once, though I had never seen it before. How many were going to Saint Ives?

The photo caption touched off a memory: *Three farmers on their way to a dance, 1914.* The date sufficed to show they were not going to their expected dance. I was not going to my expected dance. We would all be taken blindfolded into a field somewhere in this tortured century and made to dance until we'd had enough. Dance until we dropped.